ACROSS ETERNITY

THE PARALLEL SERIES BOOK 4

ELLE O'ROARK

1

SARAH'S MOTHER - 1966

Her eyes open slowly. In the dim morning light, she sees him, the man she brought home last night, searching the floor for his clothes. *Alexander.* That's what he said his name was. He looks like a movie star, but she can't really explain the depth of her attraction to him. He's at least twice her age but it's there, even now, when he's clearly planning to sneak away.

"You're leaving?" she asks.

He raises a brow. "It seemed best." His accent is slight. Where did he say he was from? Sweden or Norway. She shouldn't have drunk as much as she did when they were talking. "As I recall, you're getting married this afternoon," he adds.

She sits up, pulling the sheet to her chest, suddenly cold. "You knew?" They were together for hours last night and he never hinted at it, just plied her with wine and questions about her family until they wound up here, shedding clothes.

His smile is cruel now, not charming the way it was a few hours ago. "It's how I found you in the first place." He pulls a folded newspaper clipping out of his wallet. Her wedding announcement. "Poor Peter Stewart. Does he think you're a virgin, Vanessa? He'll be in for a bit of a shock tonight, won't he?" She is speechless, watching him shove the clipping in a pocket.

"Why did you do this?" she asks. "What is it you want?"

"I was here for information and simply partook of what you offered so freely," he says. His eyes flicker over her. "You're lovely but soulless. I can't explain the attraction...perhaps it's the time traveler in you."

That chill goes straight to her spine. He was dangerous before, but this is a different sort of danger entirely. "Time traveler?" she asks. "I have no idea what you're talking about." She meets his gaze, daring him to challenge her.

"I can see it in your eyes," he says, sitting beside her on the bed and leaning close. She's furious and yet he can feel the way she wants to yield, as if the desire for him is in her DNA. And maybe it is. He understands little about how that gene they share works, but he knows it contains multitudes no one has yet discovered. "You've tried to stop, I'm sure. But it's still there. Do you think not using it makes you better than that sister you hate so much?"

Her fist tightens around the sheet. *Iris.* Ruining everything, even when she's no longer here. Suddenly she remembers all the questions he asked about her family while they were drinking. Probably for reasons less benign than she thought. "What does my sister have to do with anything? She moved to Paris over a year ago."

He pulls something from his jacket pocket and hands it to her. It's a picture of Iris, sepia-tinted and wearing an old-fashioned dress that sweeps the floor. A man stands behind her with his hand on her shoulder. *What was Iris thinking, allowing herself to be photographed like that?*

"That's my father with her," Alexander says, "not that I'd actually call him *father* under the circumstances. It was taken in 1918, just before they held my mother captive and allowed terrible things to happen. Based on your hatred of your sister, I doubt you're surprised by that."

She isn't. Yet Iris was always her mother's favorite. It enrages her even now. "And you decided to punish *me* for it? You could have gotten me pregnant."

He gives her an arrogant smile. "*Punish?* As I recall, you enjoyed it, many times over. You were as drawn to me as I was to you, and believe me, I did not want to be drawn to anyone related to your sister." He rises and walks to the door. "But if it really bothers you, just rewind time and undo the whole thing. Because we both know you can."

She says nothing as he walks out of the room.

She swore two years ago she'd never time travel again, and now God is testing her resolve. So she will endure this memory, and her regret. But she won't get pregnant. It was just one night, and she's going to do the right thing from now on.

God just wouldn't punish her like that.

2

SARAH

Henri.

He comes into the house just after Marie has left for town. It's early fall, still warm, and his shirt clings to him from a morning's labor, unbuttoned to mid-chest. Want kicks sharply in my stomach and I swallow, trying to force it away. My hunger for him is excessive, *incessant*—it needs to be kept in its place. "I was about to see if you wanted lunch," I tell him.

His mouth lifts, a hint of a dirty smile. "I think I need a bath, little thief," he says, closing the distance between us. "And I think you need one too."

I start to reply when I hear it—that shrieking noise again, like a hand inside my skull, squeezing and twisting. *Make it stop*, I try to say, but my tongue won't obey my commands. That noise is pulling me back, somewhere else, somewhere I don't want to be.

My eyes open to find that I'm in a windowless room where the noise is worse, louder. I sit at a long table, surrounded by blank-faced women spooning something in their mouths, empty-eyed yet desperate. Stew. It sits in front of me as well, its taste on my tongue though I've no memory of eating it.

I understand their desperation. Something inside me cries

out for the contents of the bowl, as if it's oxygen and I'm short of breath. My spoon rises to my lips almost without my consent, my hand shaking with desire.

But why? The question slips forward alongside the craving. *Why do I want this so badly? Why am I even here?*

For a moment I see Henri's face. Picture his eyes, intent on mine, worried, begging me for something, as if my answer means everything to him. I shudder with relief as the spoon hits my tongue and the tension finally eases. I feel closer to Henri, now, less bothered by that endless shrieking overhead. Even at the worst of times, he looks at me as if I'm something worth fighting for, something precious. That wounded part of me, the one that still hasn't shaken off my mother's hatred, heals a little more with each moment he's near.

I watch as he unbuttons my dress, as his fingers slide down my collarbone, then dip to the base of my breasts. There's the smallest sound from his chest—a quiet groan, full of need.

"What if Marie comes back early?" I ask, but I make no move to stop him.

He laughs. "Then she will learn not to come back early."

A snap of pain between my shoulder blades jars me. The blank-faced women surround me again and something presses hard against my spine.

"Eat," a man grunts behind me. "Been here a month. Shouldn't need to be told."

My pulse jumps at the words. Even hazy and half-asleep, something inside me panics. I've been here a *month*? It's not possible. I don't even remember how I got here in the first place. I pick up the spoon, glancing quickly at the faces nearest me. Beautiful faces, with eyes only time travelers possess. They don't seem to notice me or each other—they only care about the stew. My head is too foggy to make sense of it, but I know something's wrong. I force myself to put the spoon back down, sweating with the effort.

I want this too much.

Thick-fingered and clumsy, fighting every impulse, I exchange my bowl for the empty one beside me. The woman sitting there begins to eat greedily, sending droplets of it flying.

Evil, says my mother's voice in my head. *Whatever's in that bowl might kill her.*

It's not evil, I argue. *If I don't figure this out, it might kill us all.*

Such convenient logic, my mother replies.

And I have no response to that, because this time she's right.

BY THE TIME the meal ends, the pounding in my head is worse and my skin is clammy. We are pushed down a long hall, into another gray, windowless room lined with cots, which the women move toward as if this is home. I know mine too, somehow.

My head hurts so much that my stomach rolls in response. I lie down, waiting for it to pass. When my eyes open, the room is dark, but I can make out the face of the woman on the cot next to mine.

Marie.

I whisper her name. My throat does not seem to work right. The word is garbled, and she doesn't respond. "Marie," I repeat. Nothing.

I close my eyes, sick again, longing to be anywhere else, longing for Henri. And then I am with him, watching as he slides into the bathtub, lean-muscled, still tan from summer. He holds his hands out for me. "Give me the pitcher," he says. "I'll wash your hair."

I climb in and sit between his legs, my back to his. "That's very *Out of Africa* of you."

He raises a brow. "What's African? Washing your hair?"

I laugh. "No. It's this movie with...never mind. You don't know who they are. Anyway, the guy washes the woman's hair. It's very erotic."

His hands slide around me to cup my breasts. "I'm glad you think so."

The water sloshes as my knees fall open. "Do you want more?" he asks, his hand sliding down my torso.

"Yes," I groan, but suddenly I begin to shake. I'm hot. *Sick.* This is not the way this is supposed to go. Not the way it happened the first time.

"Sarah?" he asks, his voice urgent. "What's wrong?"

I flail in the water, sending it spinning over the lip of the tub. My insides are twisting. "Don't know," I murmur. "Make it stop."

This is all wrong. I remember the afternoon vividly. I remember how Henri used his hands on me in the tub until I came, with my head pressed to his chest, and how he carried me to the mattress afterward, too impatient to even let us dry off.

But instead I am curled into a ball against him, hot and shivering at once, and I'm hearing that noise again, that awful noise. "Henri, make it stop," I beg, clutching my hands to my head. "I don't know where I am."

My eyes open and I'm back in the dark room with the shrieking noise, sweating, breathing too fast. My shift clings to me, twists around my legs. *No,* I think. *I don't want to be here. Please don't let me be here. Let me be back with Henri.*

And then I am. He's perched beside me on our bed with his hand on my brow. "It came out of nowhere," he's saying. "She was fine and now she's like this. It's been hours."

I don't understand, I want to weep. What's happening to me? Why am I in two places at once and sick in both of them?

"It's just a fever," soothes Marie, leaning over us. "You're as panicked as a new father."

"It's more than that," Henri argues, running his hand through my hair. "She keeps telling me you're with her, saying there's something in the stew."

"Stew," I whisper. "Don't eat. Trap."

She smiles at me over his head as if I'm a sleepy toddler. "We haven't had stew in weeks," she says. "You're dreaming."

My eyes open in the dark room once more. Marie is on the pillow across from mine, unmoving, her lips bled of color.

"No," I reply, though no one is listening. "I think I'm the only one who's awake."

ALL NIGHT I'M FEVERISH, going from Henri to the room with the cots, uncertain which of them is real. I'm awakened the next day by a guard who slams his gun against a metal pipe to rouse us. I'm shaking so hard it's a struggle to climb from the bed, and I do so too slowly for the guard's liking. I've just pushed myself to standing when he plants his boot in my stomach, sending me flying backward. I go to my hands and knees, certain I will throw up.

"I should put a bullet in her head," he says to the other guard. "She'll be dead by morning anyway."

I push to my feet and nearly fall in my haste to join the other women. I follow them down a long, poorly lit hallway, all metal and concrete block—back to the cafeteria, where we line up like lambs to the slaughter.

They push gruel at us instead of stew this morning, but my mouth waters with desire for it just the same. I pretend to eat, and when the woman next to me empties her bowl, I replace it with my full one.

"Watch them carefully today," says a guard who passes only a moment later. "They're decreasing the sedative. The ones we're looking for will be the first to wake."

The ones they're looking for. I know this means I need to be careful, even though it's not me they're after, but I can't. Fighting my desire for the gruel and that noise overhead, that noise that never goes away, has exhausted me. My eyes close, despite my best intentions, and remain so until I feel Henri's palm on my forehead. My eyes flicker open to find that I'm in our bed, the curtains drawn but sunlight sliding through the cracks around them.

I want to ask him why this is happening. I want to ask him if I'm being punished for my sister's death. Or perhaps just the hundreds of times I used time travel to get myself ahead—to finish a paper I'd forgotten, to learn something I didn't know would be on the test, or when I needed tuition money,

All because of time travel, I want to tell him. *My mother was right. Don't let us make this journey.*

But the words never come. A sentence in my head becomes only a gasp, a single syllable, as it exits my mouth.

Doctor Nadeau leans over me, his brow furrowed. "She's been poisoned," he concludes. "I'll give her castor oil to bring it back up."

Henri stiffens. "Poisoned? How?"

"Mushrooms, juniper berries, even too many apple cores maybe," says Doctor Nadeau. "She's American, yes? Perhaps it's not common knowledge there."

I've never seen Henri look as desperate as he does right now. He knows something else is going on—he just has no idea what it is.

Help me, I think, and his hands go to the sides of my face.

"Tell me what you need," he begs, as if he's heard my words. "Tell me what to do."

The shrieking catches my attention and pulls me away before I can answer, if I was even capable of answering. My eyes open to find I'm back in the cafeteria and being pushed toward the door. *What just happened?* Was I hallucinating, or was I—*sort of*—in two places at once?

There's a faint taste of castor oil in my mouth, but it's not until my stomach starts churning in response to it that I have my answer. I was, somehow, in two places simultaneously. I have no idea how it's possible, and I don't know why that shrieking noise doesn't entirely keep me in place. At this exact moment, I wish it would, though. We enter the hall and the first wave of nausea hits. I walk faster, but the women shuffle so slowly I can't go anywhere. When we turn a corner I vomit, letting it fall in a trail to my right as I walk.

"Which of you stupid whores threw up?" shouts a guard behind me. I hear a *thwack* and someone falls, suffering a punishment that should have been mine. I continue walking, despite the nausea, despite the guilt, as if my life depends on it—which it probably does.

We are pushed into a large room which holds chairs and nothing more. Some of the women sit, and some wander, muttering to themselves, lost in a dream world. Right now, as I stumble toward a chair as far from the guards as possible, I wish I was in a dream world too. Even if it's only in my head, a dream of Henri is better than this, with my stomach rolling, sweat dripping into my eyes.

I'm going to be sick again. I drag in air, begging myself, begging the universe for help. *Please. Not here. Not now.* It comes up anyway, but the guards aren't looking at me. Instead, they stare intently at a woman closer to them who is fading in and out —the same thing Henri insisted he saw me do.

"Did you see that?" one asks. "Kick her and see if she's awake. Just don't kick her in the stomach."

The other grunts. "I'll kick her wherever I please. There's no hidden child nowhere to be found with this lot."

Hidden child.

The words fall into my brain and doors there begin to open. Marie, the hidden child. I remember walking through Parc de la Turlure with her in 1918, wearing a dress so long it hit my ankles. We were looking for Marie's mother, who disappeared there, just like my aunt did. I remember the pain of a needle plunging into my neck.

The truth comes to me at last, so horrifying that I forget I am ill. I forget the guards and the women around me. Marie and I were taken captive, just like her mother and my aunt must have been.

And Henri—he remains in 1938, waiting for me, assuming the worst.

I've got to get back to him.

3

HENRI

Sarah.

She's the first thing I think of each morning, the last when I go to sleep. Her space in the bed is cold, untouched. I press my face to her pillow but the scent is fading.

Come back, I think. *Please, please come back.*

But no matter how hard I wish for it, no matter how many times I beg God for a different outcome...the bed remains empty and the house remains silent. I no longer see how to get through the day.

When she and Marie first left, I forced myself to go on, feigning optimism. I got Sarah's forged passport, discussed honeymoons in Greece with a travel agent. Hours, then days, slipped by without her return, and that optimism became something else, something frenzied and irrational. I focused on ridiculous things, insisting all would be well. I bought her Christmas gifts, lavish items she'd have little use for on a farm. I worried our winters might be too cold for her and dug out enough of the basement to drive pipes beneath the slab—a new way of heating the floors some American architect has been perfecting.

I worked, sun-up to sun-down, as if I could bring her home with the force of my efforts, but still there was nothing.

Now all I can do is beg. My heart is outside of my body, beyond my control, and all I can do is beg the universe to return it to me.

I eat bread and sausage for dinner, with heavy helpings of whiskey, saying a quiet prayer before I begin. *Please God, bring her back to me. It can't end like this. You have to let her return.*

After the third pour of whiskey my mind drifts. I think about the future. Living with Sarah in a flat in Paris, returning to the farm for holidays. I'll take our sons out to the Bousonne Wood to get a Christmas tree. Will our daughters time travel? Will they shimmer, like she does?

My eyes open and I'm alone in the empty house. I'd laugh at my foolishness if I were capable of it. Instead I fill my glass and drink fast, laying my head on the table when it's empty. They've been gone over a month now. How will I stand it if they don't return? Why didn't I stop them?

A memory suddenly pierces the fog in my head. Early in the fall, Sarah was ill, feverishly insisting she and Marie were trapped, telling me the stew was drugged. Is it possible she was traveling to me from 1918 then?

I sit up, jaw open, wondering why I'm only remembering it now.

"No," I say aloud, sick at the thought. "No. It was just a fever."

But only the silence of the house whispers back.

4

SARAH

I t takes four days. Four days of cold sweats and vomiting until I finally wake one morning feeling well again, or at least more like myself. We sit at the long table and I, like the others, spoon gruel into my mouth, necessary because the guards are watching and that noise is unbearable without it. I switch my bowl with that of the woman beside me as soon as I can and try to think.

I've tried to convey what's happening to Henri, hoping he can warn us, but nothing seems to work. I don't seem able to control what I tell him, and I doubt it would matter if I could. Marie wouldn't listen. Marie would still come here and need someone to save her.

I wish she would wake up so we could talk all this over. She is twitchier now that they are decreasing the drug, though she still won't respond when I whisper her name. And I'm not sure she *should* wake up. They are looking for the hidden child. Maybe it's best that she remains too drugged to give herself up until I figure out how we can escape...*if* I figure out how to escape.

We won't be able to time travel out of here—the noise keeps us all at half-strength and makes that kind of focus impossible—

and walking out doesn't look like an option either. I've only seen one door, and it's both guarded and padlocked. Though the windows are blacked out, I can see the shadow of bars on the other side, which rules out jumping.

What would Henri do in my position, surrounded by armed guards? He'd realize fighting back, outmanned like this, would be suicide, so he'd look for another way. He'd survey the information he had and create a new plan.

I squeeze my eyes shut and consider the only thing I know so far: they hope one of us carries the hidden child of the prophecy. But they must realize by now that few, if any, of us, are pregnant, so why haven't they killed us yet? And they will *have* to kill us once they have what they want—you can't set someone free if you've tortured her and she has the ability to go back in time to punish you for it.

So, they want something more. What is it?

I watch as a guard pulls a woman from her seat by her hair. They clearly aren't trying to win us to their side, which means that whatever it is they want won't require our cooperation. It's something they plan to take.

THAT NIGHT, after the lights are out and the guard sleeps soundly in the chair at the end of the room, I allow myself to go, in my mind, to Henri. I want to remember how things were, remember all the things I need to get home to.

He's coming in after the hired help are gone for the day, exhausted, in need of a shave. The harvest is nearly done, thank God. I miss my fiancé. I want him to myself once more.

I smile. "Go bathe," I tell him. "I've made us dinner, and Marie didn't even help. Which means it may be inedible, but that's beside the point."

He pulls me to him, his hands gentle on my face. "You should be resting." His mouth closes on mine. A sweet, chaste kiss. Not the kind I am hoping for. I feel the edge in him, the restraint, but I've never wanted restraint from him, and I especially don't want it now, when we've had so little time alone.

"Rest?" I ask. "Why on earth would I rest? You're the one who's been working night and day."

He pushes my hair back from my face. "You were so ill, Sarah. Your fever just broke this morning." His lips press to my forehead. "Dieu. I've never been so terrified."

I still. What is he talking about? Yesterday I helped him in the fields, and then we sat on the small porch with a bottle of wine, bickering in that way we do—more foreplay than argument.

"Fever?" I ask. "As I recall, last night you were offering me your ill-informed opinions about Matisse and I was soundly proving you wrong."

He steps back, holding a hand to my forehead. "No, love. We've never discussed Matisse. You've been ill, remember? For days and days. Out of your mind. Telling us someone was drugging you and Marie." He shakes his head. "I wonder if you're still ill."

I stare at him. I remember the past few days. I remember our bath, I remember the day we swam in the lake together, and the way he pulled me into a corner of the barn to kiss me as the hired hands drove away. I remember all of it and yet he does not.

My eyes open. Marie lies beside me, staring at the wall without a glimmer of recognition. And slowly I realize what is happening during these times I go back to visit Henri.

I'm not merely remembering what existed. I'm rewriting it.

Our amazing summer together, our fall. I'm papering over every perfect memory, and soon, he won't remember any of those days as they actually were. He'll instead recall this drugged version of me, spouting nonsense about things he's sure haven't happened.

And perhaps that's a version he won't wait for after all.

I BEGIN, the next day, to listen. Every time the guards walk past, I am cataloguing their words and their worries and their petty resentments, grabbing hold of anything that might one day prove useful, that might help me see a pattern.

They each take shifts digging a hole down the hallway. I've heard the ringing of pickaxes since I regained consciousness, but no one seems to mention what it's for. They're too focused on bickering about whose day it is to dig.

In the common room I no longer hide in the far corner but instead sit nearest the guards' desk, the most dangerous point in the room. I'm bumped, pushed from my chair, hit in the head. The guards seem to resent us for their roles here, as if they're the victims. They take a sick pleasure from the casual harm they wreak, and inside me I discover this small seed of rage in my chest, something that laid dormant until now. Every day it seems to grow a little more. Every day I become a little more like them: I'd take a sick pleasure in harming them if I could too.

Especially Gustave.

He only strikes me occasionally, and sometimes yanks my hair as he passes, but it's more in the way of a mean boy with a crush—I can live with that. But the other times, when he pushes his meaty fingers through my hair, lets them trail over my hip or chest as I pass...those times leave me feeling a type of rage that scares me.

Today he slides his hand inside my neckline to grab my breast. I force myself not to react, but fury seems to radiate out from that place of anger until I can feel it in every limb, in each finger and toe.

"You'd better not let him see you do that," warns the other guard.

He removes his hand, and I feel sick with relief. "Monsieur

Coron?" asks Gustave. "He won't be here until the end of the week."

"And when he hears that only one of them has woken, he'll be in a foul mood, so don't make it worse, eh?"

"Do you suppose once he's made his choice, he'll let us make ours?" Gustave asks, lifting my hem with his foot. He laughs. "Unlike him, I require nothing special of the women who bear my children other than the ability to lie still."

All the breath is pushed from my chest. This is why no one is trying to win us over. Monsieur Coron, or whoever he's working for, is not interested in gaining powerful allies. He's interested in creating them—infants he can shape and mold to his liking. It explains why we are all young. I've got no doubt about what happened to the older women who arrived, like Marie's mother. I've got no doubt about what they'll do with us too, eventually.

I've got to get us out of here. *Henri*, I beg silently, *help me. Show me how to escape.* My eyes open and I'm still in the common room, still surrounded by women with dead eyes. Still completely on my own.

5

SARAH

That evening, Marie's fingers begin to jerk. When she wakes the next day, for only a moment, there is a startled awareness in her eyes. It fades away to nothing before I can capture it. She's waking, and whether that's a good thing or bad, it's vital that it happens without the guards noticing, and that it happens before this *Monsieur Coron*, whoever he is, arrives.

That night at dinner, when the guards aren't looking, I knock the spoon out of Marie's hand. It falls to the floor, and she blinks before lowering her face to the bowl, to lap up its contents like a cat. "No, Marie," I whisper, pushing a roll in front of her. "Eat this."

She knocks it away and the sound, as it falls to the floor, attracts the notice of a guard.

When he moves past us, I try again. "Marie, it's Amelie," I whisper. "We're trapped in 1918. Remember? You need to wake up. You have to stop eating."

There is still no response. I glance at the guards who stand at the end of the table and then I reach for her tray.

A hand belonging to the woman beside her comes down to stop its movement.

"Are you insane?" she hisses. "Stop before the guards notice you."

I freeze, more startled than scared. It's been so long since I've heard a female voice that I'd almost forgotten it was possible. I allow myself a quick glance at the owner of that hand and voice and find the woman I saw the week before—the one who flickers in and out, the way I do. And she is absolutely clear-eyed. My heart begins to beat a little faster at the idea that I'm not in this alone. Between the two of us, surely, we can come up with a plan.

My mouth opens and she shakes her head. "Not here."

Only the dormitory offers a chance of being left alone long enough to talk, and it's late when she appears beside my bed. "My name is Katrin," she says. She's speaking French but her accent is strong. Swedish, perhaps. "We don't have long, but you must be careful. They're looking for descendants of the first families—so you can't let them know you're awake."

"I don't plan to," I reply, "but I'm not from one of the first families so maybe it won't matter."

Her brow furrows. "Of course you are. How else do you think you woke early?"

I shrug. "I was sort of in two places at the same time, after we arrived. I think maybe the drug was diluted for me."

She stills. "Two places at once?" she whispers. She leans closer, staring at my face as if she's trying to read something there. "But that's my gift."

Not much of a gift, I think, as she continues.

"You aren't from 1918." Her eyes are wide now, astonished. "If you have my gift, you must be my descendant. A daughter or granddaughter, perhaps."

I'm not sure how she's leapt to what seems, in my estimation, a fantastic conclusion. "Just because we can both sort of be in two places at once doesn't mean we're related. It's just an...aberration."

"It's the gift of all daughters of Adelaide," she says, brow furrowed. "And our gifts aren't meant to be special on their own... we are like puzzle pieces. We only make sense in combination. But surely you know this."

I shake my head. Everything I've learned about time travel came from the blank-faced girl in the cot next to mine. "My mother didn't time travel. I really don't know much about it. But I'm definitely not from a first family," I insist. "And I have no idea who Adelaide is."

She stares at me as if I might be making a joke and seems to finally conclude that I'm not.

"Adelaide was one of the four girls who left the island," she explains. "The start of the first families—four families, four gifts. And your gift could only come from one source. Me."

She's gripping my hand as if this is all very important, but everything she's saying is impossible. Yes, if this is her time, she could conceivably be my grandmother or great-grandmother... except I know my grandmothers, and great-grandmothers, or at least know of them. "I can trace my family back on both sides to the Civil War."

"What children know of their history is what their parents choose to tell them, and for you to exist must mean that I will have a child."

I want her to be wrong, and yet I feel wheels in my head turning—things I've wondered about my entire life, like the fact that I look somewhat like my mother, but nothing like my father. And while my father was not cruel, he was also never involved, and once he left, I never heard from him again. He continued to call my brother Steven, though, and paid Steven's tuition. I always assumed it was because he blamed me for Kit's death, and perhaps that was true, but maybe it was more than that: maybe it was because he knew, or realized somewhere along the line, that I was not his daughter.

But if Katrin's right, and she doesn't escape, it means the child she'll give birth to will be...Coron's.

My stomach tightens. "Maybe someone else is out there with your gift and you don't know it."

She shakes her head. "There's no other explanation, though we both wish it were true. I know what you're thinking. You're thinking the child I will have is Coron's. But you're wrong. I'm going to escape, so it can't be his."

"Escape how?"

"The infirmary is our only option. Each Sunday night they leave to take the corpses out. It's the only time the door is unlocked, aside from when the cook goes out to shop. If we convince them we're dead, we can time travel from the outside."

My mouth opens to voice a thousand objections: we would not be stiff and cold like corpses, first of all. And what if we get outside and we're too drugged to jump? Or they do something to us before they leave to ensure we *can't* jump?

She speaks before I can suggest a single one.

"If the plan fails in any way," she says, "it means we'll probably be buried alive."

"So, it's the nuclear option."

"Nuclear?" she asks. "I don't know this word."

I wave it away. "I'm just saying...we only do it if all else fails."

"Unless you're able to jump back and warn yourself, all else has already failed," she says. "Have you tried? I have, but it hasn't worked."

"I can't," I reply. "I don't seem able to get the words out, and I doubt it would do any good if I could. I came with my friend and I know she won't listen no matter how hard I warn her." There is no warning that could keep Marie from making the journey she did. And the fact that she is here at all is my fault. I'm the one who told her where her mother went, when Henri begged me not to. How might their lives have gone if I hadn't listened to my sister, if I hadn't ever ventured back to 1938 in the first place?

"Your loyalty is admirable," she says. "But I'm worried it might get you killed."

We hear the echo of a guard's boots in the hall. "You really think this infirmary plan will work?"

She squeezes my hand. "I'm not sure, but the fact that you exist, and are my descendant, makes me believe it must."

She bolts to her bed, and I lie awake, thinking too many things to possibly hope for sleep. Is what she's saying possible? Could I be her granddaughter, a product of a first family?

Or have I given her the kind of false hope that will get us all killed?

I WAKE JUST before the guards come in, craving Henri. I roll to my stomach, wishing I could dull the sharpness of missing him. My heart beats faster. I know I only have a moment, but I need this. I need one bright spot before another long day of pretending and worrying begins.

I squeeze my eyes shut, doing my best to ignore the shrieking of the alarm, and I go to him. It's early in the morning, those last peaceful days of summer before the harvest began, and the night sky has begun to dull and soften. I press myself to his back, let my hand rest on his broad shoulder.

I bury my nose in the nape of his neck to smell him, a faint hint of soap from last night's bath and summer air. I want to weep at the feel of his skin under my hand, at the smell of him. I miss him so much that the ache feels impossible to bear.

His hand comes up to close over mine. "Did you just smell me?" he asks with a sleepy laugh. I want to weep at the sound of his voice, husky with disuse. I had all of this—his sweetness, his laughter, his warm skin, his smell. I had all of it and I appreciated it, I did, but I never imagined how badly I would miss it. How desperate I'd feel, willing to give up everything just for a single piece of him. Just to carry his voice inside me, the smoothness of him beneath my hands. Just to be able to lean against his chest and tell him what is happening to us and have him direct me, or even just promise things will be okay.

I wouldn't demand all of it. Just one of those things would suffice and I can't have any of them.

I can't answer. I press my lips to his neck instead, and he tenses...but it's a good kind of tension. As if he's allowing his brain to shut down while his body picks up the slack.

"Do that again, little thief," he says. His voice huskier.

So I do, and then his hand drags mine down, down, to where he is hard and ready. "That's all it took," he says, squeezing his palm over mine, against him. And then he rolls toward me. I've been so good, lately, only visiting him at night. But, my God, I missed the look I see on his face right now. His eyes taking me in as if he will never want to see anything else as long as he lives.

"Will it always be like this with us?" he asks, his mouth moving over mine, pressing to my jaw.

"Like what?" I ask, arching into him.

"Like nothing but you matters," he says. "Like I'll die if I'm not inside you every minute we're awake."

He nudges my thighs apart with a knee and my legs fall open, more than willingly. *Yes,* I think. I don't have long but *yes.* His mouth descends on mine as he starts to push inside me, and then I hear the heavy door scraping the floor as it opens, blinding light in my face as someone flips a switch.

"Hurry," I urge Henri, but already the shrieking is making itself known and the sound of shouting is pulling me out of it.

I stumble to my feet. The women around me are already up and it's only because someone closer to the door is unresponsive that I didn't get caught.

"Fuck!" the guard roars. "We told them there were nineteen

left." He kicks the woman in the bed once and again and then a third time, much harder. My blood begins to heat. That rage in my chest has become as familiar as my own hand.

"It's not our fault she's dead," replies the other. "They still have plenty to choose from."

"Try to tell them that," the first guard replies. It's not the first death I've witnessed since I arrived, but that's not the reason I'm unsettled. The guards are often on edge, and very often enjoy their power over us a bit too much, but this is different. They're scared, and anything that scares them *terrifies* me.

We are shuffled past the corpse and on to the cafeteria, where we get our food and sit. Katrin takes the seat next to mine and we exchange a quick, nervous glance as we feign eating. For once the hunger that has gnawed at me every day, eating only the bread, is absent. I don't think I could eat even if I wanted to. I notice something floating in my gruel. A small white pellet, perhaps what they use to sedate us. When the guards aren't looking, I fish it out of the bowl and tuck it into my sleeve, though I've no idea how it could be useful.

Marie is louder this morning, more vocal. She's coming off the drug and she doesn't want to be. A guard casually hits her in the head with his gun as he passes and tells her to pipe down. And in response to the pain...her hand disappears. Only for a moment. And she moans again.

Stop, I plead silently. *Stop before they hurt you. Before they realize who you are.*

The cafeteria door opens and Gustave, the guard I hate most, bursts in, his mouth set in a grim line. "They're coming," he barks. "Be ready."

Marie moans again, and my heart begins to slam in my chest. These stupid guards don't realize she's waking, but whoever is coming seems to know more about time travel. They might. Her gruel is nearly gone and I can only think of one solution.

I switch our bowls.

My stomach lurches with guilt as she digs in, content once more. Guilt and also despair. I'd hoped she was weaning herself from the drug, perhaps getting to the point that she could be reasoned with, that we could discuss escape. And now she is calming, growing docile again. I might have saved her from being raped, but if I've just ensured that we're both stuck here forever—is that an improvement?

The cafeteria doors open and the guards jump to attention. A young woman enters. There's a man at her heels, but she's the one I stare at, because hers is a face I recognize instantly. A face so like my mother's, few people could tell them apart.

My aunt is here. And she appears to be...helping them?

I squeeze my eyes shut, wondering if I'm hallucinating, but when I open them she is still there, talking to the man behind her as they approach. I know she isn't the mastermind of all of this, because the thing that drew us here occurred long before she was born—but she is not drugged, and she doesn't look scared, which means she's not on our side, either. She left Pennsylvania when she was twenty-four, before I was even born. She never returned, which means she doesn't know I exist. Given how much my mother hated her, this is probably a good thing.

"Where's the girl?" she barks at the guard in French. Her accent is terrible, all the vowels flattened. Madame Perot, the old crone I used to read to, would be slapping her hand right now.

He murmurs something and points at Katrin. The man's eyes light up and he approaches—and places his hand on my head. "She's as blonde as you, Iris," he says to my aunt.

My heart races so fast it makes me shake.

"Not her," says Gustave. "The one beside her."

"Pity," the man replies, but his hand leaves my head and goes to Katrin's collar. "And there's no one else? A room full of time travelers and you've only captured *one* from the first family?"

Gustave begins sputtering. "We wanted to decrease the sedative more but were worried they'd get away," he says.

"They can't get away, you fool," replies my aunt. "That godforsaken alarm makes it impossible, even for me. I'll fix this."

She walks to the end of the table and throws a woman sitting there to the floor. "Cut out her eyes," she tells the nearest guard.

His jaw drops. "Mademoiselle?" he asks. "Her eyes?" He motions to his own, as if perhaps she translated the word wrong.

"Yes," she says. "Cut out her eyes, and then her tongue, and then her ears."

The guard swallows and forces himself toward the woman who has begun to sit up. He pulls a knife from a sheath on his belt and grabs her by the hair to hold her steady.

My breath stops. *If you are neutral in times of injustice, you have chosen the side of the oppressor.* Words that won't be spoken for many decades, yet they're true even now. But if I give myself up to save her, what does that mean for me? And more importantly, what does it mean for Marie? Who will protect her? Who will get her out of here?

Selfish, I hear my mother saying. *Convenient logic once more. But it's in your blood, so I shouldn't be surprised.*

The guard pushes the hilt of his knife to her eye socket and a woman near them jumps to her feet.

"Stop!" she cries in English. A fellow American. "Please stop!" The guards' heads jerk toward her at once, newly alert. She's a lovely girl, tan and luminous in a sea of pale, blank faces, and she's just given herself up.

My aunt laughs and grabs her by the hair. "I knew that would work. What's your name?"

"Luna," the woman answers, her shoulders sagging. "Luna Reilly."

"There, darling," my aunt purrs, turning to the man holding Katrin by the collar, "now I've found you two. Two of four. It's a start."

My mother always hated time travelers, and I finally see why. I'm beginning to hate them now too.

6

HENRI

The house sits empty, waiting for them.

And I am empty. I press my face to my hands. *Come home, Sarah*, I plead silently. *Come home.*

How could I have let them go? Why didn't I find a way to stop them? My God. I can't stand the possibility that it will stay like this forever. That I'll never learn what happened to them and will go through the rest of my life assuming the worst.

Father Edouard comes to the house, tugging at his collar and uncertain. His eyes widen at the sight of me—unshaven, still wearing yesterday's clothes. Empty whiskey bottles line the counter, but I let him in anyway, beyond caring.

"I hope I'm not disturbing you," he says as he steps inside.

I push a hand through my hair. I haven't been entirely sober for weeks now. I don't respect the person I've become in Sarah's absence, but at this point I'm just trying to survive. I have only the barest hope that she or my sister will return, and it's on behalf of that tiny flicker that I remain here at all, that I bother trying to make it through each day.

"Can I help you with something?" I ask.

He pushes his hands into his pockets and stares at the

ground, shockingly uncertain for a man who speaks in front of hundreds each weekend. "Marie said she'd be gone two weeks," he says. "And it's been six. I was wondering if you'd heard from her?"

It hits me all over again. Six weeks. Is there any chance at all they're coming home if they've been gone that long? Even if Sarah needed to recover, even if she needed to return to her own time for a while, Marie could easily have been home by now. The journey wouldn't even be hard on her.

"I haven't heard from them," I reply, the words gritty in my mouth.

"Surely there's someone you can call," he urges.

I press my fingers to my temples and his gaze flickers to the empty jug on the table. "It was a spur-of-the-moment trip and I have no idea where they went," I reply.

"We should call the police, then," he says, pacing the length of the room. "Border patrol can at least tell us what country they're in and how long they've been there."

Police. One way to make a bad situation worse. They will come here, find that Sarah and Marie left without luggage, without travel papers, and then I'll be tried for murder. Yet nothing could make me sound more guilty right now than arguing against Edouard's suggestion. "Perhaps," I reply.

He stops his pacing and shoves his hands in his pockets. "You're in love with her, aren't you?" he asks. "Amelie?"

I stare at the table. "She isn't actually my cousin." I take a swig off the bottle of whiskey.

He grabs the bottle and takes a drink himself. "She's different," he says, staring at the floor. "And so is your sister."

Perhaps he only means their looks, because God knows that's one thing they can't disguise. But I get the sense he means more by it. "Yes," I reply, "they are."

"I won't say anything to the police," he says. "I have faith they'll come home."

I glance at him, and recognize something of myself in his bleak, desperate face. But his faith that they'll come home makes no sense. "Why?"

"Because I'd struggle to believe in a God who'd keep them away forever," he says quietly. He takes another gulp of whiskey and walks out the door.

I wish I shared Edouard's faith, but I do not. That God of his already took my mother. I suppose I lost my faith in His benevolence long ago.

7

SARAH

For a week, I wait for Katrin's return. A week of listening to the guards laugh and complain while they hit us with the butts of their rifles, trip us, fondle us for their amusement.

You will die, I find myself thinking. *You will die and I'm going to make it slow and painful.*

Katrin returns to our room late at night, lying down in the bed beside mine, which is now free. But she is different, emptier.

I don't know what to say to her. *I'm sorry. I'm a coward. I should have done something.* But it's not enough. Nothing will ever be enough. "Are you okay?" I finally ask.

"No," she says, rolling to face the other way.

Another week passes before she speaks. I'm just drifting off to sleep when her voice floats into my ear.

"Luna..." she finally whispers. "She was from Florida. Is that near you? Did you know her?"

Under other circumstances I'd find the question amusing. Right now, I'm so astonished to hear her voice that I can barely answer. "America is a very large place, and she probably isn't even from my time," I reply.

"She had a little boy," Katrin says, turning her face to the pillow as her shoulders shake. "He's only six. He won't remember her. He won't ever know how badly she wanted to return to him."

"*Had*?" I ask, my heart thudding in my chest.

"He climbed on top of her and she just went crazy," she whispers. "She stabbed him with something she had up her sleeve and he snapped her neck." Her voice breaks. "Snapped it as if she were a doll."

Luna Reilly, the woman far braver and more selfless than I, is dead.

I couldn't have saved her. Speaking up wouldn't have prevented what happened. The guilt, though—it rests on me just the same, so heavy I struggle to get a full breath.

"He left her corpse beside me the whole time as a warning," Katrin says quietly. "He says if I'm not pregnant by next month he'll do the same to me."

I watch her thin shoulders shake. I can't begin to imagine what that week was like for her. Even if we get out of here, an experience like that...it will change her. Scar her. "But I can't get pregnant here. They hold those women in another room, and they're monitored, night and day. We have a guard who drinks heavily and sleeps soundly each night, but those women have no chance."

"I didn't realize there were pregnant women here."

"I think they were pregnant when they arrived," she says. "Maybe he thinks one of them carries the hidden child. Maybe he just wants to raise an army of time travelers. I don't know."

This is the past, and I'm sure the women all died—there's nothing I can do for them anyway—but it's possible their children survived. "Who would a child become, raised by that man?" I ask.

She doesn't reply. We both know the answer.

"You know, things are supposed to change when the first four families come together at last," she says. "It's part of the prophecy.

And now there are at least three of the four right here, and things could hardly be worse."

"Three?" I ask, my pulse beginning to race. "You mean the pregnant women?"

She raises a brow. "No, I mean us."

"*If* I'm your descendant, we only count as one family. Luna would have made the second."

Her eyes meet mine. "You're clever, Amelie, but not clever as you think," she says. "I saw your friend waking up. You gave her your gruel so they wouldn't catch her."

My heart beats faster. It's occurred to me that Katrin might give them my name, but I didn't realize she could give them Marie's as well. "But you didn't say anything?"

"No, because then I'd be no better than Iris," she says. "She's the woman advising him. I hate him, but I hate her even more—she's a traitor to her own kind."

My gaze flickers away. I haven't told Katrin that Iris is my aunt, and I'm not sure I should. How could she help but look at me differently if she knew what kind of evil runs in my blood? I even wonder it myself.

"Why is she helping him?" I ask. "What's in it for her?"

"They're getting married, I think," she replies.

"She's a fool, then," I say. "He won't let her live."

Her head rises for the first time since we began talking. "Why do you think that?"

"He can't let anyone who was here live, but especially a time traveler. Any one of us, including her, could go back and ruin everything he achieves. He won't risk it."

She looks at me, thinking something she does not say. "They're nearly done with that hole they're digging. I wonder what it's for."

I've wondered it too, and the conclusion I keep coming back to is one I haven't wanted to admit to myself. Now I'm forced to. In Coron's mind, we are all just things, and most of us are useless things at that, taking up resources. Soon he'll decide to kill those of us who haven't woken, so it's not as if he needs a cellar for food storage, or extra space. There's only one thing he needs here, now.

"The hole is for us," I say softly, with a sick kind of certainty. "For all the women they believe haven't woken. He will kill the rest of us at once and thinks it's safer to bury everyone here than to risk getting caught. It's probably the only reason he hasn't killed us already."

She looks at me oddly again. "Your mind works like theirs," she says. "I don't mean it as an insult. But you think in terms of strategy, as if people are pieces on a chess board."

I want to argue that it doesn't make me like them, but suddenly I'm not sure. I think of the rage I feel every time Gustave touches me, every time I watch the guards kick a corpse mercilessly, how endless and cruel and *cold* a piece of me is. Sometimes I feel as if I become more like them than not with each day that passes.

"They've been working on that hole for a while," I tell her, "so they must be nearly done."

"What are you saying?" she asks.

"That if we're going to escape, we'd better do it soon."

KATRIN and I begin to plan. I've found two more of those pellets floating in my oatmeal and have hidden them in my mattress. We'll use them to drug our guard once we know when we're leaving. Katrin tries to persuade me to leave Marie behind, and I refuse.

"She's my friend," I tell her. "I can't."

Katrin looks over at Marie, frowning. "Then you'd better get her off the drugs fast. If she can't time travel when we leave..."

She doesn't continue the thought, but I already know what

she was thinking. If Marie can't time travel, she might wind up buried alive. And even if I can wean Marie off the drugs enough to get her to comply, there are so many ways it could fail. What if they can tell we're not dead? What if they bag all the corpses before they take them? We might suffocate before we ever get out. What if even that small amount of the drug in our systems makes it impossible to time travel when we get outside?

The other issue is my aunt. She could, theoretically, travel back in time to stop us. I doubt Monsieur Coron would risk letting her leave the building to do it, but nothing is certain. If we had any other option, I'd be taking it right now.

The next day I don't give Marie any of my food. She is unhappy at breakfast, and by dinner time her hands twist, her body begging for something it's certain it needs.

I tell her not to eat. She looks at me with vacant eyes and picks up her spoon.

"I'm getting you out of here," I whisper. "Do not eat that." For a moment she hesitates, as if there are still gears working inside her head, listening to me. And then she dips the spoon into her bowl. I have no idea what they've given us, but it's something seriously addictive. I've only had a fraction of the dose she's had and it calls to me too, the oblivion of it. The way it would make me forget, stop aching for a future I no longer have.

I'm out of options. I push the stew onto her lap after the guard passes. Her mouth opens, as if to cry out, and I shove my bread in her hand. "Eat this instead. Do not say a word, understand me?"

A guard rushes at us and hits me so hard that I fly off the bench. I remain on the ground, letting him kick me, my eyes still on Marie, praying she remains silent.

Slowly, still fighting herself, she begins to eat the bread, but the victory is short-lived. That night she begins to thrash in bed as her body withdraws from the drug. "Need," she whispers. "Please."

"Fight it, for me," I beg. "Just for one day. I'll give you all my bread."

"Need gruel," she says, too loudly.

"Be quiet or you'll get us both killed," I hiss. "Listen to me. Henri is alone, Marie. Think how devastated he must be. We've got to get home to him. Do you understand?"

After a moment she nods. "You," she says. "You go."

"We both go," I reply. "Soon. But I need you awake, okay?"

She flinches. "But tomorrow?"

She's asking me for drugs. I'll deal with the problem when it arises. "Yes, gruel tomorrow. Just get through the night."

I give her my bread at both breakfast and dinner. After all these weeks I didn't have the energy to spare, and by the time the lights go down I'm beginning to worry I might not have the *strength* to time travel home. God knows I won't have the strength to help her. I pray most of it's out of her system by the time we leave.

Katrin is ill, too ill to be of much help. But I see the look in her eyes as I struggle with Marie—the one that says *she's going to get us all killed.* And as Marie becomes increasingly unmanageable, I find I'm beginning to agree.

We're just finishing up our evening meal when my aunt walks into the cafeteria. I hear Katrin's quiet gasp on the other side of the table, and I grab Marie's arm, punitively hard. If she does anything right now, makes a single sound, she could ruin this.

My aunt walks over to where we sit and motions, like a queen, for Katrin to rise. "Come. Your services are needed."

A guard yanks her from the table and pulls her away. This time, unlike the last, she doesn't even fight.

If I could, I'd bury my head in my hands. Selfishly, it's less about what Katrin's going to suffer than about what it will do to our plan if she isn't back soon. This may be our last chance, and it's only going to work once. As soon as the guards figure out how we escaped, they'll make sure it can't happen again. But if Katrin hasn't returned yet, could I really leave her behind? It was her idea in the first place, and if I'm descended from her the way she claims, leaving without her may mean I cease to exist the moment we go.

OVER THE NEXT two days I continue weaning Marie off the drug, but it's far harder for her than it was for me. She twists all night, sweats, retches whenever the guards aren't looking. Over dinner that second night the guard stands over us both, and we've got no choice but to finish what we were served. It takes me a day to pull out of it. Marie starts from scratch, and by the next morning is begging me for the gruel.

I begin the process of keeping her clean once more, and she's still half-drugged when Sunday arrives. The guards are more anxious than normal, and over breakfast I hear them bickering about who will drive tonight. This is it, our chance. If we go, I can save Marie but might be signing Katrin's death warrant, and therefore my own. If we wait, we could *all* die.

I spend the entire day worrying, and there are no words for how relieved I am when Katrin is shoved into our room, just after dinner. She's so pale she's nearly green, and there's a fresh bruise along her jaw.

"Are you okay?" I whisper, as we lie down to sleep.

"No," she says. Her voice is flat, empty.

"We have to leave tonight," I tell her. "I'm not sure we'll get another chance."

She's silent, and for a moment I worry she'll refuse. "Give me the drugs," she says finally.

I reach into the hole in my mattress and pass them to her. She rises, walking straight to the guard, who lounges at the desk with his mug of beer, ready for an evening nap. "I need the bathroom," she says.

He laughs. "I guess your cot will smell like piss then."

She leans toward him, over the desk. "You know he's going to kill all of you before this is done." Her hand passes over his mug.

The guard is one of the short-tempered ones. His hand flies out fast and I can hear it make impact all the way across the room. She falls to the ground. "You think just because you're his whore you can talk to me like that?" the guard roars. She clutches the sides of the desk to stand and pulls herself up.

"No," she says. "I suspected you'd react just as you did."

She returns to her cot and we lie still, waiting until we're certain the guard is passed out.

"It's time," I finally tell Marie as I pull her to her feet.

"I'm going to be sick," she whispers, and she falls to the floor and retches. Katrin and I exchange a glance. Her nausea won't be improved, lying pressed against rotting corpses for several hours. She's going to give us away.

I hold her hair back. "Get it all out," I whisper. "You can't do this when the guards load us on the truck, okay? They'll know you're alive if you do."

She nods. After a minute, when nothing more has come up, I pull her to her feet, and tell her the plan, which sounds far simpler than it actually is: hide three corpses, pretend to be dead, and time travel as soon as we're outside. "Don't wait for me," I warn. "Just go. Do you understand?"

She nods and I squeeze her hand, allowing myself to truly hope for the first time that this might work. In a few hours I might be back with Henri. I want that moment so badly I can feel it in my bones.

Together, the three of us sneak into the hall. Marie leans on me the entire way, her skin clammy and her hands shaking. Katrin is lagging too, weak and ill from her days with Coron. I can't allow myself to think about what those days entailed, and I can't allow myself to feel sympathy. Sympathy won't get us out of here.

We pass the hole they are digging, the place they will store the bodies soon. I don't want to scare Marie but I feel like I have to. She needs to understand how serious this is and right now, she's too sick and too drug-addled to get it. I point to the hole.

"You see that?" I whisper. "That's where the bodies will go after tonight. Under that big slab. Do you understand what that means?"

She nods and I pray it's enough. Because if we don't get out tonight, I'm not sure we ever will.

I open the infirmary door. The bodies lie in a pile, eyes open, mouths gaping. I wasn't prepared for the sight or the smell. Marie, though—who hasn't been conscious over these last few weeks—is far less prepared than me.

She falls to the floor beside them, dry heaving now that her stomach is empty. Katrin is green as well, but plows forward, grabbing one of the women by the shoulders.

"Are you sick?" I ask.

She gives me a tense nod. "Get the feet," she whispers.

Even with two of us, the task is far harder than I'd anticipated. It's over a hundred pounds of dead weight, and I'm so weak from days without food that even propelling myself forward is a struggle at times. I force myself to keep moving, and when we finally drop the body beneath a table at the end of the room, I have an odd, floating sensation that makes me wonder if I'll survive the journey home. We return to the corpses and grab another, both of us breathing heavily; we manage it, but just as we return for the third, we hear the heavy tread of boots in the hall. My gaze meets theirs. The guards are here early, and we don't have time to hide the third body.

Which means one of us has to stay behind.

I told Henri I would keep Marie safe, and I will. And if Katrin doesn't survive...odds are I won't ever be born.

"Lie down," I tell them.

Marie shakes her head. "No, you should go. I'm too weak anyway."

"You are not going to be able to time travel in a few weeks. You're losing your spark, and I am not. I'm still fine. Lie down. Go back to your brother. If I can escape I will. Go to America like we planned and swear on your life that you'll never return to 1918."

She presses something into my hand—her mother's necklace, the one she found in a pocket when we arrived here. She was certain it would bring us good luck, though I'm not sure it has.

I turn to Katrin. "Good luck. Hopefully this hasn't changed your future or mine too much."

She gives me the smallest, saddest smile imaginable, and runs her hand over her stomach. "Not to worry," she says. "Your future is now secure."

I blink, not able to understand, at first. And then I do: she is pregnant.

It all begins to make sense—her recent illness, her quiet. She's been pregnant since the first time she slept with him and lying about it so she'd be able to escape.

There's no time for questions and not even time to process my shock. I dive to the back of the room just as the guards walk in and hold my breath as they begin to lift the bodies on the cart, waiting for someone to notice that two of them are still warm. They don't, too busy bickering about who will drive and who gets a weapon.

The bodies are thrown carelessly, as if they are sacks of flour. The door slams as they go.

And then my shoulders shake and I begin to cry. For Marie and Katrin, my only friends here. And because Katrin has just confirmed one of my worst fears: the terrible piece of me is real. I'm a Coron.

8

SARAH

I wake to find myself being turned out of my bed. The guards are kicking my stomach, my back, my face, demanding to know where Katrin and Marie are. If I'm still here, Katrin must have survived. I hope that means Marie did too.

I accept the blows, but along with the pain I feel that familiar rage as well—blistering, making my blood heat until it's reached a boiling point. *I'm going to kill you all*, I think as they aim their boots into my stomach and back and face. *I'm going to kill you all and I'm going to make it so long and so painful you'll beg me for a quick death.*

And then I'll say no.

My body is so bruised and broken that I struggle to get back to my feet when they're done. The only thing propelling me forward—limping, unable to stand straight, drooling blood down the front of my shift—is knowing that there will be a bullet in my brain if I don't.

And a bullet in my brain means I can't make them pay.

Outside the room, I discover that Marie and Katrin's disappearance is not the only upheaval. Several guards and kitchen workers are gone, presumably fired, though they all disappeared without a word. I can only think of one reason why they'd be letting staff go: because there will soon be fewer of us here. They are preparing for the next stage—getting rid of all but the pregnant women.

There is now only a single cook and she's furious that she has to do everything on her own. She yells at us, asks the guards why they can't help, why the cattle can't serve themselves. I take my food and limp to the table.

It's too painful to chew the bread and I worry that my jaw is broken. I sip the gruel instead—I will need the drug just to get through the day. I'm not scared of getting addicted this time. Any haze it causes will be burned through by my rage.

Now I finally know why it's there. That thing inside me, first identified by my mother and then Katrin...it's his. Coron's. I can think the way he does—shut off emotion and choose self-interest again and again. And as I look at the guards or at my aunt who storms in to yell at the cook, I hate it and yet I'm glad for it too. I may die here, but I'm taking all of them out with me.

I get through the day and allow myself half the stew at night. I wake so stiff I can barely move and have to use the metal posts of the headboard to pull myself to standing.

"How do you expect me to feed them all by myself?" the cook demands when we enter the cafeteria. "Tell Miss High and Mighty to get in here and help if she's going to fire them all."

"I'd keep a civil tongue if I were you or she'll have it removed," warns the guard. "She's in a mood, Mademoiselle is. She's been made to care for the baby. And not happy about it in the least."

One of the babies has been born, then. No wonder they're getting ready to close up shop.

"I'd trade gladly. Better to watch one babe than to coddle this lot," she grumbles.

"I wouldn't fret if I were you," he says. "The other two are due any day now, so there will be far less work and soon."

I stiffen. There's only one thing that can mean: they're

preparing to kill us. Poison or a bullet to the head, perhaps. Maybe they'll just shove us in the hole and let us rot there. And it will happen without warning, the same way the missing staff just disappeared.

Which means I need to act now. I need to tell them I'm awake. I know what the result might be, and it doesn't matter. I want to live.

That night, when we reach the cafeteria, I see my aunt exchanging words with the cook. My chest is tight. Interrupting an argument isn't the ideal way to announce myself, but I'm not sure another time is coming.

"Iris?" I ask. I keep my voice inquisitive, not fearful. The way I might if I ran into her somewhere else—a family reunion, perhaps, or a wedding. "I'm your niece. Vanessa's daughter."

Iris's mouth falls open. "What did you just say?" she asks. It reminds me of the tone my mother used when I'd said something she didn't like.

A guard grabs me by the hair and I feel it all the way to my jaw.

It was a mistake, but what choice did I have? I want to live. This is the only way to do it.

"I'm Vanessa's daughter. Your niece."

Her eyes narrow. "My sister doesn't have children. And she certainly wouldn't have had any time travelers."

"I came here from 1987," I reply. "And she has—*had*—three children. My sister and I slept in the same room you and my mother did, the one that looks out on the graveyard. My mother refused to tell us anything about you."

She marches out from behind the counter and grabs me by my collar. "Related to me, and yet you are awake. We're not of the first family, so tell me how that's possible?"

"The guards broke my jaw. I haven't been able to eat much." The gruel and stew give my voice a hazy, drugged quality. I *sound* like someone who's only begun to wake up.

She regards me with suspicion, reminding me so much of my mother that I want to shrink from her. "Come with me," she says, pulling me through the cafeteria. "I'm going to enjoy every minute of this."

We go down the hall to what must be her room. I'd pictured her living like a queen, given her role here, but this isn't even as nice as the bedroom she left behind in Pennsylvania.

"Sit," she says, pushing me toward a chair while she stares at my face. "You took quite a risk in speaking to me. What's to stop me from killing you and taking your spark?"

I freeze. I have only the vaguest understanding of the rules of my kind. I've heard about this *spark* she refers to—the thing that keeps us going, and without which we die. I know only three people in a single family can have it—the rule of threes. I know that we can, in theory, take it from each other. But it never occurred to me until this moment that it was worth killing someone for.

"I'm terrible at time traveling," I tell her. "I doubt my spark would be worth taking."

She laughs. "That shows how little you know. If my body was ravaged by cancer right now and I was moments from certain death, I could stab you in the heart and be made new in seconds."

She appears to be considering it, and she has no reason to spare me, really. All I have going for me is that we have an enemy in common. "My mother hates me, so she didn't give me a lot of details about anything."

The smug smile leaves her face. "Why would your mother hate you?"

"Because I'm the reason my sister is dead. Mostly, I think, because she hates time travelers. I guess the gene skipped her."

She pauses, and then her head tilts. There's something satisfied in her expression. I suspect she likes hearing that my mother suffered. "Your mother can time travel," she says. "Did you not realize that?"

I stare at her. It isn't possible. My mother can't time travel. And if she could, there'd be no reason for her to hate me the way she does. Unless, perhaps, she thought what made me evil *wasn't* that I could time travel, but that I was a Coron.

"Are you sure?" I ask.

"Of course I'm sure," she snaps. "I grew up with the woman. What I really don't understand is how you exist at all. When I left, she was dating Peter Stewart."

I consider telling her I may be related to Coron but think better of it. Letting them know Katrin was pregnant when she left might lead them to search harder for her.

I nod. "Yes, he's my father."

She laughs. "Peter Stewart is *not* your father," she replies. "He was a dumb local boy without a drop of magical blood. There's no way his DNA produced a time traveler." She taps her lip. "A mystery to solve, which I rather enjoy. I wonder, though, why you're telling me all this? Surely you realize I have nothing to gain by allowing you to live?"

"I'm a hard worker and a good cook. I can help out wherever you need me."

She nods, undoubtedly thinking that she still wants to kill me, but perhaps also thinking it can wait until she's bled me dry working here first. "And your mother would hate it, desperately hate it, if she knew we were working together, wouldn't she?"

My eyes dart to hers. "Yes."

"Then I think I will allow you to live, niece."

That makes one of us, aunt.

THE NEXT DAY the same guard who grabbed me by the hair takes me to the woman in the kitchen. "Mathilde, here's your new serving girl," he says.

Mathilde takes one disdainful glance my way and hands me a bottle. "Place one of these in each bowl."

The pills are different from the ones I pilfered from the oatmeal, but that may be because they haven't dissolved. I do everything she says, and when the other women come in, I hand the bowls out and clean up after them without being asked. It's a long shot, but perhaps if I make her life and Iris's life easy enough, they will start to trust me.

Mathilde sits comfortably, watching me, and when the women are pushed toward the common room, a guard comes for me. "This one stays," she barks at him.

He shrugs and leaves us alone. "Finish up that washing," she says, "and I'll teach you how to make stew."

9

HENRI

It's February when it happens. I'm sitting at the table alone with a bottle of whiskey, no glass, when I hear the crash upstairs.

I'm just sober enough to know I'm not imagining things.

I run and arrive in Marie's room only to stumble to a halt. For a moment, my sister is a stranger to me. Covered head to toe in dirt, her hair matted. I take two steps toward her and she collapses against me like a small child, weeping. I want to weep myself. I really thought I'd lost her.

"It's okay," I whisper. "It's okay. You're safe. But where is Amelie?"

"I left her behind," she cries, and I feel my stomach drop. *No*, I think, *this can't be right. If Marie is still alive and was able to get out, Sarah can still get out too.*

"It was all for nothing," she whispers, as I help her to the bed. "There were no older women there. Our mother was probably dead the day she arrived. They drugged us and Amelie...she forced me not to eat the food. When I wouldn't listen, she—" Marie's head drops and she begins to weep. "She pushed my gruel into my lap, I think, and they beat her."

"So where is she now?" I demand. "Why isn't she with you?"

Marie's eyes shut and she begins to tell me a story so horrible it hardly seems possible—hiding with corpses, how one of them had to remain behind when the guards came too early. "I should have made her go in my place," Marie weeps. "It was the last night to get out."

It's not the time for blame. It's not the time to say *you forced her to risk her life to go there and then she risked it again to get you out.* But I'm thinking it. My God, I'm thinking it.

I bury my head in my hands. "What do you mean it was the last night to get out?"

"Amelie showed me the hole they were digging. To bury the rest of the dead. She said it was our last chance to escape."

I hear the finality of those words, and my brain seems to empty, go numb, before I shake my head. "No," I tell her. "No. She isn't dead. She'd find another way."

Tears run down her face. "I need the laudanum," she says. "I can't face this without the laudanum."

I shake my head. "Marie, no. Whatever they had you on, you've got to break clean of it. I need you to focus so you can show me where you were held."

She slides to the floor and curls into a ball, weeping and inconsolable. "She won't be there."

"You don't know that!" I argue. "You were the one who was so convinced our mother was trapped somewhere!"

She looks up. "Everyone was dying, Henri. That drug made us sick, something else was making us sick too. There's no chance someone survived in there twenty years. None."

I feel the pulse of terror in my chest and push it away. She is wrong. She has to be. "I still need to see, for myself. Please, Marie."

She presses the base of her palms to her eyes. "Give me the laudanum," she finally says. "Give me *one*, and I'll show you where we were held."

THE DRUGS in Marie's system made it difficult to jump after she escaped from captivity, she tells me. She had to play dead until they'd shoveled dirt over her, wondering all the while if she'd suffocate before they were done.

It's a horrible story, one that makes clear how terrible things must have been on the inside. But she remembers the building they left from, near Sacré-Coeur, so that's where we head the next afternoon.

I wear my best clothes, my father's expensive watch, and tell Marie to do the same. She's so pale and thin it's hard to demand anything of her, but for Sarah's sake this needs to be done, and done right.

"Dress up?" she asks, her words still slightly slurred. "Whatever for?"

"Because wealthy people breaking down a door can say they are inspecting it. The rest of us are merely intruders."

"I don't know what it is you're hoping to find," she whispers. "If Amelie is still there, she'd be damaged beyond anything you or I can imagine. And she isn't there. No one could have survived it that long."

"I just need to know."

"Know what?" she asks, staring at the table. "Shall we pull the cement slab aside and look for her corpse?"

I flinch. "Marie, I need to do something. Don't you understand that? I have to. So yes, if all that is left is to pull the slab aside and look for her, I'll do it."

"She'll be wearing the necklace," Marie rasps, and then begins to weep again.

"What are you talking about?"

"I found a necklace that belonged to Maman in the pocket of my dress. I thought it would bring me good luck. I gave it to her before I left. Maybe it wasn't good luck at all. Maybe it was the worst luck and I handed it off to her."

I don't believe in luck. I don't think the necklace changed a thing. But it takes everything in my power not to ask Marie why she couldn't just have left it all alone. Why she couldn't have left Sarah alone, left the one good thing in my life with me instead of ripping it away.

Marie is tense beside me as we drive toward Paris, but not as tense as me. What will I do if I find Amelie today? Who will she be after twenty years of captivity?

I suppose the truth is that I pray I do not find her today at all. Because if her bones aren't there, it might mean that sometime between 1918 and now, she escaped.

It's just past dusk when we arrive in the city. Marie stares out the window as we pass landmarks I wish I didn't need to make her face. Sacré-Coeur, Parc de la Turlure. She's too frail for this right now, mentally and physically. If anything less were at stake, I'd never put her through this.

"She kept asking me not to run ahead that day," Marie says, still staring blankly outside. "I can't believe it was three months ago. It seems like a handful of days. She was so tired and I—" Her voice breaks.

I hunger for more information. I want to feed on these memories of hers, poor substitute for Sarah that they are. Except every word out of her mouth makes it too easy to picture Sarah, forcing her limbs to move despite the fatigue. That edge of worry in her voice as she cautioned Marie. I'm glad my sister has returned. I don't want to blame her for what happened, but it grows more difficult with each story she tells.

We turn left and then right. The area is run-down. Two decades after the war, and parts of Paris are only beginning to recover.

"There," whispers Marie. I stop the car and we both stare at the crumbling building, half of it blackened by fire and caving in.

No one could be alive inside it, but I'm going in anyway, because I have to know. "You don't have to come," I tell Marie.

"I'm going in," she replies. I grab the pickaxe from the trunk and walk to the door. She follows, holding the lantern I brought along, looking so sick I'm not sure how she's staying upright.

The lock breaks easily, worn by time, and we enter. My fist is tight around the axe, ready to fight if necessary, but the building is absent of life aside from the rats scurrying underfoot. Marie's hands shake as she points me toward the room where Amelie showed her the hole.

We both stare at the cement slab on the floor. My stomach spins. *Please God, don't let me find her there.* It takes all my strength to lift the slab and the smell that rises up makes both of us retch.

As terrible as it's been, not knowing what happened to her... knowing could prove worse. I brace myself and look beneath me.

There are bodies. So many bodies, most of their clothes decayed away and what's left looks as if it was burned, probably by the same fire that scarred the building's exterior. Some are skeletons, and some retain skin, though dried and blackened. I tell Marie to hold up the lantern, and I peer more closely.

It's only a moment before a glint of metal catches my eye. I grip the side of the hole. That glint is a knife to the gut, pure terror. A piece of me wants to walk away right now, continue to hope.

I take the lantern from Marie, though, and jump in. My knees give way as I land, and I crawl until I'm beside her, ignoring the crunch of bones beneath me. I raise the lantern.

My mother's necklace glimmers in the light, nestled against the collarbone of a girl who was almost mine.

10

SARAH

I work tirelessly over the next few days. Morning til night, I am the new Mathilde. I do all the cooking and cleaning while she lounges, watching me. It's not without its benefits, however—I get undrugged food, snippets of information. I also make one potentially valuable discovery: inside the pantry is a ladder and a trap door. Perhaps it just leads to a tiny loft, but it could be another floor, one with windows that aren't blacked out, where I could call for help.

Toward the end of the week, Mathilde tells me to dish up breakfast for the pregnant woman and take it to her.

"Only one?" I know one of the pregnant women gave birth last week. We were told she died in childbirth, though I have serious doubts. But there should still be two left.

"The other died in childbirth last night," replies Mathilde, not meeting my eye. "Child died too."

It was certainly not unheard of to die in childbirth in 1918, but I'm suspicious nonetheless. I'd assume Monsieur Coron would pull out all the stops to save the child...unless it turned out the child couldn't time travel.

"Was it a boy?" I ask quietly.

"Yes," she says. "Big one too." I hear a hint of sadness in her voice for the first time, and I file that fact away. She doesn't care what she's doing to the adults, but the infants...that bothers her.

I follow a guard down the long hall to get to the pregnant woman's room. He has to unlock the door to let me in. Katrin was right. If they'd known she was pregnant she'd never have escaped.

I try to meet the woman's eye, to let her know she isn't alone and that I'd help her if I could. She snatches the bowl from my hands and glares at me. She sees me as a traitor to our kind, like my aunt, and for the first time I have to wonder if she's right.

It's just over a week later when Mathilde gives me a different tablet for everyone's stew. I glance at her when I notice the difference, and she arches a brow, daring me to challenge her. My hand trembles as I continue to drop them in. *It's probably nothing,* I tell myself. But what if it isn't? If I refuse, they'll kill me, and all these women will still receive the tablet—all these women who are going to die anyway. They are *already* dead, in my time. But I don't want to be the one who did it. *It's probably nothing,* I tell myself again.

And then the next morning, the guard bangs on the metal pipe to wake us, and I'm the only one who rises.

He and I both look at each other, wide-eyed, an odd moment of kinship between enemies. Holding my breath, I lean over the woman nearest me. She has a bluish cast, and is ice cold when I touch her.

I poisoned them. I questioned what I was doing and wanted to live so badly that I accepted the situation and moved forward. Coldly. Like Iris and Coron might.

The guard grabs my arm and pulls me from the room without a word.

"Did you know?" I ask Mathilde when I reach the kitchen.

She turns away. I can't tell if she's ashamed or ambivalent. "There was nothing to be done for it," she says. "From now on, you'll help with the meals for the staff and take care of the baby. Her highness feels it's beneath her station."

I hate her for her lack of shame, though I'm hardly better. I knew something was wrong and followed orders to save my skin. But my aunt and Coron actually planned this, and though I'd expected nothing more of them, my hands shake as I finish cleaning and go to the nursery where Iris waits. We haven't spoken since she told me she was giving me a job, but when she sees me she smiles, as if we are friends.

With my jaw broken, it's difficult to return her smile, but I try. Something comes over me as I do it. I taste metal in my mouth, feel it sliding through my veins, and the lie becomes easier. *I will kill you and I will make sure you know it's happening*, I think as my mouth moves upward.

"You'll sleep here from now on," she says, thrusting a swaddled child in my arms. "Keep her healthy and I'll let you live when this is all done."

I nod, as if I'm stupid enough to believe that, and she walks out of the room, locking it behind her.

I take the room's only chair, holding the tiny bundle to my chest. Her eyes are closed, her rosebud mouth pursed in sleep. She may survive being raised by a monster like Coron, but who will she become as a result? What kind of power will that give him, having two time travelers under his command?

I want to save her for her own sake, but that vengefulness inside me wants it for another reason: I want to make sure Coron gets nothing when this is through.

I need to get her out, this baby and the one who is due any day now, and I can think of just one way: Mathilde. She's the only one who still gets to leave. But what would convince someone who happily killed twelve women to help? It's a question I can answer with ease, since I too just helped kill twelve people. What would motivate me?

If I was helping myself.

11

HENRI

My head rests on a bar. I don't know how I got here. I remember checking Marie into a hotel somewhere, and then I was heading out, looking for anything to dull the pain.

How am I going to continue? How am I going to keep taking care of my sister, when all I want to do is end it?

"Bourbon," I demand. "Give me the entire bottle."

The bartender raises a brow but slides the bottle over to me nonetheless. It's not the first bar I've been to today. I vaguely recall being tossed out of the last.

"Sarah," I whisper, staring at my hands. Hands that held her fragile bones. I rock a little on my stool. I can't stand this. I can't survive it. I grab the bottle and drink straight from the mouth. The patrons must sense the danger leaking from my pores, the recklessness. They give me a wide berth.

When the bottle is empty, time seems to become fluid. There are other bars. There's an alley, where I'm beating the living hell out of a man far less drunk than myself because he said something about Sarah. I can't even recall what he said, but I heard him. Everyone is saying her name, shouting it at me in the streets, taunting me with it.

I catch a flash of her hair and run toward it, but it disappears from view just as I get close.

I find myself in another bar. The room is poorly lit. There are couples half-dressed against doors and on tables. Men boasting loudly and women laughing, their faces barely visible in the haze of smoke. *Sarah*, one of them says. *Sarah is here.* I round on him and catch a flash of golden hair off in the corner. Hair that could only be hers.

I hear her laughter.

It thrills me.

It enrages me.

Sarah...she lied. She came back. But she didn't come home to me. She's in the darkest corner of the room, made up like a whore, wearing the red dress that drove me mad at the town dance. And she's with someone else.

I can't help what I do next. I stumble through the room, knocking into a man who's got a woman bent over in front of him, ricocheting against the bar. Pushing, swimming through the dark and the smoke and the bare limbs to reach her.

"Sarah," I gasp, grabbing her shoulder. My grip is too rough but I don't care. How could she have done this to me? She turns. I can barely see her face in the darkness but I can make out her red-painted lips tipping up into a coquettish smile.

"Well, hello there, handsome. Care to buy me a drink?"

She's been here all along.

Letting me grieve, go mad waiting for her.

The middle-aged man she's with sneers at me. "Go find your own girl," he says.

My fist slams into his face, and he falls from the chair. The room is so dark few people notice and those who do merely laugh.

This rage is a tornado in my chest, in my brain. I wonder if they'll laugh if I hit her next. I could. I'm angry enough.

It's like lava, bubbling, burning me from the inside, roiling in my veins and demanding release. I want to weep with relief, and I want to wound her for what she's put me through, for the fact that she didn't even care enough to tell me she's alive.

"I could kill you right now," I hiss.

"Slow down there, hot stuff," she says, handing me a glass full of something. "Whatever I've done I'm sure I can make you forgive me."

I drop to my knees and grab her face, pulling her lips to mine hard. She feels different. Her kiss is different. *Because she's been here, with other men*, I think. I kiss her harder, trying to push them away, trying to erase them from her history and get us back to where she was mine and mine alone.

My face is wet. It takes a moment to realize I'm crying, like a child. "How could you do that to me?" I shout. "Do you have any idea how sick I've been? How many times I thought about ending it all? And here you were, drinking in Paris, dressed like a whore."

She pulls my mouth back to hers. "Forgive me, baby. I'm sorry. I thought you'd like it. Show me you forgive me."

"I don't," I slur, holding onto her. "I don't think I'll ever forgive you."

Her hands go to my belt. "I can make you forget what I did. Please, baby. Don't you love me? I can feel it in your kiss. Show me again."

She's right. I can't stay angry. I don't know why she did it but she's alive. I can forgive anything she's done simply because she's alive.

I kiss her, and after a moment she is pulling me up the stairs. I follow blindly in the darkness, holding on to her tightly in case she disappears. I stumble again and again, falling against the wall and pulling her with me.

"Careful, baby," she says.

I hate how flippant and careless she sounds. She's never called me that before, and it makes me feel like I'm one of many. How many men has she been with here? "Don't call me that," I slur.

She pulls me into a room and I grab her hard, trying to stay upright, angry all over again. "How many men?" I demand. "How many men here?"

She presses against me. "Only you. You're the first. Kiss me. Show your Sarah you forgive her."

My little thief. My little lying thief. I don't care what she's done. I don't care who she's become. I will love whatever she is now. I bury my face in her hair. "I love you so much. I should never have let you leave."

"I'm here now, darling," she says.

"I thought you were dead," I whisper. "I thought you were dead."

She rubs my back. "I'm here now." She pulls up her dress. "Show me how much you've missed me."

I WAKE in the morning covered in my own vomit, head pounding in a way that makes me long for death, until I remember it. Sarah.

She came to me last night. Though the light makes me feel as if I'll throw up once more, I force myself to sit. Was it a dream? I found her bones yesterday, but last night...it seems every bit as real. The room is empty but my pants are folded neatly on a chair. A woman's brush sits on the chest of drawers beside it.

Despite my hangover, my heart begins to hammer in my chest. Was she really here all along? Why didn't she come to me? I'd have let her go, if that's what she wanted, but how could she have let me believe—

The door opens. And the disappointment hits me so hard I

feel undone by it. The woman who enters is blonde, like Sarah, perhaps shares a passing resemblance to her, but nothing more.

"Awake at last," she says with a cheerful smile. "You had quite a night, didn't you?"

She's not Sarah, but she's also nothing like what I thought last night. She wears no makeup and her dress is modest. She is nothing like the coquettish woman I accused of being a whore. Maybe I dreamed all of it. I hope I did.

"Why am I here?" I ask. "Who are you?"

She gives me a shy smile. "I'd hoped to be more memorable than that."

I press my face to my hands. I'm going to be sick. "I thought you were someone else," I reply, wincing through the pounding in my head.

She perches beside me on the bed. "Your wife? She left you?"

It hits me hard, the truth. Until yesterday, I could hope Sarah would come back. And now that hope is gone.

"Something like that," I reply. I grit my teeth to force the words out.

The girl takes my hand. "I'm sorry that happened," she says. "But I'm here for you now."

The pain of it all makes me long for death. The pain in my head, the desperate need to vomit, the disappointment of discovering it wasn't Sarah with me last night. That less than twenty-four hours after discovering she is gone I've already been untrue to her memory. I push the hand away, cross the room to my clothes.

"I'm sorry," I tell the girl. "I need to get home."

12

SARAH

The final child, another girl, is born. Which means there isn't much time.

I continue to care for the babies. I name them A and B. I'm worried if I give them real names, they'll become harder to let go of.

There's a false sense of safety, sitting in the rocking chair alone with these two tiny infants, but I know that it will all end soon. I walk through the plan, all day long, looking for loopholes. There are many, of course, but I've got nothing better, and no more time to waste.

That night, as Mathilde and I prepare dinner, I broach the topic with my heart hammering loud in my chest. "Do you really think all those staff members just left at the same time?" I ask.

She looks at me sharply, nostrils flaring. "They were dismissed. What are you trying to say?"

I meet her eye. "I'm trying to say it's a dangerous place to work. If they don't mind killing us, they won't mind killing you either."

"I've got no choice," she replies. "My husband died in the war and I've got four wee ones who'll starve without this pay."

It's exactly what I hoped she might say. "I might be able to help. For a price."

She laughs. "You? The girl who serves food and does the wash? You'll be in that hole in the ground long before they need to get rid of me."

I don't appreciate her ambivalence about my death, but it hardly matters.

"It's possible I have more resources than you're aware of," I reply.

Her eyes narrow. "I can barely get out of here myself, and even then but once a week. I can't help you."

"I don't want you to help me," I reply. "I want you to help the babies. I want you to sneak them out."

She gasps. "They'd be on to me in five seconds."

I take a deep breath. This is the risky part of the plan. I'm giving her information she can turn on me. It wouldn't serve her, but I'm not sure she realizes that.

"What if you brought in two dead infants to replace them?" I ask. "Even skeletons would work. Everyone is starving after the war. You must see a child die every day."

Her eyes are wide, and then she laughs. "You've gone mad, girl. You'll get caught and then it will be my head on a platter. I won't help you."

"You might, though, for fifty thousand francs."

Her head jerks upward and she stands, slack-jawed, staring at me. Hemingway once described living quite well in Paris with his family on five hundred francs a year. If that's the case, what might ten times that buy? Her loyalty, perhaps.

"Fifty thousand," she breathes. "You can't possibly have that much."

"You're right," I agree, "but I know someone who does."

"But they'll know they're the wrong infants. Mademoiselle Iris would know."

"Not if I set the whole room on fire, she won't."

She stares at me. "If you start a fire, you'll die with them."

"I'm dying anyway, according to you," I reply. "Maybe I just want to leave the world a hero."

~

The following weekend, Mathilde leaves with her empty bags and a letter, addressed to Henri's mother.

And then I wait, with my stomach in knots, wondering if this is going to backfire. Madame Durand, at this moment, is recently widowed and has a newborn and toddler of her own to contend with. If she refuses to help, Mathilde will take my letter straight to the guards and tell them my plans, I'm certain of it.

I'm not even entirely convinced Mathilde will take her the letter at all. When I told her Madame Durand lives on a farm, she was suspicious.

"Then how does she have so much money?" she asked.

I met her eye. "She lives modestly but she is not to be trifled with, I assure you."

I'm responsible for cooking dinner on my own that night. I'm just finishing the supper dishes when she returns. Her expression is wary, and there's extra weight in the bag she carries.

She did what I asked.

~

For the rest of the week, we continue on. I take care of the babies, a job I actually enjoy, to my surprise. And it's a relief to steer clear of Mathilde and Iris and the guards, all of whom are snapping with anxiety. Given that Coron arrives next Saturday, I can't blame them, but Iris is anxious too, which puzzles me. I wonder if she's finally starting to suspect she's not as safe as she'd hoped.

On Saturday afternoon, Iris unlocks the door, telling me she's off to take a nap before her big night and reminding me I'll need to make dinner in Mathilde's stead. She locks me in, but a short time later, Mathilde unlocks it again and hands me two bags— one with the dead infants, one for the live ones.

She is pale. "How can you be so calm?" she asks.

I'm hardly calm right now, but admitting it won't help. So much can go wrong—the possibilities are endless—and I'd prefer she not realize it.

"Because this is going to work," I reply. "You're about to be wealthy."

She gives me a brisk, uncertain nod, and then opens her bag.

I gently place A and B on top of the dirty laundry, both of them so still it gives me qualms. Dosing them with a bit of the drug was necessary, but I pray to God as I kiss their foreheads that I haven't given them too much. Together we arrange clothes on top of them so they're mostly covered but can still breathe.

"You're sure she'll pay?" Mathilde asks.

The question makes my heart rate increase. She has drugged babies in the bag she carries, their faces covered with dirty laundry, and her worry is the payday. I'm still not convinced she doesn't have some scheme in mind...take the babies, tell the guards, give Madame Durand some other children.

"As long as she receives these two babies, she'll pay," I caution. "She'll know if you've given her other children, believe me."

She looks shocked that I'd even imply she might do anything else. "You really take me for someone who'd steal other babies and leave these two to die?"

I would like to point out that her character is hardly unimpeachable, given what she's done, but I refrain. "Of course not," I say diplomatically.

She walks out and I listen with my stomach knot-tight, waiting for the sound of some argument, some distress. I hear none, and then there is the creak of the door being opened and the echo as it slams shut. She is out. She's done most of her part. Now it's time for mine.

I open the bag Mathilde left, and remove the tiny skeletons. I don't want to know where she located two dead infants, but I feel nothing as I swaddle them in blankets and place caps over their heads. Who have I become, that I don't care that these children are dead? Will I recover who I was if I manage to live? Could Henri possibly still want me if I don't?

I place them in their cribs and go to serve dinner. The whole time I wait for a guard to storm in, crying that the babies are gone, but the night is quiet.

I return to the room and wait for Iris to lock me in for the night. "You don't appear to be working especially hard," she says when she opens the door.

"The children are sleeping," I reply, jumping to my feet. "Are you ready? It must be hard to impress a man like Mr. Coron. He's probably used to a different standard of living than we are. Fine clothes and jewelry."

Her eyes narrow a bit. "He likes me just fine," she says, but her eyes hone in on my necklace, just as I predicted. She's looked at it many times before.

I follow her gaze, and then I hold it out for her to see. "Would you like to...borrow it? For tonight? The diamonds are real." I have no idea if this is true, but, obviously, neither does she.

Her mouth turns up in a slight smirk she immediately restrains. "Yes," she says with the air of a queen, as if she's done me a favor. I unclasp it and hand it to her, praying she won't notice my shaking hands.

She takes it and begins to clasp it around the back of her neck, walking to the mirror to survey herself. That's when I reach for the knife I took from the kitchen, lying under a pile of blankets behind me. Aside from childhood skirmishes with my brother, I've never even hit someone before, and now I'm about to kill. For a moment, watching her smile at her reflection, I'm not sure I can go through with it. She is a pretty girl, a silly girl, besotted with a powerful man, believing she's in love and feeling as if a glorious future is just within reach.

But she is also the one who had those women killed after their children were delivered. She's the one who instructed Mathilde to increase the amount of poison, who didn't just allow but *orchestrated* the rape of Katrin and Luna.

Rage clogs my throat, giving me the adrenaline I need. She turns and I lunge, shoving the knife into her heart so fast her mouth doesn't open until my hand is already covering it. Her eyes go wide and she struggles, but she is no match for me.

With my free hand I hold onto the knife for dear life, and feel the power as it surges through me. Her power. Her spark. Now *mine*. My limbs are gaunt but they sing with life and energy. I've never felt stronger than I do now, energy coiling inside me as I hold onto the knife. I remain like that until I'm certain I will explode with the excess adrenaline, and then I spring from the floor like a wild animal, buoyed by her spark.

That's when I finally look around the room, seeing it through the eyes of someone else. Perhaps through the eyes of the girl I was when I arrived here. There are skeletons in the cribs and Iris's body on the floor. We are both covered in blood.

And it's all my doing. Does that make me like her? I don't know. But there's no time to worry about that now.

I grab her keys and then I set the curtains and crib ablaze. With one last glance, I run from the room, locking the door behind me.

I hide in the closet across the hall and wait for the guards to discover the fire. They're hardly a selfless bunch. They won't try to put out the fire for long before they unlock the door and run, which is when I will follow.

It takes them longer than I expected, though. The room I wait in and the hall outside are full of smoke before I hear them shouting in the distance. Footsteps echo, back and forth, but they don't seem to be leaving.

Why the hell are they still here?

The hall is so full of smoke I can barely see. I open my door, and that's when I finally hear what they're saying.

"Find Grenoir!" someone screams. "He's the only one with the key!"

"He's gone," another coughs. "Fire on the lock instead."

The one guard who possesses the key is missing. Maybe he left when Mathilde did. Maybe he's just fallen asleep for the night. But when the door of the nursery finally explodes and fire races along the hall, I know I can no longer wait to find out.

I drop to the floor.

Think, I beg of myself, *think*.

I hear them firing on the lock, and then screams as the fire catches them. Despite Iris's spark, I still can't time travel, not with that shrieking overhead. There's only one solution left: to go up through the entrance in the pantry to the second floor. If there's anything up there at all.

I crawl along the floor to the kitchen, desperately trying to focus on that one goal. The smoke fills my brain and my lungs; my head grows light.

Where was I going again? To Henri?

Pantry, whispers some urgent voice.

I finally reach the door. It's locked.

I lie down and close my eyes. *Sarah*, Henri asks, *are you alright?*

He's lying beside me, in our bed. I press my hands to my face, wishing I could explain, though it would make no sense to him. *The door is locked*, my head screams, *and I don't know how to get out.*

But suddenly I know what he'd tell me, if I could reach him. He'd ask me where the keys are. And I have all of Iris's keys in my pocket.

My eyes open. The room is black with smoke but I feel for the smallest of the keys and then my hands slide up the door until I find the lock. After three tries, just as I feel the heat of the fire approaching and I'm about to give up, it slides in and the handle turns. I crawl inside and reach for the ladder.

Henri speaks to me, saying something urgent. I force my hands to grip the wooden rungs, one and then the next, one and then the next. The fire is inside the kitchen now, and licks at the ladder beneath me. The food on the shelves bursts into flame, sending fiery ash flying into my hair and face, singeing my dress. I throw myself onto the second floor just as the hem catches fire and roll to put it out. Flames are already climbing through the opening as I jump to my feet and look frantically for a way to escape.

There is nowhere to go. No door. No one to beg for help.

But there's a window.

I take a deep breath. I don't know if this is going to work. But I have no more options and my aunt's spark is singing inside me, making me feel as if I could fly if I put my mind to it.

I run at the window, hard as I can, but in my mind I'm already thinking of Henri, of home. I picture the orchard, his lavish promises to buy me Versailles. I go to the night we planned for our honeymoon, and I think of waking beside him in the morning, all his miles of smooth skin, his contented murmur of pleasure at finding me there. The glass shatters and I'm in the air, plummeting toward the sidewalk. I can feel my body going light, but not fast enough.

And then I hit the ground.

13

Heaven is a noisy place.

There is constant chatter. There are beeping machines and shouting and always the sound of people talking over my head, their voices urgent and unhappy. *Anorexic*, they say. *Attempted suicide.*

I'm feverish, sweaty and then shivering. I can't reply, can't even open my eyes. I know I need to fight to return to Henri, but I'm too empty. I'm below water, and there's not enough energy inside me to climb to the surface. I fight it a little less each day. And then, at last, it stops. I'm empty, silent, my body slowly sinking toward the bottom of the ocean. And it's a relief to land there at last.

MY TIME under water seems to last forever. I wonder if this is the afterlife. I've lived through worse, but it's all just empty.

And then suddenly there is motion again, and light. I hear sounds, feel cool air on my skin, the pressure of a hand on mine. My eyes open, and I find myself in a sunlit yellow room that seems familiar. The woman sitting next to my bed seems familiar as well. My brain, still below the surface of the water a bit, tries to recall how I know her.

Cecelia. It comes at last. The woman who saved me the last time I was in 1989. How am I still in Paris with her? Did I dream it all...leaving here, going to Henri?

My mouth opens. My lips are dry, my tongue heavy. "What happened to me?" I ask. "Why am I here?"

Her hand wraps around mine. "You jumped out of a window," she says. She looks over her shoulder before leaning closer to whisper. "In 1918. Do you remember it?"

I think about the fall from the window. My body going light, and the horrible, all-encompassing pain as I hit the sidewalk. I must have been jerked back to my own time, rather than Henri's.

"I don't understand how I survived," I whisper.

"Nor I," she says. "You'll decide later on that you must have begun to time travel before your body fully took the impact of the fall, and that you had some extra energy to help you heal." My aunt's spark is what she's referring to. I wonder if I ever shared with her how I acquired it. "As it was, though, you were found in very bad shape. You broke more bones than you *didn't* break, including your skull."

"Marie," I whisper. "Did she get home?"

Cecelia nods, with a small smile. "Thanks to you, yes. Katrin did as well."

"How do you—" I begin to ask, and then I realize she knows about Katrin because, as always, at some point in *her* past I told her about it.

And in the past, Henri waits. I've got to get home to him.

I start trying to sit up and she presses her hand to my shoulder. "Not yet," she says. "You've been in a medically induced coma for quite a while now. Let the doctors assess you before you try to move. Please."

"A *coma*? How long have I been out?"

She hesitates. "You were found on March first," she says gently. "Today is September fifth."

September.

I've been gone, then, for ten *months*. Poor Henri must be worried sick. So worried I can hardly stand to imagine it. *I don't have to return to September of 1939*, I think, my heart beating harder. *I could go to March instead. The babies would be safe, and I could spare him some of the pain.*

Except it goes against everything I believe in. No matter how bad those months were for him, they're his, not mine, and they're behind us now. But I've got to get to him as soon as I can. I sit up, ignoring her hand, ignoring the way my body protests the movement. "I've got to get back to Henri."

"Stop," she commands. "Please...stop. Just listen to me."

I stare at her, and my eyes well with frustrated tears. I want Henri. I crave him. "I miss him so much I feel physically ill from it," I whisper. "So, say what you need to say and let me go."

"He's not there," she blurts out.

I suck in a breath. In all these months I spent trying to live, trying to get back home to him, it never occurred to me that it was *his* survival I might need to worry about. "What do you mean, he's not there? Is Henri... Did something happen to him while I was gone?"

She shakes her head. "He will be whole and healthy when you return. He's fighting right now. The Saar Offensive, a brief battle that will end badly for the French."

I press my hands to my face. "He's fighting? They were supposed to go to the United States. I made Marie promise. I—" I can't believe how wrong it's all gone.

"Life got in the way," she says softly, her face sad for a moment before she blinks it away. "He'll be home soon, but you're in no shape to go anywhere at the moment, and besides that...I've intervened again," she says. "You really shouldn't go back until October twelfth, which is when you originally went."

My eyes well once more. I can't believe I'm finally capable of returning to him and she expects me to wait. "How could it matter?" I ask, wrenching the IV from my arm. "I can't just sit here for five weeks. Surely you understand that."

There's worry in her face, and her mouth opens to argue, then closes. "He won't return from the front until September twenty-fifth. Stay here that long at least. You need physical therapy anyway. In your current condition, anything could happen when you jump."

I can't argue with her logic, and perhaps I should be grateful for what she's done, or for the mere fact that I survived when so many did not. But right now, I need to see Henri.

For so many reasons, but this one most of all: it feels like there's something she's not telling me.

THE DOCTOR PRONOUNCES my recovery a miracle. "You're very lucky to be alive," he says. Cecelia sits on the other side of me, holding my hand. "You healed beyond anything I imagined possible, given the extent of your injuries," he adds, yet I hear a *but* coming. A warning of some kind.

"Yes," I say, sick with worry as I wait.

"I regret to say that we couldn't fix everything," he says. "You suffered a great deal of internal damage. The scar tissue...makes it unlikely that you will ever have children."

It's not what I thought he was going to say and I wish, somehow, I'd been prepared for it. I fall back against the pillows. I think of last fall, when Henri and I watched Charlotte and Lucien...how I'd been able to see us as parents. How badly I hungered for it, out of nowhere.

I want Henri to be a father. And it's something he wants for himself. Now I'm going to return after nearly a year's disappearance, gaunt, not entirely myself, and tell him I can never give that to him.

"You can always adopt," the doctor says. He begins describing some new process that involves a donor egg and an implanted embryo. Except in 1939, everything he's saying will sound like science fiction.

I know Henri would never complain. But it's one more way I'm returning to him damaged. When I left, I could give him a family and now I can't. When I left, I was optimistic, hopeful, a little naïve, but now I've seen too many things. People have died because of me.

I wonder if he'll feel the same when he learns.

THAT AFTERNOON I'm taken by wheelchair to a gym just down the hall. My therapist's name is Guy. I force myself to smile as we are introduced, but there's a piece of me that feels unsettled, something I don't quite understand.

"You rich Americans are keeping us in business," he says, nodding behind him at a man using a walker to cross the room. "Rob," he calls over his shoulder, "come meet our new guest."

My jaw drops. The American to whom he referred is Rob Chapman, a singer whose poster still probably hangs beside my bed back home. He's even better looking in real life than I realized, but there it is again—that slightly unsettled feeling—as he hobbles over to us.

I glance over my shoulder, unnerved to be in such a large, open room. No one has threatened me, but I don't feel safe here.

"You're the other American, huh?" he asks. "The girl who fell off a building—that's you—and the guy whose motorcycle hit a brick wall—that's me. The two of us are giving our countrymen a bad name, but it will make a nice story for our grandchildren."

I smile, but it's rusty and uncertain. What I really want to do is roll back to my room and lock the door. "I'm engaged, but feel free to tell *your* grandchildren."

"Engaged?" he asks. He gives me his most charming smile. "*How* engaged exactly?"

I've spent so long looking over my shoulder that I can't seem to stop. He's flirting but I only perceive a threat, and I want Henri. I want to be home. I swallow. "Very engaged," I reply. "Excuse me."

I try to maneuver the chair but I can't get away. "Hey, hang on there," says Guy. "We haven't even worked out yet."

I can't breathe. He's holding my chair and I'm not sure what will happen if I try to walk. Even in captivity, I don't think I ever felt quite this powerless, which is illogical. But that familiar rage pulses in my chest, and if I had a knife I'd make him very sorry. "Let go of my chair!" I snap. "Let go of the fucking chair!"

His eyes widen and he steps backward, holding both hands up as if surrendering.

I suck in air, feel the pinch of tears. "I'm sorry," I whisper. "I... just got out of a really bad place."

Rob gives me a tiny, tense nod. "Is there someone I can call for you?" he asks gently. "Your boyfriend? Who will make you feel safe right now?"

I try to control my breathing. *Henri*, I think, *but he's not here.* "Cecelia," I whisper. "Or one of her bodyguards."

In under a minute, Philippe stands in the room, with his stern, impassive, wonderfully familiar face. "I'm here, Mademoiselle Durand," he says calmly. "No one will get near you without your permission."

After a moment, I'm collected enough to begin. Guy treats me as if I might shatter at any moment, and I realize he might be right, when suddenly Cecelia rushes through the doors looking frantic.

She comes to where I stand, supporting my weight on parallel bars, and her hand goes to my face. "You never told me how bad it was," she says. Her eyes fill. "But it must have been quite bad."

I nod, and tears begin to run down my face. "Yes," I finally reply. My head falls to her shoulder. "It was."

She takes me back to my room and sits with me, distressed about what happened in the gym. I'm distressed too, but for other reasons. Something is wrong with me. I've got so much fear, and anger, I don't even know what to do with myself. Yet I suffered so much less than Katrin did...I wonder how she managed.

"You told me Katrin escaped successfully and got home," I say. That knot in my gut tightens. "But was she...okay?"

Cecelia's eyes focus on my hand, still in her grip. "She never quite recovered, it seems. She stayed alive for her son, nothing more."

I hesitate. In the back of my mind, I've hoped that perhaps I'm descended from other children Katrin had later on. "She only had the one child?" I ask, my voice a whisper.

"Yes," she says gently. "His name was Alexander."

Which means Coron is my grandfather, a quarter of my DNA. The man responsible for Henri's mother's death. The reason he had to leave Oxford and give up his entire life.

She squeezes my hand. "I know what you're thinking right now, but don't," she says. "Your genetics only tell a small part of your story."

Except I'm seeing what's inside me and that rage, that cruelty...it's not small. I thought, once I escaped captivity, that I could leave that rage behind, but it's as if Coron and Iris are still inside me somewhere, begging to be set free. I wanted to kill that therapist today. The desire pulsed in my chest, so overwhelming it was all I could feel until the dust settled. I need to know why. I need to know how it could have happened, and why my family has lied about it my entire life.

After Cecelia leaves, I place the call. I haven't spoken to my mother in over a year—not since that ugly phone call a summer ago when she told me she wished I'd never been born. I have no expectation that she will want to hear from me, but I don't really care.

"Mom? It's Sarah."

The other end of the line is silent. "Oh," she finally says, with a weary, disappointed sigh—the same kind she gave every time I called, every time I asked for something. Whether it was permission to sit at the table or permission to leave it, a suggestion I might come home to visit or a suggestion it was time I should go, her reaction was always this—disgust and exhaustion, as if I was once again asking too much.

In that weary, disappointed sigh, I'm reminded all over again why I chose to cut her off, and I don't feel the need to slowly build up to the purpose of this call. "I met your sister."

I hear a muted gasp on the other end of the line. "Iris?" she asks after a moment, her voice barely audible. For once, I've managed to surprise her. "She's alive?"

"No," I reply. "But I learned some interesting things before I killed her."

She laughs—a short, dismissive bark. "As if I'd believe that. Are you under the impression that would upset me even if I did?"

"I couldn't care less if you're upset," I reply. "But I now know that Peter Stewart wasn't my father, and I'd like the truth."

The other end of the line is silent. Angry silence, I'm sure. It's the only kind my mother knows. "I don't know what you're talking about," she finally says, her voice imperious once more, "but I'm hanging up."

I anticipated this part. She thinks she's immune to the consequences of her actions, and that I've got nothing to hold over her. But I know her Achilles heel: my brother. She'd rather die than let him know what she truly is.

"I'll tell Steven. And I'll take a paternity test to prove it to him, so don't think you can lie to him the way you have been to me my entire life."

"You wouldn't do that."

I laugh. "Wouldn't I? I stabbed your sister in the chest. You think telling Steven the truth would be hard for me?"

Air hisses through her teeth. "You really want to know what you are?" she asks. "Fine. I'll tell you. You are how God punished me for being a part of that family. Your father...he took advantage of me, the night before my wedding. All because of what Iris did to his mother. And I've had to endure you and the pain you've brought into my life ever since. You're just as evil as he is. So now you know. Never call this number again."

She hangs up, and I hold the phone to my chest, feeling worse than I did before. So much ugliness had to exist to create me. How could anything but ugliness result?

14

HENRI

We are three miles over the German border when my commander asks for volunteers to scout ahead.

The battle has been brutal already. Venturing forward is a risk only an insane man would take. Or one with nothing to lose. These days, I often believe I'm both.

I start to rise and Maurice—a friend from Saint Antoine— grabs my sleeve. "What the hell are you doing?" he hisses. "You have people who need you back home."

He's right, but my responsibilities are now a burden that feels unimaginably heavy. "We're all going to die in this war anyway," I reply as I stand. "Now or next year."

The men still seated look at me as if I'm a hero, when in truth it's cowardice. God help me, but I'd welcome the end.

I MAKE it nearly a mile through the woods, close enough to spy the enemy's location, before a bullet tears into my side. I fall to the ground and slide along the forest floor, hoping I can somehow get back to my unit and tell them what I know.

Soon, though, the world seems to tilt and shift. I hear words in the wind, and night comes when it was only daylight a moment before.

"Henri," whispers Sarah, her hand on my back, "you need to wake up."

I open my eyes to find her there. Not the skeleton in burned clothing, but whole and perfect, smiling at me as if I've nodded off under an apple tree and she's come to bring me inside.

"You're not real," I tell her. "You died. I found you."

Her palm presses to my skin. "Does that not feel real to you?" she asks. "Wake up. Madame Beauvoir is here and I'm not facing her alone."

I pull her against me. "Then stay with me here instead," I tell her. "We'll sleep until she's gone."

Her lips press to mine. "It's not the time for rest," she says.

I hear voices nearby speaking French, and the moment I notice them, she's gone. That sorrow hits me all over again and my hand digs into the dirt.

Come back, Sarah. Please come back.

The voices grow closer. I'm tempted to let them pass and leave me here to die. But then I think of Sarah, who sacrificed herself for my sister. Sarah, who would never have gone down without a fight.

For her, and her alone, I call out for help.

15

SARAH

Over the next few days I become accustomed to life in the hospital, but I'm still anxious and wary everywhere I go, and I'm unable to escape it. When I sleep there are nightmares. I dream that Gustave has me cornered, that the bed is on fire, that Iris has me trapped. Sometimes I dream that Mathilde forgot about the babies, and I watch as she pulls them, still and cold, from that laundry bag where they were hidden.

It's not much better when I'm awake. Using a walker, I'm allowed to take strolls around the building and down to the park, which I do several times a day, but everywhere I look I see threats of one kind or another. There is a bodyguard with me at all times, but it's not enough.

I read everything I can about the war in my free time, and that doesn't reassure me either. I wish I knew how to fight, how to keep us safe, and I don't. Killing the guards was easy. Protecting our family from nonspecific threats for five years straight is another matter entirely.

It all makes me wonder if I'm ever going to feel safe again.

Rob comes to the treadmill beside mine three days after *the incident*, as I like to refer to it.

"I'm sorry about the other day," he says. "I didn't mean to scare you."

I shake my head. "You didn't...I just—"

He hesitates and then turns off his treadmill, which was already going so slowly it was barely moving. "Don't apologize. I don't know what you've been through, but I know it was bad, and I get how you must feel."

"You do?"

"My sister was raped in college," he says. "Walking home from class in the middle of the fucking afternoon. It took her years to feel safe again."

I swallow. "But she's okay now?"

He lifts a single shoulder. "She married a really great guy and I think most of the time now it's behind her. She never did go back to school, though. I'm sorry. Maybe that wasn't the best example to provide. I just wanted you to know I get it."

In other words, she did not recover, but she can *pretend* she's alright for the most part. I don't want to pretend when I get home to Henri. I don't want to have a panic attack any time we're around strangers.

I don't want to be this person I'm discovering inside me. The one who can rationalize away the things she's done. The one who even takes pleasure in some of it. Because sometimes, when I picture the shock on my aunt's face as I plunged the knife into her chest or remember the guards' screams as they burned alive, I feel *warmed* by it. That vicious place inside me sated, momentarily. There are times when it seems to be the only thing that brings me joy.

Henri deserves better, and I'm not sure I'll be able to provide it.

∼

THAT AFTERNOON, Cecelia joins me on one of my walks, her body-guards walking discreetly behind us. Just as we reach the park I feel a prickle between my shoulder blades and glance around us. I see the same things I do every day—old men sitting on benches, toddlers running clumsily over the grass, women smoking with a book in hand.

"What's the matter?" she asks. "Are you too tired?"

I bite my lip. I'm sure I already seem crazy, given my freak-out the other day, and what I'm about to say won't help. "I feel like we're being watched."

Cecelia pats my arm. "Louis and Philippe are here," she says. "You're in good hands."

"They won't always be," I whisper. "I need to be able to defend myself. Do you think you could get me a gun?"

She laughs. "Fragility, trauma and weapons don't mix well. My goal is to get you back to 1939, just as you arrived before, not turn you into a murder suspect."

We make a circle of the park, and just before we turn back to the hospital, I spin toward the woods...just in time to see a woman standing there disappear into thin air. My knees buckle at the sight and it's Cecelia who grabs me before I fall.

"Time traveler," I whisper. The words are barely audible. I point toward the woods. "There was a time traveler there."

"You're sure?" Cecelia asks, lifting her sunglasses to look in the direction I'm pointing. Even from here we can see the woman's clothes, lying in a heap on the ground.

"I'm sure," I reply. *Why was she here? What does she want?* I'm never going to feel safe until I'm certain I can defend myself.

"Even if I can't have a gun in the hospital," I say to Cecelia, leaning on my walker and trying to catch my breath, "that doesn't mean I can't be taught how to use one, does it?"

She glances from me to that pile of clothes by the woods. "No, I don't suppose it does."

REHABILITATION OF MY WEAK, broken body becomes secondary from then on. From sun-up to sundown, my focus is on learning to fight. Cecelia hires two different specialists: a Navy SEAL who teaches me how to shoot and use a knife, and an Israeli soldier who teaches me hand-to-hand combat.

What I appreciate about both men is that neither act like I'm a silly, scared girl. They both treat me as if I'm someone going to war, which is truer than they can even imagine. I'm taught to throw a dagger from thirty feet away, and when I can finally hit a bullseye with my right hand, I'm forced to train with my left. Using dummies, I'm taught how to immobilize my opponent, how to break a neck, where to punch to kill someone immediately—corner of the jaw or nasal cavity. Where to stab someone in the back to puncture a lung, useful because it prevents them from screaming. How to slit a throat, useful for the same reason. When Paul, the SEAL, starts showing me how to stab someone in the chest, I wave him off. "I already know that one."

Holding a knife in my hands makes me feel calm, and also powerful. It makes me wish I could go back to 1918 with my new knowledge, solely to watch Gustave die. At night I think about how I will punish Coron—how I can manage to trap him and kill him slowly. It's the lullaby that sings me to sleep on the nights when rage leaves me unable to find Henri, when I'm worried he'll find me so changed he won't want me.

But given it's the rage itself that's changed me, and that the more I allow it, the more of it I feel, I sometimes wonder if I've escaped captivity only to poison myself instead. Killing comes as naturally to me as walking must have, once upon a time, and I'm not sure that's a good thing.

Henri will fix it, I promise myself. Everything that's broken inside me won't stay this way once I'm with him again. It can't.

"So, tell me about this fiancé of yours," says Rob, on the treadmill beside mine, where I find him most days now. He has a bit of a crush—perhaps because I'm the first female who's ever shot him down. "Is he famous? He must be famous."

I smile. "No, not in the least."

"Well then, can you tell me why he isn't here?" Rob asks, arching a brow. "No offense, but under the circumstances, the guy should be here."

"He's...fighting. He's in the military," I reply. "He'll be home soon."

"Well, if something changes," Rob says, "let me know."

"Nothing's going to change," I reply.

Inside I say a silent prayer that it's actually true.

AT THE END of the second week, Louis comes to collect me, as Cecelia promised he would. Though I'm not ready to run a marathon, I can walk a mile on the treadmill at a relatively normal pace, which is more than I can say for Rob.

I pop my head in the gym as I'm leaving, clad in the jeans and a t-shirt I purchased here the summer before. Rob sees me and comes over, still using his walker.

"That's just cruel," he says, "walking in here in those jeans just to say goodbye."

I smile, choosing to ignore that. "It's been fun. Good luck with everything."

He nods at Anna, his assistant, who hands something to Louis. "Anna just gave your bodyguard all my numbers. If things don't work out with Henri, give me a call. I've got another month here before I start my European tour. You can be my plus one, no strings attached." He grins. "I mean, I'd *prefer* it if there were strings, but I'll live if there aren't."

I laugh and lean forward to kiss him on the cheek. "Good luck, Rob."

"Henri's a lucky man," he says. "I hope he realizes it."

I force a smile. The truth is that I'm the lucky one. I just hope my luck continues to hold.

~

I'M TAKEN from the hospital to another of Cecelia's beloved spa appointments, where I'm waxed and scrubbed until I shine, where my hair is cut and my nails are done and my brows are plucked. From there, I'm taken to a gorgeous flat, just off the Champs-Élysées, with all my belongings waiting for me in the master suite. I know I should relish it all, but in a day's time, I'll be back with Henri, and I hunger for it so much I can barely notice anything else.

On the day of my departure, I rise early and find myself pacing, too excited to sit still. When Cecelia arrives with a bagful of croissants, I take one and sit with her in the parlor, though I'm too nervous to eat.

She pours coffee for us while I bounce on the edge of the couch like a little girl who needs a bathroom badly.

"I have a favor to ask," she says carefully, handing me a cup of coffee, "and it matters a great deal to me."

I take the cup she proffers, nodding, ready to agree to anything as long as it gets me home to Henri. "You originally did not arrive until October twelfth," she says. "And because you were very unwell that time, you had to recover, so you remained there."

My stomach tightens into a knot. "I'm going to remain there anyway."

She doesn't meet my eye. "I know. But I'd like you to promise me...that you'll stay. To go sooner could be disastrous. I wanted to help you and make sure you got better medical care this time, though to be honest I can't remember why I wanted it—I suppose because whatever went wrong the first time has been corrected.

But the *date*. The date is important. And you could destroy everything by arriving too soon."

"I'm planning to stay forever," I reply. "I don't understand why we're even discussing this."

She averts her gaze, but not before I see that worried thing in her face.

"Cecelia," I say, forcing a calm to my voice I don't feel. "Why *wouldn't* I want to stay?"

She hesitates. "Things...may not be exactly the way you want them to be, at first. You'll need to be patient. I don't want to tell you too much, because knowing might change it all. Just please promise you'll stay."

I don't like the sound of any of this. I know Henri waited for me. What more could I possibly want? "If Marie-Therese refuses to go to America after everything we just went through, I'm probably going to kill her myself."

She doesn't laugh. She doesn't even smile. "Promise you'll stay. It means a great deal to me, personally."

I close my eyes, shutting out the concern on her face. She has no idea what's in my heart. Even if the war is encroaching and food is low, there's nothing that could make me leave Henri's side after everything we've been through. "I promise I'll stay. If he's alive, that's all I need."

She squeezes my hand. "Remember you said that."

16

SARAH

I land in the barn, as always. This time, however, I land in the loft, and send an entire bale of hay crashing into the stalls below me, nearly falling right over the edge with it.

The horses panic at the falling hay and begin to bray inside their stalls. For a moment, I just laugh, with tears in my eyes. I've made it. What kind of miracle is it that I've survived so much and finally made my way back to him? I climb down the ladder, still a bit stiff after so many months of immobility. The blanket hangs just inside the barn door, waiting for me still.

I throw it around myself and walk into the yard, under the light of a newly rising sun, just as Marie opens the door.

"My God," she grouses loudly. "What is it now?"

And then our eyes meet, and the color drains from her face. "No," she whispers. She blinks hard. "It isn't possible."

Henri appears in the door at just that moment and the two of them stare at me.

"Amelie?" he rasps, half question...half something else.

I nod and then he is crossing the yard to me, pulling me against him so hard I can barely breathe. Marie runs and throws her arms around us both, sobbing. "It's not possible," she says again and again. "We found your bones. It's not possible."

"Thank God," whispers Henri gruffly, his mouth pressed to my hair. "Oh, thank God."

He's gripping me so hard that it hurts, my body still tender and bruised from those months in the hospital, and I never want it to stop. I dreamed about him, I visited him, and yet his heat, his smell, his size...all of it was never *this*. Never entirely real.

"Henri?" A woman's voice, coming from behind them. "What's going on?"

He stiffens.

And my stomach drops. I know, even in my confusion, even as my brain begins to deny the truth, that in the woman's voice I hear possession. I hear someone who believes she owns the rights to Henri's thoughts. And his embrace.

His grip on me loosens. I look up and see dawning horror in his face, his and Marie's both.

The woman crosses the yard. She looks quite like me: my height, hair the palest blonde. But with one key difference. She is very, very pregnant.

I stumble backward, my head shaking, denying what I clearly see in front of me. I wait for Henri to explain, to deny it, but I only see apology in his eyes. Such apology.

The pain of it makes me sway, and Marie seems to realize it. Her hand goes to my back to keep me upright, while Henri stands still, pale and frozen. I was only gone for ten months. It would be bad enough if he hadn't waited that long but...from the looks of it, he didn't wait at all.

My mouth opens. I want him to tell me this is not what it looks like. That he didn't move on right after I left, while I spent month after month doing anything I could to get back to him. *Tell me she's carrying someone else's child. Tell me you did the honorable thing because I wasn't coming home.* My brain whirs with the possibilities, but no...she crosses the yard to us and he steps away from me. She takes his hand.

And he allows her to do it.

"What in God's name is happening?" she asks.

Henri's mouth opens as if to speak and then closes. It's Marie who recovers first. "Our cousin Amelie has come for a visit," she says through a dry throat. She flinches hard. "Amelie, this is Yvette, Henri's wife."

Henri's wife.

I knew, somehow, but the words...the words still take all the air from my chest.

My knees wobble and the weight of the journey descends, as I knew it would. For the first time ever, I'm glad to go unconscious.

WHEN I WAKE it's dusk. For a single moment I hear the sounds of the farm, feel the pulse of country air through the window, and I am happy.

Then I remember, and the pain of it turns me inside out. There's nothing left to me but this ache, a single sharp wound I feel in every nerve ending. I turn face down and cry, stifling my sobs with my pillow.

It doesn't feel real. It *can't* be real. Yet it is.

After everything I lived through, everything I endured to get back to him, I never dreamed the most painful moment would be arriving here. I am stripped down to nothing, empty. I should never have jumped out of the window to escape. Dying there would have been easier than this, painful but brief. Over already.

That I have returned to discover I've lost him is too much to bear. But the betrayal—*that* is the part that cuts knife-sharp. I loved him with my entire heart. I thought what we had was inviolable and perfect. Worth any sacrifice. But he didn't wait. He didn't wait a year. He didn't even wait months.

I start doing the math, wanting an answer that won't hurt, though I know I won't find it. She looks like she's almost due, which means she's been pregnant since last winter, and surely there was some courting beforehand? A month or two at the very minimum, which means he waited weeks, or perhaps days.

I cling to the rage that thought inspires. Because rage is the only thing that's going to get me out of this bed and the fuck out of here. I'm tired, but not the way I was before I gained my aunt's spark. I could survive a trip home now, I'm guessing.

I could leave. I could tour Europe with Rob Chapman. Let Henri explain to his wife how I've disappeared. It's not my problem.

I throw off the blankets. I feel a twinge of guilt at the idea of leaving without telling Marie goodbye, but surely she will understand. I can't be expected to sit downstairs making nice with Henri and his glowing wife.

Except...Cecelia. I promised her.

A part of me is tempted to ignore it. I've sacrificed enough. I've given these people a year of my life and my heart and I doubt I'm getting either of them back. I've done enough. But then I think of the way Cecelia protected me when I first arrived, how she was willing to let me cling to her when I was scared of everyone else. She was more of a mother to me than my own mother has ever been, and this is the only thing she's ever asked in return. And she wouldn't have asked if it wasn't important.

I put on the dress Marie has left. My favorite one. It was thoughtful of her, sweet to remember, except it was my favorite because of Henri. Because of the way he looked at me when I wore it, the way his eyes dipped to that small hint of cleavage like it was the Holy Land or water to a man dying of thirst. Well, let him look again. Let him get a good look at all the things he will never have again, all the things I will give away to...Rob Chapman? I want the idea of it to appeal to me but it doesn't.

And why would Henri care? He has a wife now. He chose someone else.

I go down the stairs, fueled by my anger. They are putting food on the table, and Henri is standing there when I reach the bottom step. Our eyes hold, and lock. For a moment my anger disappears and I'm nothing but bottomless sorrow, a well of grief that has no end.

"Awake at last, cousin!" Marie says with forced heartiness, looking between us like a deer in headlights. She rushes over to usher me to the table. "You must eat."

Yvette walks in, yawning, a hand pressed to her stomach as she stretches. "I thought I could nap, but you take the cake, Amelie."

I hate her. She's done nothing to me whatsoever, aside from unwittingly stealing the worthless piece of shit I fell in love with, but I hate her nonetheless.

I glance at Henri and Marie. Has Henri uttered a single word since I arrived? I'm not sure he has. "You've slept most of the day," Marie says. Her smile is so feigned it looks painful. "Your journey from *America* must have been a tiring one."

Yvette takes a seat, reaching for the bread. "What a way to arrive. I can't believe they even stole the clothes off your back."

I suppose this is how Henri and Marie explained the fact that I arrived naked, but I get the feeling she relishes the idea of my hard journey, my stolen clothes.

The tension in the room is palpable. I see it in Henri's hands on the table, holding the edge hard, in his tight jaw. The urgency in Marie's eyes. We have so much to discuss and not a word can be said with Yvette here.

"Can I help?" I ask, turning toward Marie.

She clicks her tongue. "Of course not. You need food and more rest." *So you can go where you belong.* She hasn't said it, hasn't even implied it, but they must want me gone, mustn't they? I'm just a painful, awkward thing to work around now. Another mouth to feed. My presence something they'll have to create lie after lie about because of Yvette.

Marie places bread and cheese and milk in front of me, along with a slab of ham. Yvette's eyes dip to my plate. "I thought we were saving the pig for after the baby was born."

"We'll have other foods to celebrate with then," says Henri tightly, looking at neither of us. Apparently, he *does* still have a voice, though I've rarely heard it sound as strained as it does right now. "Today we celebrate the return of our cousin."

Something inside me softens, begins to ache for him and I fight it, search myself instead for that spark of anger. Anger is all that will keep this from being the saddest day of my entire life. *He began dating her weeks after you left*, I remind myself. *He married her.*

"So much has changed since your last visit, Amelie," says Marie, joining us at the table. "We have ration cards but not much is available. It's all going to the front."

"Yes," I reply, raising cold eyes to Henri, who sits across from me, beside his wife. "I never dreamed so much would have changed." All of his promises about marrying me after I came back...did he mean any of them? Was he really that fickle or was I really that stupid? I turn from him to his wife. "When is the baby due?"

She pats her stomach with a condescending smile. She couldn't possibly know about us, but something in her expression says *I have what you want.* And the Coron in me surges. *I could take it back from you*, I think.

"Two more months," she says, smiling up at Henri.

My fork falls to my plate. If she is seven months along right now, she got pregnant in February. Which means he waited less than three months after I was gone to marry someone else. Three *months.* While I spent all that time trying to get back to him. Plotting, conspiring, starving, forcing myself to keep going. I held on, comforted only by the memory of him, the feel of him against me at night, and all along he was with someone else.

I jumped out of a window to get back to you, I want to say. *I nearly died. I will never again feel completely safe, or worthwhile, because of what I went through. But all you had to do was wait and you couldn't even do that.*

Yvette is waiting for some kind of predictable response from me about how wonderful it is that they'll be parents and I just can't bring myself to offer it.

"Eat," whispers Marie. Her hand squeezes mine for a moment.

My lips are dry and my tongue darts out to wet them. "I'm not feeling very well," I reply. I cannot look at Henri, or Yvette. The sight of them both makes me sick.

"You're too thin," she says. "You need to try."

Yvette shifts across from me. "Oh, leave her alone, Marie. She's skin and bones but she'll fatten up once she gets home, I'm sure. Americans are all fat. So yes, the baby is due at the end of November. Henri will make a very good father, don't you think?" she prompts.

I search myself for that anger before I answer. It's all that will keep me from bursting into tears. "Who knows?" I finally reply, raising my gaze to meet Henri's. "A man can seem perfect until he's tested. And then the whole charade falls apart."

Henri's fist grabs his mug so hard its contents slosh over the sides, while beside me, Marie makes a choked noise of admonishment. "You'll find, Yvette, that Amelie is full of jokes. She's teasing you now. She knows Henri will prove a good father."

Her hand rests heavily on my shoulder, as if warning me not to take this any further. For her sake, I won't.

"We thought you were dead," Henri says suddenly. He sounds as angry as I feel. "We were certain of it. Why did you wait so long to let us know you were alive?"

My body jerks as if he's struck me. Is he actually trying to deflect blame for this? Does he think I don't know how long it takes a human baby to grow? "I couldn't get away," I say between my teeth. "And then, when I finally did, I fell two stories from a window. I broke fifteen different bones, fractured my skull, and spent nearly six months in a coma." *And you were supposed to be at war,* I long to add. How exactly is he here now? Did something change or did Cecelia lie to me, knowing there's no way I'd stay until the end of October if I came any sooner? I swallow hard and look Henri dead in the eye. "I left as soon as I could. I'm sorry if that wasn't *fast* enough for you, but you certainly seem to have kept yourself occupied."

Yvette looks between the two of us. "I don't understand what the fuss is all about, Henri. You've never mentioned this cousin of yours once and now you act as if the world is caving in because she didn't write?"

All the accusations have left him. His head hangs. "You're right," he says, his voice muted, low with guilt and shame. "I have no right to complain, especially after what she's been through."

My glance flickers to his wife. "It's funny. I was only here last November, and Henri never mentioned you either. It must have been quite the whirlwind courtship. Or perhaps he just had a few special friends back then he chose not to introduce me to."

Henri's jaw grinds. "It happened very quickly," he says, staring at his plate.

"It was so romantic," says Yvette, putting a proprietary hand on his arm. "I was living in Paris when we met—I was an actress—and then he came one night and asked me to give it all up and come live with him in the countryside. You'd think I'd say no, wouldn't you? Giving up Paris for this rural life? But I knew a love like ours is a rare thing. He was worth the sacrifice."

Henri stands abruptly, clutching his side, pale beneath his tan. "Excuse me," he says, and then he turns and walks out, letting the door slam shut behind him.

The silence in the wake of his departure is so awkward Marie actually winces. But Yvette recovers quickly, giving us both a trained actress's smile. "He's just come back from the front, you know, and he was shot in the side. He was so worried he might not live to meet his child. I shouldn't have brought it up."

"I'll go check on him," Marie says faintly, beginning to rise.

I place a hand on her forearm. "I'll go."

This seems to send Yvette spinning into motion for the first time all night. "He's *my* husband. I'll go."

IT'S ONLY when the door shuts behind her that Marie turns to me with tears in her eyes. "My God, Amelie, what happened to you? We were so certain you were dead."

With Henri gone the fight has left me. I bury my head in my hands. "I wish I was. I should have just died there."

Marie's arm wraps around me. "I know this is a shock. But don't say that. You have no idea how sick we've been, thinking you'd died. I had so much guilt about leaving you. But...I don't understand. We found your body. We went to Paris and Henri climbed into that hole and found you, wearing the necklace."

"Found me?" I repeat, before realizing he must have found Iris. Coron probably buried any remaining skeletons under the floor, after that fire. Fewer questions asked that way. *And Henri found one and assumed it was me.* I shudder at the idea, until I remember how quickly he seemed to have recovered. There's so much I could tell her—about my aunt, about the babies, about all the women who died after they left. I don't have the heart. Maybe this, here, is my punishment for it all.

"I lent it to someone," I say simply. "There was a fire and I was able to climb upstairs and jump out the window. I'd hoped to time travel while I was in the air, but it didn't happen fast enough."

"I'm so sorry," she whispers. "For what you've suffered and for what I put you through when it was...all for nothing. When my mother must have been killed right away."

I've had the same thought, at times, and yet I can't blame her for wanting to know. "You'd never have been sure about her if you hadn't seen it for yourself."

"Thank God you survived," she replies. "To see you here now, in perfect health. I can't tell you what a miracle it is."

"Not perfect. I can't have children now, because of the fall." I laugh and it turns into a sob. "I guess Henri dodged a bullet, didn't he?"

She squeezes me tight. "God...this situation...I'm sorry. Henri would never, ever say he dodged a bullet, but I'm sorry. It must be such a shock for you."

"Cecelia—the woman who helped me the last time I went back—she warned me," I whisper. "She tried to warn me that things would not be as I hoped when I arrived here. She made me swear I'd stay until the end of October. I should have refused."

Marie places a palm on my face. "A piece of Henri died, thinking you were gone. You need to know...it was not the way Yvette made it out to be. Henri grieved for you. I watched him hold your skeleton. He wept like a child. I've never seen him, the way he was that day."

I feel sick at the thought. I can't imagine Henri crying. But I can no longer afford to feel sympathy for him, over anything. His words and his actions toward me were meaningless when I was here before, easily discarded. Why should anything else he does be judged differently?

Humans lie, I think. Humans do whatever makes them feel good in the moment, without loyalty, without a thought for others. Perhaps having some of Coron and Iris is a good thing. If I'd had their chilly self-interest a year ago, none of this would have happened.

"Do not expect me to feel sorry for him," I reply, my voice low and gritty with the need to cry. "If the situations had been reversed, I'd have mourned him for years, Marie. *Years*."

"It's not what you think," she pleads, clasping my hands.

"How? How is there possibly an alternate explanation?"

She hangs her head. "It's not my story to tell. But this is hard for him too. You could, if you wanted..." She stops, and her voice drops to a whisper. "You could undo it."

I blink. "What?"

"You could go back in time and warn yourself, refuse to go."

The whole stupid trip to 1918. I could go back to the previous fall and tell Marie the truth: *Your mother died immediately. You and I go, and we suffer terribly, so let's just stay here.*

"I thought of doing it a thousand times," she says, staring at her hands. "But I assumed you were dead so it would do no good."

I'm surprised she's even suggesting it, under the circumstances. That's her niece Yvette carries. "I can't," I reply, my teeth grinding. "There were two infants there. Girls. I helped get them out. At least I hope I did. Did your mother ever say anything about them?"

"Infants? Why would my mother know?" she asks, and my heart sinks. Marie was a newborn herself at the time. Of course she wouldn't know.

"Your mother is the one I wrote to. I asked her to find them homes." I shrug. "It doesn't matter. I wouldn't go back and change it all anyway."

Her head tilts. "No? Why not?"

"Because it's better this way," I reply, anger steeling my heart, making all of this bearable for a moment. "If it hadn't happened, I'd never have realized how little Henri actually cared. I'd never have realized he didn't deserve me in the first place."

∾

I SPEND much of the next day sleeping. I don't *need* it, not the way I did before I took my aunt's spark. I just don't have the heart to do anything else.

When Henri comes in that afternoon, his eyes go to me. I see misery there, and hunger too, but I no longer trust my ability to read what's in his heart. Look how wrong I must have been the first time around.

He sits stiffly beside a yammering Yvette, pale beneath his summer tan. The two of them make a lovely couple. Perhaps this is how it was always supposed to be, and I am the intruder. Watching them, I don't see how I can possibly keep my promise to Cecelia. Remain here a full month? I'm not even sure I'll make it through the next twenty-four hours.

Marie begins to put dinner on the table. I rise but she presses a hand to my shoulder and tells me to sit. Yvette, I notice, hasn't lifted a finger once since I arrived. I push the food on my plate around, wishing I had an appetite. When I look up, Henri's eyes are on me again.

"So how long do you plan to stay, Amelie?" asks Yvette. She's smiling but it's strained, unfriendly at the edges.

Henri stills, listening. "Until the end of October," I reply. "I'm meeting a friend then."

A muscle feathers in Henri's jaw at the word *friend*. Does he want to ask who I'm meeting? Does a hint of his old jealousy still exist? Good. It can only be a fraction of my own, and he deserves it.

"We love that you're here," says Marie, raising a brow at Yvette. "We want you to stay as long as possible."

"I'm sure Amelie is eager to see something of Europe other than our little farm," says Yvette. *Our* farm. I bristle at her use of the word. *It's not yours, bitch.* But as soon as the thought flits through my head I'm reminded: she's been here longer than I have. I thought of the farm as mine in a much shorter period of time. I guess she was smart to lock Henri into marriage as fast as she did, since he is obviously a man prone to quick changes of heart. "You should go see things while you're in Europe. Come back to meet your friend afterward."

"This is her home too," says Henri, hand clenched tight around his fork.

I laugh. The sound is unrepentantly bitter. "This was never my home."

Yvette looks between the two of us. She's a smart girl, a crafty one. She may not know who I really am, but she knows a threat when it's presented to her. "You shouldn't force her to stay when there's so much to see. Who's this friend you'll meet, Amelie?"

The desire to hurt Henri for this entire experience pulses inside me, swelling and growing. I know it's juvenile. I know I should be better than this.

I simply am not.

"He's a musician, beginning a European tour next month. He asked me to travel with him."

"A musician!?" squeals Yvette. "How very scandalous of you. Musicians have no money, but I'm sure you'll have a lovely time."

Resist, resist. I can't. "This one has money. A lot of money. He's got his own plane. I kept a photo of him on my wall at home, in fact, as an adolescent."

Yvette's face goes from shock to suspicion. The idea, I suppose, of some girl in borrowed shoes having a lover wealthy enough to own a plane is beyond her comprehension.

Henri rises, gripping his side, and walks straight out the door. It's only been two days, but it seems to be becoming a habit.

Marie watches him go, flinching, and then she grabs a pail off the counter and hands it to me. "I forgot to milk the cows," she says. "Can you?"

I reach for the pail but she doesn't release it until I meet her eye. I know what the look says. *Hash it out. Have your fight so you can stop bringing it under my roof.*

I give her a tight, barely visible nod and walk out of the house to find Henri.

～

HE IS PACING, out by his bale of hay. Our bale of hay. I will never look at it without thinking of the last time I was here, of all the promise that lay ahead. His life is still full of promise, though, isn't it? Brand new promises he made some other woman the moment my back was turned.

He watches me approach with his hands in his hair, tugging at it viciously. "Did you mean what you said? You're going to leave here and go off with some musician?"

I laugh. "I already gave up my entire life for you. I dropped out of college for you. I gave up my chance of escaping that hellhole so your sister could get home instead. Perhaps I deserve a few months of touring Europe with a famous musician as a consolation prize."

He looks gutted, which would be laughable were it not so outrageous. He presses the base of his palms to his forehead. "Don't do this," he pleads.

"Oh, I'm *sorry*," I reply. "It would be better for you if I'd died, wouldn't it? That way, no one would get a sample of the things you *chose* not to wait for."

In two lunging steps he's in front of me with his hands gripping my arms. "Stop this. Stop. You're—" His lips press together tightly.

"I'm what?"

He closes his eyes and gives me the smallest shake of his head. "Nothing. I know how this looks. You just need to believe that I was in a bad place when you and my sister were gone. And I did wait. I did. Marie was certain you'd died and I insisted you hadn't. I hunted for you. I dragged her back to Paris to find that house. And then I found your body. I held your skeleton in my hands. I—" His voice breaks and he stops talking entirely.

My heart gives an unfortunate lurch of sympathy. I'm incapable of seeing the bad in him even when I'm the victim of it. I'm angry at us both for that fact.

"Do not ask me to feel sorry for you," I say between my teeth. "You waited less than three months after I left to fuck someone else, Henri." My voice trembles. "Do not expect me to believe for a single moment that you were *devastated* by my loss."

"I was," he says. His hold on my arms tightens. "I still am. Look at me. Do I look well to you? Happy and healthy?"

I shake free of him, swiping an angry hand over the tears that are in my eyes. "I will not feel sorry for you!" I cry. "I won't. You've been sitting here married and planning for your new family, while I—do you even have any idea what it was like, where we were held? Or did Marie spare you all that?"

He stiffens, bracing himself. "She didn't remember, mostly."

I look him in the eye. "We were drugged and beaten. I had to pretend for months that I was asleep so I wouldn't be raped. I had to let the guards hit me and put their hands down my dress and maul me as I passed, without ever reacting once. And I had to watch all the other women die off, one by one. You know what they were doing there?"

The cords of his neck stand out with tension. "Marie thought they were raising children who time travel."

"No," I correct. "They were hoping to *breed* children who time travel. They assumed those of us able to fight off the drug were more powerful, and the rest were expendable. I finally had to give myself up simply so they didn't kill me off."

He staggers backward and leans against the wall, holding his side. "God," he groans, dragging a hand through his hair. "Please tell me they didn't..." He can't even say the word.

"No. But how could it possibly matter at this point?" I reply. "You have a new, unsullied wife."

His shoulders slump, and a kinder person would stop right now, but I can't. That anger inside me isn't abated at all by what I've said. It's like a fire, finding more things to burn, taking on new life.

"They were drugging the food, so I starved myself to keep a clear head. I was so weak from hunger toward the end, but do you know what kept me going, Henri? You know what kept me from eating, kept my feet moving each day no matter how hard it got? It was *you*. It was the idea of getting back to you. And I could visit you in part, but not without changing your memories of our time together, so I came while you slept. I would lie down, half this past version of me and half the present one, and weep at how much I missed you. So don't tell me how *hard* and *sad* it was for you here on the farm for a few months before you forgot me. Because I never forgot you. Not for a single day."

His hand goes to my shoulder. "I'm so sorry. I never meant for any of this to happen, Sarah."

His apology is a slap in the face. *I never meant for any of this to happen.* How many weak, worthless men have used that phrase before, and how *dare* he offer it to me now?

"Don't use my name."

"You already gave it to me," he says.

I stand up straighter, buoyed by my rage. "I gave you a lot of things," I snap. "And now I'm taking every one of them back, and I'm giving them to someone else. Don't ever use my name again. You didn't deserve it after all."

I walk away and he lets me. Everything I said was perfectly cutting. It made me feel no better at all.

17

SARAH

The next day, Henri is absent. Yvette stays in with us, knitting baby booties while Marie-Therese and I cut and chop and can. She spends the entire afternoon musing aloud about baby names for the child she's convinced is a boy, until I think I can't stand it anymore.

"Shall I name him Henri?" she asks us. "Would my husband like a junior around the house?" I picture Henri as a toddler—that adorable, rosy-cheeked boy I once saw chasing chickens through the yard, plump-legged and gleeful—and suppress a shudder of pain. That little boy should be mine, not hers. *That child wouldn't be mine regardless*, I remind myself.

I don't answer the question so Marie-Therese replies for me. "As long as he's healthy, I doubt Henri will care what you name him."

"And you, Amelie?" asks Yvette. "What do you think Henri would like?"

My eyes raise to hers. "I'd have to care what Henri likes in order to form an opinion."

She smiles then. It's so obvious that I'm wounded by this situation and she enjoys that fact. She feeds on my unhappiness like a monster. I can't hold it against her, entirely, because I'd happily feed on hers as well.

In the afternoon, when we're done with the canning, Yvette enlists me to help her sew small, adorable little baby gowns in white linen. I think of refusing her, and yet a piece of me now seeks out the pain, as if something might break inside me once there's been too much of it.

So, I sit with her while she muses aloud about Henri and the baby and their blissful future. My needle jabs into the fabric haphazardly, and jabs into my own thumb more than once. I almost enjoy that pain too. I like feeling something other than the wound she and Henri have created.

"Your stitching is atrocious," she says, clicking her tongue at my handiwork as I bring my bleeding thumb to my mouth. She pulls it from my lap and rips the seams out. "Try again."

She hands it back to me, regarding me with those cat eyes of hers. We've fooled her not at all with our pretense of being cousins. She knows Henri and I were more. How could she not? Some piece of us exists in every glance he and I exchange.

"What do you think of the name Andre?" she asks, watching me carefully for a reaction. "Or Pierre? Pierre Durand. He sounds like a politician, does he not?"

I look up from the gown, wondering what, exactly, she wants from me. Does she want me to weep and beg her to give him back? Does she want me to lash out in a jealous frenzy? If she knew what I was capable of, what I'm tempted to do, she'd stop pushing me.

"I like Ted Bundy for a boy," I reply, focusing once more on my stitches.

"Tedbundy?" she asks, as if it's all one word. "It's an American name?"

"Yes." I'm not completely evil. I'd stop them if she actually considered it. Probably. "It's really popular."

"What an odd name," she replies. "I think I prefer Pierre."

I'M in the barn when Henri finds me. He pauses before walking in. "Dinner is ready," he says.

I don't glance up from the cow I'm milking. The mere sight of him hurts. I will stay until the end of October, as I promised, but if I avoid him, avoid looking at him, maybe I can stop wanting him too. "I'll be in when I'm done."

He goes nowhere, however, and I'm finally forced to glance up. His brow is arched, and he's looking at me in the old way, not as if I'm a victim or a torturer, but as if I'm a naughty child in need of a spanking, one he's too amused by to deliver. "Who is Ted Bundy?" he asks.

"A serial killer. He murders a bunch of women in the 1970s and has sex with their corpses."

His mouth twitches. "Yes, I suspected as much. Please stop offering my wife input."

That word—*wife*—siphons every ounce of joy from this conversation. "Then tell her to stop asking for it," I reply.

He still stands there. "You shouldn't be doing so much," he says quietly. "You're still too thin." I rise—not because I'm done but because I have to get away from him.

"Do me a favor," I reply, handing him the half-full pail. "Don't try to pretend you care. I think you've proven quite conclusively you don't."

I enter the kitchen with Henri on my heels. He hands the pail to Marie, mumbling something about how I shouldn't be working as hard as I am. He looks as if he should be working less hard himself. Exhaustion is etched into the corners of his face and he walks away with his hand pressed, as always to his side.

Yvette looks at me as I take a seat, her eyes raising slowly, cunning as always. "He's right, of course. You do work too hard, but I understand it. We are just scraping by here. It must be awful to feel like you're another mouth to feed at a time like this, when our family is growing."

She wants to hurt me. The smartest thing I could do right now is not give her the satisfaction of knowing she's succeeded. But I lash out instead. "If times are so hard and you're barely scraping by, perhaps you shouldn't have decided to grow a family right now. That seems like a far larger problem than my temporary visit."

Her cheeks suck in and her eyes narrow, just for a moment, before she stretches like a cat and looks at me from beneath her long lashes. "Henri does not give me a moment's rest, even now, in *that* regard. Pregnancy is unavoidable with a man like him."

She wanted to hurt me and she has. *My God,* she has.

I realize only now the lies I've still been telling myself to dull the pain. I wanted to believe he'd used her to drown his sorrows, but that wasn't it at all. I close my eyes and push away from the table. I can't sit here. I can't remain across from them for another meal, watching Yvette's eyes dancing across his broad shoulders, counting the moments until she gets him alone.

"I think I'll go for a walk," I tell Marie. "I'm not really hungry."

I ignore Yvette's Cheshire-cat smile and walk out the door. Marie finds me a short time later, sitting by the hay bale, and places bread and cheese and ham on a plate in front of me. "Eat," she says. "You still look as if you're a moment from death's door."

I brush the tears off my face. "Unlike the luscious Yvette, who is blooming."

She laughs. "Even as starved as you are, Yvette's face can't hold a candle to yours, which you must realize. If it could, she wouldn't be so tediously jealous."

"Jealous?" I scoff. "What's she got to be jealous of? She's married to Henri and having his child. He apparently rushed off to Paris to beg her to marry him and can't keep his hands off her now."

Her smile fades. "Surely you realize that Yvette stretches the truth a bit?" she asks. "Does Henri strike you as being unable to keep his hands off her? They're rarely even in the same place."

"Because the grapes are coming in and he's busy." I think about the day he undressed me in the middle of the vineyard, during Madame Beauvoir's visit. How desperate he was, how reckless. Yvette was right. Pregnancy *is* unavoidable with a man like him. "Believe me, he finds a way to work around *that*."

Her hand covers mine. "No matter what Yvette says, he does not share with her what he did with you. I shouldn't tell you this, but theirs was no great romance, the way she made it sound. He got her pregnant by accident and she showed up on our doorstep two months later. He did the right thing."

I wrap my arms around myself, blinking away tears. "He told me he'd wait forever, Marie. Instead he got her pregnant three months after I left. So, no matter how you spin this story, he's not the innocent one in it, is he?"

"No," she says. "I suppose he's not."

I LIE DOWN THAT NIGHT, realizing something that is equal parts pathetic and terrible: I miss the days of captivity. Not all of it, but just these moments at night, when my head first hits the pillow. Because at least then I had something to dream about, something to want and to return to. There was hope, and now there's none. Even if I'd died, I could have died knowing I was deeply loved by someone—all a lie, of course, but I didn't know that then.

It's weakness on my part, but I allow myself to travel to Henri's bed the summer before, back when I was still wanted there. I nestle beside him, breathing in his scent of soap and fresh linen and whiskey. He's naked under the sheets. My hand slides over his arm, his back, his hip. Already he is growing hard, and in a moment it will wake him, and he will roll me on my back, still half-asleep. He'll wake slowly, his thrusts increasing in tempo, a hand gripping the headboard and his jaw tight as he tries not to come, waiting on me.

And maybe I should do it. Maybe I should lie here with my eyes open at last, quietly taking something from Yvette the way she now takes from me.

I shudder away from him instead, and return to myself, this pathetic husk of who I was, now sleeping in the guest bedroom upstairs while below me, he fucks his wife.

18

I help Marie with the morning's chores. When Yvette finally rises, she sits at the table and waits to be served. I ignore her but Marie is far too nice and asks if she can get her something. Yvette only wants coffee. She pats her stomach and says she doesn't want to get too fat with the baby. "Though God knows his father doesn't seem to mind my new curves," she says with one of those smiles I hate.

I ignore her, continuing to pound the bread on the counter with unnecessary violence. Why do I have to stay until the end of October? As far as the war is concerned, the next months are calm. *Drole de Guerre*, they call it. *The phony war*. Yvette will be eight months pregnant at that point, so I'm sure they won't want to travel to the United States yet. There is absolutely nothing I can do for them that Marie cannot. My teeth grind at the thought of remaining here, suffering the sight of Yvette's hand on Henri's, her head on his shoulder, night after night. It's not even fair to ask it of me—after the way I suffered to get back to Henri, to get his sister home to him, have I not done enough?

And yet...what if I'm wrong? Cecelia wouldn't have given me a specific date without a reason. As angry as I am, I don't want any harm to come to Henri or Marie-Therese, though I can't say the same for Yvette.

"I'm sorry he's had so little time to spend with you, Amelie," she muses, looking at me over her coffee mug. "I hope you won't take it personally. This is just a very busy time for us on the farm."

I stop what I'm doing. I haven't seen her do a goddamn thing since I arrived. "*Is* it a very busy time for you?" I ask pointedly.

If she understands my implication, she pretends she doesn't. "Very. Though I told Henri he must hire more men next year. It's crazy that he's working so many hours. Especially wounded the way he is."

My work stops again. Wounded? I think of the way he holds his side every time he sits and rises. I've wondered about it but didn't want to ask—it's no longer my place and he's no longer my concern. "You said he'd been shot." My voice cracks as I say the words. "Hasn't it healed?"

She waves her hand, dismissing it. "It's fine. A scratch at this point."

Relieved, I focus on the other part of what she said. "You mentioned hiring people *next* year?" I look from her to Marie. "I assumed you'd go to the United States once the baby was born."

I don't know why they haven't gone already, to be honest. There were months and months where Yvette could have traveled safely, and they must have realized the window was narrowing. Why the hell didn't they go?

Marie shifts uncomfortably, cutting a quick glance at Yvette and away. "I'm not sure what the plans are. We can't do anything at the moment."

Yvette's jaw has dropped. "Moving? From France?" She laughs. "But of course we'd never move. Whatever gave you that idea?"

I ignore her and stare at Marie. After everything we went through, solely so I could get them to safety...they're *staying*?

Tears sting my eyes, and I'm not sure if they're from rage or sadness. I whip the apron over my head and march straight out the door.

I go to the fields to look for Henri. I find him, sweat on his brow though the weather is on the cool side this morning. He looks older than his age right now.

He stops working when he sees me approach. There is a moment—there is always a moment—when a certain light enters his eyes at the sight of me. As if he's forgotten about our time apart, forgotten what he's done. And I understand it because there's a moment, when I first see him, that I forget too. And then I have to live through the hurt all over again as I remember.

"Why didn't you leave?" I demand. "You should already be in the US."

His tongue darts out to tap his lip, the way it does when he's thinking through an answer...or concealing one. "I just wasn't sure about some things, and I doubt Yvette wants to go to the United States."

"Does she want to *die*? Does she want your kid to die? Does she even know you're half-Jewish?"

His jaw tightens. "Of course she knows. You think I'd conceal something like that—"...*from my wife*. He doesn't say it, but the unspoken words ring in the air between us, and God, I hate him for them. "It was my decision, and what's done is done."

I squeeze my eyes shut. I'm so angry at him, but that's not what matters here. In four weeks, I'll be back in my own time and I can deal with my anger and sorrow then. "So, what, exactly, *is* your plan?" I demand.

"We can't do anything until the baby is born," he says. "And no infant should be on a crowded ship with God knows what being transmitted. Besides, I can't just abandon my country. I need to stay and fight."

I dig my hands in my hair. It's all still make-believe to them. They see the future as survivable because it's human nature to assume you'll be the exception...but World War II held far fewer exceptions than any of them can dream.

"Henri, I read about this when I was home. It's so much worse than even I knew. There will be internment camps for the Jews in France. Two big ones right outside Paris, and all those people will get deported to the concentration camps I told you about in Germany."

His eyes close. "Is there anywhere safe aside from America?"

"Switzerland, if you can get there. At least get yourself south, to what will be the free zone, and figure things out from there. It'll buy you some time."

He nods, sighing heavily. "How long do we have, before it starts?"

"The Germans will cross the Meuse on May thirteenth. After that, nothing is safe. They don't just bomb Paris. They fly low over the civilians trying to escape and shoot them as well. And then they take over and you're trapped."

"I will be eligible to take leave again in the spring," he says. "I wouldn't want to go before then anyway. I have no idea how hard it will be to find lodging, and I can't risk it with a newborn."

It's all about the baby for him. No crowded ships because of the baby. No risking a trip south because of the baby. I'm sure I'd make the same decisions in his place, but that doesn't lessen my bitterness. It's on the tip of my tongue to remind him of his carelessness, that he has created a situation that might get them all killed. His sagging shoulders and pallor hold me back. He already knows this is his fault.

Then he does something I've never seen him do: he sags against the trellis, as if he's struggling to stay upright. The color bleeds from his face.

"What's wrong?" I ask.

"Nothing," he says, eyes closed and teeth clenched. He is holding his side.

"Is it your wound?"

"It's fine. I'm just recovering slowly."

"Bullshit," I reply. I reach out and pull up his shirt before he can argue. The bandages covering his wound are soaked through —yellow, plus fresh blood as well. "Henri," I breathe. "You realize your bandages shouldn't look like that, don't you?"

He shrugs and starts to pull away but I hang tight to his shirt and begin to pry the gauze loose. His wound is red and swollen, oozing. "It's infected, you idiot," I hiss. "How long did you let it go like this?"

"There's work to be done," he says.

"And who will do this work for your family next year when you've gone septic and died?" I demand. "Get back in bed."

He ignores me. "I can't. The harvest is in. This has to get done."

My arms fold. It reminds me of last summer, when I had no leverage here, no control over the situation. Except this is serious...and I do have some control. I'm glad right now to have this anger in my heart. It makes it easier to use cruelty and threats to get what I want. No, not just easier. It makes it *enjoyable*.

"Get back in bed or I'll tell Yvette about us."

His head jerks toward me. "You wouldn't."

"Try me," I reply. "If you think things are tense now, just wait until I give her enough details about the two of us to make her stomach turn."

He heaves a sigh and wipes at his brow again. No wonder he's sweating, with the fever he must have from that infection. "She's pregnant. Please...just don't. It'll be bad for the baby."

As if I care about your stupid baby. I turn on my heel. "Then you'd better beat me back to the house."

Within seconds Henri is beside me. "I have a farm to maintain," he spits. "You can't just blackmail me to get your way."

I stop and laugh unhappily. "This farm will not be yours in a year, Henri!" I cry. "Don't you get it? The Germans are coming, and they are going to take everything, and then they are going to kill you and Marie and probably this kid you're being so precious about, and where will any of this have gotten you?"

His jaw drops, and he looks at me as if I'm a stranger. "This isn't like you," he says quietly. "You've changed."

"No shit," I reply, walking again. "Try discovering that the love of your life gave up on you, three months in. See how much of yourself remains when it's done."

I continue inside and he follows. Marie and Yvette glance at us in shock. I'm sure we both look mutinous enough to scare almost anyone.

"Henri's wound is infected. He has a fever." I glare at Yvette. She slept beside him. In theory he can't keep his hands off her. *How* could she fail to notice it? How fucking stupid is she? "I need gauze and tape and some kind of alcohol," I tell Marie. "And we need an antibiotic, so call Dr. Nadeau."

I push Henri toward the room. "Lie down," I demand.

His mouth opens to object but then he glances at Yvette, standing in the doorway, and complies. I begin to unbutton his shirt.

"I'm his wife—" she begins, but when she sees the gauze soaked through, her words fall away and she turns slightly green. "It might be best for the baby if I, um, wait outside."

I take the alcohol Marie's handed me and soak a fresh piece of gauze with it before applying it to the wound. He stiffens, but his eyes never leave my face.

"I wasn't trying to say you were worse," he says through gritted teeth. "Just that you've changed."

I prefer the angry Henri. The kind one makes tears spring to my eyes and I have to keep my head down so he won't notice. "I know I've changed," I reply. "And I'm definitely worse."

Marie returns to the room. "Dr. Nadeau says there's nothing he can do," she tells me. "They made him send all his penicillin to the front."

"And you believe him?"

She's as wide-eyed as a schoolgirl. "Why would he lie?"

I shake my head. How she can have such faith in human nature after what we went through? Perhaps because she wasn't conscious for it. I envy her that.

"He has children, and grandchildren," I answer. "Do you really believe for a moment that he didn't set something aside for his family?"

She blinks. "But then it's for his family."

"No," I reply. "Anything he has is mine, if I want it to be. And right now, I want his goddamn antibiotics."

If they're unsettled by my harsh answer, neither of them say so. Marie walks out and I continue to bandage Henri's stomach. "How do you know so much about this?" he asks.

"I don't," I reply. *But I apparently know more than your useless wife.*

I smooth the gauze down and tape it, thinking of the last time he lay in bed like this, shirtless, in daylight. I'd been making scones when he called out to me. I came to the room to see what he needed and found him much like he is right now, naked from the waist up, pants unbuttoned.

"You made it sound like you were injured," I'd said, perching beside him.

"I'm in a great deal of pain, which is similar," he replied with a grin, his hand moving between my thighs. "Let's discuss a cure."

"Perhaps you're dehydrated."

His fingers slid beneath my panties, sliding in small, torturous circles. "How fortunate for us both that you're not."

It was like that with us. He just had to touch me, and I'd abandon every other plan.

Now he is someone else's, but I want him just the same, and he's looking at me with the same expression he had that day. His eyes hungry, desperate. He is gravely ill from a gunshot wound, yet looking at me like all of this—his wound, his marriage—is as meaningless as the scones that burned that day and stunk up the house until nightfall.

"You shouldn't be looking at me like that," I tell him, rising.

"I know," he says, flinching. "I'm sorry."

I feel his eyes on me, though, until I've walked out of the room and shut the door behind me.

In the kitchen, Yvette's gaze sweeps over me, head to foot, and she gives me a tight smile. "Already done?" she asks. "Such a treat. My husband never takes a day off. I'll go see if he has need of me."

My jaw grinds. There's absolutely no question in my head what kind of *need* she means. And yet I resume my place at the table, because a part of me wants to hear it. Wants to hear his noises, wants the pain of accepting that he loves her and enjoys her as much as he did me. I want to scrape myself raw with his sounds until I finally accept that it is over with him and meant as little as it must have for him to have moved on the way he did.

But within a few seconds, Yvette returns. "You could have told me he was asleep," she says with pursed lips.

Henri couldn't possibly be asleep yet. Which means he's pretending to sleep to avoid his wife.

I feel hope begin to stir in my stomach, though I wish it would not.

LATE THAT NIGHT I walk to Dr. Nadeau's house. I could have driven but I know petrol is rationed now, so I imagine Henri wants to save it for his wife and the baby. I try to ignore the surge of irritation I feel at that thought.

Dr. Nadeau's office is in the back of his home, so I climb the fence and then peek in the window. I could time travel inside, but I'd rather not get caught in here naked if I don't have to.

I push at the window and it slides open. The mere idea of

breaking into a home like this would have terrified me before. Now I just feel relieved that it's an option. It takes me no time at all to find some penicillin—the idiot didn't even take it out of his medical bag. How ill might Henri have gotten if I hadn't come for this? Would Nadeau have let him die, simply so he could hoard the drug for himself? I feel a small throb at my temples. Nadeau deserves to be punished for that lie, for his selfishness. My hand closes hard around the two bottles and syringe I'm taking. He's lucky I have other places to be right now, and he's lucky I'm leaving soon. I have a feeling that, if I stayed in 1939, this wouldn't be the last time he pissed me off.

When I return to the farm, Henri is sitting on the front steps, waiting in the moonlight. He rises when I walk up, his jaw clenched tight. "Where did you go?" he demands. "I was worried sick."

"Worried about what?" I snap. "That I might go fuck someone else the moment your back was turned? No, Henri. Only you do that."

He reaches for me and I find myself spun, pressed tight to his chest. He's holding my arms tighter than he should and I see that thing in his eyes again—pain and hunger and a touch of madness, as if he no longer cares what happens. I understand all of it. It's how I feel most of my day.

"I thought you might have left."

We're so close, closer than we've been since I arrived. His eyes flicker to my mouth and I feel that glance all the way to my bones. I want him. And I've missed him so much. Why can't I just have a little of what I came here for?

He swallows, everything in him taut and desperate, the cords of his neck straining as if he's lifting an impossible weight. And then he releases me.

"I got you penicillin," I say, stifling a disappointment so vast it feels like it could knock me off my feet. I pull the vials from my pocket, along with a syringe.

His mouth falls open. "You stole it?"

"Well, yes, since Dr. Nadeau wasn't offering another method, the lying bastard. Come inside so I can get this over with."

He takes a chair at the table and I draw up the medicine. I have no idea what size dose he needs, but for tonight I decide one small syringe will be a good start. He watches me the whole time, and I'm reminded of the way he used look at me that first summer together, when we pretended to hate each other—as if I was passing by too quickly, but he was trying hard to see me anyway.

I inject the penicillin into his arm, and then drop the bottle and syringe into my pocket. "I'll call someone in Reims tomorrow and find out the correct dosage," I tell him.

Before I can pull away, he grabs my hand, and presses his lips to my knuckles, holding them there longer than he should. My pulse skitters in my throat at the contact, at the way it makes me long for more. It's unfair of him to do it to me, to keep me here on this fine edge of pain and desire all the time. It would be kinder if he'd just tell me he didn't want me. Kindest of all if he'd told me, right from the start, that he just didn't care enough.

I pull my hand from his grasp and walk up to my room. And then, just for a moment, I let my lips rest where his did, on my knuckles. It's almost as if I can still feel him there.

19

SARAH

The next time I see Henri, walking into the kitchen midday to tell us the hired hands have arrived, he looks like his old self again. I feel an odd sort of joy at the sight of him healthy once more, and when his eyes find mine across the room it's a struggle not to smile.

"When, exactly, do you meet your musician?" asks Yvette suddenly. I'd forgotten she was even in the room and my gaze returns to the apples I'm peeling.

"A few weeks."

Her mouth pinches. "I only ask because you're sleeping in the baby's room, you know."

"We'd never discussed having him sleep in there," says Henri sharply.

Yvette's laughter is forced. "Well, where else would he sleep, Henri? Would you have him stay in the barn all winter instead?"

"I assumed he'd be in with us at night," Henri argues, "so we can hear him."

Yvette waves her hand. "No, no. I'm going to need to rest. Babies should learn to get through the night on their own anyway."

"*Babies*, perhaps," says Henri. "Newborns, no."

I don't enjoy their minor squabble as much as I'd have expected. If anything, it only makes them seem more married than they already did.

"I'll be gone by then," I tell her. "You don't need to worry."

Henri's jaw is tight and even Marie looks unhappy. "We want you to stay," she says softly, casting a small, scolding glance at Yvette, who seems to neither notice nor care.

I don't reply. Instead I rise, set the peeled apples on the counter and go outside to help with the harvest. It seems kinder than reminding them all that I am desperate to leave.

All afternoon I work alongside Marie and Henri and the help. I try to focus on filling my basket, try to forget that this is the last time I will do this with them. It would probably be the last time anyway. There's no chance they'll still be here this time next year; not like this, anyway.

"You should be resting."

My head jerks up to find Henri standing there, casting a long shadow over me. His voice is gentle but firm.

"I like being outside," I tell him.

"You're pushing yourself too hard," he says. "Sit on the porch if you want to be outside. Not this."

He crouches beside me and reaches for the shears I hold in my hand. I cling to them. "Don't worry," I tell him. "I'll be out of your hair as soon as I'm able."

His face falls. "You can't possibly think that's what I want," he says, his eyes searching mine.

I avert my gaze. "If it's not, it should be. You're starting a family, remember?"

He sighs and after a moment, he rises. "Yes, I remember," he says. "It's a little hard to forget."

∽

WE EAT a dinner of cheese and bread and fruit from the orchard, plus the last of the ham, because Yvette did nothing useful while we were working.

"It was so dull here all day," says Yvette. The three of us are so bone-tired it's hard to dredge up a response. Or perhaps it's just that all the responses that fly to my lips involve ways she could have entertained herself, while perhaps relieving Marie and me of some work.

"It's apt to be like this the rest of the week," says Marie. "I picked up some books at the library. Perhaps one of them will appeal to you."

Yvette sighs. "Poor Marie. Your life here has been so quiet you hardly know what people do for fun." She reaches for Henri's hand. "You know what we should do this weekend? Go to Paris. We could stay in a hotel, take a mini honeymoon at last. Amelie and Marie don't mind, do you girls?"

Henri's eyes glance up for the first time through the entire meal. They flicker to me before they return to his plate. "No," he says flatly.

"But why?" she pouts.

"Because it's the harvest and I'll be working all weekend," he says between his teeth, sliding his hand away from hers. "This is what life on a farm is like."

I see her eyes flash before she pins her anger beneath a strained smile. "Well, at least there's the dance on the twelfth."

The date catches my attention. Cecelia made such a big deal out of October 12th, the day I was supposed to arrive. As if something monumental occurs on that date. Is it something the dance will set in motion, perhaps?

Henri's gaze returns to me before it goes back to his plate. "I doubt we'll attend that either."

"Not attend?" she gasps. "But we have to! And it's sponsored by the church, so there's that. Let poor Marie and Amelie find some nice young men while I have one last hurrah."

I glance at Marie, poor Marie. Still so in love with Father Edouard and still so unwilling to admit it. Her face has been alight since the word *church* was uttered. If she'd bend an inch the poor man would give up his collar and take up farming in the blink of an eye.

"Yes, let's go," I say firmly.

"You see?" cries Yvette. "Amelie is the guest and it's what she wants, so it's settled."

I don't want to be on the same side as Yvette for anything. It makes me wish I'd disagreed. Yvette, however, smiles at me as if we are now friends. And as soon as Marie and Henri go outside, she corners me in the kitchen and gives me a hug.

"Thank you for making Henri see reason," she says. "I'm going crazy here."

I shrug, turning away from her. Thinking *I didn't do it for you.*

"You have so much influence over him," she continues. "But I guess you've known the family a long time. Did you ever meet Henri's mother?"

I'm slow to answer. I don't know what Marie and Henri have told her and it feels like a trap of some kind, but captivity has left me suspicious of everyone.

"Yes," I reply cautiously.

"What was she like?" she asks. "Henri gets distressed when I ask about her. Her death is such a sore subject with him, even now."

"I'm not sure anyone fully recovers from the death of a parent," I reply mildly, hoping she drops it.

"I want him to give me her wedding band and he will not," she says. "He says it's an heirloom and should go to Marie."

Ah, this is what she's after. "I doubt the ring was anything to write home about," I reply. "They married in the early 1900s and had no money."

"His father had a Cartier watch. Henri wore it the night we met. You know how much a Cartier watch costs? Besides, you don't keep trinkets in a safe deposit box," she argues, her voice laced with irritation.

My head jerks up as a sudden memory sweeps over me.

Just days before I left for 1918, Henri went to Paris. I'd asked if I could come and he'd said no, that it would be a dull trip and also a dangerous one, since part of the day involved being around the unseemly sort of men who forge documents and procure things—by which I'd assumed he meant condoms—from the black market.

Marie asked him, grinning, if he'd be going by the safe deposit box, and his face lit up with a sweet, boyish smile, quickly suppressed.

"Yes," he'd told her. "I thought I might."

It could have meant anything, but even at the time it felt odd. Even at the time I'd asked what was in the safe deposit box and ... what was it he said to me?

That's for me to know and you to find out.

Was Henri going to give me the ring? And if so, why is he refusing to give it to his wife?

YVETTE IS ALREADY IN BED, after a long day of doing nothing, when Marie comes into the kitchen with the red dress in hand.

"That won't fit," I tell her. I've gained weight since I arrived and was glad to see the return of my cleavage, but I'm still much thinner than I was the last time. "And I don't think I'm going anyway." I'm not spending the whole damn night watching Henri care for his pregnant wife, watching Yvette with her proprietary hands all over him.

"Oh, but you must," urges Marie. "It won't be the same without you. The dress can be taken in."

"I'm just not in the mood to—"

"Henri won't feel comfortable leaving you here alone," she says, wincing. "If you don't go, none of us go."

"Why would he care if I'm here alone?" I ask.

Her smile is brief, and sad. "Because he's scared you'll leave."

It makes little sense, but I don't push her on it. I try on the dress and she pins it along the sides and the hips so that it skims the curve of my waist rather than obscuring it entirely. I'm standing on a chair while she touches up the hem when Henri walks in.

He stands in the threshold of the door with a look of pain and want on his face, and I wonder if he's remembering the last time I wore it. That night when he came up behind me in this dress, his breath along the shell of my ear, and told me I was exquisite. When he told me he'd been worried about what would happen that night.

What did you think would happen? I'd asked him.

That everyone would discover a secret I wanted to keep for myself, he replied.

Our gaze locks and the memories of it swirl between us, and then I jump from the chair without a word and go to my room, where I weep into my pillow, still wearing the dress, the pins digging into my skin.

I cry for all the moments in our past that meant nothing. How deeply I felt them all and how badly I wish I had never left. I suppose I should consider myself lucky to learn just how shallow his feelings for me actually were, but I'm not. If someone would allow me to go back to those days, to return to my ignorance, I'd accept the offer gladly.

20

SARAH

On the morning of the dance, Yvette and even Marie are aflutter, girlish and giggling.

I am not. What could possibly change in the next few hours? I admit to myself, reluctantly, that I'd hoped the change might have to do with Yvette. People died in childbirth in 1939, still. Especially women in the country. I've tried not to actively wish for it, though there's part of me that would like to. But I did, at the very least, wonder if it might fall in my lap.

But Yvette is the very picture of health. Still not due for six weeks, and ready to dance. So, what exactly is coming tonight that somehow requires me to be here?

Preparing for it seems to eat up the bulk of the day. Marie does my hair and I let her apply cosmetics before I start work on hers. She's glowing tonight. Perhaps what *should* happen is that I tell Father Edouard to open his eyes. But even that wouldn't require that I stay another two weeks.

I descend the stairs when we're finally ready, and my eyes go to Henri, so beautiful in his suit—the shirt crisp and white, the jacket straining around his broad shoulders. And he is looking at me too, as if he's helpless to do otherwise, as if there is no one else in the room. It's not until Yvette coughs politely that I realize she's here as well, also in red, and looking none too pleased to see me.

"Poor Amelie," she says. "You're truly skin and bones, aren't you? And tan as a day laborer. But don't worry. Someone will still dance with you, I'm sure. Henri, who's that friend of yours always going on about wanting a wife? Gerard? Will he be there?"

Henri's jaw sets. "I have no idea what you're talking about," he says, walking out of the house.

I sigh, internally. As bad as the last dance was, this one is shaping up to be worse.

THE DANCE IS HELD in the same mansion where, once upon a time, I watched Henri flirt with Claudette Loison. It's still daylight when we arrive, and it seems as if the entire town is walking there. I raise a brow at Marie. "Are we the only ones who drove?" I ask.

She cuts a quick glance at Yvette. "Most people are saving their rations in case they need to flee."

Henri parks right in front of the mansion, and together the group of us enter the ballroom, where there's no sign of war or deprivation. The mood is festive, and there's a glass in every hand.

"I can't wait to dance," squeals Yvette, squeezing Henri's hand.

Henri and I have only danced once, really. In the moonlight, while he hummed a tune next to my ear. *If anyone comes out here, they'll see you dancing with your cousin,* I'd said.

He'd smiled at me then, a smile I'd come to know well, once we became intimate. *I'm sure you realize they think we're doing a lot more than that,* he'd replied.

The memory steals the breath from my chest and I turn,

pushing through the crowd to escape them, only to find myself face-to-face with Andre Beauvoir.

"I would like to apologize," he says.

I stiffen. I'm not interested in Andre's apologies. A man who was completely sober when he shoved his hand up my skirt and then called me a whore has not *suddenly realized* he behaved unbecomingly. He's just realized he should have been smarter about it.

As much as I'd like to offer him a few choice words, though, and as much as I'd like to tell him that I'm now capable of far worse than swinging a crutch at him to defend myself—I can't make things worse for Henri and Marie. Andre's family employs much of the town, and with the Germans coming, he'll have even more to hold over the Durands' heads than he did before.

"What I did was unforgivable," he adds. "I was misinformed about you and your cousin, but that's no excuse. I just don't want there to be any ill will between us, as I understand you've decided to stay."

You're so full of shit, Andre. It's only for the Durands that I offer him a tight smile. "No harm done," I reply. "I appreciate the apology. But I'm definitely not staying."

His gaze flickers to Henri and Yvette—who both watch us. Henri's eyes are so dark they look black from where I stand.

"Not everything was as you thought it would be?" he asks.

Yvette's hand rests on her stomach and she smiles up at Henri. It's a full-wattage smile, but it strikes me, suddenly, how normal she is. A pretty girl, certainly, but without the advantages Marie and I share. She doesn't glow when she smiles. A man wouldn't slow to look at her or whip his head back as she passed. It should make me feel better, but instead does the opposite. After all of Henri's assurances that normalcy was overrated and that there was nothing wrong with my gift, she's the one he chose. Not me.

"It's exactly as I thought it would be." I can hear the sound of my teeth sliding against each other. It's exactly what I should have expected. My mother taught me countless times that no one could truly love me as I am, and it turns out she was right.

With another forced smile I go to the bar. The gift that saved my life, the one that keeps me from getting drunk—it's not absolute. I was still drugged in 1918, just not as much as the others. So perhaps drunkenness isn't an impossibility for me.

I'll just need to work a little harder at it than anyone else.

"Four shots of whiskey, please," I tell the bartender.

"Make it eight," says a voice behind me.

Luc Barbier stands there. I met him at the last town dance, where he flirted and bought me a drink and tried to convince me to run away to Paris with him. He hasn't changed much in the past year but he looks older—in a good way. His boyish charm is still there, but it's a bit more roguish now, and weary.

His hair is shorter and there's a grim determination behind his smile that wasn't present back when we met. "You've changed," I comment.

He holds my eye for only a moment. "I enlisted. I'm home on leave after six months defending the Maginot Line." He pulls one of the shots off the bar and raises it. "What are we drinking to? The reunion of old friends? Or the blessings of fertility?" he adds with a nod toward Henri and Yvette.

"All of the above," I reply, slamming the first shot and proceeding to the second.

"I won't even have to try to get you drunk," he says. "You're doing my work for me."

I look at Luc, who was handsome before and is extremely handsome now. I gave myself to Henri without a second thought, under the impression that it was special somehow, and he only waited three months to replace me. So, perhaps I shouldn't wait another year to replace him. Perhaps *special* is a myth that serves no purpose.

"Who says you'd have to get me drunk?" I reply.

His eyes sweep over my face, slowly. His lashes are long, and his smile is languid and sad all at once. As if he knows, like I do, that the end is coming, and recognizes the only thing to be done for it is to live while you still can. His hand goes to my hip, something slightly possessive in the press of his fingertips.

"I don't actually take advantage of drunk women," he says. "And I don't take advantage of heartbroken ones, either."

I shrug. I like him better for how unexpectedly honorable he's being right now, even if it's not exactly part of my plan. "Your loss," I reply, throwing back the third shot.

"Not so fast," he says. "Give me a chance to fix your heart first. Let's go to Paris."

"How is Paris going to fix my heart?"

He grins. "Drinking and dancing in the world's most beautiful city can cure more problems than you might think."

Luc's friends Jean and Marc slap him on the back. "You know he only enlisted because beautiful American girls love soldiers," says Jean. "Don't let him fool you with his idealistic nonsense."

"You're talking to my future wife, Jean," Luc replies. "Let me keep the magic alive through our honeymoon." He winks at me. "Paris?"

The whiskey is beginning to work its magic. I don't feel like I've had three shots, but I feel like I had one and it's a good start. And no one said I had to remain in Saint Antoine for whatever Cecelia is so worried about. Except Henri has been watching from across the room the entire time, and right now his jaw is clenched tight. I've got no doubt he'll try to stop me, and I'm not in the mood for his paternalistic bullshit tonight. I glance behind me at a door that is painted so that it appears to be part of the room.

"Why not?" I reply. "But I might need some help getting out of here without an argument from my family. You three go out the front and I'll meet you."

"You're going to make a perfect wife," he says with a grin, and my heart folds in on itself. Because Henri said those words once too, and he apparently meant them no more than Luc does now. Perhaps it's time I came around to this way people have of saying things they don't mean. If I'd realized sooner that this is how the world works, I'd be so much better off right now.

I FIND Luc and his friends within two minutes of exiting the hidden door and am quickly shuffled into his car. "How do you have the petrol for this?" I ask. "I thought everyone had to save it."

He gives me another of those smiles of his. "I have my methods."

Jean leans between us from the back seat. "He means he has his father's checkbook and can buy whatever he wants on the black market."

Luc merely laughs. "Yes. That's the bulk of my method."

Jean and Marc try to open a bottle of champagne out the window and I glance at Luc. What kind of man is wealthy enough to afford things no one else can and decides to enlist in the military anyway? Shouldn't he be like Andre, coasting on the family's success and assuming it puts him above the rest of us?

"How did your family feel about you enlisting?" I ask.

I see a hint of that sorrow in his eyes again. "My father passed away last fall," he says. "He was never especially proud of me in this world. I can only hope he'll become proud of me in the next."

I sigh. Luc joined up out of guilt, but that's the kind of guilt that will get him killed, and I'd like to see him survive what's coming.

"There will be lots of chances to prove you deserved his esteem," I say. "Don't blow it all on this."

He glances at me. "I feel I should say the same to you," he says. "I can't imagine why Henri chose Yvette. If it's any consolation, I feel certain he's regretting it now."

I'm inclined to agree with him, but it doesn't change anything. "He's not regretting it enough for my liking."

His mouth tips up at the corner. "Keep spending time with me." His palm spreads over the back of my hand for only a moment. "I can assure you we'll make him regret it more."

WE ARRIVE AT LE TIGRE, a bar deep in Montparnasse a little over an hour later. It's a relief. Twenty years may have passed, but the idea of being anywhere near Montmartre, where I was taken captive, terrifies me.

Looking around, you'd never know there was a war going on. Women are dressed more flamboyantly than ever, and most of them carry strange satin bags or boxes with them. "What are those things?" I ask Luc as we walk to the table. "I was here only a year ago. Handbags that large can't have suddenly become fashionable."

He looks at them and shakes his head. "Those are gas masks. It's become all the rage among rich women to carry them in matching bags for exorbitant amounts of money."

I sigh. "They should be saving every penny for what's coming."

"What do you mean?" he asks. "This phony war won't continue much longer."

"Your country just lost a decisive battle and went running home with its tail between its legs. You can't still be under the impression the Germans aren't a threat?"

"We were trying to punish them for what they did to Poland and we lost. But they'll never get into France. The Maginot Line is well defended, and they can't possibly get through Ardenne. The terrain is too difficult."

It's the very philosophy that will allow the Germans to invade without obstacle next spring. I'd like to tell him that, but I can't, and it's a reminder that there is a vital piece of me he can never know, much as my last boyfriend could not. That was the beauty of being with Henri, or at least part of it—I didn't have to hide from him.

He hands me a glass of champagne and I drink it to the bottom and place it on the counter.

"I think you should teach me to dance," I say.

"I'm happy to teach you anything you want to learn," he says with an intentionally lecherous grin, which makes me laugh. Luc may not be everything I ever wanted, but he makes me happy, and it's been so long since I felt happy that I barely remember the experience.

We each finish another flute of champagne and then he pulls me to the dance floor, painstakingly teaching me how to do the Lindy Hop. Henri once suggested I should know the dance because it was named after Charles Lindbergh, and the memory —even though we were fighting at the time—saddens me. It led to what followed, when he came up behind me, his breath at my ear, and finally let me know what was in his heart.

Did it mean anything? Did he say the same sort of thing to Yvette a few months later? Somehow, even after what he's done, I'm incapable of believing it.

Luc lifts my chin. "Where'd you go, Amelie?" he asks. I see pity in his eyes.

I smile too broadly. "Sorry. I'm easily distracted. Show me again?"

We dance, and it feels as though if I can keep moving, I can stave off my sadness. But once we sit, it returns. Despite all the champagne and the shots, I am painfully sober again, and desperate for some new answer. Could Luc be it? He'd sleep with me tonight if I asked it of him, I'm sure. Why shouldn't I? I saved myself all those years for nothing, for a man who didn't wait three months for me.

"The next time we come I'll teach you to tango," Luc says.

I shake my head. "I leave in two weeks."

His hand covers mine. "Stay. Give me a chance. I can make you forget him."

My eyes flutter closed. It's late. Something Cecelia wants badly is on the cusp of happening.

Is it this? I can't have children, so she isn't my daughter...but do I raise her with Luc? None of it makes sense, but maybe it doesn't need to. Everything seems meaningless at this point. Maybe I should give into it and have some meaningless fun with a man who isn't lying to me about it to make it happen.

The words *why don't we go somewhere private* rest on the tip of my tongue...and fall silent when my eyes open again. Henri looms over the table, glowering at the two of us as if we've been caught naked together.

"I came to bring you home," he says, his jaw stiff as steel, his mouth flat.

I've been through too much to be treated like a child with a curfew by anyone, but especially by him. "You came all the way here for that?" I ask incredulously. "I'll ride home with Luc."

A muscle twitches just beneath his cheekbone. "Amelie," he says softly. "Please."

I thought there was nothing he could say to sway me, and yet he's found it. That single word, *please,* is imbued with so much desperation, so much pain, that I'm unable to deny him.

I'm probably not the *meaningless fun* kind of girl anyway. I turn to Luc. "I'm sorry. I should go."

He grabs my hand. "I'm here when you've figured this out."

I lean down and brush my lips against his cheek. "Thank you," I whisper, and then I turn and follow Henri outside the bar.

The car sits just down the street. He holds the door for me and I scold him as I climb in. "I can't believe you wasted the petrol on this trip. After the baby comes, God only knows where you might need to drive, and drive quickly. Why are you even here?"

He slides into the driver's seat. "That's a fast crowd," he says. "I'm sure it seems innocent now, but they do things I don't want you exposed to."

My fists clench. His overprotective bullshit was bad enough back before he'd ever hurt me. Now, it's unbearable.

"What kind of things?" I ask. "Will one of them take my virginity, talk about marrying me and then knock someone else up instead? No. Only you sink that low. I'm going back."

My hand goes to the door but he catches my arm. "Sarah," he whispers. "Please."

I jerk away from him. "I told you not to use my name again, and I don't need your help. Have you forgotten what I lived through over the past year? A situation like this is laughable by contrast. And I'm capable of disappearing at will, remember?"

His eyes narrow. "Yes, turning invisible in front of the men from my town is just the kind of attention my family needs."

"Is that why you're here?" I demand. "Because you're worried I'll *embarrass* you?!"

His shoulders sag. "No." He sighs heavily, staring at his lap. "I'm here because the idea of you with one of them tortures me. And I know how unfair that it is, under the circumstances. Marie told me so, a hundred times before I left. But I've never claimed to be a saint."

"Tortures you? How could that be true? You're married, for God's sake."

He glares at me. "Do you really think this marriage of mine could possibly change how I feel about you?"

"If you felt *enough*," I reply, my voice choked, "you'd never have married her in the first place."

"You're wrong," he says. "What I told you was true, about finding your skeleton, how it destroyed me. What I didn't tell you is what happened afterward."

I wait, and my heart begins to thunder in my chest. The

shame of whatever it was weighs so heavily on him I can see it like a visible scar.

"I put Marie up in a hotel," he says. "And then proceeded to get so drunk that I don't know what bar I was in or when I left. But I thought I'd found you. I remember that. I remember believing I'd found you—out having a drink in Paris. I was enraged. I couldn't believe you'd been in Paris all along, hadn't even told us you were safe. But you apologized and I was so happy that I couldn't stay mad. And you kept begging me to forgive you. I remember that. You kept saying, 'show me you forgive me.'"

My pulse is in my ears now and I stop breathing entirely.

"And then I woke up beside Yvette. She's never admitted to trying to trick me that night, and I was so drunk that I can't be sure enough to accuse her of it. But two months later, she came to the farm and told me she was pregnant."

The image of it hurts so much I press my hands to my heart. "So you married her," I whisper.

He reaches out and slips his fingers through mine. "What else could I have done?"

I can think of several alternatives, but they are nothing he'd have ever considered because he's honorable, and because he will always do the right thing, no matter how much it hurts him. I love that about him.

"Are you even sure the child is yours?"

He stares straight ahead. "Only time will tell. But I didn't even know her last name until we filled out the marriage certificate. We'd never even shared a meal. I knew nothing."

I wish I'd known. I've been so broken up over this, and I'll remain broken, but knowing he cared might have made it bearable, at least. "Why didn't you tell me this when I first came here?" I ask. "I've spent *weeks* believing you just moved on."

His tongue darts out to his upper lip. "Because she is still my wife. It seemed...disloyal...to admit that I don't love her, and that this marriage is not what I'd have chosen."

And yet, he's never going to leave her. He's never going to abandon this child that may or may not be his, and all I'm doing here is causing trouble. And making my own situation worse. Was I seriously considering sleeping with Luc just moments before? Sleeping with him and *remaining* in this time instead of my own? It was insanity.

"I'm going to go home," I tell him. "This situation...it's only going to cause us both pain."

"I thought you were staying until the end of the month," he says. His voice rasps, a quiet plea.

I shake my head. "There's no point. I don't know why Cecelia insisted I stay, but nothing good can come of it."

He closes his eyes. "Will you ever come back?"

There's a fiction we tell ourselves when we're saying goodbye to someone we love. We always pretend there will be another time, because it would be too painful to acknowledge it's the last. But I want to feel the pain of my answer, because I think it might haunt me less to get it out of the way right now. "No," I tell him. "I won't be coming back."

The ride home is mostly silent, beautiful and also painful. One last chance to be with him, knowing what we had before wasn't all a lie, and knowing it's going to end. "What are you thinking?" he asks as we turn onto the side road that leads to the farm.

I lean my face against the window. It's surprisingly cool. "I wasn't thinking, really. I was just pretending this is how it would always be." His hand reaches for mine before he realizes what he's doing and pulls it back.

"It's what I've done every time we're alone," he says.

He turns toward the farm and we both see it at the same time. It's late, but every light in the house is on. We exchange a shocked glance. Something is very wrong.

Marie-Therese is out the door the moment we climb from the car, tugging at her hair the same way Henri does when he's beyond upset. "Mon Dieu! I *told* you not to go after her!" she screams. "The baby is coming. Go get the doctor!"

He takes one last glance at me, and then he is gone.

INSIDE YVETTE IS SCREAMING. Not that she ever struck me as the stoic type, but her face is lined with agony right now. "Make it stop," she begs, again and again. She hardly seems to notice us, but when her eyes fall on me she flails in the bed. "Get her out! I don't want her in here."

I walk from the room, pacing in front of the windows, waiting for the sight of Henri's car. I'm torn. I can't wish ill upon a child, especially not a child of Henri's. But the baby is early, and I'm not sure how he'll fare here, without an incubator and oxygen and whatever else preemies need, and if the baby doesn't survive... would Henri stay married?

I squeeze my eyes shut, trying not to think it, trying not to allow that secret hopeful piece of me to exist. I need to be better than that.

"Shouldn't we take her to a hospital?" I ask Marie when she steps out of the room. "The baby is six weeks early. You're not equipped for that here."

"A hospital?" Marie asks with an unhappy laugh. "The nearest one is in Reims. Even if we had enough petrol to get there, I doubt we'd make it in time."

My jaw tightens. "I didn't ask him to come after me, if that's what you're trying to imply."

She sighs. "Of course not. You've done so much for us. And you're doing so much by remaining under these circumstances. It's him. Henri. He's about to be a father. He can't go running off to Paris after a girl like a schoolboy."

Which he did because of me. The birth must be why Cecelia insisted I stay...but why? As far as I can tell, I've only made things worse.

Henri arrives moments later with the doctor, who goes into Yvette's room with Marie and shuts the door behind them. Henri turns to me, with the weight of the world on his shoulders. "It's too soon," he says, slumping into the chair beside mine and placing his head in his hands. "The child won't live."

"He might," I reply. But all I can think of is JFK's first son, who will be born more than a decade from now, six weeks early, and will not survive because his lungs aren't developed.

"I've made such a mess of things," he whispers. "I'm not sure how it's possible for one man to make as many mistakes as I have, and to potentially ruin as many lives without trying."

My heart twists. Only a few years ago, he was at Oxford with a magnificent future ahead of him. He's tried to do the right thing, again and again, even with Yvette, and his life has detonated instead. I live in a time where every teenager and college kid expects good things, and even expects the bad to be followed by good. But how can I promise Henri it will all work out when I know what lies ahead?

My hands reach out to surround his. "Don't lose hope just yet," I tell him. It's the best I can do.

It seems only a few minutes later that Yvette's cries stop, and, after a half-second of silence, we hear it: a tiny, fledging wail, warbling and pathetic. Henri jumps to his feet, and rushes to the door. When it opens, Marie is smiling. "You have a daughter," she says with tears in her eyes. Henri's eyes hold mine for a moment, scared and hopeful and apologetic before he follows her into the room.

I breathe deep, brushing a hand over my dress as I rise and go to the family room. This is a time for family, and I'm not family. Now, especially. Marie and Henri share a blood link to Yvette. Their loyalties will be to her and the baby. It's how it should be, and maybe that makes this the perfect time to leave. No drama, no weeping goodbyes. A chapter that ends just as a far more exciting one opens.

My chest hurts at the thought of it, but I wanted to know what it was like to love someone so deeply that it felt like I couldn't breathe when he walked into the room, and I got it. I will never have this again, I know. But I had it once—how many people can say that?

I'm writing them a note when Dr. Nadeau and Henri exit the room, Henri carrying a tiny white bundle so small it hardly seems possible there might be a baby inside. I walk toward them gingerly.

"A girl," he says to me with awed eyes, so full of love already for this tiny thing. His life has moved on, as it should. And if I care about him at all, I need to let him have this moment, not ruin it with my bitterness.

I force myself to smile, though all I really want to do is weep. "Congratulations. Do you have a name?"

He shakes his head. "Perhaps Rose, after our mother, but I have to discuss it with Yvette when she wakes."

Doctor Nadeau hoists his bag and frowns. "She is very early, and very small. You'll need to be extremely careful with her if she's to survive the next few months. Constant tiny meals. Her stomach is too small to hold enough yet. And if she stops breathing, use the pump I gave Marie-Therese. She'll show you how to use it."

The possibility that she might stop breathing is enough to make me take a step backward. In spite of all the death I witnessed in 1918, it's not those women I picture...it's my sister, being carried out of the lake. And I don't want to live through that again. I don't want to be at fault if it all goes wrong.

Henri holds the bundle out to me and I take another step back. "I'd better not."

"Nonsense," he replies. "She's barely two kilos. I think you'll manage." He pushes her at me again so I really have no choice. I curve my arms beneath her inconsequential little body, holding her gingerly as a grenade I might drop, and as desperate to get rid of her as I would a grenade as well. I bounce her in my arms for a second or two and try to hand her back but he doesn't take her. "I have to drive the doctor home. Can you watch her just until Marie is done getting Yvette cleaned up?"

My mouth opens to refuse but I can't think of an excuse. They leave and I take a chair in the living room. Reluctantly, I pull back the blankets from her face, though I'd rather not see her. She has dark hair like Henri's but otherwise I can't tell which of them she resembles. Her mouth purses and makes a sucking motion. I find my eyes stinging as I watch her. I loathe Yvette, and I strongly suspect that this pregnancy was not an accident, on her end—but this baby is innocent and when she opens her tiny slits of eyes to look up at me, I see faith there. This baby trusts me to care for her, to keep her safe. In spite of all the evil things I've done, and wanted and thought, she believes I will keep her warm and safe and fed. And she is right—I would. Holding her reminds me that there is good inside of me along with the bad. That the good is capable of winning, and I want it to. That rage inside me has been satisfying at times, but ultimately, I'd rather feel peaceful. I'd rather be a person worth this tiny human's faith.

When Henri returns, he takes the chair beside mine. "I'm sorry. I thought Marie would be out by now."

I shake my head. "It's fine." I hand her back to him and the two of us stare at her. "She is what will make this all worthwhile, you know."

He swallows, glancing from me to her. "I hope I'm able to believe that one day."

"Can you hire a nurse to help you, for the next few weeks?" I ask. "Since she's so small? If people in town ask where you got the money you can tell them I left it for you."

He stills. "You're not going to stay? I thought maybe this...I thought you might change your mind."

I stare at my lap. "You have a family now. You *are* a family. My presence just makes things worse. But I'll check on your daughter throughout her life, and make sure she has what she needs."

His head hangs but he doesn't argue with me. When he yawns a few minutes later, I take the baby from him and cradle her. It feels natural to me already.

"I want to keep this in my head forever," he says, watching us. Our eyes hold. I want to hold it in my head too. *This is what it would have been like to have a child with him.*

Marie stumbles out of the bedroom just then, her clothes painted with blood and yawning. "How is my niece?" she asks, smiling down at the little face.

"Excellent," I reply. "But getting hungry I think."

Marie swoops her up with graceful efficiency. "Let's go see your maman, lovely Cecelia."

Henri's brow shoots up. "What did you call her?" he asks.

Marie smiles knowingly. "Oh, the baby? Yes. Yvette has named her Cecelia."

He and I stare at each other, dumbfounded as it all comes together. This tiny beautiful thing in Marie's arms, this child who isn't yet five pounds, is the woman who has saved me twice. And someday she'll be the richest woman in France.

"Is it the same person?" Henri asks incredulously.

I never, in a million years, would have put it together before, but I know that it is. "She knew you. She knew me as Amelie. She knew about Marie and what we could do. Except I—I don't understand. She knew where to look for me based on my stories. Like the hospital...she came to save me from it."

"She wouldn't have heard them from me," he says quietly, placing his hand on my knee. "Which means you told them to her yourself."

"I don't see how that's possible," I whisper. "I'm leaving. I'll be gone in a few hours."

Marie stands, holding Cecelia, and her eyes go to Henri's hand, which still rests on my knee. "Henri," she says, "you should probably go see your wife. Take her the baby, will you?"

He looks at her blankly for a moment, as if he'd forgotten she was there, or forgotten, perhaps, that there was a wife in all this. And then he rises, gently fixing Cecelia's blankets before he carries her away.

Marie takes his place on the couch. I expect to be chastised— I shouldn't have left for Paris tonight, and Henri and I shouldn't have been sitting the way we were. But instead, she squeezes my hand. "Don't you see?" she asks. "Something must occur in the next two weeks that changes your relationship with Cecelia. Something that changes the course of your life and hers."

"How is that possible?" I ask. "In two weeks she still won't be talking. I'll look out for her, Marie. You know I will. But from a distance. There's nothing I'll be willing to do for her in two weeks that I won't be willing to do now."

"Obviously there is, because two weeks somehow turns her into a person you *know*. A person you tell your stories to, who knows you loved her father and he loved you. And she's not that to you yet."

Marie has no idea what she's asking. That staying here means feeling like an outsider while waiting on Yvette hand and foot, means watching as Henri becomes a family with someone other than me. "I can live without telling these stories, believe me."

"You might live, but will she?" Marie asks. "Tell me something: if you return to your time, and there is no more Cecelia Boudon...if she is poor, or broken, or worse? If she's dead, you can't fix it. What then?"

I can't imagine what difference two weeks could make. It's not as if Cecelia and I will be having any life-changing heart-tohearts during that time. But can I guarantee it won't change things? No.

I sigh. "Fine. I'll stay."

She squeezes my hand once more. "Thank you. For everything. You saved my life, and now perhaps you'll save my niece's life too. I think there was a reason God brought you to us. Maybe this is it."

God didn't bring me, I think. *I brought myself. And I'd be better off if I hadn't.*

Cecelia is a sweet baby. Taking care of her is lovely and painful at the same time. No matter what Marie believes, I'm not going to be a permanent part of this child's life. She's another thing I will love and let go of, like the infants in 1918, like my sister, like Henri.

She eats and sleeps and does little else her first day of life, but she wants to be held. Always. The second we lay her in the crib Henri built she wails, and none of us—not Henri, not Marie, not myself—has the stomach for it. Yvette, similarly, also sleeps all day, and when she's awake and not being showered with attention, she too wails. She wants praise and coddling. She wants food and wet washcloths. She does not seem to want much to do with her daughter, as far as I can tell, but who am I to judge? I'm not the one who just shoved an entire human out of a small hole.

The next afternoon I get the apple and cheese Yvette has requested, and force myself to say the polite words that feel like grit in my mouth as they exit. "Congratulations. She's beautiful."

She smiles at me with eyes that remain cruel and distant. "That's kind of you to say. It must be so hard for you."

I plant my feet to the floor, bracing myself. "What must be hard for me?"

"Seeing how Henri has moved on."

My stomach sours. I grab the door frame for dear life. *I could end you in moments*, I think. *Just give me a reason.*

But then I think of Cecelia. Of how she looks at me and how I feel when I hold her, as if all that is good and right exists in her, and also in me. "I have no idea what you're talking about."

"Of course you do. It's obvious you were in love with him. Do you think I missed those calf eyes you make each time he walks through the room? And your visit here was all for nothing, wasn't it? Because he chose his child over you."

"What you're saying," I reply, my voice deceptively soft, like the hiss of a snake, "is that *you* aren't even a part of the equation. He didn't choose me. But he didn't choose *you* either."

Her smug smile grows more strained. "Well, he's mine either way, and you're alone and pathetic."

I laugh. "That may be true, but when a man marries me, it won't be out of pity and obligation. So don't assume you're any less pathetic than I am."

I turn and walk out the door, certain my words hurt. We both know they're true.

"I won't wait on her again," I tell Marie as I walk through the kitchen and return to Cecelia's crib.

22

SARAH

Every day with Cece makes it harder to leave. I change her diaper, thinking I'd be so much better off if I'd left before she was born—before I realized what it was like to care for Henri's child—when I'm suddenly pulled from my selfish thoughts. Cece's chest rises and falls in a way I don't think it did before. Is she breathing faster than she was? Why am I noticing it so much more now?

I continue to change the diaper, distracted now. My thumb stings as the safety pin jabs into my skin, but better me than her. And the more I watch, the more certain I am that something is wrong. I call for Marie and she comes, looking as exhausted as I feel. Neither of has had more than a few hours of sleep in days.

"Look at her," I say, my jaw set hard.

Marie glances at Cecelia, then me. She is gray with fatigue and her face doesn't change. "I don't understand," says Marie. "She looks fine."

"No," I breathe. In the span of five seconds I've gone from uncertain to convinced. "Her chest is sinking in when she breathes. It's concave. It wasn't concave before."

Marie bites her lip. "Perhaps it's just that she's taking bigger breaths as she gets stronger?"

The hair on my arms goes on end. No. It's not right. I know nothing about babies but this isn't right. "Think of the strongest person you know. Henri, for instance. Does his chest sink in when he breathes?"

She looks at me, her green eyes pale and frightened. "I'll get the pump."

She runs from the room and returns seconds later, but it seems to make no difference. Cecelia still struggles. "We'll need to take her to Reims. One of us should go with Henri..." She hesitates. "It should probably be you. Yvette..."

Hates me and won't want me here to help. She also won't want me with Henri, but her preferences matter little to me.

I leave Marie and run into the field, where Henri is cutting back vines. He takes one look at my face and then stands straight, bracing himself. "What is it?"

"We need to take Cecelia to a hospital," I tell him. "I think she's struggling."

His mouth opens. "Doctor Nadeau..."

"Acted ambivalent as hell about whether or not she survives, and probably should have known this was a possibility. And he's the same man who lied to us about penicillin for you. Is that really who you want to trust with your daughter's life?"

He looks lost for a moment, then gives me a small nod. "Get the baby. I'll start the car."

Five minutes later I sit in the back seat holding Cece in my arms, using the useless little pump to no avail.

His eyes meet mine in the rearview mirror. "How is she?" he asks.

My stomach tightens. "Alive. But pale. Drive faster."

He flinches. "I'm already driving as fast as the car will go."

Her eyelids have a bluish cast now, reminding me of Kit, when they pulled her from the lake. "You're going to be okay," I whisper, my pinky sliding into her tiny, clenched fist. It sounds more like a plea than a promise.

I don't know if I've done enough. Yes, Cecelia was alive in 1989 just a short time ago. But that doesn't mean I've done everything I was *supposed* to do. Perhaps I should have been more adamant. Perhaps I should have jumped back to earlier in the morning or even the day before to warn them.

And now it's too late. If I time travel from this car, I won't land back at the farm. I'll land naked and alone on the side of the road.

The fact that Cecelia was alive the last time I saw her as an adult doesn't reassure me at all. It just means that if she isn't alive the next time I go, the fault for that will rest on my shoulders alone.

CECELIA IS TAKEN from us at the hospital, and Henri and I stand there in the hallway, shell-shocked, watching her go.

It feels wrong, handing her off to a complete stranger. Henri's hand slides through mine and I don't pull away. I need the grip of his fingers every bit as much as he needs mine.

We wait, sitting side by side, for hours. It's a chaotic place, a mixture of mothers scolding children over something minor, and mothers weeping as if they'll never recover.

Every time a nurse enters the waiting room, we both hold ourselves still, bracing for bad news. After what feels like a very long time, a doctor walks out and asks us to come with him.

Henri's hand is so tight in mine that it hurts.

We are led to his office and take seats across from him.

"You must be very worried, Madame Durand," he begins.

"I'm not Cecelia's mother—she's still too ill from the birth to travel."

His eyes flicker to our hands again. Despite that, Henri's grip does not loosen.

"She is very ill," he says. "Her lungs aren't fully developed yet and she's caught a virus of some kind."

I flinch. I could have brought her in sooner and maybe I still should. We could call Marie and tell her to jump back a few days to warn us all. Except that might be the wrong decision as well.

"I imagine her country doctor didn't know any better," he continues, "but a child of her gestation...has little chance of survival under the circumstances, without assistance."

"Is she going to be okay?" Henri asks.

The doctor leans forward. "The next twenty-four hours will tell us much. If we can keep her alive for the next week then she is likely to survive."

"What do we do now?" Henri asks.

"Go home to your wife," he says, a gentle admonishment. "I'll call you if anything changes."

Henri goes pale. I understand why...I can't imagine leaving this tiny infant here among a hundred others with only a hope that she will be okay. Knowing she might not even live through the night.

We drive home, the two of us too panicked about Cecelia to think of any other topic we could possibly discuss. When we arrive, Henri goes straight to the barn, and Marie is in the garden, which leaves me alone with Yvette when I walk in.

"Did you enjoy that?" she asks with a miserable little smirk. "Creating some drama about my daughter to get time alone with my spouse?"

"You know what's interesting?" I ask. "Your daughter nearly died today, and she may not live through the night, and the only person who doesn't seem to care about that is you."

~

I'M unable to sleep that night. I lie awake and eventually dress and go downstairs, where Henri sits, staring at the fire. I take the seat beside him on the couch.

"Is she going to be alright?" he asks.

I squeeze his hand, briefly. "Yes," I say firmly, because it's what he needs to hear. And what I need to hear.

He gives me a small smile. "If that's so, then why are you awake?"

"I just miss her," I tell him, and it's true.

"Me too," he replies.

Behind us, the bedroom door opens, and we both turn guiltily though we've done nothing wrong.

Yvette stands at the threshold, her eyes narrowed on me. "Isn't this cozy?" she asks. "I hate to disturb you, but I need my husband's assistance."

He rises and leaves, while I remain behind. Is it wrong that we were sitting together? Is it wrong that I squeezed his hand, that I wanted to comfort him? No. But that doesn't mean it was innocent either. Nothing about the two of us is.

I wake early, on little sleep, and dress to go to the hospital, only to find Yvette waiting downstairs when I arrive. "Your help won't be necessary today," she says.

Henri looks at me with apology in his eyes. "Get some rest, Amelie," he says softly. "I'll call the minute there's news."

Marie and I wait near the phone but it does not ring. Instead, not three hours after they took the one-hour journey to Reims, they return. My hand goes to my throat. "Cecelia, is she..."

Henri shakes his head. "She's alive. Still on a ventilator."

"Then why are you here?"

Henri looks straight ahead, and I realize for the first time that he's holding himself apart from Yvette, painfully stiff.

She shrugs. "It was so dull there and I *did* just have a baby," she says. "I suppose you'll never understand since you can't have children, but sitting for long periods like that is hell after childbirth."

I stiffen, shocked that Marie told them. Has Henri been pitying me this whole time? Has he been thinking he's lucky things turned out the way they did?

Henri is staring at Yvette as if he finally sees her for the monster she is. "Have you taken leave of your senses?" he asks her.

Her eyes go wide. "What? All I said was that—"

"Everyone in this room heard what you said," he replies, opening the door to walk away. "Please have the decency not to repeat it."

I walk out to the hay bale, sick over the whole thing. I know I'm a bad person and maybe I deserve my losses. But Yvette's no better. Why should she get everything I want? Henri, Cecelia, his future children?

Footsteps approach and I recognize that heavy tread before I've even looked up. "I'm sorry," Henri says. "It was thoughtless of her to have brought it up."

It was far worse than thoughtless. It was intentionally cruel. I wonder if Henri sees how bad she really is.

"Marie shouldn't have told you," I reply.

"She was trying to help," he says. "She wanted Yvette to be more sensitive."

I rise to face him. "So you've all been quietly pitying me this whole time. Poor, barren Amelie? And thinking you're lucky to end up with a child after all."

I start to walk off and his hand lands heavily on my arm, holding me in place. "Don't presume to know what is in my heart," he snaps. "It's a terrible situation, but if you think for a moment I could be capable of finding a silver lining in all this, you do not give me enough credit."

I blow out a breath. He's right. My capacity for self-pity has been endless, but there's no reason to look at everything in the worst possible light. "I'm sorry."

He looks at his hand, still gripping my arm. "No one could be more sorry than I am," he replies, letting me go.

THAT'S the first night I hear Yvette and Henri fight. Mostly, it is she who fights. Her words are hissed, inaudible but for their intent.

The next morning, I wake just after sunrise and dress for the hospital. He's waiting downstairs, looking as if he hasn't had much sleep.

We ride to Reims and then wait side by side in the pediatric ward. Henri asks if we might be able to see Cecelia today, and the nurse frowns and tells him it's unlikely, but that she'll check.

He grips my hand, and he's still holding it hours later when the doctor we met three days prior finally walks into the hall. The two of us spring to our feet as he approaches. "She's been off the ventilator for nearly twenty-four hours," he says, his face breaking into a smile. "I think she can safely go home."

I burst into tears. Henri's arms wrap around me. Neither of us care, a single bit, about the fact that we shouldn't be holding each other so tight or so long.

THE WHOLE RIDE home I hold her in the back seat, marveling at her perfect fingers, her darling mouth, her steady breaths. Marveling at the fact that there ever could have been a time when I didn't want her to exist.

Yvette makes a show of being relieved that Cecelia is home, but it's not long before she's complained of fatigue and retires to her room. I take the baby and feed her in the parlor while Henri looks on—worried, hopeful. I place her on my shoulder and she gives the loud, satisfied burp of a much older and larger child. Henri and I both grin at each other. When I lay her down in the crib, now deeply asleep, the two of us just stand there, watching her.

"She's the most beautiful thing," I whisper.

He turns and his eyes go from my hair to my eyes to my nose to my mouth. "She's one of them."

He looks at me as if I'm the world's only source of light, and it hurts. It hurts so much that I can't have this. I feel my eyes sting and avert my gaze. I cannot stand here like this with him. I can't.

"I should—"

He moves toward me and his palm curves along the side of my face as he leans in, pulling me closer. There's the gust of his breath and then his mouth is on mine. Soft and hungry and desperate and careful all at once.

I should stop him but the part of me that has waited long, long months for this, that spent one night after the next in captivity *dreaming* of this, does not care. That part of me says *take. She hasn't earned him and you have, so take this while you can.*

My mouth opens under his and we tangle, mouths and tongues and hands, and he moves me until I'm pressed to the wall, pinned like a butterfly under his weight. If I'd ever doubted that he might have missed me the way I missed him, I no longer do. It's in the urgency of his mouth, the pained sounds he makes. His bones, like mine, are hollowed out waiting for this, waiting to be filled again.

When he finally pulls back, his body still pressed to mine, I can feel the restraint it takes. I feel it in the rigidity of his arms, in the bulge that presses hard against my abdomen.

"You can't—" I begin.

"I know. But I'm not sorry," he says, stepping away. "God help me but I'm not sorry."

23

SARAH

Things are different with us in the morning. All along I've existed on this raw edge of pain and want and restraint and heartbreak, but now...I can feel him pressed against me. I feel his desire in my cells and hear the pain of his groan no matter what else is going on around me. And each time I look up, his eyes are on me, with a hunger like I've never seen in him before. Not even last fall, not even at our most reckless and desperate, did he look at me the way he does now, like he wants me so much he's sick, mad, with it.

They fight again that night. Yvette's screaming wakes Cecelia, who still sleeps in the parlor. I creep down the stairs to the crib and bring her to bed with me. She falls back into a contented slumber, and I stare at her in the moonlight, this little girl who feels like mine though she is not, listening to the sound of things being thrown in the room below. "That's enough," Henri finally says. The front door slams, but things continue to be thrown.

∾

THE NEXT NIGHT, when it starts all over again, I go downstairs to get Cecelia before she wakes. I hear Yvette's words clearly this time. She tells him she wants me to leave, and that she doesn't want me around the baby. *Whore*, she says of me when all her other words get her nowhere. *She's a whore and a witch and you look at her as if she just made the sun rise.*

I carry Cecelia upstairs, and wonder if it's truly time for me to go. I'm the thing making Henri's life harder right now, creating friction between Cecelia's parents. How could it possibly be a good thing?

On the third day, all of us are hollow-eyed from the fighting. I'm so tired I can barely remain awake through dinner, and Henri hardly looks better. Only Yvette, who continues to rest most of the day, appears refreshed.

I'm just drifting off that night, my thoughts scattering like ash, when, from downstairs, Yvette's voice wakes me.

"You stared at her all night!" she cries. "You stare at her every night, just as you did at the dance! Does it torture you, the thought of her with Luc?" Cecelia begins to cry and I go downstairs and scoop her up. I can't hear his words but I hear the anger in them, the inherent threat.

"Did she spread her legs for you like she does the rest of the town?" Yvette screams. "She did, didn't she? Did she spread her legs like the whore that she is?"

Their door opens and he stands at the threshold, unaware of my presence, so I hear every word he says in reply. "No, she didn't. But you did, and the child that resulted is the only reason I allow you to stay."

It's only when he turns that he sees me there, with Cecelia. His face falls.

"I have her," I tell him.

He tugs at his hair with those hands of his, tortured and desperate. "I'm so sorry you heard that."

"It's fine," I tell him, though as I say it the weight of this whole thing seems to press down on me. Loving Henri and his daughter when I can't keep either of them, watching Yvette take everything I want in the world when she's not even grateful for it...it's too much. I feel like marsh grass in high wind, barely able to stay upright, sustaining one blow after the next and feeling as if it will never end. "But I'm leaving in the morning."

I TAKE CECELIA UPSTAIRS AND, tucking her into the crook of my arm, the two of us fall asleep. I hear more shouting, later, but I'm so exhausted it doesn't matter and Cecelia will sleep through anything as long as she's being held. At some point, Marie comes in and takes her from me, and the next time my eyes open the house is blissfully quiet at last and flooded with sunlight.

I walk down the stairs to find Marie sitting at the table. Her hands are idle for the first time ever, and she stares out the window.

"Is everything okay?" I ask.

She blinks, as if surprised to find me here. "Yvette is gone."

"*Gone?*" I ask.

"She left early this morning. She says she's going back to Paris."

My head swivels. The crib is empty, and it feels as if everything inside my chest is sucked out by a vacuum all at once. "Cecelia?" I gasp.

Marie gives me a small smile. "Yvette left her. Said the baby was our problem, not hers. Henri is walking her. He thought we should let you rest."

I collapse into a chair, leaning forward. My limbs are still shaking from that single moment of terror. "Thank God."

When I look up there are tears in her eyes. "I'm so sorry," she whispers.

"For what?"

"For all of this. It's because of me that you went to 1918 in the first place. It's because of me you got stuck there. Because of me that Henri thought you were dead and wound up with her at all. You've suffered so much and it's entirely my fault."

I shake my head. "All of those things had to occur for Cecelia to exist. How can we regret any of them?"

Her eyes close. "I know. But now Yvette's gone and I hope—" She trails off.

"You hope what?"

"I hope you'll stay," she says. "I wouldn't blame you if you didn't want to. And with the baby...all our lives are in jeopardy in a way they weren't before. Whether Henri remains here or goes off to fight, Cecelia will need a woman's care, and she can't jump with us, which means one of us will always have to stay behind. What I'm trying to say is that I hope you will stay, but I'm asking far more of you with that request than I once was."

I'm not sure how to respond. The truth is that I am still so in love with Henri I feel like I can barely breathe at the thought of leaving him. But I am also hurt, even if I shouldn't be. I know that I will probably stay—how can I not, under the circumstances: with his whole family in danger, with a new baby more defenseless than the rest of us?—but I'm not sure how it will be with us. Or if it will ever be the same.

The door opens. Henri stands there with Cecelia on his shoulder, so impossibly tiny by contrast with her father. His eyes hold mine and I freeze, without a clue what to say. It is Marie who swoops in, brushing her hands against her dress and walking briskly toward him. She pulls Cece from his arms and begins cooing to her as she walks outside, shutting the door firmly behind her.

"You heard?" he asks. He hasn't moved an inch.

My eyes slowly lift to his. I suppose I should tell him I'm sorry, but the words don't come. Cecelia has lost her mother, but Yvette was already proving not to be much of one. "Yes," I reply. "I heard."

My tongue goes to my lips. I'm not sure what he wants of me now. I'm not sure if he wants to pick up where we left off, not that it's really an option, or if he's actually grieving the loss of his wife. Based on his silence, I guess maybe it's the latter.

If he can't even bring himself to ask me to stay, then it's the surest sign I shouldn't. "The two weeks I promised are nearly up," I say quietly.

For a moment I'm greeted with another of his silences, and it feels like agreement. My chest begins to cave in on itself.

But then he takes three large strides to where I sit, and he drops to his knees in front of me. His head falls to my lap, like a child's might. His voice is strangled when he finally speaks. "Please don't leave me. I will find a way to earn your forgiveness. Please, just give me a chance."

My eyes burn, and all that pain I felt in my chest a moment ago is still there, but it's different. It's pain mixed with relief. He still wants me. He will do what is necessary to fix what's gone wrong. Tears slip down my face and I bury my hands in his hair, rest my face on the back of his head.

"I can't just...it's going to take me some time," I finally say.

He raises his head. "I will give you all the time in the world," he pleads. "Just stay."

I nod, feeling heartbroken and ecstatic at once. "It's all I've ever wanted."

MARIE COMES IN, not much later, and we all move somewhat awkwardly around each other for the rest of the day. Henri takes care of the chores and Marie cooks and I take care of the baby and not a single one of us mentions how things are going to be from now on.

I watch Henri walking toward the house at dusk, and it's the first time, in all these long weeks since I arrived, that I truly allow myself to appreciate him. To take in the sheer masculinity of those shoulders and his unshaved jaw and that swagger as he walks, and allow myself to want him again, want him in the way of something I might actually have.

When he comes inside, his smile for me is almost bashful. "How was she today?" he asks, nodding at Cecelia.

"Happy," I reply. "I think she actually tried to hum when I sang to her. And she smiled. A real smile. Not just gas."

He nods, biting his lip. "Thank you...for watching her."

He's never thanked me for this before. It makes things between us feel oddly formal, *transactional*, even. I don't know what to make of it. "Of course."

I'd hoped things might improve over dinner, but they do not. During the past weeks with Yvette here, we've gotten out of the habit of casually discussing things related to my time, or traveling, or anything beyond the mundane conversations you might hold with a stranger. We talk about the weather and the farm, and Cece most of all. Which is wonderful—there is plenty to discuss—but it doesn't make me feel closer to him.

Henri still looks at me the way he has now for weeks. Hungrily. And as if the sight of me causes him pain. But I can't go from a long discussion of Cecelia's eating and pooping habits to ripping off his clothes.

"I'll take her tonight," says Marie with an awkward look between me and her brother.

Internally, I quail at the idea. There is not a chance I'm sleeping with him when his wife hasn't even been gone twenty-four hours. I guess I still haven't quite forgiven him after all, not entirely.

I shake my head. "You both barely slept last night and I'm used to having her with me. I'll take her tonight."

Henri's shoulders, hunched over the table, grow still as I

speak. His head remains facing down when I'm done. "Thank you," he says formally. "I appreciate how much you've done for us these past few weeks."

I smile politely in response, feeling as if, somehow, we just took a large step backward.

Another day passes. Another night where I make excuses about Cecelia and sleep in my own room, longing for him yet unsettled by it all as well, though I don't understand why.

On the third morning, Marie stops me. "What exactly is happening with you and my brother?" she asks.

I flush, moving Cece to my left shoulder. "I don't know. I guess we're getting to know each other again."

"And how do you think that will happen when he's so scared you're going to leave that he's treating you with kid gloves, and the only topic you're willing to discuss with him is his two-week-old?"

"I don't know what you want me to say. Do you think I want things to be like this?"

She pulls Cece out of my arms. "I'm taking her for a walk into town," she says. "Please find my brother and solve this before I get home."

"It's not that easy," I object, but she continues walking. I watch as she puts Cece into the pram on the porch and heads for the road, and then I look toward the fields, steeling myself. What am

I supposed to say to him? What would I have said to him before? I can't even recall who we were, and the discomfort isn't entirely one-sided. The truth is that before I left, if I walked into the fields to find him, he'd have wrapped his arms around me before I could say a word. Now, most likely, he'll wait with a pained look on his face, or ask me how Cecelia is.

I take a quick glance in the mirror and then walk out the door and head through the fields. It's unusually warm, as far into the fall as it is, and when I finally spy him in the last row, I find him stripped down to a t-shirt, which clings to his chest and shoulders and abs in a way that would make any female stare. His head raises and when our gaze locks, he has that look on his face once more—hungry, desperate, restrained.

He begins to move toward me and I toward him, so scared and so needy I feel sick with it.

I mentally comb through all the mundane topics to discuss with him—the weather, how much Cecelia ate this morning—anything to put us in a normal place, a place where he isn't looking at me the way he is right now. My brain is empty today.

"It's a nice—" I begin, and the words are stopped short as he grasps my face in his hands and kisses me. Kisses me hard, with a low moan of need.

That *sound*. My God. When he makes that noise it's all I can do to stay on two feet. I cling to him, under the sway of my desire, hands clawing at his shirt, desperate for purchase, desperate for the feel of his skin after these months apart. His mouth is on my jaw as I untuck his shirt and slide my hands beneath it. My palms press flat, wanting to savor him, but I can't hold still long enough. I want more, everything, as fast as possible and when his lips move to my neck, every nerve ending seems to light up. I arch against him as I gasp, wordlessly begging for more.

"I can't wait another moment," he says, tugging at my dress, too reckless and needy to stop for buttons. "My God I've wanted this for so long." I hear the back tear and it matters not at all.

We pull each other to the ground, his mouth on my breasts as I reach for his belt. My fumbling hands are too slow. He shoves the pants down on his own and lays me back in the dirt, kneeling between my parted thighs. My panties still separate us. He tears them in half and pushes inside me.

My God.

I'd remembered it, and yet I hadn't. The feeling of being stretched by him, being so impossibly full.

If either of us had hoped to go slow, I realize now we're not capable of it. The moment he slides out I'm jerking my hips to meet his again. We are gasping and senseless, teeth and tongues, swallowing the other's sounds greedily. He's too desperate to be gentle with this. His belt hits my thighs with each thrust, the rough canvas of his pants abrading my skin. I'm not gentle with him either. I rut against him, hard and frenzied, wanting to somehow drive out the agony of the last year.

My back sinks farther into the lumpy ground beneath me, my legs wrap around him tighter and tighter and his murmurs, entirely in French, grow frantic and barely intelligible. He tells me he's missed me and that he loves me. I feel a sharp pang in my gut, as if my body is opening, preparing for flight. His words change, grow filthy and desperate, things I never dreamed I'd hear him say. I clamp down around him and cry out. He jerks inside me once, and again, and a final time, but slower.

My eyes open. I'm a little shocked to find us in the dirt, with the sun overhead. To find my dress in ruins and most of his clothes still on. He blinks, and his eyes are wide, alarmed, when they meet mine.

He slides out of me, averting his gaze. He's still hard, and the old version of Henri would have stayed where he was, would have told me he'd be ready again in a moment, but this one is uncertain. He looks at me like someone he just fucked by mistake.

"Are you...okay?" he asks haltingly. My thighs are sticky now and the bottom of the dress is wet with us, which hardly matters since it's too ripped to be salvageable.

"Yes," I say, sitting up, staring at my hands. "I'm fine."

His fingers trail along a point just above my collarbone. "I bruised you. I'm sorry."

He sits back, pulling up his pants. I pull my knees together and try to hold the dress around myself. "I didn't notice. It was fine."

How can it be so gruelingly awkward between us now? I want to fix it, but the girl I was before everything happened would have launched herself in his arms—would have demanded he tell her every thought in his head no matter what it was—and I'm not her anymore. That girl didn't have to ask if he was comparing her to his wife, didn't have to wonder if she had, by comparison, failed.

He runs a hand over his face. "I—" he begins.

"I need to get back to the house," I cut in, terrified of whatever is about to come out of his mouth. "Marie will be back soon. I don't want her to see my dress."

He nods, shoulders hunched as if defeated somehow, and no wonder. I'm sure he never thought sleeping with me could possibly make things worse, but it definitely has.

FOR THE REST of the afternoon I stay inside with Cecelia. It's unnecessary since Marie is home, but the truth is I'm scared to run into Henri again. I'm scared of how uncomfortable things are between us. I'm scared of the weight of my desire, which even as I sit here burping Cece, has me feeling like I might come out of my skin with wanting him again. I think of it every time my bruised back hits the chair, every time my thighs—abraded by friction—rub together. I'm a disaster and I only want more and more, with someone who could barely look at me when it was over.

Yvette. Does he miss her? She was a conniving little bitch, but men are stupid about things like that. She certainly didn't enter into a relationship with him quite as innocently as I did, and maybe I'm just not...enough. I don't have *tricks*. The little I know about sex I learned from Henri. Maybe he's come to appreciate the value of an experienced partner.

I think of the things he said to me just before he came, filthy things that shocked me and probably could have made me come even if he were just whispering them over the phone, and wonder if he said them to her as well. Did he get carried away at the end and forget who he was with?

My stomach drops. "Of course he did," I whisper aloud, horrified. "Of course, of course, of course." I'm embarrassed for myself, for the way I reacted...thinking I'd somehow *elicited* that reaction from him. Mostly, I'm just sickened by the fact that he had that kind of relationship with her. That they were so open with each other, so filthy. So *unlike* us.

When he comes in, I busy myself with Cecelia, and after dinner is cleaned up, I fake a big yawn and announce I'm turning in for the night, Cece pressed to my chest like a shield.

He follows me to the bottom of the stairs, while Marie busies herself in the kitchen as if she doesn't notice. "I'm sorry," he says tentatively, "if I was too...rough. I got carried away."

It all feels like a euphemism now. Like he's really saying *I'm sorry I confused you with my wife*.

"It was fine," I reply.

25

SARAH

T he next day things are more uncomfortable than ever. It's unbearable that it's gotten this way. I love him, I love his daughter, and I want to stay. But how can we continue like this?

When he comes in at lunch he barely looks at me.

"I need to go into town," I say, rising.

"I'll give you my list and the two of you can go," says Marie. "I'll watch the baby."

I want to be alone with him, and yet I also don't. I'm scared that he'll apologize again, or even worse...that he'll imply there's something about Yvette he misses.

We walk in silence. It's not until we've reached the town that he turns to me.

"Can we talk about yesterday?" he asks suddenly.

I tense. "What about it?"

He closes his eyes and exhales heavily. "It's not how I'd have wanted our first time to be, and I feel as if it ended badly, but when I try to discuss it with you, you end the conversation."

"I don't know what you want from me," I mutter. "I told you it was fine."

His laughter is short and bitter. "Yes, that's what every man wants to hear. *It was fine.*"

Tears spring to my eyes. "I'm sorry," I snap. "I'm sure Yvette was much better at demonstrating her appreciation." I start crossing the street toward the general store.

"Amelie, wait," he says.

"Just leave me alone," I hiss over my shoulder. "I'll meet you at the butcher shop."

I walk into the store, trying to compose myself. This is a small town and it'll just take one person seeing tears in my eyes to get the rumor mill running.

And who am I fooling? It's already running full speed, I'm sure. A year ago, the whole town was gossiping about Henri's possessiveness of his cousin, and as soon as the cousin returns his wife runs off. It's easy enough to imagine what they are all thinking.

I grab a package of pins and then ask Madame Fournier for ten yards of cotton for diapers. She tells me to give her a moment, so I turn to walk down the aisle and run right into Luc.

He looks startled to see me, and then glances at the pins in my hand and gives me a small smile. "And?" he asks. "Are the rumors true?"

"What rumors?"

"That Yvette left. She told Claudette Loison that you and Henri were lovers and she caught you together."

"No," I gasp. "Of course not. Yvette was...unhinged. She was constantly making accusations and had no interest in being a mother. Her departure had nothing to do with me."

He steps closer. "My leave is nearly over. I haven't seen you in town once, though."

"I've been taking care of the baby," I argue. "She's still fragile. None of us have been around."

He nods and then his hand slides out to grab mine. "Just be careful," he says. "Please. His wife is gone and I'm sure he's ready to take you back with open arms, but he's hurt you once and that situation is a landmine. The woman just had a baby. Her emotions are all over the place but she's going to come back. Surely you realize this." As he says the words, I realize I've been saying them to myself as well. Asking what will happen if Yvette changes her mind. Cecelia is her daughter and Henri will go where she goes. "You're beautiful, and I'm not saying he doesn't care, but if he has to decide between taking her back or losing his daughter, what will he—"

Luc's words die off suddenly, and before I can ask him what's wrong, I feel Henri move behind me, standing too close.

"Drop her hand," he growls.

Luc's eyes darken. "I'm getting tired of these little interruptions, Henri," he replies, his hand still on mine. "Perhaps if you took better care of your things, you wouldn't need to guard them so zealously."

Henri's hands go to my shoulders and he starts pulling me behind him, which means, no doubt, that he's anticipating a fight. Madame Fournier and her assistant peek around the corner at us.

"Stop," I hiss, locking myself tight so Henri can't move me easily. "Both of you. We're making a scene."

Their gazes flicker toward Madame Fournier, but I get the feeling neither of them cares all that much at this precise moment.

"I should go," I say to Luc, slipping my hand from his. "Thank you for your concern." I turn away, all but shoving Henri in the opposite direction. We haven't bought anything we needed, but I sense an explosion coming—his or mine, I'm not sure—and it can't happen here.

I march back toward the farm and he's on my heels.

"Is that why you were so eager to shop?" he asks, the words hissed more than spoken. "Your secret meeting with Luc?"

"*Secret meeting*?" I demand. "Are you kidding me?"

I walk ahead as fast as I can and don't say another word until we're just outside of the village and on the quiet road to the farm. "I spoke to him for all of a minute before you steamrolled over us both."

"He held your hand!" he shouts. "Don't pretend for a moment you were merely talking!"

"Did I *fuck* him?" I demand. "Because until I *have*, I still won't have caught up with you."

He pulls me off the side of the road, into the grass. "Is that what it's going to come down to?" he asks, gripping my shoulders. "Will you need to punish me for it before we can move forward? Do you need to go be with Luc so things are *even*? Fine. Do it. Just stop throwing it in my face again and again when there's absolutely nothing I can do to fix it!"

"So, you *want* me to sleep with Luc."

"Of course I don't want you to sleep with him!" he cries. "I want you *back*. I want you to stop hating me for what I did, and if this is what it will take, then I'll learn to live with it. You're mad, and you have every right to be. But I'm mad too, Sarah."

My jaw drops. "*You're* mad? About what?"

"I begged you not to go. My God, I begged, and you didn't listen. What I wanted was meaningless, and you will always be able to disregard my opinion, won't you? You will always be able to leave for a year and return, buffed to perfection after a trip to your own time, talking about some musician you were with."

"I didn't leave you," I tell him, and now the tears are rolling down my face whether I want them to or not. "You left me and you'll leave me again if she comes back." My chest aches as I say the words. This fear has been knife-sharp all along, the thing I can't get past, the reason I don't want to trust him.

His arms come around me. "Is that really what you think?" he asks. His voice breaks. He sounds devastated. His lips press to the top of my head, to my temples, to my eyes. "Sarah, I could barely make myself stay when she *hadn't* left. There's not a chance I'd take her back now."

"What if she threatens to take Cecelia?"

His lips move over my cheeks, slick with tears. "She won't take you, or my daughter, and God help her if she tries to do either one."

I stare at his chest, tucking my chin to keep the wobble out of my voice. "I don't want you comparing me to her...not with *that*."

He looks truly dumbfounded. "Are you talking about sex? How could I possibly compare the two of you when I can't remember ever being with her in the first place?"

"She said you couldn't keep your hands off her."

He sighs. "And you believed her? She was petty and cruel and jealous. Why would you believe a word that came out of her mouth?"

"When we were together," I say, finally glancing up at him. "The things you said at the end..." I shake my head.

He raises a brow. "You seemed to like the things I was saying well enough at the time."

"Yes," I cry, "until I realized you weren't even thinking of me when you said them! That was nothing you *ever* did with me. And if you're going to be pretending I'm her, I'd rather just leave."

He pulls my face to his. "The way I was with you last time, Sarah...it's because I was desperate. It's because I'd thought of nothing but you for a year, and because I'd fantasized, and because I hadn't had sex I was sober enough to remember *once* since you left."

He holds my face in his hands as if nothing has ever been more precious to him and he kisses me. An apology, a plea. His mouth moving slowly over mine as if relearning its every dip and curve. My mouth opens and he steps in closer, his tongue gently making me forget where we are and what we were discussing. My coin purse falls to the ground and his palm slides to my ass as he pulls me toward the trees on the side of the road.

I arch against him, seeking friction, and his mouth moves over my neck. He undoes my first two buttons and, when it's still not enough to reach my bra, he leans over and pulls at my nipple with his teeth through the fabric of the dress. I reach for his belt.

"Please," I beg him. "I need more."

His hands are up my dress, sliding up my bare thighs. In a moment he'll discover that I'm so wet it embarrasses me. My legs spread in anticipation as I undo his pants.

But he stops, his chest rising and falling quickly. "No."

"No?" I ask. I'm humiliated by how distraught I sound right now.

"It won't be just like last time," he says. "I won't let this be rough and frantic and perfect only to end with you unable to look me in the eye."

"Fine," I say, reaching for him. "It won't be."

"No," he insists. "No more sleeping in another room. No more awkwardness. No more using Cece as an excuse to avoid me. The next time we do this, we do this in *our* bed, in *our* room."

"Have you even changed the sheets yet?" I ask, bitterness in my tone.

"Marie did the day she left."

I frown. "I still hate that she was in there, but fine. I'll sleep in your room."

I reach for his pants a third time, let my hand splay over his cock, jutting against the material. He hisses air between his teeth, but then his fingers twine with mine and he pulls my hand away. "I want it even more than you do, little thief, I assure you. But if this is what I have to do to have you back in my bed, begging for it, I will."

I arch toward him. "I'm begging right here."

He laughs. "Not good enough."

WHEN WE RETURN to the house, Marie looks at us askance. "You've been gone nearly two hours and you return empty-handed? Dieu. You're both absolutely worthless." Henri ignores her, grabbing the key to the truck off the peg by the door.

"Where are you going now?" I ask.

A hint of a smile graces his mouth. He leans over and presses a kiss to his daughter's forehead, and then a kiss to mine, before reaching for the door. "Just a little insurance policy."

"Were you fighting?" asks Marie after he leaves.

"No," I say, lifting Cece from her crib. She burps loudly and I grin at her as if she just got into Harvard. "Such a good girl," I coo.

"He didn't say anything? You don't think he—" Her question trails off as she looks away, and I know what she was going to ask.

"No, he didn't go to bring her home. *That* I am certain of."

Hours pass. Marie continues to fret, and it's time to put Cece to bed but...well, I promised. And more to the point I *want* what he promised me if I stayed in his room. The truck pulls up at last and he comes in, moving past us but flashing me a quick grin. Seconds later, he's pulling the mattress from the room. He dumps it outside, without ceremony, and then drags in a new one, wrapped in plastic sheeting.

"Henri," breathes Marie, "what on earth?"

He ignores her, going to the linen cabinet just off the hallway and grabbing clean sheets. And then holds out a hand for me, formally, as if he's a foreign prince meeting his new bride. "Marie, do you mind very much taking Cecelia tonight?" he asks, never looking away from me once as he pulls me into his room.

When the door shuts behind us, he begins pulling a fresh sheet over the mattress. "I was already going to sleep in here, you know," I tell him. "You didn't have to take it quite this far."

He meets my eye with a single brow raised. "Just so we're clear, you'll be lucky if you do *any* sleeping."

I blush, feeling suddenly shy and uncertain. Somehow, we never went through this awkward stage the first time around, but

I'm going through it now. I reach for the door. "I should check on—"

He comes to where I stand and presses his left palm flat against the door so it stays shut. With his right, he begins unbuttoning my dress. "Stop avoiding me, Sarah," he says. His voice is a low growl, one that unsettles me as much as it makes me want everything he's promised.

"We still haven't finished making up the—"

"Close enough," he says, pulling the dress over my head and swinging me onto the mattress. He tugs my panties down, then slides down until his head is between my thighs, letting his tongue dart out to taste me while his fingers push inside.

"Henri," I groan. "Oh my God. It's too much. Just come up here."

He laughs. I feel the pulse of his exhale against me, just where his tongue is still flickering so, so perfectly. "All in good time, little thief. But first I'm going to taste your tight, wet-"

"*Henri*," I warn.

"I know you like it," he says. "And I want to make sure you know whose tight, wet, delicious-"

"*Henri*. Stop."

He laughs again. "Why?"

"Because," I reply, pulling him toward me. At last he complies. "You're going to end it before it starts." I tug his pants down and pull him on top of me before they're even mid-thigh. He pushes inside me and the two of us groan at the feel of it. I lean toward his ear. "*Now*," I whisper, arching upward to meet his thrust. "*Now* tell me."

WE ARE exhausted but unwilling to sleep. I doze off, and when I wake in his moonlit room, I'm certain I am dreaming, convinced I'm still a captive and have time traveled to him the way I used to.

He rolls toward me and holds my face in his hands. "You have no idea how many times I've prayed I'd open my eyes to find you here," he whispers, and it comes to me—Yvette and the pain of finding her here, Cecelia's birth and the way it healed me. A small burst of anger and pain and forgiveness, emotions I run through so fast it's hard to tell them apart. I can't wish it away, not when Cecelia couldn't exist without it, and while a part of me wishes things were still pure and unsullied between us, the way they were a year ago, I know that we are stronger like this. Even the best foundations have some dirt mixed in. That's what makes them harden into something solid and unshakeable.

He was sure of me back then, yet worried I would someday choose to leave, and now he knows better. I was sure of him back then, yet a piece of me still wondered if he wouldn't be better off and happier with some normal girl he could count on. But now I know a part of him belongs to me, craves me, in a way that wouldn't be satisfied by someone else.

I press my mouth to his. In a moment this will lead to other things—to me, rolled on my back and him pushing inside me. But for right now, just in this moment, our kiss is something else. A seal, a promise. The start of a new, and better, version of us. Coron and Iris may be a part of me, but I will never allow them to take over. With Henri and Cecelia by my side, I can close the door on that side of myself. Forever, I hope.

26

SARAH

For the next month, the war seems so far away it would be easy to forget about it entirely. The Germans don't advance. The French don't attack. There is rationing, yes, but it affects us little on the farm—between the canned goods and the livestock we have plenty. Henri and most of the young men in town are considered active duty, forbidden to leave the vicinity, but there's not much to it at the moment—daily drills out in the fields on the far side of the village and some target practice, nothing more. Henri still can't quite believe that Marshall Petain, a decorated war hero himself, will just surrender to Hitler with nary a fight after becoming president, but I shudder when I think about what lies ahead. If Henri died during World War II, that means he'll die again no matter what I do. I comb my memory for the conversations Cecelia and I had during the visits to my own time—*will have*, in her case—about her father. She was so careful not to give me a single detail. But did she ever speak of him as if he was someone she knew? Did she ever tell me a single thing implying that they'd been together, shared a meal or a conversation?

I don't think she did.

I try to content myself with the days I have right now and, for the most part, I'm happy, but I still bear scars from my time in captivity that might never depart. I still wake at night with my heart pounding, certain Gustave's hand is on my ankle, that Mathilde let the babies die.

Henri quietly soothes me on those nights, running a hand down my back until my heart settles again. "What happened to you there?" he always asks, his voice tight.

"Nothing," I reply each time. "I don't want to talk about it."

One night he asks whose body he pulled out of the hole, wearing his mother's necklace. I lie and tell him I don't know, because in spite of everything, our lives are good and I'm not that person now, the one who killed with glee. *I refuse to feel guilty about it,* I will say to myself sometimes. But what troubles me isn't that I feel guilt—it's that I feel nothing but a quiet, simmering pleasure when I remember most of the deaths I was responsible for.

And I'm not the only one who bears scars from our time apart. On those afternoons when he walks into a silent home—when Cece is napping and Marie is in town—I get a glimpse of something haunted in his eyes, the ghost of last winter when the house was empty and threatened to remain so. Then he finds me and it's gone, replaced by his staggering relief, and quickly followed by the suggestion that we should go to the bedroom while we have a few moments to ourselves.

On one of those afternoons though, after he's silently undressed me and pushed me back to the bed and we're lying together with my head on his chest, he brings up a topic we haven't discussed in a long while. "I want you to marry me," he says.

I lean up on my forearms. "I hate to ruin an otherwise perfect moment by pointing out the obvious, but you're already married."

"I filed to have it annulled," he says. "I'm not sure how long it will take to come through, but when it does, on the *day* it does, I want you to marry me."

"Are you going to try to claim it wasn't consummated?" My laughter is meant to sound lighthearted but comes out bitter instead. The truth is that even the most oblique references to Yvette bother me. "There's some obvious proof it was."

"We never once had relations after our wedding. And therefore, the *marriage* was not consummated."

I study his face. They were married from March to October, sleeping in the same bed. It's obvious Yvette was more than willing. "Not *once*?" I repeat. I want it to be true. The thought of them together is something that never stops eating at me.

"I told her I wasn't comfortable with the idea of it because of the baby. Thank God she left before I had to come up with a new excuse," he says with a relieved exhale. "So? Yes or no?"

Once upon a time it seemed too soon. Now it seems like I've waited forever for it. I smile and place my head back against his chest. "Yes," I reply. "There's nothing I want more."

ON THE LAST weekend of November, all of us head to town dressed to the nines for the baptism of the newest Durand. Since Cece's birth, Marie's been attending mass alone. Cece is too fragile to be taken into crowds just yet, but that's not the only reason Henri and I have been avoiding mass: in the aftermath of Yvette's departure, Henri has become *the man who threw over his pregnant wife for his own cousin*, and I'm now *the American who seduced her own cousin away from his pregnant wife*. I could live with it, but I'm glad we're leaving so I won't have to.

Father Edouard, unlike the rest of the town, doesn't appear to hold it against us. His main source of trouble this day, it seems, is Gerard—a friend of Henri's from grade school who will serve as a godparent alongside Marie. Every time Gerard makes Marie laugh, offers her assistance or even stands beside her, Edouard's square jaw flexes until I'm certain he's going to crack teeth. At one point, most unpriestly of all, I catch him rolling his eyes.

The service begins and, after a few prayers, he asks who the parents are. Henri grips my hand and we step forward. "We are," the two of us say in unison. Henri squeezes my hand and I truly feel, in this moment, that I don't have a single regret. I'm a mother because of what happened. Might I have had my own children if it hadn't? Perhaps, but it no longer matters to me. I couldn't love Cecelia more than I do, and I wouldn't trade her for a hundred children I might have had otherwise. The sun floats in through the stained-glass windows, and Cecelia, happy in my arms, smiles at me, as if she knew long before I did that this was exactly what was meant to be.

After the service we invite everyone back to the farm for a small party. Marie goes to the vestibule to get Cecelia's pram, and Gerard follows, complimenting her smallest actions—*you're so good with the baby, so careful, I wonder if she'll be as lovely as her aunt.*

"He's making a fool of himself," Henri groans as we exit the church.

Edouard's face has been strained for some time. He cuts a quick glance toward Marie and Gerard. "Yes," he growls. "He is."

"Well, he'll need to work fast," I reply, smiling to myself, "given how soon we move." We are due to travel by ship from Calais to England in April, when Henri will next have leave and Cecelia will be big enough to withstand the trip. Once Henri gets us settled—a friend from Oxford has already found us something to let in the British countryside—he will join General de Gaulle's London-based forces, though I wish I could dissuade him.

Edouard's face jerks toward mine. "Move? Move where?"

"England," I reply. I'm surprised Marie hasn't mentioned it. "The countryside is safer there, until the war concludes."

He looks at me with a hint of confusion and then—worry.

"Most say the war won't affect us," he comments, watching my face. "But you feel otherwise."

I hesitate. "People are putting an awful lot of stock in the Maginot Line and ignoring the many other ways the Germans could break into France. They've already taken over Poland. They beat us conclusively at Saar. It would be naïve to assume they won't make every effort to take France. They need our ports if nothing else."

"But surely moving so far..." He glances back at Marie, that worry in his eyes deepening. "Moving so far is extreme. Even if the Germans want the coastline, and take it, they'd have little use for a small town like ours."

"Saint Antoine rests just between Germany and Paris, and just between Germany and the Normandy coast. And if the Germans do come, there are...other concerns."

His brows come together for a moment, in confusion, and then he nods. "Because Madame Durand was Jewish?" he asks.

Henri stiffens beside me. "I'm surprised my sister chose to share that with you."

Edouard frowns. "She didn't. It's been mentioned to me by others in town." We all walk together in silence, letting that sink in. People in town are already discussing it, this meaningless piece of Henri and Marie's past, though it nets them nothing. Which means that once Saint Antoine is occupied and those words have value—and can be exchanged to curry favor—people in this town will be lining up to share them.

Marie's friend Jeannette waits at the house when we arrive with Lucien and Charlotte in tow. A widow since the Saar Offensive, she looks much thinner and older than she did when I left a year ago. Worry lines crease her lovely face and her smile flickers out now as soon as it's begun. The children, thank God, are unaffected as yet by the change of circumstances, and have both grown so much—Luc now an adorable, rosy-cheeked toddler, walking on unsteady legs through the house, knocking things over. Charlotte, age five, is as graceful as a princess when she holds Cecelia for the first time, but her face breaks into a wide grin, one that's missing several teeth, when Cecelia burps.

The sight of it squeezes my heart so tight it hurts. We've found ways to help them with money and food, but we cannot convince Jeannette to leave. She, like everyone else, believes this war will come to nothing, and refuses on the most ridiculous bases: she can't leave her mother and grandmother, though she only sees them once every few months, and she wants to stay close to people she knows—even though *we* are the only people here with whom she's friendly; and being a practicing Jew, most of this town will turn on her the minute the Germans arrive.

Today I try to convince her to get the children passports, which she insists is unnecessary. I suggest she could bring her mother and grandmother with her to England, and she laughs.

"They'd never go. The English don't practice good hygiene, you know," she argues. "Covered with lice during the war."

I sigh. "Don't you think, maybe, they were covered with lice *because* they were in the middle of a war?"

"No," she says very seriously. "My mother still talks about it. They just refused to bathe."

I feel despair as I watch Lucien and Charlotte run around the room. No one, *no one*, is taking the threat of Hitler as seriously as they should.

Gerard emerges from the bathroom, asking us all where Marie went. Jeannette and I exchange a quick glance—both Marie and Father Edouard are absent, suddenly, and there's no good reason for either of them to have snuck outside alone on a bitterly cold November afternoon.

Gerard goes in search of them. Henri, playing with the children on the floor, notices nothing, which is for the best since Marie and Edouard both look dazed and unsteady when they return a moment later with Gerard. Edouard takes his leave, but the whole time he's congratulating Henri and myself, his eyes are on her...different than they've ever been before.

"So, where did you and Edouard go this afternoon?" I ask later in the day, when the guests are gone and Henri isn't listening.

She blinks and a flush colors her cheeks. "He just wanted to see the orchard."

I raise a brow. "In November?"

Her gaze rests on her hands rather than on me. "Yes, that's what I said too," she murmurs.

I hesitate, torn between pushing and letting her have her secrets. I finally decide to let her keep them for now. If something did happen, she has a lot to think about. As much as I did that first time Henri kissed me, certainly, and I wasn't ready then to mull it over aloud.

The truth, I figure, will come out in time. I just hope she doesn't make a mistake she can't undo before then.

27

SARAH

Early in December, Henri and I take the truck out to the woods and chop down a fir. In truth, he deals with the tree and I stand by, worried it will fall on him. He laughs at me. "Is that what people worry about in your time?" he asks with a crooked smile.

No, it's what *I* worry about. Now that I have him again, I can't help but think about the ways I might one day lose him. But it's not the time for my depressing thoughts, my anxiety. I return his grin. "Now I *hope* the tree falls on you just to teach you a lesson."

"And if the tree breaks my back, how will you carry me to the truck?"

"What makes you think I'd bother?" I reply. "I'll just take your keys and drive into town to see if Luc is free."

He rises, pacing toward me with a light in his eyes, amused and dangerous at the same time. He pulls me against him. "Say that again," he growls, his mouth an inch from mine. He takes my lower lip between his teeth and gives it a small nip.

It's a dare, a challenge, and my heart thuds hard in my chest. "I said that I will drive into town," I reply, meeting his gaze, "and go find Luc."

His fingers go beneath my coat, to the button of my trousers. My mouth falls open. "You wouldn't," I say.

He pops the button, and his hand—cold, calloused—slides down the soft skin of my torso. "Tell me again how you'd seek out Luc," he hisses against my mouth. His long fingers slide between my legs. "You're so wet and warm here. For him or for me?"

I gasp as his fingers push inside me. "You."

His mouth lands on mine. I arch toward him, toward his flickering fingers, wanting more and more from him, as excited by the unexpectedness of it as I am the ferocity of him right now, the way jealousy and possessiveness strip him of his normal civility. I come with a sudden, sharp gasp and he turns me around, pinning my hands to the trunk of the tree as he shoves my trousers down to my knees.

The air is so cold it bites into my skin, and I don't care. With one arm he hooks my waist, pushing my ass toward him. With the other he frees himself from his pants and then he is there, pressing between my legs.

"This is mine," he says against my ear as he shoves inside me. "Mine and no one else's."

His thrusts come sharp and fast, and my face is pressed to the trunk of the tree but I hardly notice it with him inside me, slick and hot and pulsing. He's barely started and I can already feel that cord in my abdomen, the one that seems to pull tight just before I come.

"I dreamed of this when we were apart," he rasps against my ears. "Every place I set foot that year, I pictured you. Bent over or on your back."

"I'm coming," I gasp, and he thrusts faster, the tendons of his arm pressed hard to the tree, taut with the strain, and the moment my shoulders settle he pushes me to my knees and I open my mouth for him.

"This," he hisses. "I dreamt of this too."

He flinches as he comes, crying out, holding my head in his

hands. After a moment, his shoulders settle and his eyes open again, but at half-mast, as if drugged or in need of sleep. Slowly, his fingers unwind from my scalp and he helps me to my feet.

I have no regrets whatsoever, but something in the way he's avoiding my eye makes me think he does. His fingers brush my cheek. "You've got a scrape there. Did I do that?"

I smile at him. "I think my cheek was pressed against the tree —it was well worth it."

His shoulders sag. "I'm sorry," he says, his voice earnest, as if we're discussing a broken bone or stab wound instead of something so minor I didn't notice it until he brought it up. "I should have been more careful."

"Stop," I command. "You *should* have. Don't ruin it by taking it all back." I can tell he's still troubled, however. "What's wrong?"

His hands palm my face. "I was too rough, Sarah," he says. "There are times when it hits me, how much I've missed you and how desperate I was, thinking I would never see you again and..."

"And what?"

"And that you're keeping secrets from me, and I don't know what those secrets mean. I don't know if they mean I'll lose you again."

I grow still. "What are you talking about?"

"You'll need to go back to your own time again soon," he says, averting his gaze. We haven't discussed it much, but I know he's right. If I want to maintain my ability to travel to the future, I'll need to return sometime in the next year. "And when you're keeping things from me, I have to wonder if the secret is something there. Something that might mean you don't come back."

"Of course not," I reply. "When I go, it will be for as short a time as possible, and I'll come right back."

"That's not all," he says quietly. "It bothers me...that you've never told me what happened when you were gone."

I look away, wishing he would just let it go once and for all. Why does he insist on revisiting this topic? "They're ugly stories I don't care to remember, and how could they possibly matter now anyway? It's in the past."

He pushes my hair back from my face. "It changed you," he says. "In small ways, things I barely see now, but I know they're there. And no matter what they are, I will love you. I will love you just the same, I swear it. But until you know that, it will always be between us."

I meet his gaze, so open and full of love, and feel the ugliness of everything that lies inside me. He would never look at me the same way again, if he knew. He thinks he would, but only because he has no idea how dark this piece of me really is.

"I love you," I tell him, "and there's nothing more to say."

He is still for a moment and then nods. I try to pretend I don't see disappointment in the gesture.

CHRISTMAS IN SAINT Antoine is a quieter affair than I'm used to at home. Not that my mother ever made the holiday particularly festive, but there were always ample decorations in town, carols playing in the stores and a flurry of parties leading up to the event itself. I don't miss any of it, however. It's the first time I've ever been part of a family that actually wants me, and that alone makes this holiday the happiest I've ever experienced.

On Christmas Eve, Marie goes into town for mass and Henri, Cece and I remain behind. There's been something fragile about Marie since the baptism that I can't put my finger on, as if happiness has stretched her too thin, turned her into something that might shatter with the smallest provocation. Edouard has always struck me as a good man, a decent person. I was sure that if he made his feelings known to Marie, he'd offer some kind of commitment, yet nothing has changed. When I see her high color and the feverish glaze in her eyes now, I worry he's going to break her heart, but I can hardly caution her about what she's doing if she won't admit she's doing it. She practically skips from the house, and as soon as she's gone, Henri pulls me by the hand over to the tree we decorated simply with some fine glass ornaments that have been in the family for decades and popcorn and cranberries strung together.

"Perhaps this is a good time to exchange gifts," Henri says, with a smile that strikes me as slightly mischievous. We agreed to exchange handmade gifts, a rule I broke in small ways and, based on the pile of presents Henri has unearthed from a secret hiding place, he broke in vast ones. First, he gives me things he purchased the winter before, a fact which makes my heart ping with a tiny ache. There's a beautiful dress I will have few places to wear until the war ends, and lingerie I'll wear a great deal. There's a mink stole and muff, a hat from Givenchy.

For him, I've purchased a warm winter coat, heavy boots, the most recent book Evelyn Waugh.

I kiss him once our gifts are opened. "This has been my best Christmas ever."

"It's not over yet," he says, producing a small black velvet box.

My eyes meet his. Jewelry, under the circumstances, would not be wise. We have a long voyage to another country and a war to get through.

"Open it," he urges.

Slowly, I pop the box open to find a diamond ring that makes my breath stop, and I know, before I've even asked, that it's the very one Yvette wanted so badly—his mother's. It is no trinket, as I suggested to Yvette when she brought it up, but a large emerald-cut diamond set among smaller ones.

"But—" I stare at it. A ring like this will attract notice anywhere, but in Saint Antoine it will be the talk of the town. "I thought we wanted everyone to think we're poor."

"In four months, it won't matter as much," he says. "And if anyone asks in the meantime, we'll just tell them you were forced to buy your own ring with your obscene American wealth." He grins at this. Most of the town is now asking why I haven't used my money to help the Durands fix up the farm, never dreaming that in truth I'm the one who's got nothing.

I slide it on my finger and it fits perfectly—as if it was meant to be mine all along. "But...wasn't it in Paris? You haven't been to Paris once since I returned, aside from the night you came when I was out with Luc."

"I got it last year, before you left," he says. "And then, when I thought you were dead...I buried it. Under the hay bale. Stupid perhaps, if this farm will no longer be ours soon as you say, but I couldn't stand the thought of anyone else wearing it."

I press my mouth to his. "Now we just need the annulment," I tell him.

"Wear it now anyway," he says. "I dare anyone alive to tell me you are not my wife, wedding or no."

28

SARAH

1940 arrives. Everyone toasts to a new decade and, in town, people have already begun to move on with their lives, as if the uneasiness with Germany was a brief moment of ugliness that has nearly passed. We continue preparing to leave, however, and offer Jeannette the farm in our absence. It means she'll have fresh milk, fruit and eggs for the children, but it still feels like we haven't done enough to keep them safe.

Marie spends so much time at the church that I worry she will balk at leaving too, but when I press the topic, she changes it entirely. It seems only fair to leave her alone when I'm so immeasurably blessed. Cecelia, who now sleeps in my old room upstairs, smiles all day long and makes every waking hour a happy one for me. Each day, I see a little more of who she will become, and a little more of who Henri will be as a husband and father. When I watch him give Cece her evening bottle I marvel that I ever believed I could marry someone else.

I want to relish every moment we have together, yet my approaching return to 1989 weighs on us both. I need to maintain the ability to travel forward because there may be times when we want to know what's coming down the road or when the ability to skip ahead could help or even save a life. And it's best that I do it before the war begins in earnest and it's just me and Marie, alone in the British countryside.

As much as I hate the idea of leaving, it bothers Henri far more. It's a small source of friction between us, just like those nightmares I won't discuss, and I wish I could fix it.

"What will you do there?" he asks one night, though I am not leaving until the end of March, still a month away. His face is grave, as if we're discussing something far more serious than a two-week trip.

I shrug. "I really don't know. Why?"

His glance flickers away. "I was just wondering."

"It was more than that," I reply. "What aren't you telling me?"

He holds my gaze. "What aren't you telling *me*?" he asks in turn. I see hurt in his eyes and look away. I wish, so badly, that I could answer.

IN THE MIDDLE OF MARCH, a letter arrives for Marie. She tears it open right there in the doorway, and then staggers backward, holding onto the small table in the entryway for support.

"Marie?" I ask. "What is it?"

Her eyes fill. "Edouard's been sent away," she whispers.

Henri's head jerks toward her. "Sent away where?"

"They wouldn't tell him," she says, staring at the words on the paper as tears fall freely. "He says a priest from Reims arrived this morning to take him to see the monsignor in Paris, and he was told to pack his things."

Henri rises, flinching as he pinches the bridge of his nose. Slowly, his eyes go to hers. "Why," he asks, with something unhappy and dangerous in his voice, "would he write you personally about this? Because Edouard must have done something wrong to be sent away like that, and it seems very suspect that he found time to write *you*, of all people."

She raises her head from her hands. "You're still married and living in sin with another woman! How dare you judge *anything* he does?"

"I'm not a priest," he says, nostrils flaring. "And your overreaction right now leads me to think he wasn't acting like much of a priest himself."

She raises her chin. "He loves me," she says. "He asked the church to replace him here so we could be together. There's no shame in it."

Henri holds a hand to his forehead, appalled. "God, Marie," he says softly. "He's a grown man. He didn't need to ask anyone's permission to be with you if that's what he wanted. Did he...take liberties?"

Tears stream down her face. "You just don't understand! I knew you wouldn't!"

"Answer the question," he demands between his teeth. "Did he, or did he not, take liberties?" He makes no effort to disguise the violence underlying the question.

"No," she says, and then she runs from the room and up the stairs, weeping and heartbroken.

"Dieu," says Henri, collapsing onto the couch. He glances up at me. "Did you have any idea?"

I bite my lip. "I suspected. She's been in love with him for a long time."

His jaw falls open. "And you didn't tell me? If I'd had even a hint I'd have put a stop to it, believe me. And if I discover he laid a finger on her I'll see that he regrets it."

I roll my eyes. "Yes, it's truly astonishing that I didn't run right to you with my suspicions. You're handling it so well."

"How am I supposed to handle it?" he exclaims. "I've dedicated most of my adult life to keeping my sister safe and hidden so she can fulfill the prophecy, only to discover the parish priest has been wooing her and making false promises before he left town! What if they'd run off together? What happens to your precious circle of light then?"

I know he's just frustrated, and worried, but none of that will help the situation. "First of all, it's not *my* circle of light. If you'll recall, I'm not even interested in time travel. Second, what you and your mother wanted was for her to be able to make her decisions without influence or pressure or baggage, and that's what she did, didn't she? Or did you only want her to make decisions influenced by you?"

"He's a priest," he mutters, running a hand through his hair. "If she's been carrying on with a priest then perhaps she *needs* me to influence her decisions. But you just expect me to say nothing?"

"What good would it do at this point anyway? Edouard is gone."

He leans forward, his forearms to his knees, and stares at his clasped hands. "I can't believe I didn't see it," he admits. "We've been in this little bubble, you and me and Cece. Marie's been a ghost here for months and I've been so focused on my own happiness I didn't notice."

I squeeze his hand. "She didn't need you to notice, nor would she have wanted you to. She isn't as fragile as you believe, and she deserved a chance to lead a life of her own design for once. She still does."

He sighs. "Fine. But if I find out they had relations, Edouard is a dead man."

I restrain a smile. "Yes, relations before marriage would be appalling. Something you would *never* do."

He narrows his eyes. "It's different with us. I'm not a priest. And I would marry you tomorrow if I could."

"It sounds as if Edouard would marry Marie as well."

"But I'm not a priest!" he says again, irritated and amused at once.

"I'm well aware," I reply, scooting beside him. "No priest would say the things you do in bed."

His eyes slant toward mine, his mouth tipping into a reluctant half-smile. "And you love every one of them."

"I do," I reply, pressing my mouth to his jaw. "So have no fear. I will never take up with a priest."

"I never realized it was something I had to worry about prior to today," he says, pulling me toward him. "But thank you for letting me know."

FOR THE NEXT WEEK, we see little of Marie. She continues her duties at the church but spends most of her hours at home on the cusp of tears, and every time the post arrives she dives for it, only to retreat, small and broken and disappointed when there is no letter from Edouard. It's a terrible time to go to 1989, given the way my trip has Henri's nerves frayed, but I can't cut it any closer to the day we leave for England than I already have.

The night before I go, Henri and I lie in bed, unable to sleep. He makes love to me with a desperation that borders on violence, again and again. Yet early in the morning I can sense something that remains dissatisfied in him.

"What is it?" I ask, lifting up on my forearms to see his face.

He stares at the ceiling, thinking hard before he finally voices what's in his head. "Whatever it is, whatever it is you won't tell me —does it have to do with someone in your own time?" he asks. "Is it the musician?"

My stomach sinks. I hate that he'd even think it. I hate that I can't tell him the truth. "No," I tell him. "Nothing ever happened with that musician and I only brought him up to make you mad."

"Then why won't you tell me what it is?"

I could. I could risk it. But how would he respond, if he knew what I did? If he learned that the people responsible for his mother's death and his sister's captivity share my blood? It would change things. A piece of him, even if it was a small piece, would start to distrust me, just like my mother did.

"Because I like the way you look at me now, and I'm not sure you still would if you knew."

His lips press to the top of my head. "I will love you no matter what you tell me, Sarah, I swear it."

I wish I could believe that. I just don't.

Just a few hours later, it's time to go. I feed Cece, memorizing the solid weight of her in my arms, still heavy with sleep. She smiles around her bottle and reaches for my face. My eyes sting. How am I going to leave her? How am I going to leave Henri?

"I'll be back as soon as I can," I tell her, my voice rasping.

Henri walks me to the barn and I say the same thing again, this time crying in earnest.

Time travel is so much easier for me now that I have my aunt's spark, but we both know, after my time in 1918, that there are no guarantees. That anything could go wrong in my absence, on his side or mine. "I love you and I *will* wait as long as it takes," he says, begging once more to be forgiven for something I forgave long ago.

"I know," I reply, kissing him once before I let my body go light. The impulse to return to my own time hits me as hard as ever, but it's tempered by my sadness at leaving him. Even when I've completely disappeared, I can see him standing there, staring at the space I just vacated, his face bleak, and I have to force myself to go.

29

SARAH

When I reach 1989, I land with ease for the first time. I'm still in the barn, though it's now quite modern, and once I've confirmed that no one is around I scurry to the woods for the clothes I buried there years before.

It's technically spring but still feels like winter, and I'm thrilled to find warm clothes in place of the ones I left—including a Burberry coat, hanging from a branch. No sooner am I dressed than a limousine pulls up and Cecelia climbs out, shielding her eyes from the sun, looking for me.

She's dressed impeccably, as always, in a coat and dress that match—designer, I'm sure—and stiletto heels. That she is the same baby who pressed her tiny palm to my face only a few hours ago absolutely stuns me, but I can see it, in the set of her mouth and her eyes, even in the way she glances around.

"Cecelia," I whisper from behind a tree and she smiles and hurries forward, wrapping a big coat around me.

"You have teeth now," I say, and my eyes fill with tears.

Her eyes well over too. "You have no idea how wonderful it is that you finally know who I am."

I shake my head. "You shouldn't have saved me the last time," I tell her. "It could have gone so, so wrong."

"You've already saved my life once," she says, "and not for the last time. Don't ask me not to keep you from harm when I can."

We both climb into the back and I smile again. "I can't get over the fact that it's you. I just fed you a bottle. Your father says hello."

She swallows and then she smiles. A brief smile, a flicker. "Does he?" she asks.

She changes the subject. Maybe she does so because her father is alive and she speaks to him daily. Or maybe she does so because the subject is painful and she doesn't want to give too much away.

I lean back against the plush leather, tired but not exhausted the way I've been in the past. I couldn't time travel right now, but it feels like I won't need ages to recover, either. "Do you know how long I'll need to stay?" I ask. "How long it takes me to get all my ability back?"

She smiles at me fondly, and it's as if our roles are reversed. "A little over a week," she says. "But try to make the most of your time here. You've never gotten to enjoy Paris when you were completely healthy."

We're entering the city now, bright and pristine, old and modern simultaneously. And it's perfect, but I don't want to be here. I want to be home with Henri and our daughter. "I just want to get back," I tell her. "Once we leave for England everything's going to change and—" I shrug. "Our lives are very peaceful now. I'm not sure they'll stay that way."

She continues to smile pleasantly. Am I imagining the strain I see behind it?

We pull up in front of the flat where I stayed the last time, and Philippe comes out to open the door. "I'll see you again before you leave," she says.

"You're not coming in?"

She squeezes my hand. "As much as I'd like to, I think it's best I don't. I see you trying to read the future in every word I say, like a child who says she doesn't want to know what's in the box but keeps peeking inside anyway."

I hesitate. "Do I want to know? Will I regret not asking later?"

She shakes her head. "There is not a single thing about your life you would change, Sarah," she says. "Your life will be filled with more magic than you can possibly realize."

THE NEXT MORNING, I am shepherded out of Cecelia's flat early in the day for another of her beloved spa appointments. My skin is waxed and scrubbed and steamed until it shines, and then I'm led back to the car and taken to yet another spa to get my brows done and my hair cut. I know Cecelia well enough by now not to argue. She's so used to her modern-day life that she doesn't realize a hot shower and some tropical fruit alone seem like the height of luxury to me.

After my haircut, I ask Philippe if I can walk back to the flat and he agrees, though I know he'll be following at a distance. The brisk air whips the coat around my legs, and I breathe deep, happy and sad at once. I want to be here, but I miss Henri. I miss our daughter. And time spent without them can only be bittersweet.

I turn the corner to Rue Courtalon. The limo is in front of the flat already, and as I step off the sidewalk to cross the street, I stumble to a sudden halt. There's a woman beside the building, staring intensely at the limo...and I recognize her. Even though I only saw her once, very briefly, I recognize her face.

I recognize the malevolence that seems to radiate from her, just like the last time.

She's the time traveler who followed Cecelia and me in the park, the last time I was here. I remain frozen a moment too long, and then I dart across the street. I have no plan in mind. I just know she'd better have a damn good explanation for why she's following me. She was watching the limousine, but when the car I jump in front of lays on its horn, her head jerks in my direction.

Her nostrils flare in disgust, her eyes narrow, and then she begins to run.

She's already turned into an alley by the time I reach her side of the street, and I know it's a lost cause. If we go to that alley we'll only find a pile of clothes once more. Philippe is by my side within seconds. "It would make my job easier if you wouldn't throw yourself in front of cars for the remainder of your stay," he suggests.

"I'm sorry." I hug my arms to my chest. "I don't suppose Cecelia would allow me a gun during this visit?"

He laughs. "Not if you intend to start shooting women who just happen to look on when a limo pulls up to the building."

It's nothing I can explain to him, but she didn't just *happen* to be here. She's watching us. And I want to know why.

At my request the next morning, Cecelia comes to the flat once more.

"I understand you've been using my pillows for target practice since yesterday," she comments, trying not to smile.

It would be hard to deny since there's currently a knife sticking out of one. "Just the bedroom pillow. It's not expensive, right?"

She laughs. "I wouldn't care if it were. My issue is more with the fact that you are suddenly feeling like you need to defend yourself. I fear you've hurt Philippe's feelings."

I take the seat across from her. "I saw that time traveler again yesterday," I admit, twisting my hands. "She was watching the limo. I guess she was waiting for me to get out. And I know this will sound paranoid, but she's bad. I can feel it. She needs to be stopped."

I see a hint of knowledge in her eyes. And concern.

"Did I tell you about her?" I whisper. "During my visits as you were growing up, did I ever mention this girl? Or have you seen her lurking around?"

She gives me a single terse nod. "I've noticed her once before. And yes, you've mentioned a time traveler following you in the past."

"Is there anything you want to warn me about?" I ask.

She meets my gaze. It's only a moment before she smiles and tells me there's nothing. But I saw it.

She hesitated first.

30

SARAH

For the rest of my time in Paris, there is no sign of the time traveler. But I never leave the flat without a knife in my pocket and Philippe or Louis by my side, and it's a relief to say goodbye to Cecelia and climb into a limo for Saint Antoine once my abilities are finally restored.

When I arrive in 1940, to a warm April day and a cloudless sky, I want to weep with relief. I run to the house and find Henri in the living room pacing. "Thank God," he says, crossing the room to hold me tight.

I laugh against his chest. "I was only gone a little over a week."

"I know," he says. "And Marie reminded me a thousand times that nothing had gone wrong. I just—"

He trails off, but he doesn't need to complete the sentence. He's already lived through a time when our plans failed and I didn't return. His mouth presses to mine and I inhale him, wishing I could stay just like this with him for hours and days, until I finally feel full. "How's our daughter?" I ask when he lets me go.

"Napping at the moment," he says. We creep up the stairs to her room and peer in on her. She sleeps flat on her back, arms overhead, fists curled, mouth open and sated. My heart lurches with love for her. She seems happy in 1989. I just pray the years until then will be happy for her too.

We quietly slide from the room and go back downstairs. I fully expect him to pull me to the bedroom—he seemed ready enough for it before when he was kissing me, but instead he takes my hand and leads me to the parlor.

He runs a hand over his face, as if weary. "There has been a small change to our plan," he says.

My stomach drops. "Is it Marie? Is she refusing to go?"

He bites his lip and leans toward me, pressing his forehead to mine. "No. The Germans have attacked Norway and sent troops toward the Maginot Line. Petain is ordering half of us there, and the rest to Norway. I leave Sunday."

I freeze. "No," I argue. "I read everything about this. The Germans don't attack until May twelfth. Until then, the French assume nothing will happen."

"Perhaps it changed," he says. "Or perhaps history books have it wrong."

I try to breathe but can't seem to manage it. Even with all the reading I did, even knowing the goddamn *future*, I messed up somehow. But I wasn't wrong—I know there is no battle yet, not for another month. So why is this happening? "It's a diversion," I whisper. "Hitler's making you all think he's going to attack at the Maginot Line and then he's going to push through the Ardennes."

"I still have to go," he says. "Which means you and Marie and Cecelia will need to travel to England on your own."

I flinch. If it were just me, I'd refuse. But now there's Cecelia, who can't blink and disappear into another time at the first sign of danger. Henri is an adult and I have to let him make his own decisions, even if I disagree. But Cecelia can still be saved.

Which means these two days I now have left with Henri may very well be the last ones we share.

HENRI'S MILITARY-ISSUE backpack is carefully packed for a long, cold winter. I pray it's not that long until we see him again, knowing even as I pray that seeing him *after* the winter would be a best-case scenario, a stroke of incredible luck. The early battles are vicious and there are so, so many casualties. All who survive are taken prisoner, sent to work camps in Germany.

Henri tries to persuade me that all will be well, but when I wake at night to find him watching me, or catch him leaning over Cece's crib with a lost look on his face, I know what he's doing. He's trying to memorize us, as if this is the end. I'm devastated, but also angry. Angry at myself for not researching more thoroughly, irrationally angry at Henri for his refusal to disobey orders. Angry, most of all, because it keeps me from bursting into tears.

We rise early on Sunday, before dawn. Anger abandons me and I weep like a child, pressing my face to his chest. "Don't let them send you to Dunkirk," I whisper, frantically trying to remember what I read. "It's a massacre."

He pushes my hair back from my face and kisses me. "I have no control over that," he replies. "All I can promise you is that one day it will all be over, and I will come to England to bring you home. No one will fight harder than I to make that happen."

I want to ask him to promise, but I don't. Everything that's happening now is beyond our control. Everything that's happening now has *already happened*. I can only pray that it all turned out well.

31

SARAH

The first day without Henri feels endless. Marie is upset too, and we avoid each other's eyes as we get through the day. All our valuables—the money, the jewelry, my wedding ring—are packed, leaving us little to do. In a few days, we will watch Jeannette's children while she goes to Paris to say goodbye to her dying grandmother, and I wish the children were already here—it would be good to have something to fill my head right now other than thoughts of Henri.

That night, as I sit down to dinner and begin feeding Cecelia a bit of mashed apple and ham, Marie's eyes fill. I've spent the entire day trying not to cry, but if she starts now, I won't be able to stop. "Please don't cry," I rasp, my voice beginning to wobble. "I'm keeping myself together right now for Cece's sake, but barely."

She presses her hands to her face. "I'm not crying over Henri," she says.

I grip the spoon in my hand with unnecessary force. Henri may die, while Edouard is ensconced safely behind the walls of a church. It seems as if, just this once, Marie could think of someone else. "Edouard again?" I ask, struggling to keep the acid from my voice.

Her tongue darts to her lips and then her eyes close. "I'm pregnant," she whispers.

The spoon in my hand clatters to the floor. I stare at Marie, unable to even process what she's said.

"I didn't want Henri to know," she says, putting her forehead in her hands. "He'd blame Edouard."

I shake my head, so dumbfounded it's hard to find my voice. I thought they might have exchanged sweet words and perhaps a kiss. Never, ever, did I think Edouard would allow it to go this far. *He shouldn't have.* He shouldn't have slept with her, and should have been careful if he did and...I have so many criticisms, so much judgement, I don't even know where to start.

"How could he have slept with you and then just left?"

"It wasn't his fault," she says. "He tried to stop it and I wouldn't let him."

Edouard is a grown man, and a priest. Marie *was* a twenty-two-year-old virgin who, as far as I know, had never even been kissed. I'm hard-pressed to imagine she's solely at fault here. "There's no possible way he doesn't bear some responsibility."

"He asked the church to relieve him of his duties and find him another position. They said no. All his training is in theology and he's not qualified to do anything else. He's been looking for teaching positions, but with the war, no one is hiring, and he won't marry me until he can support me. He thought I would be safer in England with you until he found something."

You'd also be safer if he hadn't knocked you up. "Does he know?"

She shakes her head. "He's only been able to get me one very short note because they're punishing him for breaking his vows, but he's still looking for a way out."

Edouard and Marie were careless only in the same ways Henri and I have been—but this changes everything. Now there will be two babies to care for in the British countryside, where food will be scarce, and doctors even more so. Perhaps some of the bitterness is more selfish: I want nothing more than to have

Henri's child one day, something that will never happen, while everyone around me seems to get pregnant unintentionally.

I force myself to take one calming breath and then another, because Marie is not at her most rational and there's no place for my unhappiness in this conversation. What now? It's possible that this is the prophecy unfolding—that Marie is the hidden child and will now produce the circle of light. But even if she isn't, Edouard deserves to know about his child.

"You need to let Edouard know before we leave," I sigh. "Maybe he refuses to let a woman support him, but when he realizes it means his child will be raised fatherless, he might relent a little."

"I don't know how to find him," she whispers. "I suppose I could ask Monsignor DuPree in Paris, but I'm worried I'll get Edouard in trouble."

I couldn't care less if Edouard gets in trouble, I want to snap. *Edouard deserves to get into trouble*. But it's not a response Marie will listen to. "Then lie," I tell her. "Tell him Edouard is your cousin and you fled from Germany hoping to find him in Saint Antoine."

"You want me to lie to Monsignor DuPree?" she gasps, wide-eyed.

"Oh, so lying to a priest is a greater sin than sleeping with one?" I snap. "I love you like a sister, Marie, and I'll support whatever decision you make, but this isn't the time to be quibbling over minor ethical dilemmas."

She stares at her hands for a long time, saying nothing. And then she rises with tears in her eyes. She kisses Cece on the forehead, and then me, in turn. "I'm sorry," she says, heading for the stairs.

32

SARAH

It seemed odd, Marie's tearful apology.

But it all made sense when I found the letter she'd left the next morning. She wasn't apologizing. She was saying goodbye.

Dearest Amelie,

I hope you will find it in your heart to forgive me. I would not be doing this, but you and Cece no longer need me, and my place is here, or wherever Edouard is. I know he will find a way to be with me and take care of his child no matter what the circumstances, and even if it means I'm stuck in France during the war—even if it means I don't survive the war— that's preferable to an entire life without him. I'll write you in England once I'm settled.

All my love,

Marie

I stare at her neatly formed words for several long minutes, jolted from them only when I hear the sound of my joyful daughter babbling in her crib. The house already feels quieter without Marie, and the truth is I'm terrified to be doing this alone, even though it's me, not Marie, who cares for Cece, and there's little to be done on the farm in the week before we leave the country. Instead of three adults with one baby, it will be just me and Cecelia. Now that the troops have been mobilized, I won't be the only person fleeing the country, which means the ship may be crowded and porters may be scarce. I don't want to undertake it alone.

Mostly I'm frightened for Marie. In a few weeks, bombing will begin and there will be a mass exodus from Paris. People will wind up abandoning their cars and their belongings, sleeping by the side of the road and dying there too, from hunger and thirst and German attacks. Marie will either be a part of that, or worse —she'll be a Jew trapped within the Occupied Zone when the war begins, unable to get away.

As far as I can tell, she left everything behind—all the cash we took from the accounts, everything of value. She's floated by her entire life with someone there to catch her when she fell. Her mother and Henri and, during captivity, me. I doubt it even occurred to her how badly things might go.

She isn't a child, but in some ways she's as ill-prepared as one. How am I going to leave without knowing she's okay?

THREE DAYS PASS WITHOUT WORD. I call the monsignor's office and they refuse to tell me Edouard's whereabouts, which means they probably refused to tell her too. So why isn't she home?

The next morning, I meet Jeannette at the train station in Saint Antoine to take Lucien and Charlotte. The station is far more chaotic than normal. "What's going on?" I ask when I find her, as people push past us, carting trunks and hatboxes.

"Everyone is fleeing Paris for the countryside," she whispers over the children's heads. "They think the Germans will punish us for assisting Norway. But where's Marie? She didn't come to help you get the children home?"

I hesitate. It's still possible Marie will return with her tail between her legs, either unable to find Edouard or having discovered he wasn't as honorable as we thought. She won't want the whole town knowing she's pregnant with the priest's child. But Jeannette is a friend, and not a parishioner. It might seem slightly less risqué to her than it would to others.

"Marie has left," I admit with a sigh. "She's in love with Father Edouard and has gone to Paris to find him. She says she's not coming on the trip."

Jeannette's mouth forms a small, shocked circle. "Does he reciprocate her feelings?"

Does he? I'd have sworn to it, once upon a time. But now he's slept with her and left, and perhaps his excuses make sense, or perhaps they are merely excuses. Though I don't have much experience with men, Marie has far less, and her love for Edouard is so unshakeable I don't think she'd be capable of doubting him regardless of the situation. I shake my head. "I don't know. But there's nothing to be done," I tell her. "The monsignor won't give me any information, and she's an adult. I can't force her to come with us."

"I'll go to the monsignor's office myself once I've seen my grandmother," Jeannette offers. "Have no fear, my friend. Unlike you and Marie, I'm not scared of priests. Nor am I attracted to them."

I sigh. "I'm no longer finding Edouard so handsome myself."

She pulls Lucien and Charlotte close, pressing her lips to their foreheads in turn. "Behave for Amelie, my angels, and I will be back to put you to bed." Lucien's eyes tear up and he clings to her leg, refusing to let her go. It makes me wonder how I will ever be able to leave Cecelia the next time I return to modern days, when she's older and aware of what is happening.

I drop to the ground. "She'll be back tonight," I say, pulling him against me. "Shall we make a pie to celebrate her return?"

He's too young yet to understand the concept of pie, or to be bought off by it, but when he sees how excited Charlotte is, he dries his eyes.

I walk home, pushing Cece in her pram while Lucien and Charlotte hold hands beside me. The walk is peaceful, but once Lucien is at home, I realize just how much my life will change once Cece is his age. He's a human missile, endangering himself constantly, and I soon give up on the idea of pie and devote myself mostly to keeping Charlotte entertained and Lucien alive.

Late in the afternoon, I begin to anticipate Jeannette's return and collect their things, but dusk comes and goes with no sign of her. I serve the children a cold dinner of tinned ham and milk and bread, the best I can do given the situation.

Soon, it's Cece's bedtime, but I can't allow Lucien to run wild while I put her to bed, so all three children are awake—and cranky—as the hours pass.

By nine PM, the last train from Paris has arrived and moved on, and there is still no sign of Jeannette. That's when the small, niggling fear in my chest that began this afternoon and seemed paranoid at the time begins to bloom and grow.

Jeannette is a good mother, a *careful* mother. She wouldn't have failed to return, and she wouldn't have failed to call...but she did.

We have forty-eight hours until we must leave for Calais. I sit in silence, watching Lucien pull books from the bookcase, finally allowing myself to ask the question I've been avoiding all night. *What happens if she's not back in time?*

~

THE NEXT MORNING, Charlotte is waiting by the door for her mother, and Lucien climbs into my lap. "Maman home soon?" he asks. His hopeful little face makes my heart twist in my chest.

"I'm not sure," I tell him. "Sometimes the trains are slow."

I long for Henri, or even Marie. I don't want to be the only adult in this house, the only person to make the decisions I must. If we don't leave for Calais tomorrow, we will miss our boat, and once the war begins in earnest in a few weeks, we may not get another chance to go. But who can I possibly leave Charlotte and Lucien with? Jeannette had no other friends in town, and right now, thanks to the war, anti-Jewish sentiment is running high. I doubt anyone would even be willing to take them in. Finding her mother in Paris and delivering the children there is really the only reasonable option, though I shudder at the idea of the children in Paris a few weeks from now.

I find Jeannette's address book in one of the boxes she brought over. Her mother is listed simply as *Maman*, no last name, no address. I dial the phone number listed there. It rings and rings but no one picks up—I can only assume because she's at the hospital with Jeannette's dying grandmother. And I can't exactly call the hospitals in Paris asking for *Maman*, a woman whose first and last names I don't know.

As night falls, I finally admit the truth to myself. Jeannette is gone, and all my careful plans will need to be abandoned. Until something changes, I remain one hour from the enemy, with three children considered Jewish under German law.

33

HENRI

On the morning of May 20th, I'm the only man smiling as I line up for morning rations. It's the day Sarah, Marie and Cecelia are due in the Cotswolds, after several weeks in Cambridge with friends of mine. And though we've not received any mail here yet, when Sarah arrives at the house we've let, my hope is that she'll find a stack of letters waiting from me. I've written each day since I left.

"What's with the smile?" asks my commanding officer. "You're aware we're at war, Durand?"

It would be hard to miss. The sound of artillery fire is ever present, and growing louder by the minute. The Germans will take Norway any day now. "My fiancée arrives safely at the house we let in England today," I tell him. "I'm just relieved."

"Well, soon you'll be able to wave to her from the other shore."

I glance at him. "What shore?"

"Haven't you heard? Germans have our boys trapped on the Normandy coast. We're sailing out tomorrow to reinforce them."

I think of Sarah's warning. I feel a prickle of unease at the base of my spine. "Where in Normandy?"

He shrugs. "Place called Dunkirk," he replies. "We leave at first light."

Dunkirk. The one place she begged me not to go.

IT TAKES a little over a week for us to reach the channel. The trip is relatively peaceful, and I spend it picturing my girls. I imagine Cece taking her first steps in the long grass, Sarah hovering, waiting for her to fall. I see them unaffected by rationing, though it's unlikely, and not too worried about me, though I suppose that's unlikely too. I picture coming home to them most of all. How long will it be? Will Cece be walking then? Will she remember me? *It doesn't matter*, I remind myself, *as long as they're safe.*

When we reach the channel, I stand portside, looking north. With a looking glass, I might see England's shores. My family is so close I can almost feel them, and it's harder than being far away.

Within an hour of entering the channel, we begin to hear the sounds of war, sharp after a week away from it. Soon, there are German bombers swooping low in the distance, and plumes of smoke over the water, indicating that they've hit their target.

I think of everyone trapped below decks on that boat in the distance, underwater and panicking, no exit in sight. Soon, their target will be us. *Please God*, I beg, *let me return to my family.*

The men crowd the top deck as the sound of bombing grows louder, and the rowboats are lowered, though we are far from shore and the water is rough. For some reason, I think of the story my mother told us as children, about a rickety old boat that survived an impossible storm. Of all the fantastic parts of that story—and there were many—the boat was always the bit I found most implausible.

Over the loudspeaker, we are told to man the boats. There

aren't enough for all of us, however, which means the men push forward toward the ladder in a desperate mob, throwing elbows.

Only four boats are filled when a bomber swings low. I hear its whine long before it reaches us and I can see the future unfold as surely as Sarah once did. I watch as the bomber's hatch opens and two missiles are dropped in quick succession. *Everyone* watches—horrified, spellbound, praying for some act of God to save us. The water will be ice cold, and we are too far from shore to swim.

Sarah warned us about the war. She warned me how Germany would break into France, and she was right. She warned me about Dunkirk, and she was right once more. She seemed convinced I would die. I pray that just this once, she was wrong.

I dive off the boat because there's no other option. I do it praying I'll survive. Praying Sarah will forgive me if I don't.

34

SARAH

I t's August, a rare moment of quiet in this house. Cecelia has cried all day, victim of one of those mysterious crying jags parents always blame on teething until the real culprit presents itself. Lucien and Charlotte helped me pick fruit all morning and are now drawing at the kitchen table, a level of contentment that won't last long. They are sweet children—but they are still children, constantly in motion.

I peek out the window. This is how I spend my days now: looking after children, watching the road. And waiting. Waiting for the Germans to arrive and discover Lucien and Charlotte hidden here, waiting for them to take the last of our meager resources or ask for Cece's papers. And the thing I most dread, because it's the one I can't defend myself against—waiting for a courier to tell me Henri is dead.

There's been no word, though I wrote to tell him we weren't able to leave. I try to reassure myself that he hasn't received my letters and is healthy and whole, still writing to us in England. But as the days drag on it's harder to believe it.

They'd have told me if he was dead, wouldn't they? I ask myself this question ten times a day. *Yes*, I always reply. *And at least he wasn't at Dunkirk.*

The tragedy at Dunkirk was in all the papers. The French and British forces were pushed to the shore and forced to evacuate while German bombers circled, taking out one ship after another. I'd read about it in my own time, of course, but it's different now that I can picture the men. Luc Barbier and his friend Marc were there, and no one has heard from them. They were just boys. Too young to die. They'd barely even lived yet.

I watch the road all day long, in a constant state of readiness, but my mind often drifts the way it does right now, and I picture Henri coming home. In the distance, I'll see a tall man with dark hair. It could be almost anyone, but something inside me will say *it's him*. I can feel it, the way my breath will still, the way I'll try so hard not to let myself hope while my heart beats harder and faster. I picture him cutting through the field and then that flash of his smile, the one he saves only for me.

I picture it so hard that for a moment it seems possible I can *will* him here. But the road remains empty, and my stomach drops, back to that pit of dread and fear that almost seems permanent at this point.

How could it all have gone so wrong?

I think back to April, when Jeannette left. Lucien and Charlotte didn't have passports, so I couldn't have gotten them to England, but we could at least have headed south to the free zone before the bombing started, back before there were zones at all, back before travel papers were required—travel papers denied to Jews. Except I was so certain that if I called Jeannette's mother enough times, someone would pick up. I even considered going back a few months to get the address from Jeannette, so I could leave the children there. And then, one day, I found the address on a letter tucked in a book, and discovered the entire block was now rubble. Which meant that, had I time traveled to get the address, the children would be dead. Because of me.

If the Germans come for them in Saint Antoine, that will be because of me too.

What I might do, and what I might do wrong. The topic consumes me. I could go back to the days when Jeannette first disappeared, and tell my previous self to take the children to the free zone—but now fear holds me in place. Anything could go awry on the way and I wouldn't be able to fix it, not if it meant leaving three young children out in the open, without supervision. We are alive now, and I'm terrified I might change that, the way I nearly did once already. I could travel back to the day before Marie ran off and explain to her why she shouldn't leave— tell her I need her to take Cecelia to England so at least one of the children is safe—but if I do, I may be stripping her of a life with Edouard. And who knows what might go wrong instead?

The questions make my gift feel more like a curse, and I'm angry about all of it. We shouldn't be trapped. Lucien and Charlotte, children who've just lost their mother, shouldn't have to live like fugitives. Charlotte shouldn't have to stare out the window each day, hoping her mother might come back. I shouldn't need to sleep with an ear open each night—waiting for the Germans or the constant threat of intruders, those who escaped Paris on foot and come through the farm now stealing chickens and fruit.

I shouldn't have to fight off this black-heartedness all over again. I don't want to let the ugly piece of me back into the light, and I worry with every day that passes I'll eventually have no choice.

EARLY IN SEPTEMBER, Charlotte stops staring out the window. For days she is quiet, her small face unreadable. I try to draw her out, bribe her with bits of rationed chocolate or a game, but nothing quite works. Then one afternoon, while Cecelia is pulling herself up on the bench, and Lucien marches around the room chanting some nonsense rhyme he's made up, Charlotte climbs into my lap and presses her head to my chest. "Are you going to be my mother now?" she asks.

I hesitate. In a way it feels like a bigger promise than I should make—if a relative appears I might be forced to give the children up, and I don't want her to count on me if she can't. But what does she need most? Does she need some tenuous promise of care until a better option arrives, or does she need to believe there is someone in the world who will always love her? Agreeing means far more than she could ever realize: it's an unholy alliance with that dark piece of me. The one that will kill what stands in my way, including anyone who tries to take her from me, even if their right to her is greater than my own.

"Would you like me to be?" I ask. Charlotte will be eleven when the war ends, and Lucien will be seven. He won't even remember another mother but me. I picture some hapless, well-intentioned relative finding us and trying to take them from me and taste metal in my mouth, blood pumping heavy and fast in my veins, surging with that desperate need to destroy.

She nods, and I squeeze my eyes shut.

"Then yes," I say, pulling her close. It feels like the right decision, and the worst choice I've ever made, all at the same time.

A WEEK later the Germans come. There isn't enough time to hide Charlotte and Lucien in the barn, and Lucien is still too young to stay quiet when asked. As the Germans are pulling up in front of the house, I rush the two of them to my room and lower them out the window closest to the woods.

"Run to the end of the vineyard and wait for me," I tell them. "Hold hands, and don't make a sound."

I climb back in and head toward the door, placing the gun under a dish towel on the table. That dark piece of me doesn't want to hide the gun at all. It wants to hurt them for doing this to us, for scaring me, for forcing me to tell a two-year-old and a five-year-old to run for their lives.

I open the door and find two soldiers there, boys themselves. They both look embarrassed.

"Good day, madame," one of them says politely. "I apologize, but I've been sent to retrieve your cow and your chickens."

I swallow hard. I'm not a citizen, and no one knows Lucien and Charlotte are here, which means Cece is the only person in this house who receives a ration card, and it's a half-ration at that. Without the cow and chickens, we will lose our eggs and milk and cheese. The vines and trees will soon be bare, so we'll be left to subsist on tinned food and nothing more.

I could kill them both in a heartbeat and be done with it, I think. Except they are barely children themselves, doing a job they don't want to do. And killing them will only bring questions that will cause more trouble.

"I need eggs and milk for my daughter," I reply. I want to wince at the sound of begging in my voice.

He frowns. "I'm sorry, madame." He flushes and looks at the soldier beside him. "Perhaps you might be allowed to keep one of the chickens?"

He's asking the other soldier more than he's asking me, and taking a risk. His compatriot's eyes widen and then he gives a small, terse nod.

I watch as they load the chickens into a cage, leaving me one, and then drive away at a snail's pace, the cow tied behind them.

Once they're out of sight I place Cece in her crib and run as hard as I can to Lucien and Charlotte. I fall to the ground when I find them, pulling them against me tighter than I should.

I can't lose them. I can't lose Cece. The thought terrifies me.

And the terror makes me angrier than I've ever been. Angrier than is probably safe.

35

SARAH

November.

Not even officially winter, and already it's unbearably cold. Our heated floors and fireplace offer me little comfort. I can only think of Henri. Where does he sleep now? Was he taken prisoner? Is he floating at the bottom of the sea?

At night, after the children are asleep, I weep for him, asking one question again and again: *Why can't they just tell me what happened?*

Our lives have tightened and narrowed until it feels like there's almost nothing left. Because I anticipated that Jeannette wouldn't plan sufficiently, I'd already stocked the cellar with nonperishables last spring, and we live off of that and almost nothing else. I rarely get into town to buy anything more since it means leaving Charlotte and Lucien here alone, and when I do go, I only see resentment—*Why should a homewrecking American be getting rations?* they wonder.

It's not that all, or even most, of the townspeople are bad, but it only takes one of them to feel their own lot might be improved by lessening ours. And that one will give our names to the authorities, if they haven't already. It's inevitable. The revolver now sits on a high shelf near the table, waiting for the moment it will all come to a head. The girl I once was believes murder is wrong. But I still plan to kill anyone who enters our home and beg her forgiveness later.

I set dinner on the table, and Charlotte's small face falls when she sees another bit of tinned ham with powdered milk. I don't blame her—I understand how lucky we are to have it, but I'm sick of it too.

She picks at her food and then helps me clear the table. "What will it be like when we get to England?" she asks.

I smile at her. It's one of our favorite topics these days. "We will live in the country, like this," I tell her. "You will go to school, and while you're there, I'll take Lucien and Cecelia to the market and we'll buy lots of food and when you come home each day, I'll have a big supper waiting."

"Will there be pie?" she asks.

"More pie and cake than you could ever want to eat. With fresh cream."

"But no tinned ham," she says firmly, wiping her hands against each other in a perfect imitation of me.

I tuck in my smile. "If anyone suggests we eat tinned ham, I'll kill them myself with my bare hands."

She laughs. "What about powdered—"

There's a sound outside. Boots on the front step.

And the door is still unlocked.

The plate in Charlotte's hand falls to the ground and shatters. I stand frozen before I remember my plan and spring into action, darting across the kitchen for the revolver.

Kill whoever is at the door, the first part of the plan. It doesn't feel real now, even as I repeat the words.

The door opens. I point the gun just past it, ready to fire. "Halt!" I yell.

In spite of my fear, the desire to punish our intruder throbs in my veins. If he sets one more foot inside this house, I will put a bullet in his head, and some part of me will enjoy it.

"As you wish, little thief," comes a low voice in reply.

My hands shake. It's too much. It's too good to possibly be real. I'm scared to believe it.

"Henri?" I breathe.

He steps into the light. Thinner, and tired, but him. As beautiful as ever. "Is there another man who calls you little thief?" he asks, with a smile I've missed more than I even knew. "I thought in that one way, I might have been original."

I set the gun on the counter behind me and run to him from the kitchen, throwing myself into his arms, weeping like a child. He seems impossibly tall now, perhaps because he's so thin, but he's still my Henri. His clothes are in tatters and stiff with dirt, but beneath it is the same skin, the same smell, the same broad hands against my back, holding me as if I'm all that's keeping him from falling overboard into a stormy sea.

"Don't leave us again," I whisper.

"My poor little thief," he says. "Has it been awful here?"

"It's been awful wondering if you were alive or dead for the better part of six months," I reply.

"I'm home now, though I wish to God I hadn't found you here," he says. "When Marc told me you'd stayed behind I—"

Cece begins to cry too, unsettled by all the excitement, or perhaps just feeling left out. I release her father and his face lights up at the sight of her before he takes in our other guests and turns to me with a raised brow.

"Our family grew while you were gone," I tell him quietly.

He blinks once, putting it all together, and then smiles, twining his fingers through mine. "I always wanted three children," he says.

I lead him to the table and he sits with Cece in his lap, chatting with Lucien and Charlotte, while I get him a plate.

He glances up at me as I place the food in front of him. "It's late. I'm surprised Marie isn't home."

My teeth sink into my lip. Marie's been gone so long I'd almost forgotten he would expect her to be here. There's a lot he doesn't know, and he will definitely not be pleased. "She's...gone. She went to Paris right after you left. I—"

"She *left*?" he repeats incredulously. "She left you here in this situation *alone*?"

I shoot a quick glance at the children. "The situation here didn't change until she was gone, and it's...complicated."

He looks sick. "But she's alright?" he asks. "She survived the bombings?"

I bite my lip. "I assume so. I think we might have heard from Edouard if she didn't."

He raises a brow. "Edouard?" he asks. "Why would we hear from *Edouard*?"

"You're going to be an uncle," I tell him, and his jaw falls open as he puts it together. I can see his thoughts even before he voices them: in his mind, his sister is painfully sheltered and innocent, still fragile from the ordeal in 1918. If she's pregnant, it's because she was forced, or manipulated. "I know you want to blame Edouard, but Marie played a heavy role. She admitted it herself. And the fact that she never came back means they're probably married by now," I reply.

His nostrils flare. "If he hasn't married her, I'll—"

My hand folds over his. "I know. But right now, you need to focus. The child she carries might be...what everyone has waited for. You're home and safe, and hopefully she is too. Under the circumstances, it's more than we could hope for."

We both take a quick glance at the children: Cecelia, who could easily have been swept away by Yvette, and Lucien and Charlotte, who'd lost both their parents before the war had even begun in earnest. "You're right," he says softly. "There were many times when I thought I'd never have a moment like this again. Thank God I was wrong."

He digs into his food, eating like a starving man, which is likely not far from the truth. He tells us he dove from his ship just before it was sunk, swam in icy water for hours before he was rescued by three British soldiers, and then was taken captive. He managed to escape in late September, and has been traveling by night ever since.

"How did you eat?" I ask, grinding my teeth not to cry. Now that he's here, and safe, I'm finally able to picture how awful it must have been.

His eyes—the softest green—meet mine. "I managed, little thief. But I'm so glad to be home."

~

I DRAW him a bath and then take the children upstairs to bed. When I return he's still in the tub. "You have no idea what a luxury clean water is," he says with a laugh, "and *warm* water, no less."

My eyes fill at the sight of him there and I go to the tub's edge. "I'm shocked the water's so clean."

"I've had to empty and refill the tub twice," he admits, and then his crooked grin fades. "What happened to Jeannette? If you stayed back because of the children, she must have died before the bombings even began."

I sigh. "I'm not sure we'll ever know. She went to Paris two days before we were due to leave. There was a stampede at the train station and many people died, but I have no idea. And by the time I knew where her mother lived, the whole block had been destroyed. But someone could come for them after the war. There might be aunts and uncles," I tell him, before taking a deep breath. "I won't give them back if that happens."

His tongue darts to his lip, considering what I'm saying. "Legally, I'm not sure you'll have a choice."

"I don't care what the law says. Anyone who would take children from the family that's raised them for more than half their lives doesn't deserve them."

He presses a kiss to my forehead. "You're my wife in spirit, if not in name, and I trust your decisions," he says.

My eyes sting. I'm not sure I deserve his faith. In fact, I know I don't. But I feel so unspeakably lucky to have it. I kiss him, unable to say all the things I'd like to say. "Give me the pitcher and I'll wash your hair," I tell him.

He hands it to me, and I fill it with clean water, trying not to look at his naked lower half. He's exhausted and half-starved from his journey, so certain things may need to wait.

I tip the pitcher over his head and fill it again, before lathering the soap in my hands. He groans as my fingers press to his scalp.

I still. "Am I hurting you?"

"Just the opposite," he says. His hands rise to clasp my face and pull my mouth to his. He holds me there, exploring me with his lips and his tongue, dragging his teeth over my lower lip on his way to my neck. "Christ, I've missed you. Night and day, for months, I've missed you. And now you're here and it seems almost too perfect to be real."

"Henri," I gasp, as his lips pull at the skin of my neck, "I have to rinse your hair."

He slides under the water and then emerges, climbing to his feet and towering above me—leaner than before, bruised and glorious. I want to eat him whole.

It must show in my face.

He grins at me. "I can work with this position, but I sort of pictured us starting off in bed."

~

I WAKE NESTLED AGAINST HIM. He is too warm and too perfect to be a dream, yet it still doesn't feel quite real. Will there ever come a time when I don't wake grateful to find him here? It's hard to imagine.

Lucien rises and comes into the room before our clothes are on. "This will be an adjustment," says Henri with a raise of his brow, holding the blanket to cover himself as he searches for clean clothes.

By the time I've dressed, Henri has a fire roaring on the hearth, and sits at the table with Lucien in his lap while Cecelia is being helped down the stairs by her adoring big sister.

"We don't have coffee anymore," I tell him. "Or sugar, I'm afraid."

He smiles at me. "I have my family," he replies. "That's all I need."

I feed him eggs and bread and the last of the canned ham and watch him eat with the same sort of delight I once felt when Cecelia was finally taking a full bottle. When he's done, he plays with the children: chasing Lucien around the room on all fours, growling, swinging Cece up in the air and catching her in his arms, and teaching Charlotte to play *jeu de barbichette*, a horrible game that involves reciting a rhyme—and hitting the first person to laugh.

I frown. "What kind of game encourages children to hit each other?"

"French games," he replies with a grin, "and this one was always my favorite."

"And what happens when she plays that at school and gets expelled for slapping someone?"

He laughs. "Are all people in your time so soft?"

"Yes," I tell him, but it feels like a lie as soon as I say it, and my smile falters. People in my time are soft, but I no longer am, not the way he thinks.

"You're happy again," says Charlotte when I put her to bed that night.

I smile. "Wasn't I always happy?"

She shakes her head. "No," she says. "You were waiting to be happy."

A chill runs up my spine. She's right. I had moments of happiness here with them, but they were brief. I was waiting for Henri to come home until I took a full breath, and once we're settled in England and he leaves to fight, I'll wait once more. If he dies, I'll wait forever because there'll be no other option.

"I don't want you to fight," I whisper to him much later, as we both lie awake in the dark, unwilling to be separated by sleep. "Once we are settled in England, I want you to stay with us."

He rolls to face me. "I can't hide like a coward and let others fight for my country. But I'd never have gone if I'd known you would remain here, so defenseless."

I laugh unhappily. "Defenseless? You know what I can do. There isn't a woman in France better defended than me."

"Except you're no longer interested in defending yourself," he replies. "You're defending them, and in that you are as vulnerable as the rest of us."

I want to argue but a part of me can't deny what he's saying. "There's not much to be done for it now," I tell him. "We're here and we'll have to deal with it as it comes."

"Yes, but you can be prepared if nothing else," he argues. "You need to know how to defend yourself. And how to kill."

I freeze. Henri can't conceive of the version of me who stabbed her own aunt in the chest or allowed people to burn alive, who wanted Yvette to die and even considered killing Dr. Nadeau when I discovered he'd lied to us about the penicillin, and I hope he never does. That part of me was successfully locked down when Cece was born, and I'm not letting her back into the light.

"I don't want to learn how to kill," I reply.

"And I don't *want* to have to teach you how, but now it's necessary," he says. "We'll start small. I'll go hunting and you can come with me."

My heart pounds in my chest. How would he look at me if he knew? Would he forgive me? He might. He'd excuse it as self-defense. But what if he really understood where it came from? My grandfather and aunt are the reason his mother is dead. They're people who wanted to hurt others, who enjoyed it. And there is a part of me, a part I sometimes feel pulsing just under my skin, that wants that too.

"No," I reply. "I can't leave the children to go, and I'm not interested anyway. That's just not who I want to be."

"You realize I've killed men, yes?" he asks softly. "Do you judge me for it?"

"Of course not. You were at war."

His hand glides through my hair. "And, if someone comes here to take the children, will you not be at war too? You had a gun in your hands the night I came home."

I squeeze my eyes tight. If the children were hurt or threatened, there would be no end to my rage, to my need for revenge. But until that time, I want to remain who I am: a person who went to a dark place and came back from it. A person capable of evil but refusing to give in. "That's different," I whisper.

"Only because it's hypothetical," he replies. "Once it happens it won't be different at all."

I stretch alongside him, allowing my hand to splay across the flat plane of his stomach. "Is this really what you want to discuss with me right now?" I ask, as my hand begins to slide lower.

"Yes," he says with a groan, "but I suppose it can wait."

36

SARAH

Our lives don't change dramatically with Henri home. He will be arrested if the Germans know he's here, so he and Lucien and Charlotte still can't be seen and we still need to listen, always, for the sound of approaching cars. But he fills us, as if our family was a slightly deflated balloon and he's a huge burst of air. He sets traps in the woods to augment our paltry staples, and because he's here, I can finally go into town, using our pathetic ration cards and a little bit of our money to buy food on the black market. His presence also means the world to the children, Lucien in particular, who never even met his father. For the first time in his life there's someone around to wrestle on the floor and carry him on his shoulders.

I love having him home, and I love that, with him back, I'm no longer in this alone. Regardless of what skills I've acquired over the past year, I'm still only twenty-three. I need opinions other my own, and there's no one alive whose opinions I trust more than Henri's.

We go over the situation at night, once the children are in bed, and agree that we need to get out of the country. The "free zone" is hardly that—there are Germans in every town, and Jews are losing their jobs and their businesses everywhere. As no ships can sail out of Calais now, we will either need to get on a ship from Marseilles—more difficult, as the Germans are unlikely to let Henri board—or we can go through Spain to Lisbon and leave from there. But in order for that to happen, we need travel papers, ones that claim no one in the house is Jewish.

"I'll ask around," he says. "My Paris contacts will probably have gone underground. But there's always Monsieur Roche in town."

My teeth sink into my lip. I've only met Roche a few times, but he's never struck me as either helpful or trustworthy. "Are you sure it's safe to let him know Charlotte and Lucien are here? Is it safe to let him know *you're* here?"

"For enough money, Roche will keep anything quiet," he replies. It's a struggle to accept that answer. Not when the children's lives—and his—are at stake.

"People can be so much worse than you think," I tell him, looking at my hands. Iris wasn't merely the sister my mom disliked. She was evil, almost inhuman. My mother was a liar. Mathilde and the guards all looked perfectly normal but were willing to kill innocent women and newborns for a paycheck. And he has no idea how bad I am either. "You can't trust anyone."

He comes to where I stand. "Of course you can," he says. "I trust you."

I'm not sure you should. I keep the thought to myself as I rest my head on his chest, but something in the way he stiffens makes me feel like I said it aloud.

AT THE END of our first contented week together, I sit in the chair near the fire to give Cece her evening bottle, and Henri sits on the couch across from me, with Charlotte beside him and Lucien in his lap, telling them a bedtime story. His stories are normally about three children named Charlotte, Lucien and Cece, who go on amazing voyages and wind up living somewhere made of candy.

Tonight's story, however, is different. He tells them about a distant island, lost in the middle of a stormy sea, with waves so huge that no ship's captain dared approach for fear his boat would be dashed upon the high cliffs. "But one day a boat did arrive," he tells them. "It was a rickety boat, and no one understood how it had survived the water, much less the waves, but it had. Aboard the boat were four girls. They were dressed strangely and claimed to remember nothing of the journey or their life before it, aside from their names."

"What were their names?" Charlotte asks excitedly.

He grins. "No Charlottes in this bunch, I'm afraid," he tells her. "Their names were Lea, Scylla, Aisling and Adelaide."

My head jerks up. *Adelaide*. The woman Katrin told me we were descended from. *The start of the first families—four families, four gifts*. Could it be the same story? It must.

"The four girls," he continues, unaware of my surprise, "were taken in by families in the village. Eventually, each fell in love, and married. But no children came, and one by one they each went to the priest seeking answers, and he told them no children would come until they left the island, because they'd each been given a gift, one that was meant to be shared."

Charlotte's small face falls. "But were they able to come back?"

"That's what the girls asked too, because they were sad about leaving. And the priest told them, 'You will all return home when the circle is complete.'"

"So, did they?" asks Charlotte. "Did the girls ever come back?"

"Pieces of them exist all around you," Henri replies, "waiting to be called home. I feel certain they'll get back eventually."

"But where did they come *from*?" she persists. "They had to have parents."

"No one really knows," Henri says. "No one knows how that boat could have survived the storm, either. Perhaps it was magic."

"I don't believe in magic," she replies. "If magic was real, someone would stop the bad things from happening."

"Personally," he tells her, "I believe that when the circle is complete, there will be enough magic in the world to do just that. Maybe that's the reason it exists at all."

Charlotte continues to ask questions and then complains bitterly at how unfair the priest was as we take the children upstairs. I lay Cece, now heavily asleep, in her crib and then, after pressing a kiss to Charlotte and Lucien's foreheads, follow Henri to our room.

"Is that where the first four families came from?" I ask. "The woman who escaped with Marie—Katrin—she told me she was a daughter of Adelaide."

And that I was too. I wish I could tell him.

He shrugs, unbuttoning his shirt. "It's the story our mother always told us, growing up. And maybe it's a fabrication, but most origin stories seem to contain an element of the truth. I hope so, anyway."

I do too, except if it's right, I'm not sure how the pieces will ever come together. Luna Reilly, who was brave when I was not, may have been the last of her line. And since I can't have children, Adelaide's line may end with me. I perch on the end of the bed, feeling as if there is something important in what he said, something I'm missing. "What did you mean when you told Charlotte the girls could go home when the circle is complete?"

The shirt comes off and the undershirt follows. For the first time in the years I've known him, even the sight of his perfect, bare chest isn't enough to distract me. "There are time travelers who believe that being a part of the prophecy confers some kind of immortality," he says. "That they will all go to the island in the end."

"I wonder if that's what Coron was after," I say. "I thought maybe he wanted to produce an army of time travelers, but maybe he just wanted to assure his place in their afterlife."

Henri's mouth tips into a sad smile. "If that's true, then many people died over a fairy tale."

"So you don't think it's possible?"

He crosses the room and pulls me to stand. "I don't need to believe in any kind of afterlife. I'm happy with what I have right here and now."

His hand weaves through my hair, pulling me forward so that his mouth can press to the top of my head. I'm happy with what we have right here and now too. But that doesn't stop me from wishing I could keep it forever.

December comes. Henri speaks to the few people he trusts in town about getting travel papers, but comes up empty-handed, which leaves us stuck with only one option: Monsieur Roche. Henri heads to the woods to meet him one afternoon. The danger for him is much greater than it is for any of us—he's as likely to be shot as arrested if he's caught.

I wait for his return, feeling sick to my stomach, and rush toward him when he walks through the door, only to freeze at the sight of the bloody bag he holds. "Rabbits, for stew," he says, but his smile is strained.

"What happened? Is he going to get us papers?"

He closes his eyes. "It seems Roche has got himself into some trouble with the British. He doesn't want money in exchange anymore."

I stiffen. I don't trust Roche. "Then what does he want?"

"He doesn't have all the details, but the Brits need some airmen escorted to the Pyrenees."

My anger bubbles. I close my eyes, trying to rein it in. "Why can't Roche take them himself if he's created this problem?"

"Because it's dangerous," Henri says with a sigh, "and he's banking on the fact that someone will be desperate enough to do it for him."

"Which you're not," I reply.

He rubs a hand over his eyes. "I know, little thief," he replies. "I'll look for another way. But we can't hide in the open forever. It may be our only option."

"If that happens, then I'll take them. I can do things you can't. I can escape."

Henri shakes his head. "Absolutely not," he says. He gives me a small smile. "You weren't even willing to hunt rabbits. Larger prey might prove quite a struggle for you. We'll find another way."

THE WEEK BEFORE CHRISTMAS, the children are all struck down with some mysterious ailment that involves a sore throat and fatigue. It may be strep throat, but it lingers and all three of them have flushed cheeks and glassy eyes that don't seem to improve. I call Dr. Nadeau, asking if I can bring Cecelia in.

"I cannot see you," he replies. "Don't call my home again."

Coward, I think, fury bleeding from my pores. He would let an infant he personally delivered die simply because she's a quarter Jewish. And yet I can't say a word to him about it because, like the rest of this town, he holds us in the palm of his hand. Eventually, he, or someone else, will suggest to the Germans that they look more closely at us than they have been.

"He refused?" asks Henri, his voice quiet but livid as he walks in behind me. I nod, so angry that I don't dare speak.

"When he stands before God," he hisses, "he will regret the decisions he made during this war."

Not soon enough, I think. It would be so easy to make Nadeau

pay for this now. And why shouldn't I? The man doesn't deserve
the comfortable life he has, and he'll clearly never be of use to *us*
again.

Henri is watching my face. "What are you not telling me?" he
asks.

"Nothing," I lie.

He grabs his coat. "You know what I miss?" he asks softly,
heading for the door. "The days when I was certain you were
telling me the truth."

What he said bothers me, and the tension between us that
lingers afterward, even more so. It's as if a part of him has closed
off to me. And yet, I suppose, he feels as if a part of me has closed
to him as well. It's there when we go to sleep at night, and the
next day, even though nothing seems to have changed.

It's just the stress, I tell myself. *It's just that the children are sick.*
But I'm not sure it's true, and when he leaves the next day to get a
Christmas tree, hoping to buoy everyone's spirits, my stomach
sinks as I watch him walk away. I don't want to lose him to the
war, but I don't want to lose him to *me* either, to this piece of me
I'd rather he not know.

When Cecelia and Lucien go down for a nap, I pull my coat
on and cross the yard to feed the single chicken now in the coop.
I've just reached for the feed when I hear the low purr of a
vehicle approaching and freeze, fear flooding my system.

Henri is gone. The gun is inside, on the high shelf. I could
time travel to warn us, but what if something goes wrong and by
the time I fix things, one of them is dead?

I take a single step out of the coop just as the jeep pulls up to
the front door. Three German soldiers, in crisp new uniforms,
medals gleaming. Their eyes lock on me, and I panic. I want to
race inside for the gun, but I would be leading them straight to
my family.

I need to get them out of here before Henri returns. Alerting
them to his presence is as good as signing his death warrant.

"Bonjour, mademoiselle," says the one who climbs from the back of the car. He's older than the others, clearly in charge. "You're alone here on this farm?"

"No, my daughter is inside sleeping," I tell them. "But she's quite ill."

"Perhaps a visit from the doctor is required," he says. I glance at him, wondering if he's toying with me, if he's already aware the doctor won't come. My anger begins to coalesce, sharpen.

Even if I were able to get the gun, I could only kill two before the third killed me. So, whatever I do, I can't let them into the house.

"Perhaps," I reply. "Is there something I can help you with?"

He looks at me as if it's an invitation, his eyes roaming from my mouth to my chest to my legs, capping it all off with a small smirk. I grow colder inside, watching it. He'll die first.

"We are surveying the properties here," he says. "How many rooms have you?"

"Three rooms," I reply crisply. "All taken, I'm afraid."

He laughs. "My math skills are failing me, madame. Explain to me how a child and a woman require three rooms?"

"My sister-in-law will return soon from Paris. The third room is hers."

He raises a brow and begins to approach. "In these difficult times, I'm sure two women and a child could share a room." He circles me. "Or my men would be happy to share with you if you'd rather." His baton lowers, slides just beneath the hem of my skirt. It reminds me of Gustave, and my hands begin to shake with fear and rage at once. That coldness inside me grows —the part that hates them for making me scared. I picture how they will die when this is over, the same way I used to picture the guards' deaths. It makes me feel powerful, except attacking them could bring more problems than it solves, and the driver is just a boy, unable to meet my eye. Nearly as much a victim here as me.

The commander's baton goes to my palm, pushing my right

hand in the air. "No ring, I see, but you claim to have a daughter. Are you married?"

The ring is still packed, waiting for the trip it appears we will never take. The soldiers behind him shift uncomfortably. Obviously, they've dealt with him before. They're well aware that no answer I can provide will satisfy him.

"Yes," I reply. "I lost the ring."

"Let's go inside and have a look around, madame," he says with a smirk. "Perhaps together we'll find it."

I brace myself, ready to spring for the door if necessary. "No."

"No?" he repeats. His hand flies out, striking the side of my head, and then he pushes me to the ground. "Do you really think you can just tell me *no*?"

He plants one boot on my chest and shouts something in German to the others that makes them both freeze in place. It's not until he withdraws his gun that the youngest comes forward, with absolute dread on his face, and drops to his knees between my legs, pushing my skirt around my waist. With eyes shut, he whispers something in German that sounds like an apology. He is a child following orders. His pants fall to my bare thighs, and then two things happen so close together it's hard for me to determine which is first: the blast of a gun, and the spray of something solid and damp across my face. The soldier's eyes go wide and he falls on me—his eyes now sightless—as the gun blasts again and again.

Suddenly, Henri is there, pulling the soldier off me, his eyes as wide and shocked as my own. The three Germans lie dead on the ground around me. "Are you alright?"

The rage is still so strong inside me I shake with it. I nod, wrapping my arms around myself.

His hands go to the top of his head and he tugs at his hair. He's furious, but not only with the soldiers. "You didn't even jump!" he explodes. "You told me you'd leave if something went wrong and you didn't move a muscle!"

I close my eyes and try to hold myself together. "I panicked," I reply, grinding my jaw. "And I couldn't just leave the children inside, undefended. I don't know what you want me to say."

"I want you to say that you won't panic next time!" he shouts. "That you'll use your head!"

My arms fold around me again, but when I feel the dampness of the blood on my sleeves I jerk them away. It's smeared now, all over my coat. There's a vicious piece of me that likes it. That likes that they're all dead, even the innocent one.

Henri goes to the German soldiers on the ground and lifts one up by his hair. The man's eyes are still open, his jacket so soaked with blood it appears to be black. He's the one who was polite, initially. Just following orders. I can't look at his face.

"Grab his knife," he says. "If you're going to survive this war, you've got to stop being so precious about death and the idea of harming anyone. He'd have raped you and killed all of us, given the chance, but you panicked and now you're standing there, unable even to look at his corpse."

I press my hands to my face. "You don't understand," I hiss. "Just leave this alone. I'll be fine when the time comes."

He drops the German and grabs the knife himself, pushing it into my hands. "The time just came and you failed!" he cries. "Stop making promises you won't keep. If you'll be *fine*, then prove it. Show me how you'll kill him the next time."

The adrenaline and rage inside me gather to a head, then explode. I grab the knife from him and slice the soldier's jugular vein. Blood pours from the wound and I feel absolutely nothing. I grip the knife harder and bury it in the soldier's back, hearing the slight hiss of air as his lung punctures. I pull it out and send it whistling ten feet away, where it buries into the base of the commander's neck.

Henri's jaw hangs open.

"What just happened?" he asks.

"I did what you wanted," I reply. My voice doesn't sound like my own. "Put them in the jeep. I'll be right back."

I go inside and get the keys to the truck. When I return, he's loaded all three bodies into the jeep and waits for me, still astonished, still wanting answers to questions I wish he wouldn't ask. *I'm made of the ugliest things, Henri. Please don't make me say it aloud.*

I push away my self-pity. I don't deserve his forgiveness and there's not time for it anyway. If this isn't executed perfectly, it will blow up in our faces, and it needs to be done before the children wake. I throw him the keys to the truck. "Follow me," I tell him, climbing into the jeep.

"What are you doing?" he demands. "If anyone sees you..."

"I can time travel away and the jeep will crash." I don't wait for him to continue questioning me but push down the clutch and take off, heading for an embankment about a mile down the road.

I'm terrified, my heart beating too fast, but that feeling is pushed down hard as the jeep picks up speed. Something cold and methodical comes over me—maybe it's the Coron blood. Maybe it's simply that a part of me thinks it might be easier to die right now than tell Henri the truth. Either way, it's a relief to feel something other than fear. I drive toward the sharp turn at the top of the hill and focus hard on the embankment. The car slows as my feet disappear but has enough momentum to continue without me. I fade entirely just as the jeep tips over the side of the hill and land, naked, twenty feet away.

Henri's brakes screech to a stop nearby. "Sarah!" he cries as the jeep rolls into the ravine and lands upside down at its base.

I ignore him, scrambling toward my clothes, which flew out of the jeep before it rolled over, thank God. I clutch them to my chest and reach into my coat pocket for the matches I placed there. The match is struck and thrown toward the brush near the jeep. There's a risk that it will die out before it reaches the gas tank, but I'm hoping to give myself some time to get away. I run hard up the hill, feeling the heat of the fire behind me. For a moment, I'm back in 1918, climbing a ladder in the pantry that may or may not lead to safety. Henri pulls me over the edge just as the jeep explodes, staring at me like I'm someone he doesn't know, a demon who's possessed the girl he thought he loved.

"What in God's name were you thinking?" he shouts. "If that jeep had caught fire a moment sooner you'd have been blown to bits!"

Now that it's over, my hands are shaking. I cut it close—ridiculously close. I lean over, certain I'm going to vomit but simply shake instead, cold sweat dripping from my forehead. "There will be an investigation into the deaths," I reply, forcing myself to pull it together. I grab the dress and tug it over my head. "If they found bullet holes, they'd be looking for culprits. Now they might believe it was just a dangerous turn taken too fast."

"I thought you were dead!" he shouts, grabbing my arm. "I watched the jeep go over the edge and I was certain—"

"Yell at me later," I say, jerking away from his grip. "The smoke will attract eyes. We've got to get out of here."

He follows me to the truck and drives home in silence, but once we arrive, he slams his hands against the steering wheel. "I want answers," he says, his jaw tight. "I've known you for two years. You stay awake all night worrying when our daughter has a cough. You can't watch me break a chicken's neck, and gag at the sight of dead rabbits, but suddenly you know how to kill, and how to *disguise* a killing, with ruthless efficiency. How is that possible?"

Finally, I feel something. *Despair.* Because the truth is vast and ugly and he's making it unavoidable.

"I don't have time for this," I reply. I channel my mother, using that haughty, imperious tone she intimidated me with a thousand times as a child. "The children are going to wake soon and I'm covered in blood."

He's out of the truck and blocking my path before I can reach the door. "Enough evasions!" he shouts, gripping my arm. "Talk to me! Tell me what this is!"

A choked laugh escapes my throat. After everything we've been through, after fighting so hard to get back to him and so much time spent hiding what I am, he's going to force me to ruin it.

"Let me ask you something," I say, brushing angry tears away with my free hand. "Those people who held us captive, who killed your mother—what if I told you I was like them? What if I told you I was *one* of them?"

He shakes his head. "Why are you asking me this? You're neither of those things!"

"I'm both of those things," I reply. "The man in charge was my grandfather. The woman helping him was my aunt."

There is horror on his face. I'd held out the tiniest shred of hope that he might look past it, might be able to forgive me. Now I know, looking at him, how naïve that was.

His hand releases me. I turn and walk into the house before he sees me cry.

BY THE TIME I emerge from the room in clean clothes, Henri's got Cecelia in his arms, and Lucien and Charlotte are both sitting at the table with mugs of powdered milk. He looks at me for a long moment when I walk in. I can't tell if it's disgust or despair I see in his face. I suppose it doesn't matter. Neither is good.

I throw my clothes into the fire and then, without saying a word, he hands me Cecelia and goes outside. A few minutes later he brings in the fir he cut down, which I'd forgotten about entirely. The children, still so ill, rouse a little at the sight, and we feed them dinner and help them string popcorn and cranberries for the tree, saying not a single unnecessary word to each other.

Perhaps I should be grateful for the silence, but I'm not. It feels like the lull before the storm. Does he hate me now? Does the revelation make me someone he won't want around his daughter? I swallow hard at the thought. I have no idea what I'll do if he asks me to leave.

Cecelia falls asleep in my arms. "I'll put Lucien and Charlotte to bed," he says, without looking at me.

I lay Cece in her crib and then go to the bathroom, shutting the door behind me. I wait for the tub to fill, my heart beating hard. What will I do if he tells me to leave? How will I keep all of them safe through the war if he won't let me near them? If he were anyone else, threatening to separate me from him and the children, I'd be planning his death. But my Coron blood is nowhere to be found at the moment.

I wash my hair, listening for the sound of his heavy tread all the while. I never dreamed the day would come when I'd be more frightened by the sound of Henri's footsteps than a stranger's, but I am right now. He holds everything I care about in the palm of his hands.

When I finally hear him coming down the stairs, my forehead presses to my knees. *Don't cry*, I tell myself. *Use your head.* But the part of me that was so sharp and certain earlier has abandoned me. I feel like the child I once was—small, alone, despised, defenseless.

The door opens. His eyes are cold and hard. "Is your bath done?" he asks.

He's going to throw me out. It seemed possible before. Now it feels certain. Inside, I am scrambling, wondering how I can prevent this from happening. But the voice that comes out is my mother's again. Cold and careless. "I'll let you know when I'm done."

"You're done," he snaps, striding across the room. He lifts me from the tub as if I'm a child, while I fight, slippery and desperate, pounding at his chest but getting nowhere. His grip tightens.

Tears run down my face. "You can't make me leave!" I scream. "You can't!"

His body jerks and stills, suddenly. "*Leave?*" he asks. He places me on my feet, holding onto me with one arm. "You think I want you to *leave?*"

"Why else are you pulling me out of the tub?" I cry, still tense and braced for a fight.

To my utter shock, he laughs. A small, slight sound, but a laugh nonetheless. He wraps a towel around me. "I'm tempted to question your sanity right now. How could you possibly think that?"

"I told you everything and you—" my anger gives way and my voice breaks – "you couldn't even look at me afterward. You didn't even speak to me all night. What else was I supposed to think?"

He pulls me to him with the towel, which he holds tight around me. "I didn't speak tonight because sometimes, in anger, it's best to say nothing. And I'm *still* angry. First, because you didn't trust me enough to tell me the truth about all this. Most of all, though, because I had to watch today as you were very nearly raped and then very nearly incinerated, and both were entirely your fault. You took unnecessary risks, and I'm furious at you for it, but that's the opposite of wanting you to leave, isn't it?"

"I did what I had to do to keep us all safe," I reply. "But it's as if you haven't even heard what I said. You saw what I'm capable of today and you know who I'm descended from. How can you still want to be anywhere near me? How can you still care what happens to me?"

"You stabbed a man who was already dead," he replies. "That hardly makes you Hitler."

I stare at his chest, no longer able to meet his eye. "I've killed before this. It was my aunt you found in the pit, wearing your mother's necklace. I probably didn't even have to kill her, but I wasn't sure I'd have the strength to time travel home without her spark. I set the fire that killed all the guards. And I helped them. I started working in the kitchen, and I was the one who poisoned the other women. I didn't know it was poison, but I knew something was wrong and I did it anyway."

He listens to my words with his grave face, but when I finish I see no judgement there. "If it's because you did those things that you managed to come home to me," he says softly, "then I'm glad for every one of them."

He takes the towel and crouches, drying my legs, between my toes. As if I'm still something he treasures. Tears run down my face, watching him, and then he rises and wraps his arms around me.

"My mind works the way theirs did, Henri," I whisper. "It's cold and methodical, and killing made me feel...powerful."

His lips press to my temple, and then my cheek. "You're not going to scare me away, Sarah," he says. "I know you. Killing might make you feel powerful, but it's not your driving force, and even if it were, God help me, but I'd love you all the same. If you are soft and sweet and need protection, I will love you. And if you are a weapon capable of destroying people in ways I haven't even dreamed of, I will love that version of you as well. Whatever it is you are, I want you and I wouldn't change it."

He holds me there, with the towel wrapped around me, until my tears have slowed.

"You're shivering," he says. "Come." He pulls me to our room and tucks me into bed, wrapping the blankets around me, before undressing to slide in beside me.

He finds my hand and lifts my palm to his lips. "Tell me everything."

Haltingly, with my head pressed to his chest, I do. I tell him about Katrin, and her suspicions that I was her descendant. About Luna Reilly, who tried to stop the guards while I just sat there in silence. I tell him about Mathilde and the babies, and how I swaddled dead infants and felt absolutely nothing as I did it.

I tell him that I thought of killing Yvette and Dr. Nadeau, that there was a time, before Cece was born, that I hoped she wouldn't survive. And he listens, running a hand over my back the entire time, soothing me, even as I tell him things he should hate me for.

"But how does any of this make you related to Coron?" he finally asks when I'm done.

"Katrin... I think she knew what I was even before I did. She said something about it, the way I was able to think the way Coron did. She was one of the women he raped and she was pregnant when she left. I confronted my mother about everything when I got home and she admitted that Peter Stewart wasn't my father."

"Sharing Coron's blood doesn't make you what he is," Henri says.

"In my case, it does. It felt like it went away, when Cecelia was born, but it's back. I feel it every time we're threatened. That ugly side of me wants to be set free."

"That side of you might just turn out to be what saves the children's lives if I'm not here," he says, pushing my hair back. "Perhaps everything you've lived through was necessary to survive what's to come. And I need you to survive. So please, never do what you did today. Don't risk yourself like that."

His lips brush mine, once and then twice, and his hand rests on my hip, pulling me closer. My mouth opens beneath his and I feel him respond to it, groaning as I arch against him, before he pulls back.

"I should let you rest," he says, flinching. "After what happened today—"

I pull him on top of me. "Nothing happened today," I reply. "And I'm not fragile."

With a small shudder he pushes inside me, leaning over to

find my mouth. I feel split open, mentally and physically. He knows the ugliest things in my soul and he loves me in spite of them. It is more than I could have hoped for, and it changes something between us.

Being with him tonight is more than love or lust.

For the first time ever, it feels holy.

38

SARAH

I wake the next day feeling sore, but in the best possible way. With the secrets between us finally gone, something that seemed impossible to improve upon is even better.

But our situation remains the same, possibly worse. Did that commander who visited yesterday tell anyone where he was going? Surely, the fact that they died two miles down the road will force someone to at least look at the farm. All day long my eyes flicker to the revolver on the high shelf in the kitchen, to the knives on the counter. Lucien knocks over a broom behind me and I jump.

"We can't continue like this," Henri says.

I shrug, as if my heart didn't nearly shoot out of my chest from the sound of a broom falling. "I'm not sure we have a choice."

"Unfortunately," he sighs, "we do. I'll stay through Christmas, and then I'm going to run Roche's little errand."

I shake my head. "No," I whisper. "Please. Don't."

"I'll be gone two weeks, perhaps three, and then we'll have everything we need. We'll take the train to Marseilles and be on the next boat to England. Think of it, all of us together, where the children can run outside without fear."

There's a part of me that wants to believe him, that wants to fall into this pretty picture he's creating. Already, I can imagine summer nights when the children catch fireflies in jars and swim, Henri and I watching them with our hands clasped, the worst behind us. I hunger for it in a way I can hardly even express.

But nothing that's happened over the course of my life leads me to believe our happy ending could be so close at hand, or acquired so simply. If it were easy, Roche would be doing it himself.

By Christmas, Lucien and Charlotte are better. Cece is still sick, but she's younger and more fragile, so it stands to reason she'd heal more slowly.

Though the holiday is not Charlotte's and Lucien's, they are part of our family now, so we get them a few gifts we managed to scrounge up, resolving to teach them about their own traditions when the war has passed and it's safe again.

It's a struggle to remain cheerful all day, however. Tomorrow, Henri will leave for this mission of Roche's. I can't stop wondering if this might be the last Christmas we share, but I don't want to ruin our time together with my sad thoughts.

Once the children are in bed, I curl up against him. *Don't talk about tomorrow. Don't ruin this.* "Tell me about our honeymoon," I say.

"We'll go to Greece," he says. "After the war, when the world is finally safe again."

"Will we take the children?" I ask.

He smirks. "Is that a serious question? Absolutely not. Think how awkward that would be, with you in bed the whole time."

"The *whole* time?"

"Don't worry," he says, twisting a strand of my hair around his finger. "I'll make sure you still have a lovely view of the sea from our room."

"Ah, so only *I* will remain in bed?"

He laughs low. "I plan to exhaust you to the point that you won't be able to leave. I'll venture out to get you food and perhaps take a quick dip in the water, but nothing more."

I grin. "Maybe I want to be the one to venture out for the food while you remain in bed."

He pulls me above him. "Are you offering to do all the work, little thief?" he asks, his voice dropping an octave, smooth as silk. "I'm happy to agree. But first, perhaps, you should show me what that entails."

I try to smile but it falters. "Please don't do anything stupid on this mission."

"Everything I do is brilliant," he says with a cheeky grin, trying to make me laugh.

His ploy works but the laugh catches in my throat and becomes a sob. I am already thinking of last summer, of those months when I didn't know if he was alive, the terror of them. We got lucky once. Will we get lucky again?

His lips press to my head. "Don't cry. In two months, we'll be sitting at our cottage in the British countryside and this will all be behind us. Have faith, little thief. I have a feeling our story isn't over just yet."

39

HENRI

I head to Paris on foot, through the woods. I'm provided directions to the safe houses along the way by Roche's contact before I'm led to the airmen I'll be guiding.

Any optimism I felt diminishes once we meet. One of the two Brits, Reginald Price, is shifty-eyed and sullen. Nothing about him engenders trust. The other, Thomas Stevens, is quite ill, struggling with a foot he thinks he may have broken upon landing. He's not willing to remain behind, but a journey like this is taxing on even the strongest of men, and I don't see him making it through Pyrenees without assistance. The American, Michael Quinn, is neither ill nor untrustworthy, but he's brash and loud and behaves as if this is some kind of lark, which leaves him, in my estimation, the most likely to get us all killed.

We sneak out of Paris by the skin of our teeth, one block at a time, hiding in the shadows the whole way. We walk all night and most of the day, making our way through the woods instead of using main roads. Our progress is slowed significantly by Stevens, who is dragging his foot like a heavy bag behind him.

"He's slowing us down," Price says under his breath. "We need to leave him behind."

My lip curls. They're not just countrymen—they flew together and were the only two of their crew to survive. I don't trust any man with so little loyalty to a soldier he's fought beside. "No one's getting left behind."

"It's your funeral," Price mutters.

Our funeral, I long to correct, but say nothing. Fighting will only delay getting them to the final safe house, which will delay the one thing I want right now: to get home.

"You got a girl, Durand?" asks Quinn as we settle into the first safe house, which is little more than a shack and provides no protection from the elements.

My eyes are closed. I don't want to talk right now. I want to picture Sarah waiting in bed for me or the smile on her face when I walk through the door. I want to think of the way she looks as she sits with Cece in the rocking chair or brushes Charlotte's hair. I still don't understand how she could have thought I'd want her to leave, but I suppose being raised by a woman who hates you is hard to shake.

"Yes," I reply. "Amelie. You?"

He shrugs. "I did have one, before the war started. When I volunteered, she found herself some college boy who didn't enlist. You got a photo?"

Reluctantly, I reach into my jacket pocket and pull out a copy of her passport photo, taken just before she was held captive. She's in the blue dress, though it simply looks gray in the picture, and she smiles at the camera with a certain look in her eyes—the kind that promises all sorts of delights once I've put the camera away. Only a few days have passed, but I miss her badly.

Quinn lets out a low whistle. "Sweet Jesus. She have a sister?"

I laugh unwillingly. "No."

"Hope you stashed her somewhere safe."

I fight the uneasy feeling in my stomach, closing my eyes to remember how fierce Sarah was that day the Germans came. When she threw that last knife with nary a glance, but still managed to sever the commander's brainstem. If anyone can protect herself and our children until I get back, it's her.

The next morning begins several very long days, as we make our way to the free zone. Once we finally arrive, Quinn starts to cheer and I silence him. "Don't let the name fool you," I warn. "Vichy isn't as free as you might hope. And we have a long walk to the Pyrenees ahead."

He quiets down, but his unfailing optimism remains firmly in place, which is still far preferable to Price's weasel eyes, constantly shifting between the group of us. He suggests more than once, under his breath, that Stevens should be put out of his misery. "It would be the kindest thing to do," he says.

If the situation weren't so grim, I'd laugh. Sarah killed bad people in order to save her own life and thinks she's evil and violent because of it. But true evil is surrounding us right now in men like Price, men who kill for selfish reasons and tell themselves it's heroism. I can't even judge him too harshly for it. Every day I spend in his company has me justifying reasons to put a knife in his back too.

On the ninth day of our journey—four days behind schedule—we finally see the Pyrenees rising in the distance. This time, I'm able to share Quinn's broad grin.

"Nearly there," he says.

I laugh. "We're still two days from the base."

"Don't ruin this for me, Frenchy," he replies. "I'm picturing a big steak dinner and a pretty girl waiting at the bottom of that mountain and you won't persuade me otherwise."

Stevens, his bad foot now dragging audibly behind him, does not share our happiness. Climbing those peaks seems a daunting task even to me, and in his current state I can't imagine what it will take to get through it. I argue with myself for the next two days, but when we reach the safe house in Carcassonne, I finally pull him aside.

"The journey so far has been easy, compared to what it will

be," I tell him. I flinch, thinking of what it will mean if he accepts the offer I'm about to make. It will add a week or more to the time I'm gone, at the very least. "If you'd like to rest here and gather your strength, I'll come back for you."

He scrubs a hand over his face. "My son turns three next week, and my wife's due at the end of the month. I suppose I won't be there for either of them, but it'd be a hell of a surprise if I were, wouldn't it? I've got to try."

I give him a brief nod. I disagree with his decision, but it's not mine to make. "It would," I agree. "I'll do my best to get you there."

We sleep all day by the fire and set out at nightfall with fresh bread and tinned ham in our packs, skirting the main road so we don't miss the trail that will lead us into the mountains. As sunrise approaches, the terrain grows steep and the air thins. Stevens struggles to keep up, his breathing harsh and irregular.

"Come on, mate," I urge quietly. "I see the trail ahead, which means we'll be stopping soon."

"Not at the rate he's moving," snarls Price. "And the Krauts are all over this damn place, so if we're still out at daylight we're good as dead."

"Fuck off, Price, you selfish bastard," says Quinn. "Where's your fucking loyalty?"

Price rounds on him as I turn onto the trail. "You shouldn't even be here. The British government is trying to get *us* home, not—"

A floodlight blinds us and I jerk to a stop, squinting into the glare. Five Germans stand there, blocking the path ahead, their rifles trained on us.

And then they tell us to drop to the ground.

40

SARAH

January is the coldest month I've ever endured. So cold that I can feel it in my teeth if I stand near the window, and so gray it's hard to imagine there was ever a time when it was otherwise.

I wake each morning feeling as if I'm holding my breath, waiting for Henri's return. How could anyone survive in this weather for four weeks? Lucien climbs up to the window several times a day with those sad brown eyes of his, ever hopeful that Henri will be walking around the corner. I can hardly fault him— I keep hoping for it too.

Cecelia, my poor sweet baby, is sicker by the day. I really thought she was turning a corner, around the time Henri left. But then the crying began, a heartbreaking wail I can't seem to fix. She needs real milk, real meat, real fruit. All three of them do. They haven't had food that wasn't from a tin for weeks. When the last day of the month comes and goes with no sign of Henri, I know I can't keep waiting on his return to get us something in town.

And I can't keep waiting to find out what happened to him.

Before sunrise the next day, I grab every ration card we

possess, along with an obscene amount of money, and leave Charlotte in charge of Lucien. I know I should put them in the cellar in case we have visitors, but it's so cold I can't stand the thought of it. I promise Lucien chocolate if he is very good while I'm gone, and then bundle Cecelia into her pram. A month ago, she'd have been far too restless to lie down in the stroller the way she does now. A week ago, she'd have wailed until the entire town was staring at us. Now, she doesn't fight and she doesn't cry. My stomach clenches into a knot so tight that it hurts as I look at her.

I walk through town in the darkness until I arrive at Roche's home, on the less savory side of Saint Antoine. I lift Cece from her pram and knock on the door. He looks me over with interest for a moment, and then his eyes narrow and he grasps me by the arm so hard and so suddenly I nearly drop Cece as I'm yanked over his threshold.

"I know you," he says. "You're Durand's whore. And if you mean to threaten me by showing up like this, let me assure you I don't take threats kindly."

I pull Cece closer to my chest, my heart hammering hard. With her here, I can't do any of the things I'd like to right now. "I'm not threatening you. I want to know where my husband is."

He looks me over again, head-to-toe. "He's not your husband, as I recall. He's someone else's. He didn't even try to get papers for you, you know."

Anger makes my vision begin to cut in around the edges. "Answer the question," I reply between gritted teeth. "Where is he?"

"There's been no word," he replies. "I'm assuming that means he failed and got them all killed, but you'd need to ask my contact in Paris to be certain."

Killed. I restrain my desire to shudder. He's not dead. Maybe he's captured, but he's not dead. He can't be.

"Well, in order to speak to anyone in Paris, I'll need those travel papers you promised."

He arches a brow. "I agreed to create those papers in exchange for a job he has not yet done. When the airmen reach England, then he shall have his papers." His eyes roam over me. "Unless you'd like to strike another sort of deal."

Rage boils in my blood. This man is risking Henri's life but won't hold up his side of the bargain, though it will cost him nothing. "I'm not striking another sort of deal with a man who still hasn't honored the first one."

He grasps my elbow and pulls me to the door. "Then we have nothing to discuss. Come here again and I'll see that you regret it."

The door slams behind me and I stand for a moment, feeling the pulse of fury in my brain, the desire to destroy. Cece is heavy in my arms, reminding me how ill she is—not since she was a newborn could she have slept through an exchange like that one. I place her in the pram and force myself onward, to the queue at the grocer's.

If Roche knew who he was dealing with, I think, *he wouldn't have been so high-handed.* And God knows I'm tempted to show him.

I reach the grocer's just as the sun is rising. The women in line eye me with suspicion. In better times, they were friendly enough, but now I'm the worst of all possible things—a home-wrecker, an American, and tainted by association with the Durands. The only way I could make it worse at this point is if I were also a Nazi, and then at least they wouldn't be openly rude. Claudette Loison, the girl who fancied Henri so much back in the day, is among them. She whispers to the woman behind her and then turns back toward me. "Whore," she mouths, so I can see.

I'm not someone you want to trifle with, I think, and then force my gaze to Cecelia—a visible reminder that I must be level-headed right now, my best self. I get our things and proceed to the butcher's. His wife offers me canned sardines and I lean toward her so I won't be overheard. "Is there anything else you might be able to spare for fifteen francs?"

Her eyebrows go up. "Since when do the Durands have fifteen francs to spend?" she asks.

I'd almost forgotten Henri's charade of being poor. "They still don't," I reply. "But I do."

She gives me an almost imperceptible nod. "I can give you a ham. My husband will meet you in the back."

Within a few minutes, I'm on way with a ham wrapped in paper beneath my arm. The basket is heavy but when I picture how delighted Lucien and Charlotte will be with my haul it all seems worthwhile.

I walk along the main road, ignoring the eyes on me as I pass, and breathe a sigh of relief as I turn toward the farm. Finally out of sight, I set the basket down, rubbing the welt it's left on my inner arm.

"Nearly there," I tell Cecelia, who looks up at me with pale eyes, more listless than she was even when we left. I slide my finger against her palm, and her hand tightens around it, a reflex. "When we get home, I'll mash you up an apple and some ham and you'll be right as rain." My voice cracks on the last word. I no longer believe my promises to her.

I reach for the basket, and straighten, but just as I do, something slams into the back of my head. The pain makes the world go black, and I fall. It's impossible to think, to understand what's happened. For a moment I don't remember where I am.

Cecelia.

Panic has me struggling to push my face up from the ground. My sight returns but I'm so dizzy that my stomach rolls as I climb to my feet. Cecelia is still in her pram, thank God, but my basket and the ham are gone.

I sway, trying to make sense of it. Until this moment, I thought it must be an accident. A falling branch, perhaps. But it was intentional. A hit hard enough to kill me. Whoever ran off didn't care that he was leaving an infant here to freeze while her mother bled to death on the ground.

That rage—simmering for weeks—boils over, staining everything, spilling poison in my brain. Not just for my assailant, but for all of them: the Nazis, the French police doing their dirty work, the women in town whispering slights as I walked past. Monsieur Roche and this job he's made Henri do. Jeannette and Marie for leaving. Doctor Nadeau for refusing to help us.

Right now, my capacity for harm may exceed anything my grandfather or aunt ever dreamed of. I want to kill everyone who has ever hurt us, though I'd settle for jumping back in time a few minutes and teaching whoever struck me the most painful lesson he's ever endured.

Except the children are at home unattended and Cecelia needs to get inside. *Focus*, I tell myself. *You have to put them first.*

My hands shake as they wrap around the handles of the pram and I begin to limp home. My ears still ring from the hit and my vision remains slightly blurred. I haven't touched the back of my head but it feels wet.

I get to the farm and walk in the door to find the bookcase on its side and broken. Charlotte and Lucien are both crying but unharmed, and I want to cry too.

What am I going to do? How am I going to get us out of this mess?

"Your head is bleeding," Charlotte says through her tears.

I know she's talking about the cut, but it feels like so much more than that.

I DON'T NORMALLY PRAY and I'm not even sure what I believe in, at this point, but once the children are in bed that night I fall to my bruised knees and beg anyone listening for help. "Please help Cece get better. Show me what to do for her. Please bring Henri home and help us find a way to get out of here." I ask and ask, but when I'm done the house is silent. Absolutely nothing has changed, and I know it's not going to. And that feels like an answer, in and of itself.

No one is going to help. No reinforcements are coming. But God left us a weapon, one it's high time I used.

Me.

41

SARAH

I get off the floor.

My tears have dried and I feel empty now, and calm. My blood slows and my sight sharpens. Fear is replaced by cool certainty, and I welcome it.

Nadeau *will* cure Cecelia. Roche *will* tell me how to find Henri and provide me the documents he owes us.

I just went about it all wrong. And time travel will allow me to do it again, the right way.

Normally, when I time travel, I do so from the barn. Tonight, though, I just go into the kitchen. I close my eyes and go back to the evening before. Some previous version of me sleeps nearby and I freeze for a moment, worried I'll wake her. But there isn't a sound. She continues to dream, blissfully unaware of how terribly her day is about to go.

I dress in trousers and a sweater that hang by the fire and I sneak out of the house, sliding through the shadows in town to Roche's home. When I reach his locked door, I know I should be terrified, and perhaps some distant part of my brain still is, but anger is like an ice-cold drink on the hottest day. It makes me feel new again, and capable of anything.

I consider my options—knocking on his door or time traveling inside on my own. I go for the latter. He's stronger than I am and may be armed, so I want the element of surprise on my side. I focus on the interior of his house, and fade, landing inside perhaps a second earlier. He's a sound sleeper, which is unwise given his profession, and unwise given the enemy he's made in me, though he's not aware of it yet. His snores continue unabated while I open his door to get my clothes from his front stoop, and don't stop until I'm standing beside him, pressing my blade to his neck. He gasps as it punctures the skin. "I'd be very careful, were I you," I tell him. "I'm barely a millimeter from a very important artery. And before you do something stupid, know this: you won't be the first person I've killed, and I sort of enjoy the experience when warranted. Now tell me where Henri Durand is."

It sounds believable. Perhaps because every word of it is true. His nostrils flare but, to his credit, he doesn't try to attack me. "He met the people in Paris. That's all I know."

"So how do *I* reach the people in Paris?"

"I don't know," he says. "They contact me, not the reverse."

I press the blade against his neck more firmly and allow it to nick his skin. "How sad for you, then."

His teeth grind together before he concedes. "Go to the Café de la Mairie. Tell them you're tired of chicory and long for a single sip of real coffee, then ask for Robert. Now get that blade off my neck."

"Not so fast," I say, leaning closer. "There is still the matter of the papers you owe Henri."

"I don't have your papers!" he shouts. "And Durand didn't get the job done, so you won't be getting them."

"Sit up," I hiss. "I'd like you to watch something."

Still holding the blade to his neck, I pull another knife from my jacket with my left hand and throw it at the rosary hanging from his bookcase. My gaze remains on him as the chain breaks and the beads spill to the floor, and then I lean in close. "I am capable of doing things you can't even dream of, and I want my fucking papers."

I've spent years asking nicely and pleading for what I need.

As he unwillingly moves to his desk to get what I've demanded, I realize I should have done it this way all along.

JUST AFTER SUNRISE, a few hours after I've left Roche's house with our papers, I go to the site of the attack. Whoever threw that brick at my head is about to pay dearly for what he did. I hide in the bushes, longing to warn myself as Cecelia's pram comes into view. That brick comes sailing through the air, striking with a force that makes me wince as I watch it happen.

Someone rushes up to grab my basket. It's only when she turns to flee that I see her face.

Claudette Loison.

Claudette left me on the ground bleeding and perhaps dead, left my sick daughter out in the cold to freeze. Somehow the fact that I *know* her only makes my fury greater. If I'd planned to let her off the hook—though I really hadn't—this discovery would have put an end to it.

I spring from the bushes, felling her with the same brick she used on me. She's knocked unconscious by it—which is probably for the best—and I pull out my knife.

It would be so easy to kill her right now. My blood hums with desire for it, and she *deserves* just that for leaving Cece so vulnerable. It takes all my restraint to hold back.

It's not her life I need right now, though—it's her finger.

I cut off her pinky and place it carefully in my pocket. And then I leave her on the ground, to die or not die, just like she left me.

FOR THE LAST stage of the plan, I return to regular time. Dr. Nadeau doesn't sleep as soundly as Roche and is fumbling for his glasses when I walk into his room—holding Cece on my left side and a gun in my right hand.

He winces at me and turns on the lamp beside him, flooding the room with low, flickering light. "What the hell are you doing?" he sputters. "Put that thing away."

"I'd be happy to," I reply. "As soon as you treat my daughter."

"You really think you can threaten me?" he asks. "I could destroy your entire family with a single word."

"I could destroy yours as well. And if my daughter isn't cured tonight, I will. I know where your son lives. He's a dentist in Reims, correct? I met him and your sweet little grandson at mass once."

For the first time I see fear in his eyes, and I relish it. I've been terrified for a month because he refused to help Cece. It's about time he discovered what it's like. "You wouldn't," he says, though he doesn't sound certain. "He's just a child."

I laugh. "The little girl I hold in front of you is just a child, yet you were willing to let her die."

He snorts. "That wasn't *murder*. You could have found another doctor. I would never hurt someone intentionally."

"Well, you and I are different in that regard," I reply, pulling Claudette's finger from my pocket and placing it on the night-stand. He'll know who it belongs to by now. I'm sure the whole town has heard about this morning's attack on Claudette, and I'm sure she made herself sound absolutely blameless.

His jaw drops. "Claudette—" he says with a gasp as he puts it together. "How could you?"

He was willing to let a one-year-old die simply because she's a quarter Jewish, yet Claudette's loss of a *pinky* is the true crime? "Because *you* have placed me in a desperate situation." I bring

Cece forward. "Figure out what's wrong with my daughter and fix it. *Now*."

He barely even looks at her. "Rash and listlessness following a case of strep throat," he says. "It's rheumatic fever."

Which happened because you refused to treat her. He is responsible for this and he doesn't care—feels no guilt at all, even with her sweet little face staring up at him. "Fix it," I hiss.

He raises his hands. "You need penicillin for that. I've had none since the war began."

This stupid man still believes he's in charge.

"Would you like to see something interesting?" I ask with a smile. "Something you can't even imagine possible?" I walk to the far end of the room, place the gun on the desk, and lay Cece on top of my coat.

And then I disappear. I hear his gasp as it happens and he's still sitting there, thunderstruck, when I reappear beside him. I'm naked now, of course, but he's so stunned he hardly seems to notice.

"How did you—" he begins.

"It doesn't matter," I say, returning to my clothes, which sit on a pile on the floor next to Cece. "You're under the impression that you can warn your son and grandson before I get there, but guess what? If I don't walk out of here with enough penicillin to cure her, I can go back to the previous day and do what I want to do. I can go back a year. I can go back *thirty years* and make sure your son never even exists." I finish dressing and pick Cece up, holding her close. "So, I suggest you figure something out."

He shuffles across the room to a drawer and hands me a vial of penicillin.

"More," I demand.

He raises a brow. "I know some of your secrets too, you know. I saw you walking home with Jeannette Olatz's children that day she disappeared. I know they're at your house."

I still. This man who now hates me, and hates my daughter,

knows about Charlotte and Lucien. And he thinks he can threaten me with that information.

It makes what might have been a difficult decision quite easy.

I pick up the gun and fire.

42

HENRI

Stevens is dead. They shot him only an hour after we were caught, and the rest of us had no choice but to keep moving, bound together as we are with a German rifle at our backs. By the time we stop for the night, we've been marching for twenty-four hours straight. If I were to guess I'd say we're heading northeast. Probably toward the labor camps in Germany.

"We're moving fast now," Quinn says to Price as we're led out of town. "Is it everything you hoped it would be?"

We stop in Mirepoix and are handed over to a commander there, who has a much larger group of prisoners under his command. We're held there nearly a week, unfed, huddling in a ditch for warmth, as more prisoners arrive. Occasionally, someone is dragged into the square, seemingly at random, and shot. It's how the Germans remind the townspeople that even here in the free zone, they are not actually free.

At the end of the week, we are led onto a road heading east. We walk in silence all day. It's only when the soldiers are off cooking their evening meal and setting up their tents that we dare speak.

"You're looking unhappy these days," Quinn says.

I glance at him. It's sometimes hard to tell if he's mentally defective or just endlessly optimistic. "I imagine we're all looking pretty unhappy these days."

"Don't worry," he says. "Your girl will wait."

"That's not what I'm worried about," I reply. In truth, though, what scares me most does relate back to Sarah. He'd just never believe it if I told him.

I'm worried she'll come get me herself.

43

SARAH

We arrive at the first checkpoint outside Saint Antoine just after sunrise. I never dreamed I'd set out for Paris with a suitcase that holds mostly food, leaving the children's things behind, but we can't drive once we reach the city—it'll invite too much suspicion—and with Cece in my arms, I won't be able to carry much else.

Though it's February, I'm sweating as if it's the height of summer. Nerves, possibly, or perhaps just the fact that I have wads of cash stuffed between my skin and the dress.

All my confidence from the night before is gone. The desire to kill is still there, and still strong, but when I faced down Roche and Claudette, I only had to worry about myself. Even with Cece there, I was confident I could take on Dr. Nadeau. Now, though, there are three children to protect, and at any one of these stops it could all go awry. I have two knives on me and a gun hidden under the seat, but I'm still human. I can only kill so many people at once and will be assuring my own death if I attempt it. What happens to the children then?

The whole plan feels increasingly uncertain. Though I managed to get Edouard's location from the monsignor's office—

violent threats once again saving the day—there's no guarantee Marie is there, since Edouard is apparently still a priest. But whether she's there or not, Edouard owes my family a debt. He'll find a place for us to stay or pay heavily for his failure.

The line is backed up. My gut tightens as I watch a soldier force the couple ahead of me to get out of their car and walk to the side of the road. Their luggage is removed from the trunk, and I begin to panic.

What if they do the same to us? Time travel would be useless here. Yes, I could jump back a day or a week, but I'd still land *here*, an hour from Saint Antoine. Who would I even warn?

The soldier off to the side gestures me around the car being searched.

"Destination?" he asks, taking my papers.

I swallow. "Paris," I say. "To see my brother."

He looks over the first pass, mine, and then someone begins yelling behind him. Both our heads jerk at the sound. The man who was pulled from his car is down on his knees and the woman is weeping. Already that same fury is coming over me. If I didn't have to protect these three children, I'd grab my gun and fire as many shots as I could.

The soldier's eyes return to my papers, and then he frowns. "There's an error," he says, in heavily accented French. "You will need to pull off the road."

My heart beats so hard I feel sick from it. "An error?" I ask.

"There is no stamp on this," he says, holding my travel papers in the air.

The whole world seems to still in this moment. Roche screwed us over. Intentionally. He had to have known that stamp was important. And there are no good options available to me. If my travel papers are bad, the children's are as well. If he intentionally messed up the travel passes, then their passports are probably no good either.

My hand slides beneath my seat, feeling for the cool metal of the gun. "Oh, the magistrate's office must have made a mistake. I'll just go back to get it fixed."

He starts to shake his head when the sound of gunfire draws our attention. The male of the couple, maybe forty at most, lies on the ground bleeding, and the woman weeps and falls to her knees beside him.

The soldier looks behind us, at the line of cars now backing up down the road. "Go," he barks. "Make sure you've got a stamp before you return."

I'm shaking so hard I can barely push the accelerator down, but I manage to drive another twenty minutes, trembling all the while. We need to get out of this car, but I don't know how we'll make the journey to Paris on foot. The cash against my skin is soaked with sweat when I finally drive off the road and cut the engine.

"Are we in Paris?" asks Charlotte.

I open the door and throw up in the grass. "No," I reply. "I think we'll walk through the woods the rest of the way."

IT TAKES us most of the day to travel that remaining few miles. Our suitcase is gone, left behind when it became necessary to carry Lucien in one arm and Cece in the other. "Not too much farther," I tell Charlotte. "I wonder if there's anywhere in Paris that still has pastry."

Her excitement at the idea breaks my heart a little. These children who've lost their parents, who've spent nearly a year in hiding...they are still children. They still light up at the smallest pleasures and *my God* what I wouldn't give to get them to a place where those pleasures were possible.

We stop in the woods to eat, and I tear a bit of bread to feed Cece. The penicillin is already doing its job. She smiles for the first time in weeks when I place a piece in her mouth.

Charlotte rests her head on my chest. "I wish we were home," she says quietly. She's had the hardest day of the three children, and I imagine her feet are as blistered as mine by now.

"Not too much farther," I reply, praying it's true.

THE CITY, when we reach it, is greatly changed. Massive swastikas hang from the buildings, and German soldiers patrol the streets, fill the cafes, sometimes strolling arm-in-arm with girls, as if the city is now a luxurious resort destination open only to them.

We pass through Saint-Germain-des-Pres, where Henri and I once spent a lovely day together, bickering and pretending not to enjoy each other's company. It's overrun with soldiers now, but for a single moment longing fills me. I want another day like the one Henri and I had. I want to do the things I refused to do with him at the time—a walk through the Orsay, the Louvre, the sculpture garden at the Musee Rodin. I thought at the time that I wanted to save those experiences for Mark. I realize only now that I was scared: I didn't want to share anything special with a man I already liked more than I should.

It's another mile to Edouard's church, which is in an undesirable part of the city. People won't meet my gaze as we walk toward the doors, and inside, the church is ice-cold and in grave need of repair. Edouard is clearly being punished with this assignment, and I can't say I'm sad about it. I knock on a door to the right of the altar, hoping I might find someone who can lead us to him, and the nun who answers gasps at the sight of us.

"Amelie," she says. "My God."

Marie. Marie is here and she's now...a nun?

"What on earth are you doing here?" she asks, ushering us in. She looks as shocked to find me as I am to find her.

I feel relieved tears stinging my eyes. I didn't realize until just now how scared I was that we wouldn't find her alive.

"You're a *nun*?"

She flushes. "It's a long story." She looks over my shoulder and panic flickers in her eyes. "Henri...he's still fighting? Or captured?"

I sigh. "He's been captured, I think, but that's a long story too."

As she leads us to a set of rooms in back, my relief at finding her alive is quickly tempered by anger. The past ten months would have been so much easier with her there, or if she'd gotten Cece to England. She is not married, and there appears to be no child—so what was it all for?

"We've walked all day and the children need to be fed," I say stiffly. "Can you help us?"

"Of course," she says. She removes her headpiece and takes Cece from me. "She's so big."

"It's been ten months," I reply coolly. "That's what happens."

Her shoulders sag. "I had no idea—" She glances at Charlotte and Lucien. "I thought you were in England."

I'm too tired to stay angry and it's as much my fault as hers. "Where's Edouard?" I ask.

She blushes. "He's giving last rites. He won't be home until late."

Home? I understood her fascination with Edouard and even the affair, though Henri did not. But living together like this, while he's a priest...is a tough sell even for me.

"And Henri?" she asks. "What makes you think he's been captured?"

I tell her about his journey south and the fact that he never returned. Saying it aloud forces me to see just how bleak the situation is. He didn't come home, which means he was caught somewhere, and being caught in his position is more likely to end in death than imprisonment. I shake my head, unable to face the idea of it. "I'll know more tomorrow when I speak to his contact," I conclude.

Marie sighs and nods her head. "If that fails," she says, "Edouard may be able to make some inquiries."

"So, apparently he's still a priest?"

She flushes again. "He was going to leave the priesthood. But once the shelling started, people began depositing orphaned children here. Most could be sent safely to other parts of the country, but the Jewish ones could not, and had to remain."

"They're here?" I whisper. "Inside the church?"

She nods. "But we all leave in two weeks. Someone has found us a safe place outside the city."

"And when that happens, Edouard will leave the priesthood?" I ask. I don't really care whether or not they're married—how could I, when Henri and I aren't either? Living with someone isn't considered risqué in my time, the way it is in hers. But I dislike the fact that he's still a priest. Until I've seen him put Marie first—before priesthood, before God even—I will doubt him.

"He would already have left," she says. "When I told him about the baby, the decision was made for him. But then the war started in earnest and I lost the baby and—" She stops, pressing her face into her hands. "It was my fault. The baby. It was all my fault."

"That can't be true."

"It is," she says. "I time traveled. I didn't even think about it...you know how often I do it, and the baby was just gone when I landed. I suppose because he or she couldn't travel with me." She bends her face to her hands and begins to cry again.

It's an aspect of pregnancy that never occurred to me until now: if males can't time travel, what happens if you do it while you're pregnant with one? But if that's the case, how did Katrin escape while pregnant with my father?

"You couldn't have known," I whisper.

She nods, drying her eyes. "Once we leave here and are safe, we will try again."

I sigh. "Marie...no place in France is safe. Not until the war is over. Where, exactly, are you going?"

"Chateau de Nanterre. To the west of Paris. We have someone working on getting the children forged papers, but until then I believe we'll be well hidden."

"Could your contact help get us papers as well?"

She shakes her head. "It's a lengthy process. You might be better off asking Yvette. She's the companion of a German colonel now. Very well-positioned. She could probably help you."

"Why would Yvette help *me*?"

"She wants to see Cecelia. She's helped Edouard get medical supplies and food when we were under attack. She isn't entirely bad."

I seriously doubt that, and allowing Yvette to see Cecelia seems like a bad idea. "You think she'd really help Lucien and Charlotte?" I ask.

Marie nods. "I know she is lazy and selfish, but she isn't a monster. She liked Jeannette and she liked the children."

"What if she tries to take Cece?"

Marie smiles. "The benefit of time travel is that we can undo what goes wrong, yes?"

I nod. But something about it just doesn't sit well. I'd say the odds here are not in our favor.

44

SARAH

The next morning, I find Roche's contact in a small room behind the café he directed me to, a room from another time. They use candles for light, a fireplace for heat.

Three men sit inside, all staring me down as I enter. One keeps his hand on his gun.

"I'm looking for my husband," I say. "Henri Durand. You sent him off in early January to get three airmen to Spain. He should be home by now."

The man closest to me sighs. "I'm sorry to tell you, madame, but they were taken near the base of the Pyrenees. They were last seen being held in Mirepoix."

He says it as if he's delivering the weather or informing me that a sale has ended. *Too bad, so sad*, he might say in my time. I want to lash out, but I force my anger down.

"Taken," I repeat. "But not dead."

He shrugs. "Good as dead—they'll be marched to the work camps over the border, and those who survive the journey rarely survive the camp as well."

It's not his words that enrage me—it's his apathy. The only man I have ever loved may die because of this stupid mission, and he couldn't care less. I feel it again, that fury and fire, and the way it takes everything terrified and weak inside me and makes it hard, and certain. I lean forward, placing my hands on his desk. "*He* will survive."

He frowns. "I don't think you understand the severity of the situation."

"No," I reply. "You don't understand. You're going to show me where he's headed, and I'm going to bring him home."

His jaw swings open. "*You?*"

"Yes. Me. Now show me the route."

He is reluctant, but fortunately for us both, he's too apathetic to fight me. He pulls out a map—there is only one major road leading northeast from Mirepoix, so they're undoubtedly somewhere along it. The road forks at Valence, and though they will probably continue north, toward Lyon, there's no guarantee.

"So you see," he concludes, "there's really nothing you can do."

"I can wait for them off the side of the road, south of Valence."

He laughs. "And then do *what*, madame? Will you fight the German soldiers with your bare hands?"

I stand to leave. "You have no idea what I'm capable of."

My confidence, however, is failing. He's right. How the hell am I going to fight off several German soldiers single-handedly in order to free Henri? I walk with brisk steps down the Champs-Élysées , trying to come up with a plan that won't get us both killed. My head remains empty.

When I glance up, I realize I'm standing beside the shop Henri took me to so long ago. The store is closed now, but I press my face to the window as if I can still see him just as he was that day—so handsome in his suit as he leaned against the wall. Sneaking glances across the aisle at me, his mouth curving upward when I caught him looking.

It hits me in the center of my chest, a vacuum that makes me want to fall to my knees. *He can't be dead. He can't be. I won't survive it if he is. I have to free him.*

A policeman barks at me to move along. I glance at him and swallow down the urge to challenge him, to fight, to punish. Killing Nadeau didn't cure that urge. It fed it. *Focus,* I say to myself. *Get Henri first. And then you can make everyone pay for what they've put you all through.*

~

EDOUARD IS home when I return. He greets me, equal parts wary and unrepentant. He shouldn't have slept with Marie in the first place, but what's done is done and he didn't judge me when Yvette left, so I suppose I should extend the same courtesy to him.

I lay out my plan to save Henri: I will take a train south. Once I've found him, we'll escape on foot. Of course, it requires a substantial contribution from Marie and Edouard as well. "While I'm gone, I would need you to watch the children. We'll get to Nanterre as fast as possible, but there's no way I can do this with them there."

"There's no way you can do this regardless of whether they're there," Edouard says softly. "How can you take on an entire unit of soldiers singlehandedly? And what if Henri is injured? You can't carry him home, even with the abilities you have."

My eyes widen. Marie was pregnant with his child so she could tell him about *her* ability. I just didn't realize she was going to tell him about mine too.

Marie doesn't seem to notice my surprise, however. She's too busy agreeing with Edouard. "It's a suicide mission."

"Can't you just jump back in time to warn him what's going to happen?" asks Edouard.

Marie and I exchange a look and she answers for me. "No. Because there's a chance he's alive right now. Any change we make will lead Henri to different decisions, ones that could be fatal."

It's the part of our gift I hate the most, that potential to make things worse. He nods, though I get the feeling he doesn't really understand. "At least speak to Yvette before you go," he says. "See if she'll get the children papers."

I hesitate. If I die on this suicide mission, as Marie calls it, talking to Yvette could at least ensure the children are safe from the concentration camps. But Cece is back to her old self—currently toddling around the room on chubby legs, smiling her gap-toothed smile. I'm not sure how any woman who saw her wouldn't want to take her from me. And Yvette would have the right to.

THE BUILDING YVETTE is staying in is crawling with soldiers and seems like more of a headquarters than a home. I walk with my head down and covered, fully prepared for this meeting to go poorly. I don't see how it won't. Yvette hates me, and more importantly, I hate her. The desire to kill still hums in my blood like a song I'm singing to myself. With each step I take, the sense of foreboding grows.

Her door is guarded by two German soldiers who take their jobs very seriously. Yvette's companion must be important—another reason not to act on my rage while here. I'm ushered inside a large parlor, with stiff velvet chairs and walnut tables. She makes us wait, of course, but when she finally swans into the room in expensive clothes and silk hose, the smug look on her face falls away.

"Cecelia?" she whispers to my daughter, appearing stunned that the infant she left fifteen months ago could have turned into a little girl. She reaches out. "Come to mama, darling."

Cece tucks her head into my shoulder and tightens her arms

around me. Did Yvette really think her daughter would remember her? She was barely involved in childcare even when she was around. "She's been sick, and she's also a little shy," I tell her. "Give her a minute to warm up."

Yvette frowns and looks as if she plans to argue before reluctantly taking the seat across from mine. "I'm surprised you dared come here," she says, opening a small case and withdrawing a cigarette.

"Edouard said you wanted to see her."

She lights her cigarette and takes a long drag, observing me. "Have you enjoyed it? Playing mother to my child when you can't have your own?"

My elbow brushes against the pocket of my coat, where a knife rests.

"She's a very good baby," I reply.

She takes another drag off her cigarette and exhales. The smell of the smoke makes me gag, and I hate that Cece is breathing it all in when she's still recovering.

"And Henri?" Yvette asks. "I suppose you got your claws in him too, didn't you? As you can probably tell, I don't care. I'm far better off without him." The lie is obvious. Her bitterness and jealousy show in every line of her face, which leaves me with no good way to answer. She'll know I'm lying if I deny it, and she'll be livid if I confirm it.

"I know you don't like me—" I begin, and she cuts me off.

"Don't like you?" she repeats. "You cannot begin to imagine the depths of my hatred for you, because if you did, you'd never have dared come here in the first place. Do you know who my benefactor is?"

Benefactor...what a pretty word to describe what you're doing, and with whom. She sees the disdain on my face.

"Ah, of course you do. Do you think you're so much better than me, Amelie? That's rich. It's *I* who look down on *you*. I could send you off to the concentration camps with a single word. And what's to stop me from doing it? It's more than you deserve."

She blows a plume of smoke from the corner of her mouth. "You may think he loves you, but it wasn't you he wanted any more than it was me."

I still. "What makes you say that?"

Her eyes flicker toward Cece. "The night she was conceived he was so drunk I was surprised he was able to...you know. Oh, but the whole time it was about Sarah. Him crying for Sarah, shouting her name at the end. I don't even think he knew I was there. You and I, we are the same. Just poor substitutes for her."

It only makes me love him more, hearing this version of events. My throat tightens, and Yvette laughs. "How does it feel, cousin?"

I would like to shatter her moment of misplaced triumph, but that's not why I'm here. "Cecelia will need help to get out of Paris. She needs travel papers that don't identify her as a Jew."

She stubs out her cigarette. "You don't need to worry about my daughter anymore. Hand her to me."

I freeze. If I refuse, she'll call the guards and have them take me away. If I time travel, I'll probably *still* land in her apartment, and there will *still* be guards outside. My best bet is to go along with it, and reverse things once I reach the church. I shudder at the idea of leaving Cece in her care for even a few minutes, but I'm not sure what choice I have.

Yvette makes the decision for me, yanking her away. Cece begins struggling to get free, and when her flailing hand strikes Yvette's face, Yvette drops her. For just a heartbeat, we both stare in horror at Cece on the ground, and then she begins crying and scrambles to her feet, running back to me.

"Guards!" Yvette cries. "Hurry!"

For a moment I'm frozen. Boots approach quickly from the hall and the door flies open.

Yvette looks at her daughter the same way she looks at me—

with disgust. "The child is a Jew and the woman is a conspirator," she says. "Take them away."

There is no time for finesse or escape. I close my eyes and give in to the urge I've felt since today's journey began. I picture the moment Yvette opened the cigarette case and I jump, and then land...naked, in front of her.

That earlier version of me looks as shocked as Yvette does, pulling Cece close, as if I might be another enemy. I lunge forward, grabbing the knife from the coat pocket.

"*I'm* Sarah," I tell Yvette, and then my arm swings in a wide arc, slashing through her jugular vein.

The fully dressed version of me watches all this with Cece's face pressed to her chest, staring at me in horror. That's when I realize the biggest problem with what I've done: once the guards find Yvette's body, they'll be looking for me. If I hope to leave the city at all, I need to get out today.

45

SARAH

Lyon is 300 miles from Paris. The ride there feels much longer than it is, waiting as I am for Germans to board and take me away. I was panicked as I snuck onto the train at Gare du Nord. Now, between the rocking motion of the car and the smell of the people on board, I'm almost too sick to care if I'm caught.

Could I have handled the situation with Yvette better? Undoubtedly. I didn't have to kill her, but I can't bring myself to regret it. She fueled that fire inside me, and she deserved to die. I just wish I hadn't added so much danger to an already tenuous situation. And I wish I'd had more time with the children before I left. Instead, I shoved what I could into a bag, kissed them each on the head, and ran. If this all goes wrong, that careless, panicked goodbye will be their last memory of me, if they remember me at all.

I arrive in Lyon late in the afternoon, and take another train from there to Valence, a hundred miles to the south. It's dark when we finally pull into the station. No place in this country is safe for a female traveling alone, especially at night, but I'm just glad to be off the train. Soldiers patrol the platform, but I keep my head down and walk away as if I don't notice them, clutching my bag to my chest.

"Mademoiselle!" a voice calls behind me.

I stiffen—mentally searching for the weight of the knife in my pocket though I force myself not to grab it. He's done nothing yet, but that bloodthirst inside me suggests I stab him anyway.

I turn. He's holding out a gray wool glove. His smile is almost apologetic.

"Yours?" he asks.

I shake my head. "No. But thank you."

"You have somewhere to stay in town?" he inquires, flushing. He's a boy with a crush, and one who probably did not want to fight, yet a part of me wants him to die anyway. It's as if I've let the lid off something that refuses to lay dormant again.

"My aunt is right around the corner," I reply.

He tips his hat. "I hope I will see you again."

I scurry away, my breath coming fast, and head out of the city, looking for a place to sleep—with the trip behind me, I'm so exhausted it's a struggle to even push forward. About a mile outside of town I find a barn and sneak in, burrowing into the hay for warmth. It still feels as if I'm on the rocking train and my stomach revolts. I try to put my mind on other things, better things, and as always, I think of Henri, remembering those early days with him, after he'd caught me trying to steal an apple from his barn. How I loathed his nickname for me back then.

I'm not a thief, I once said.

Not a good one, anyway, he'd replied with one of his arrogant grins.

My smile at the memory fades quickly. What would he make of the things I've done this past week? As forgiving as he is, I can't picture him accepting that I've killed two people he knew well.

～

I'M UP BEFORE SUNRISE, crouched in the woods just off the main road, shivering despite my wool coat and the tights I wear beneath my trousers. There is little traffic these days aside from military vehicles, and Henri is not with them, but none are safe from me. That rage, that urge to destroy, leaves me both fearless and bloodthirsty. I fight against the desire all day long, and retreat to the barn after nightfall, dissatisfied, hungry for it.

I wake with my stomach in knots, too tense to eat, and spend another long day shivering by the side of the road. Snow begins to fall. It will make us easier to trace when we escape, and increasingly this feels like a fool's errand.

That day passes, and then another. The snow melts, and finally something happens. A distant sound shatters the silence of the woods—a vibration at first. Boots, hitting the ground. Many of them.

The rumble of it grows, and the ground seems to tremble as they approach, until they are walking right by me—ten German soldiers and around fifty prisoners, tied together in groups of three or four. They are a ragged bunch, many limping and wounded. One of them is Henri if I'm lucky, and if he's as bad off as some, he might not survive the escape. Am I saving him or dooming him? If he died during the war, I can't change that. But if he survives…I could ruin it.

I creep through the brush alongside them, unable to distinguish one from the other through the haze of trees. A few minutes down the road, a soldier stumbles, and the men on each side—already struggling themselves—try to hold him up. It only takes a moment before a German soldier sees what's going on and shouts at them to stop. The prisoner is cut loose and my breath holds, hoping for a miracle, until he is tossed on the ground. Casually, as if lighting a cigarette or waving to a friend, the German pulls a revolver from its holster and shoots the man in the head.

My hand reaches for the gun in my pocket. *He deserves to die*, I think.

Except there are only five bullets in the chamber of my gun and there won't be time to reload before I'm caught. I should at least go to the man after the prisoners disappear. I could hold his hand, look for the name of a loved one to inform. But instead I leave him there, wondering if that makes me as empty as the soldier who shot him in the first place.

I REMAIN behind the prisoners for the rest of the day. They take only one break, during which the German soldiers mostly laze about, smoking and laughing, while the prisoners sit, dazed and thirsty, saying nothing. When the break ends, they begin again. My legs are in agony, and I have blisters I didn't notice until we stopped. How long have they gone like this? How long have they marched with their shoes falling apart, deprived of water and food? I feel like I'll barely survive a single day of it.

It's dark when they stop for the night. The prisoners are huddled together in a ditch, in groups of three or four, while the Germans cook something over a fire. The smell of it turns my stomach—tension has made it difficult to keep food down this week—but it must be torture for Henri and the others.

Eventually, half the soldiers retire, while the other five patrol the road, pointing their shotguns toward the ditch. I wait until it's late, until I'm certain all but the patrols are sound asleep, and then I creep forward, trying to get close enough that I can see the prisoners' faces in each small group. My coat catches on a bush and a soldier's head swivels, looks right toward where I stand before he resumes his watch.

How the hell am I going to save Henri when I can't move a foot without being overheard? I wait for the wind to gust before I move on to the next group, and soon a light rain begins, making it easier.

I spot someone with Henri's dark hair, his size. Hope rises in me as I creep closer, and closer. And then the hope vanishes. The man has Henri's build but not the full lips I love, not the cheekbones that rise so sharply from that square jaw, the aristocratic nose.

I begin again, angry at myself for not planning better. I have no idea what I'll do when I find him, *if* I find him. Pulling him out of the trough will wake everyone for miles.

I spy another dark head and crawl on hands and knees to get a better view.

Henri.

My heart swells at the sight of him until it feels as if my chest can hardly contain it. He's sound asleep, almost boyish at rest, despite the beard that's come in after these weeks in captivity. I can picture, looking at him, the child he was. The son we might have had.

He's in a group of three, with about four feet between them and the next group of prisoners. Three German soldiers patrol this end of the road and they'll notice someone climbing free of the ditch. I could risk it, but the days of doing things the *proper* way are long over. I'd rather kill them anyhow.

I throw my knife into a tree on the other side of the road. The nearest soldier's head gives a half turn toward the sound but ignores it. Thank God for the rain.

I close my eyes and time travel, aiming for the tree, so certain it will go poorly that I'm a little surprised when my bare feet strike the mud at its base. I grab the knife and spring toward the closest soldier. He gives only the smallest gasp as the blade slides into the back of his neck, and then he falls forward.

I've retrieved my knife and am grabbing his gun when another soldier calls out to him. I freeze for a moment, and then begin crawling toward the sound. I'm ten feet away when his flashlight sweeps over me.

There's no time for finesse or even forethought. There isn't even time for panic. I throw the knife the way I was trained, so fast it's more instinct than strategy. It lodges between his eyes, but as he falls backward into the ditch with the prisoners, he makes far more noise than I'd like.

I leap in after him, retrieving my knife and scrambling toward Henri, who is awake now and wide-eyed.

I cut through the ropes that bind him to the others and am about to speak when he pushes me down and lunges over me, tackling a third soldier I hadn't even heard coming and snapping his neck. I climb from the ditch with him on my heels, snatching up my bag and clothes as we run into the woods.

"My God, little thief," Henri says behind me. "What have you done?"

I don't answer, focused on moving as fast as possible without leaving a trail. It's only when the woods grow dense, blocking the moon and making it hard to see, that I stop to search for the flashlight.

I reach for the bag but instead he pulls me against him and his lips find mine.

He isn't gentle. He holds onto me like I might vanish at any moment, and his kiss is hard and urgent, telling me more about his anxiety and what the last weeks have been like for him than any words ever could. It's the way he kisses when he's inside me and his restraint is at its breaking point, senseless and desperate. I should stop him but I don't. I've missed this. I've missed *him*. Even now, in the panic and chaos, he fills that emptiness inside me in a way no one else ever could.

A twig snaps and we both swivel. The two prisoners he was with are coming our way, making far too much noise and breaking too many branches. They've made it easy for the Germans to follow us. And I don't want them along anyway. They mean more mouths to feed, more noise, more potential for failure. I could give them a bit of bread and tell them to go elsewhere, but they might ignore me. Or I could kill them...that would be the easiest.

Henri steps in front of me. "Put on some clothes, Sarah."

"It's pitch black. I hardly think my nudity is our biggest issue."

He looks at me over his shoulder. "It's an issue for me. Please."

I ignore the undergarments and scramble into my pants, sweater and shoes while weighing our options. I don't have enough food for the interlopers, and they'll only cause problems. The coldness that hardened me as I killed the Germans comes upon me once more. I step out from behind Henri, reaching for my knife, but there is shouting in the distance and no time for what must be done.

"Come," I command in English, turning north though I have no idea where I'm going. "And stop breaking every fucking branch."

For fifteen minutes we run, but Henri's breathing is labored and he's moving more slowly than he should. We reach a stream and I stop him.

"Are you hurt?" I ask.

I get a small, tense nod. "Just go," Henri says, in a hoarse whisper. "Please. Jump out of here."

"Tell me what's wrong," I demand.

His mouth pinches hard and he opens up his shirt. A slash along the side of his rib cage bleeds freely. "I was stabbed a few days ago. It's broken open again, but it was already infected." I stare in horror while the crashing of the underbrush grows louder.

I grab the tights I didn't put on earlier and wrap them around his rib cage as snugly as I can. It's not perfect, but it's the best I can do.

"We should walk through the stream so they lose our trail," Henri says to the other two prisoners. He turns to me. "And you need to leave. Please. If something happened to you...just please."

He looks so desperate and panicked as he asks that it would be nearly impossible to deny him. And I nod, though I have no intention of letting him do this on his own.

"Head to your left and walk as far as you can stand it," I tell him. "I'll cross into the woods on the other side and leave a trail for them to follow."

"No," he says. "You need to go."

"I will," I reply. "I'll time travel once I've gone into the woods."

I hand him the bag and with one last hard kiss, he wades into the water, the prisoners following. I step into the stream and stand in the icy water, watching him go before I climb up the muddy bank on the other side and begin crashing through the brush, swinging a flashlight so the Germans will follow.

As I run, a plan begins to form. I will lead them as far from Henri as I can and then attempt to time travel back to the stream and find him. The problem is that I've never jumped particularly far. I'm just as likely to land in the middle of the woods, naked and lost, as I am to land at the place where we separated.

When I've gone as far as I dare, I stop and wait for the Germans to close in.

Their shouts grow louder, and when the distant glow of a flashlight hits my face, I take a deep breath and picture the stream. The branches around me shake as they close in and begin to fire, but at last I fade, landing on my ass in the freezing water only a moment later. Naked and shivering, I push myself up and begin to run. The rocks are ice beneath my feet, moss covered and slick. I fall again and again, but my shins and feet are soon so numb I barely feel it.

By the time I find muddy boot prints on the bank, I'm so cold I can barely stand it. I do my best to erase the trail they've left as I follow it, branches whipping against my skin the whole way.

Fortunately, it doesn't take long to find them. They're so

exhausted, and trampling so loudly, they don't even hear me approach.

"Henri," I whisper. In the moonlight I see three astonished faces turn. None more astonished and distressed than Henri's. "Can you give me the clothes and boots inside the bag?"

He marches toward me. "You promised to go," he snaps. "You *promised*."

"I lied."

His hands land on my shoulders. "Please, Sarah," he begs. "Go. I don't want you here for this. You've done all you can."

I know he's trying to save me. I know my presence here scares him more than the threat of death. But he needs me and if he was being honest, he'd admit it. "You know I have skills that can help you."

He exhales sharply and tugs at his hair. "You won't listen no matter what I say, will you?"

His companions shuffle impatiently and I ignore them. "You can't claim you didn't know what you were in for."

His mouth twitches. "I suppose I did."

"Can you two banter later on?" asks the Brit, his words clipped. "We need to get going."

My blood heats and I smile, *hoping* he wants a fight. Hoping he plans to keep annoying me. *Give me an excuse to kill you.* "You saw how easily I took care of that soldier guarding you? Don't imagine for a moment I can't dispose of you just as easily."

His mouth closes and he turns north.

I'm disappointed that he gave in.

46

SARAH

Soon, the sky begins to lighten, but we continue to move. I haven't seen anywhere for us to stop, and I'm not sure how long the Germans will search for us before they give up. But I'm troubled by Henri's labored breathing. He barely reacted to the news that Marie is living with Edouard and pretending to be a nun, a testament to his exhaustion if I've ever seen one. My makeshift bandage isn't doing much for him, and his wound may be the part of this that is out of my hands.

At midday we stop. I pull out the bread and cheese and divide it in sixths, handing one portion to each of them and saving the remainder for tomorrow. I'm feeling too sick to eat right now and they need the food more than I do, but eventually it's going to be an issue, trying to feed four people on what I brought for two.

"I assume the *rest* of that food is just for you?" Price asks.

Henri's eyes were growing heavy, but they flicker with fire suddenly. "Watch yourself," he growls. "She saved your miserable life, but I'd be happy to end it if your attitude doesn't improve."

IT'S NEARLY dusk when we finally come upon a deserted homestead. Whether we can afford to stop or not, we have to. I'm worried Henri will collapse soon if we don't. He is stumbling now, his skin almost ashen.

"We'll stay here for the night," I tell them.

Henri looks at me with heavy eyes and nods. "We should sleep in the barn, though. If the Germans come, they'll search the house first. It will give us a small advantage."

"You *killed* people," says Price. As if I killed *good* people. As if we aren't in the middle of a fucking war and I didn't save him from a work camp and certain death. "They aren't going to just ignore it. We need to keep moving."

"Feel free to keep moving," I reply. "I'd prefer it if you did." That goes for both of them. Quinn's unwarranted self-confidence is nearly as annoying as Price's sense of entitlement. The only *smart* thing I've seen him do yet is steal the German's canteen.

Henri and I walk into the barn and when he lowers himself into the hay, his whole body seems to sag, his eyes sunken with fatigue. He needs so many things I'm not sure where to start. I turn to Price and Quinn. "Can you see what's in the house? I need alcohol to clean the wound."

"Or you need a head start to get away from us," says Price.

I'm about to reply when Quinn grabs him. "Even *I've* had about enough of your mouth. Come on."

They leave and I start to pull off Henri's boots but he reaches for me. "Come here."

I go to him. "What is it? Are you in pain?"

He tugs me toward him and presses his lips to the top of my head as he pulls me to his chest. "My sweet, insane girl," he murmurs. "You could have died."

His eyes close, as if the act of talking is too much for him. I pull away and grab the penicillin from the bag. Henri doesn't even seem to notice the needle as it enters his skin.

Quinn walks in and throws me a dress. "To bandage the wound," he says, taking a heavy drink from the bottle in his hand.

"I'll take the alcohol too," I tell him, reaching up for it.

He hands it over, nearly emptied. Henri is obviously in pain and the selfish bastard only saved enough for me to clean his wounds, nothing more. "You worthless piece of shit," I mutter. "You could have left some."

"Henri, I pictured you with a refined little lady," Quinn says. "This one has quite the mouth on her."

Henri gives a quiet laugh, and then flinches. "Yes," he says, "that was my first impression as well."

Quinn and Price retreat to the loft and I make Henri lie down on a makeshift bed of hay and the single blanket. Using the dregs of the alcohol, I do my best to clean the wound and dress it with strips of fabric.

"How do you feel?" I whisper.

"Lucky," he says. "And scared."

"Scared of what?"

He forces his eyes open and pushes the hair back from my face. "If I die—"

I shake my head. "You're not going to die. Once the antibiotic kicks in—"

His eyes close. "Sarah," he says quietly, "you know how this works. If this is when I'm supposed to die, nothing you're doing will matter. If that happens, swear to me you'll go with the children and stay gone. A promise you actually keep."

I curl up beside him and press my nose to his neck. He smells of soap and hay and sweat and the combination reminds me of a thousand other times I spent with him in the barn. "I swear."

And this time I mean it. Except if he dies, I'm not sure how I will possibly go on.

∾

THE NEXT TIME my eyes open, it's daylight, and our bag is gone. So are Quinn and Price.

They have everything we need aside from my knife—our food, Henri's penicillin, our money. Everything.

They fucked with the wrong girl.

"What is it?" asks Henri, groggy, struggling to open his eyes. Do I dare leave him here while I go back in time to take care of this? What if he's found while I'm gone? I flinch at the idea, but then again, I can't defend him here without that bag.

"Nothing," I reply. "I have to go take care of something."

Just then I hear whistling. Obnoxious, *brash* whistling. Quinn walks into the barn and sets the bag down beside me

"Where did you go?" I ask.

"I caught him with your stuff about a quarter mile from here. Bastard offered to split it with me."

My hands are shaking. Price deserves to die, and it would be so easy. So unbelievably easy, if I time traveled to earlier in the morning.

"What is it?" asks Henri, sitting up and wrapping his arm around me.

"He deserves to die," I reply between my teeth. "He should die for taking that bag."

Henri looks at me for a long moment, studying my face. "He'll likely die anyway," he says. "He's got no food, no weapon, no money."

I pull my knees to my chest, taking deep breaths. "He deserves to die *painfully*."

"Little thief," Henri says against my ear. "We need to go. Killing him doesn't move us forward."

And I know he's right. But the desire still burns in my chest. The Coron in me is getting stronger. It feels like it's overtaking everything I am.

～

AFTER ANOTHER NEAR-SILENT day of travel, we find shelter, though the home is in such disrepair it's hardly better than sleeping in the open. Henri cleans up at the pump, already much better than he was yesterday, and returns without his shirt. Despite his wound, the sight of him like that is as appealing as it ever was—miles of smooth, tan skin, all muscle. My core clenches in response, but right now, he needs a good night's rest.

"Lie down," I say. I give him the shot of penicillin and then start putting a clean dressing on his wound. While I work, he asks the questions he was too tired to ask the night before, and I finally tell him about the worthless forgeries Roche provided.

"He'll pay for that," Henri says. "As soon as I'm back home."

Home. My hands still before they resume their work. I'm not sure we *can* go back to Saint Antoine after what I've done. Claudette will never know for certain that I cut off her finger, but she might guess at it, and my sudden disappearance on the heels of Nadeau's death will be suspicious. At the time it all seemed so necessary, so well-deserved, and it still does, but in both Saint Antoine and Paris, people may now be looking for me. Every bad thing I do seems to have a ripple effect.

"What's the matter?" he asks.

I swallow. "Nothing. I tear one last strip. "I'm nearly done. I think your wound is looking better."

"Do you remember when you did this before?"

I laugh. "Last night? Yes, I remember it well."

He presses my hand to his chest and holds it there. "No, not then. In Saint Antoine. When you bandaged my gunshot wound. Do you remember? I wanted you so badly it felt like a fever."

"You *did* have a fever," I reply with a small laugh, tying the last strip around his rib cage.

"That might be," he says, "but I was hard the whole time." He wraps a hand around my neck and pulls his lips to mine. A kiss that is clearly meant to lead to more. And God knows I'd like it to, except I don't want him to tear his wound open again, and Quinn is across the room.

I pull away, wanting him so much it's painful, and go to the pump to wash up. *He's injured,* I say to myself on repeat. *He needs to rest.* When I return to the house, Henri appears to be asleep. I sneak in quietly and lie down beside him, relieved and disappointed at once. His arm urges me closer. "I need you," he whispers.

"You should rest," I argue, but he's already tugging at my pants.

"I'll rest when I'm dead," he says.

He pulls me on top of him. Even wounded and starved as he's been, his strength amazes me. His hands go to the button of his trousers and he pops it open. "Please, little thief. I've dreamed of you every night since I left."

I pull the trousers down low enough for him to spring clear of them, while his hand slides between my legs. When he finds me bare there, free of my undergarments and ready for him so soon, he groans. "My God, I've missed this."

He lines himself up and grabs my hips. I try to resist, to go slowly and he makes a noise of exasperation.

"Don't be gentle, Sarah," he says. His fingers dig into my hips, lifting me, pushing me back down, doing the work for me. "Please. I've dreamed of this for too long."

I take over, trying to maintain some sense of sanity despite the desperate press of his fingers and the fullness inside me. It's only been two months, but it feels like a lifetime.

"Faster," he grunts, the boards beneath us squeaking loudly.

"Quinn will know," I whisper.

"And he'll know several times more tonight," he says with a sound that is half laughter and half groan. "Come closer. I want to see your face when you let go." He pulls me down, pressing his teeth into my shoulder, buried to the hilt, and I stop trying to be gentle. I ride him as if he is here only for my pleasure, to use as I wish, and in seconds I feel it coming, my stomach tightening, my heart hammering.

"Yes," he hisses. "That's it."

I gasp, my head going backward, eyes squeezed shut. His hips lift, chasing mine, and then his hands pull me hard against him as he comes with a low, sustained groan. I collapse on top of him, resting just for a moment before I start to pull away.

He grabs my hips once more. "Stay. Just for a moment. Stay."

I lean over him, careful to avoid his side, and he presses his lips to my forehead. "My beautiful, insane girl," he whispers. "Of everything I've suffered and witnessed over the past two months, being apart from you was the hardest."

I listen to his steadily beating heart, torn between two contradictory emotions: so full of love for him I could weep, and so terrified of losing him that I feel violent and desperate in response. I need to tell him what I did. *But not now*, I think. *Just let me enjoy this while I can.*

I don't realize I've fallen asleep until many hours later, when Henri shifts against me, hard as stone. "We'll perhaps need to find you undergarments tomorrow," he whispers. "It might help."

I laugh. "Yes, our first job, before we find food."

He rolls on top of me, pushing the sweater around my waist. "If you're awake enough to make jokes," he says, sliding inside me, "you're awake enough for this."

WE RISE at first light and begin moving north once more, following the road at a distance. My spine prickles and I look over my shoulder.

"What is it?" Henri asks.

"I...do you think someone could be following us?"

He gives a short laugh. "I think many someones are following us."

"No," I whisper. "One person, on foot. Watching us."

He frowns. "It's natural to feel that way, under the circumstances. But an armed person would already have acted. An *unarmed* person would die if he attempted anything."

I know he's right, but I still feel it for hours—that unsettling nudge at my back. It reminds me of the time traveler I encountered during those last visits to my own time, her eyes on me as if she was just waiting to strike.

The sensation abates after a few hours, and by the tail end of dusk, when we find another abandoned farm, I've almost forgotten it entirely.

We eat another insufficient meal, and then Henri goes to the woods to set traps while I enter the house, scouting for things we can take with us. The closet is full of dresses, but what I want most is the mattress—a week of sleeping on hay and the bare ground has taken its toll. I tug it down the stairs and drag it outside.

"That's for the best," says Quinn. He's leaning against a wall, whittling. A useless endeavor if I've ever seen one. "If I have to spend one more night listening to the squeaking boards while you and Henri make whoopie I'm going to put a gun to my head."

"Now there's a thought," I grunt, struggling with the weight. It's filled with goose down and spectacularly heavy, but he doesn't offer to help, naturally.

"You really don't like me, do you?"

I let the mattress fall, suddenly exhausted. Within a day, we'll have parted ways. Once we reach Clermont-Ferrand, Henri and I head north for Nanterre while Quinn will turn toward the Pyrenees. It can't come soon enough. "I have no feelings about you either way, aside from the fact that you are one more mouth to feed and one more person to defend while I try to save my husband."

He raises a brow. "You make me sound like a child who can't

take care of himself. Has it ever occurred to you I might be of some help if there's a fight?"

"No," I reply. "I can honestly say that's never occurred to me. Which reminds me: Henri and I are staying here to rest an extra day, so if you want to head out on your own, feel free."

We're near the Occupied Zone, and once inside it, we will need to move fast. I want to be certain Henri is sufficiently recovered before we go, though if his stamina last night was any indication, he'll be just fine.

Quinn shrugs. "Sure, I can rest," he says. I roll my eyes as I turn away. I was really hoping we'd get a day here without him.

Henri is just returning from the woods, so I cross the yard to him. He nods at the mattress. "Are we moving in, then?"

"We could use a good night's sleep."

His eyes rake over me. "I'd like a soft mattress as much as you, though for very different reasons."

I shake my head, hiding a smile. We are in a terrible situation —walking across the country, in danger, separated from our family—and yet simply because he's here, I'm happy.

"What reasons would those be?" I ask.

He pulls me toward him. "Let's go get the mattress," he says, "and I'll show you every one of them."

I WAKE in the middle of the night and stare at the moon through the open beams of the roof. Between the blanket and Henri's warmth, it's cozy here. But it eats at me, the things I haven't told him.

I don't realize he's awake until his mouth brushes my temple. "What's troubling you, Sarah?" he asks. "I can sense it, you know, when you're keeping things to yourself."

I roll toward him. He's going to learn it all eventually. It may as well be now. "Marie wanted me to go see Yvette when I was in Paris, so I did."

"*Yvette?*" he asks. "Why?" There is incredulity in his tone, and I don't blame him. When I say it aloud, it sounds insane to me too.

"She...was sleeping with some high-ranking German and Marie thought she might help us get papers, at least for Cecelia. But she wouldn't. She got mad when Cece wouldn't stay with her and called the guards on us both."

"You killed her?" he asks softly.

I nod, my breath holding as I wait for some sign of disgust or condemnation. Instead he pushes my hair from my face and his palm rests there, against my jaw. "You didn't think I'd blame you for that, did you?"

"She's not the only person I killed," I whisper.

He tugs me even closer. "It won't matter. There is nothing you can say that will change how I feel. So tell me."

My hand curls into a fist against his chest as I begin. I tell him about Cece's illness, Nadeau's threat, Claudette's attack...and what I did in response.

Slowly, as I speak, he unfurls my fingers and rests his own hand over mine.

"I should never have left you alone," he says when I conclude. "I put you in that position, leaving you the way I did."

I shake my head. "It's something inside me, Henri. It grows a little more every time I hurt someone, like a weed. I'm worried it's going to take over."

I want him to tell me that's not the case. I want him to tell me what I feel is normal and will go away. But for the first time, he doesn't try to reassure me.

"Can you stop?" he asks. It's an honest question—not a suggestion, not a reprimand. "Can you just let me defend you instead?"

"I'll try," I tell him. I wonder if he doubts me as much as I doubt myself.

I RISE in the morning and walk into the house, hoping to get clean clothes before I wash off. And hear a single footstep somewhere behind the kitchen.

"Show yourself," I announce, reaching for the gun tucked in my waistband. "Or die."

The steps are light, unhurried, as they approach, and then a child walks into the room. She's young—maybe eleven or twelve—and wearing clothes I recognize from the room upstairs. Her eyes lift to mine...and I take a shocked step backward. She has the eyes of a time traveler—green eyes, like Henri's—and then a brilliant, sweet smile lights up her whole face.

"Who are you?" I demand.

Her mouth opens and then closes, uncertain. "I'm not sure I'm supposed to tell you. *Am I* supposed to tell you?"

I lower the gun. "You must be...Marie's child?"

She laughs. "Mom, it's *me*," she says in English, without a trace of an accent. "Quinn."

I blink several times, wondering if I've heard her correctly. So much is wrong here. She called me *mom*. And she is definitely not Cecelia or Charlotte. And if I did have a child, why the hell would I name her Quinn?

"*What?*" I ask, but already I'm seeing it: I see Henri in her, and also myself. She has his thick hair, his olive skin, his green eyes, but with my bone structure and build. She's as much a product of the two of us as any child could be.

"How is this possible?" I whisper.

"Well, you showed me all these places when we came last summer and I wanted to see what happened so..." she trails off, and her eyes grow wary. "Are you mad?"

I shake my head, still trying to understand how she could possibly exist. And then I begin to put things together: the way certain smells have been making me gag, the constant rolling of my stomach. The fatigue. How have I not realized until now?

I'm pregnant.

I've been pregnant since Henri left Saint Antoine, and the girl who stands before me is the result.

She's still waiting, wondering if I'm mad, when I don't understand how she possibly managed to arrive in the first place.

"But how did you get *here*?" I ask.

She shrugs. "I jumped. Last summer you showed me some of the places you stayed. I jumped to one of them, but you were leaving."

"My God," I whisper, pressing my hands to my face. "You've been following us all this time?"

She shakes her head vigorously. "Just a little while yesterday but I had to go home."

"Home? You live here? Outside Lyon?"

Her head tips to the side, as if she doesn't understand what I'm asking. "No, we live in Virginia."

"Virginia," I repeat. To go back to a specific date, to a specific place on the other side of the world with almost no landmarks to guide you...the skill it would take to orchestrate it is almost unthinkable. "Are you saying you time traveled all the way from Virginia and managed to land *here*?"

She nods, looking a little uncertain. "You always tell me the story about the soldier and I wanted to see him."

I feel the air whistling through my lungs. "What soldier?" I whisper.

"Henri, the one who fights off all the Nazis." Her face grows wary. "I always thought maybe he was...my dad? I just wanted to see him. I wasn't going to talk to him."

The shock nearly sends me to my knees. She's saying she's

never met her father. And I can only think of one reason why that would be the case.

I take a deep breath, trying to focus, trying not to fall apart in front of this girl who says she's mine. Who *must* be mine. Even standing here I feel a connection to her, as if something has us tethered. I want to ask her so many questions—*What happened to Henri? Are the rest of the children okay?* But she is too young for all that, too young even to realize how her simple visit could thrill me and break my heart all at the same time, and that she's endangered herself by coming at all. Only moments ago, I was ready to kill her myself.

I grab her hand. "It's not safe here, so I need you to swear to me you'll go home and that you will never come here without telling me again. Do you swear it?"

She nods. "But...my dad is the tall one, isn't he? The one with eyes like mine?"

I feel the sting of tears and nod quickly. "Go now, okay?"

She throws her arms around me. "See you at dinner," she says, pulling away with a wide, fearless grin, so like her father's. She closes her eyes, and just as quickly, she's gone. Leaving me so stunned I can't even remember why I came into the house.

She time traveled over an *ocean*. How is that possible? Marie has a talent, like I do, but nothing along the lines of what I just witnessed.

Suddenly I recall Madame Durand, reciting the prophecy to me so long ago: *In France there will be a hidden child, born of the first family, conceived during a great war and born on the other side of it.*

This will be a child born of *two* first families, conceived during a great war, but not born on the other side, unless...

Unless I chose to go to my own time to have her. If she's the hidden child, nothing could be safer than hiding her five decades into the future, could it?

But no. I would never leave Henri and the children. Let someone else be the hidden child. It does not have to be her.

I walk back to the barn and lie down next to Henri, who is still sound asleep. I curl up against him as if I can somehow cement us together. I wish I'd asked if he was alive when she was born. Because if he wasn't, it means we have less than six months left.

He rouses. "Well, hello there," he says. I start to pull away, but he holds onto me. "Not so fast."

"I need to check your wound."

"And I need to enjoy the feeling of you wrapped around me like a blanket."

"Fine, but no more sex."

He laughs. "Not even married yet and you're already denying me."

It hits me all over again: I am *pregnant*. I want to tell Henri, but...it would also mean telling him he will not know his daughter. It means telling him he might die in the next few months.

"I'm not feeling well," I whisper, and then I press my face to his chest and begin to cry. I don't want to be part of the prophecy. I don't want to be the mother of the hidden child. I just want Henri and our life, and even now—as he swears to me everything will be fine—I suspect I'm not going to get it.

IN THE AFTERNOON, Henri goes out to check the traps. "Perhaps you'll eat if I can find you something other than meat in a tin," he says.

I bite down hard on my lip, watching him walk away. Going off into the woods is a risk, and so is building a fire to cook the meat. I should tell him about the baby, but this is a perfect example of why I'm reluctant to do so. He'll take risks he shouldn't, and he'll coddle me in ways that are unnecessary. Most of all, I'm worried he'll ask me to leave, because this is a terrible time and place to give birth. Even finding a doctor will be an issue, and what if she comes early like Cecelia did?

I return to the house, looking for anything that might prove useful for the last leg of our trip, and find myself facing a mirror in the bedroom upstairs. Now that I know I'm pregnant, I'm not sure how I could have failed to see it. My face has changed, and so has my body. I turn to the side and pull up my shirt just enough to see that the perfectly flat plane of my stomach, the one I've had all my life, has disappeared. It won't be long until Henri sees it too.

"Well, well, well," says a voice. I let the shirt drop and round on Quinn. Why the hell I would name any child after *him* is beyond me.

"I didn't think you were *capable* of sneaking up on people," I snap.

"When the occasion calls for it, I manage." He glances at my stomach, his mouth set in a grim line. "So whose is it?"

"I don't know what you're talking about."

"A woman doesn't stare at her stomach in the mirror the way you just did unless she's looking for one particular thing. Is it his or not?"

I glare at him. "Don't be an idiot. Of course it is. You really think I'd risk my life trying to save someone I'd been cheating on?"

His arms fold. "Then why doesn't he know?"

"Because I just found out myself," I snap. "And because it will complicate things. I'll tell him when we get to—"

The purr of vehicles approaching silences me. Quinn and I stare at each other, our constant animosity gone for once, and rush down the stairs.

"Two vehicles," he says, peering out the window. "Six soldiers. With at least one machine gun."

I pull my gun out of my waistband, a quiet, ugly thrill in my veins. I know I told Henri I'd try to stop, but this is different. "I'll go around the back of the house and shoot from the side. You go to the window."

He grabs my arm. "Are you nuts? They turn that machine gun on you and it's over. Do you not even care about the baby?"

I should, but the desire for revenge is humming in my blood, louder than any other sound. "We can do this," I hiss. "I can get the three in back, you take the three in front."

He shakes his head. "No. Just run. I'll surrender and tell them I'm alone. Maybe it'll give you enough time."

I blink. Since we met, I've seen him do little that isn't selfish or boorish. But here he is, unexpectedly noble. I don't understand. "Why would you do that for us?"

"Henri is a good man," he says, and for the first time he seems like the adult he might be one day—decent and responsible. "He deserves to know his child."

He walks out before I can stop him. His hands are up. *I can reverse this*, I think. *I can still save him.* And then the soldier with the machine gun rises and begins to fire. I watch as Quinn falls to the ground.

It feels as if it lasts a very long time, but in truth it's probably only a second before my shock morphs into dark rage. I should care that I'm pregnant, that what I'm doing is suicidal, but making them pay...it surpasses everything else.

I run out the door behind the kitchen with one gun, hoping to kill the three in back before they realize where the bullets came from.

I slide along the wall, and once I'm close enough, I take aim. I'm almost calm, empty, as I open fire. The first soldier falls, and then the second. The third swings toward me and falls...but the bullet isn't mine.

Henri, just on the periphery of the woods, has begun to fire. And it feels as if the world is falling apart as they turn toward him, rather than me. It was different when it was just my life at stake, or even mine and Quinn's. But now it's Henri's, and all my confidence and rage abandons me in a sudden rush of panic.

The soldier who holds off the Nazis, our daughter said.

Is it *this*? Is it because of me? The questions and the fear flood my brain and it's impossible to think clearly. Had I listened to Quinn, had I not given into my hideous anger, this wouldn't be happening.

The machine gun is directed at Henri, and even the tree he stands behind won't protect him for long. Somehow I manage to shake off my terror and jump to the house, grabbing the weapon Quinn left behind. I aim at the soldier with the machine gun and strike him in the head, but his gun swings wildly as he falls, and a bullet comes through the window a foot from me. I dive, and when I stand again, I see Henri, coming at the remaining soldier at a run.

Once again I'm paralyzed, unable to think, unable to fire. I watch as the soldier turns toward him, takes aim.

Henri lands in the jeep, on top of him. The gun explodes and then they are both still.

I freeze. *I can't stand it if he's dead*, I think. *I won't be able to survive it.*

Another shot is fired, and then...a miracle. Henri lifts himself off the soldier, and his eyes go to me, standing in the doorway, naked and stiff with shock. He climbs from the jeep and crosses the yard, pulling me tight. My knees buckle with relief.

He pulls away just enough that I can see the fury in his face, and the fear behind it. "You could have died. Why didn't you leave?"

Why didn't I? I could have stopped Quinn and time traveled back a few hours to warn us what was coming. Quinn is dead because I made the wrong choice. Because I wanted to kill more than I wanted us all to live.

I lean my head against his chest. "I wanted to kill them," I admit. "And now Quinn is dead. He surrendered and I just watched him go. I should have stopped him."

"This makes no sense," he whispers. "Why didn't he fight? It isn't like him just to give up."

My chest tightens with regret and sorrow. Henri's right. It wasn't like Quinn to just give up, but he was willing to make sacrifices for my family even I wasn't willing to make.

"He did it for you," I whisper. "You and our child. He thought he was buying us time to get away."

He stills. "Child?" he asks. "I never told anyone about Cecelia."

"Not Cecelia," I say gently, looking up at him. "*Our* child. I'm pregnant. I figured it out this morning and he figured it out right after I did."

"Pregnant," he repeats, his eyes alight, but wary at the same time. "You're certain? Because I thought the doctors said it wasn't possible."

"They said it was unlikely," I amend. "And I'm very sure, because I met her."

He blinks. "What? You mean, in the future?"

I shake my head. "Here. *Today*. Henri, she crossed an ocean to get here and her powers were...extraordinary. I think she may be the child mentioned in the prophecy."

His jaw falls open. "*Conceived during a great war and born in its shadow*," he recites. "But it's not possible. This war will continue for years."

"For some reason, I must jump forward," I reply, and then my head hangs. I don't want to tell him the rest.

He uses his index finger to tip my chin up, and then he studies my face. "What is it?" he asks.

"She was here to see you," I tell him, looking at the ground once more. "She said you'd never met."

I feel him stiffen, and then, slowly, his hand cups my jaw, forcing me to meet his eye. "And that's why you wept this morning?" he asks. When I nod, he presses his lips to my forehead. "Nothing is set in stone, little thief. Maybe there's another way."

I nod, swallowing hard to keep from crying and praying he's right.

"But this changes everything, Sarah," he continues. "You've *got* to protect our child and leave the rest to me until she's born. You've got to escape dangerous situations instead of staying behind to fight."

Quinn's body rests twenty feet ahead. He lies at an awkward angle, impossibly still for a man who was so very alive a few minutes before. I cross the distance and pull his dog tags up to the light.

Michael Robert Quinn. Waco, Texas.

He had no reason to sacrifice himself for us, but he did, and it's time for me to give things up too. That ugly part of me has to be set aside so I can bring this child into the world and keep her safe.

I understand now why I named her after him. Not just because he sacrificed himself for us, but so I'll always be reminded of what happens when I give in to the dark.

47

SARAH

Over the next week, as we head to Nanterre, we come to terms with our news. We have to stay quiet during the day, but at night we discuss the future—what it means that this child is the product of two first families. I tell him about the time traveler I saw lurking during my last visit to 1989, and we come to the same conclusion—there's no assurance that our child will be safe, regardless of the decades she's raised in.

He insists on taking more breaks than I need and coddles me as if I'm fragile, but I don't really mind. Our time together feels more precious than it ever has. No matter what we tell ourselves, we both know it may end soon.

On our final night together, there is no shelter to be found—not a safe one anyway. We make a bed of leaves and then lie down with the blanket pulled around us and his arm beneath my head. It's still cold out, but growing warmer now, with the barest hint of spring on the way. And all I can think is that by the time it gets cold again, I may be gone.

"I'm probably due in October," I whisper.

"I can't imagine a life without you, little thief," he says, reading into my words and my sudden melancholy. "I refuse to believe that's what's in store for us."

"You once said something about the island." I glance away, as tears threaten. "About being reunited there. Do you think there's a chance it's true?"

He's quiet for a moment. "I'm a practical man," he finally replies. "I struggle to believe in the concept of heaven, and the island sounds, to me, like another version of that."

I suppose I mostly feel the same way. I just wanted him to convince me otherwise. I wanted him to convince me there was time.

IT's afternoon when we finally crest the hill and see Chateau de Nanterre. My stomach drops at the sight—it's mostly rubble, destroyed either by time or German bombs.

Henri, who's been tense all day and trying to restrain his fury about Marie and Edouard's predicament, stiffens in a way that does not bode well.

"They can't be living here," I whisper, squeezing his hand. "There must be an explanation."

"I hope for my sister's sake it's a very good one," Henri growls.

We proceed down the hill. The grounds are surrounded by a twenty-foot wrought iron fence with spiked posts and the gate is locked.

"I'll just time travel to unlock it," I suggest.

His eyes flicker with anxiety. "What about the baby? What happened to Marie—"

"Won't happen here," I say softly, squeezing his hand. "I've been time traveling throughout this pregnancy, and this child's abilities surpass all of ours, remember?"

Before he can argue further, I fade and land on the other side.

He raises a brow at me. "Just keep in mind that you're supposed to avoid time travel for the next six months."

I grab the bars of the fence and smile at him. "I thought I'd mostly agreed to stop killing people."

I unlock the gate and, once I'm dressed, he takes my hand and we proceed down the long gravel path. The grounds are overgrown but flourishing in the March air—rose bushes budding, tulips already springing up in the beds along the exterior.

The remains of the chateau hardly look stable, so we head to the back. Crawling through a break in the eight-foot hedge, we emerge to a wonderland on the other side—a reflecting pool and long yard with cottages along its periphery and woods behind them. In the grass, at least twenty children stand frozen, staring at us in shock.

One small figure breaks from the group and barrels toward us —Charlotte, brown curls flying around her joyful little face. "Mama!" she cries, throwing herself into my arms. I kneel in the gravel and pull her close, breathing in her smell of soap and grass and sunshine.

Tears spring to my eyes. It's only now, now that we've finally gotten home to them, that I recognize the empty space that's been inside me since I left. Lucien runs next and then the four of us are on the ground, entwined.

"Please don't go away again," whispers Charlotte against my ear. My chest squeezes tight at her solemn, tear-stained face. She already lost one mother and spent the last several weeks worried she'd lost another. I wish I hadn't put her through that.

"I hope I never have to," I tell her, turning my head to see Cecelia toddling forward, led by Marie.

"Mamamamama," she cries when she's close enough to see my face, releasing Marie's hand and running on chubby little legs, her arms outstretched. She lands with a thud against me, wrapping her arms around my neck and scrambling into my lap with such force that she knocks me flat on my back. I lie on the ground, laughing while her arms squeeze me tight, until Henri lifts her up and turns to face his sister for the first time since he left to go fight.

Marie no longer wears a nun's habit and is flourishing in the early-spring air. Her eyes glow, her cheeks are rosy, and she is smiling widely.

And he looks torn. He loves his sister and a part of him is clearly relieved to find her safe here. But there's something else going on with him, a tension I've seen in him ever since last winter, whenever her name has come up.

I rise and nod toward the children playing in the grass. "None of them would be here were it not for what Edouard and Marie did," I remind him softly.

"It's true," says Marie. "You can't blame me, under the circumstances? And we'll be married as soon as he's defrocked."

His jaw grinds. "You think this is about the fact that you're not married?" he asks incredulously. "What about the fact that Amelie nearly died for your sake and you repaid her by abandoning her in Saint Antoine? She and Cecelia could be safely away in England right now if it weren't for you."

And there it is, the real source of his distress. He just wishes a few of us were safe.

Marie's smile fades. "You left her alone in Saint Antoine too, did you not? Don't hold what I did against me when you *also* did it twice."

I see Edouard approaching, out of his priest attire, and for once it's me who keeps a level head. "No one knew what was coming," I say quickly, "and it all worked out for the best." This child that grows inside me is there because I stayed. If we'd made it to England, none of this would have happened.

I feel his urge to argue, and then it releases as his lips brush over my hair. "You're right. Our family is perfect just as it is."

He and Edouard shake hands, both of them tense. I think they'll be friends in time, which is good, because they have more in common than they know. I've been piecing it together—that glow to Marie, the flush of her cheeks.

I'm not the only one here who's pregnant.

THE CHATEAU BELONGS to Genevieve Lepin, one of the country's wealthiest women and—ostensibly—a Nazi sympathizer. Her mansion in Paris is at the heart of wartime society, a salon for German officers to mingle with the city's prettiest girls while drinking its best liquor and dining on foie gras, which gives Genevieve many privileges most French citizens don't have. One of those privileges is that her property is left alone, and I'll admit that a bombed-out, gated off home makes a good hiding place for the time being. While the ten cottages that sit on the periphery of the rolling green lawn are a bit rudimentary, they provide room enough for everyone—twenty children, plus Marta and Rachel, two Jews who fled from Germany to France—and in the one section of the house that remains standing there are two baths and part of a kitchen. Genevieve is still trying to help them get papers for all the children, but in the meantime it seems as good a solution as any.

Marie shows me to the cottage Henri and I will share with Charlotte, Lucien and Cecelia—it's a single large room with a curtain used to partition off the beds—a double for me and Henri, and another large bed for the three children.

"So it seems we're both pregnant," I say, turning to face her.

Her eyes go wide. "But I thought—" she begins.

I shrug. "I thought so too. I don't understand it. But...I've met her. She visited us when we were on our way here."

Marie sinks onto a bed. "A time traveler then," she says.

I hesitate. For the past two years, Marie has believed—as we did—that she was the hidden child of the prophecy. I never got the feeling that it mattered to her, but I can't swear that it *didn't* matter either.

"I think it's more than that," I reply. I explain about learning that I'm from one of the first families, and then witnessing our daughter's powers firsthand. "I think she may be the hidden child," I conclude.

Her jaw falls open as I speak, and when I'm done, she buries her face in her hands and begins to cry. I'd thought she might be disappointed, at most, but I never expected this. "I'm sorry," I whisper, placing my hand on her shoulder. "Nothing is certain...I had no idea you'd be so upset."

She raises her tearstained face to mine and laughs. "I'm not upset," she says. "I'm relieved. All this time I've been thinking the child I lost might have been the circle of light or whatever it is, and that I ruined it. The prophecy my mother died for, that *we* nearly died for." She wipes her eyes. "What you're telling me means I haven't ruined anything at all."

Poor Marie, carrying so much guilt for no reason. "I'm sorry you ever thought it," I tell her.

She steps back, frowning again. "But if the war isn't ending for years still, does it mean you'll go forward in time to have her?"

"I don't know," I admit. "We haven't decided."

Her hand grasps mine. "I'm sorry the responsibility has been placed on your shoulders," she says. "But so many people have lost their lives or their loved ones in order for this to happen. If you're truly having the hidden child and you're supposed to go forward, I hope you'll think it through."

THAT NIGHT, we put the children to bed and then retreat to our own.

"I told Marie about the baby," I whisper, pressing close to him. "She seems to think it's my duty to go home to have her."

He stiffens. "How convenient for her to suddenly preach to you about duty while she sleeps with a priest."

"Henri," I chide, "she was just being honest."

"If she wants honesty," he growls, "I'll have plenty for her and Edouard in turn."

I shouldn't have brought it up. He's mostly made up with Marie, but if he thinks she's pressuring me to leave, his anger will ignite once more.

My palm presses to the side of his face and I tip my head just enough to press my lips to his.

"If you're trying to use sex to distract me," he says, pulling me closer, "you'll probably succeed."

I laugh. "We can't have sex here," I whisper. "Until the war ends, we may never have sex again."

"Of course we will," he says, sliding down the bed. "You'll just need to learn to be quiet." He lifts my nightgown up and spreads my legs.

"Oh, I'm the one who makes too much noise?" I ask drily, pushing up on my forearms.

He grins. "Shall I prove it to you?" His tongue darts between my legs, over me and then in me and I gasp, holding the pillow over my face.

"Fine," I whisper. "It's me. Keep going. I'll learn to be quiet."

48

SARAH

Spring arrives. We fall into a routine, and our days are busy but happy. Food is scarce—mostly tinned food sent by Genevieve, augmented by what Henri and Edouard manage to trap in the woods—but there are luxuries that come our way occasionally. Flour, sugar, chocolate, fresh fruit. It certainly doesn't feel as if we're suffering.

All the adults take turns teaching, though our cumulative knowledge is less useful than we'd like, and nights are spent sitting at the long table Henri and Edouard built. The children eat with us and then play until it's dark, making our time here feel, in some ways, like an extended vacation, albeit it one with terrible food and cramped accommodations.

Tonight, before dinner is even over, Cecelia grows tired and climbs over Charlotte's lap to reach me, yawning as she rests her head against my chest.

Charlotte plugs her nose. "She needs a diaper change."

I start to rise, but Henri takes her from me. "I'll get it," he says. "You sit. You've been on your feet all day."

Rachel's eldest, a twelve-year old named Daniel, frowns. "I'm never going to change a diaper."

"When we get married," Charlotte informs him, "you will need to help."

Henri makes a sound that is either laughter or choking, perhaps a little of both.

"You're six years younger than me," says Daniel, flushing. "I can't marry you."

"When I'm eighteen, you will be twenty-four," she informs him. "And it won't seem like so great a difference."

"Charlotte will be a beauty one day," Marie says later, after the children are in bed, "and Daniel will wish he hadn't been quite so dismissive."

I squeeze Henri's hand. "You'll have to beat back so many boys who come for Charlotte and Cecelia both."

"So you've decided to go forward after the war to have your child?" asks Marie. Her voice is so hopeful and grateful it makes me wince.

"No, she hasn't," Henri snaps. "We don't even know that this is the hidden child she carries."

"Of course it is!" cries Marie. "What are the odds that two of the four first families would come together to produce a child?"

"If Sarah can get pregnant once, she can get pregnant again," Henri says, staring hard at the table, apparently ignoring the fact that it was our daughter herself who told me she'd never met him. "And we don't owe it to anyone to keep the child in another time."

Marie's jaw drops. "Henri, be reasonable. This is about more than the two of you. It's about more than any of us. Have we not seen firsthand how much harm a powerful time traveler can do?"

Henri's nostrils flare. "Who, Coron? He wasn't a time traveler."

"You're right," she snaps. "But imagine how much worse it could have been if he were. Imagine a powerful time traveler with bad intentions—or even a *family* of time travelers. They would be undefeatable if they wanted something. If they fail, they can just keep going back."

"You're speaking in hypotheticals," says Henri. "I'm talking about the flesh-and-blood woman I love." He's so resistant to the idea he can't think clearly, and I suppose I am too. Even if it was only four more years, that's four years without Henri. Cece would be six when she caught up with me, Lucien, seven, Charlotte, ten. And if I have to return to my own time, it would be so much longer. I'd need to wait until our child was eighteen before I returned to them. They'd all be adults by then. Adults who barely remember me.

"I'm sorry," Marie says. "I'm not trying to ruin these months for you. I hate that this may mean Amelie is leaving. But...what's being asked of her is a gift. Don't you see? Anyone, anywhere in the future could appear and take this away from us. They could go back to kill us as children and even remove the times we've already had. With this child coming, I understand now why our mother hated that so much. I wouldn't want to be in Amelie's position, but if I were, I know what I would do."

"The prophecy is a *prediction*," Henri says. "If the child is supposed to be hidden, it should happen naturally, because circumstances dictate it. Not because we followed what it said like a play book."

He's right. And yet, when I think of all the people who died or suffered, hoping to bring this to fruition...a part of me thinks I owe it to all of them to do this the right way.

Henri and I retreat to the cottage a few minutes later, both of us worn down by worry and guilt. Maybe Marie is right, but when I picture raising this baby alone, away from Henri and the children, I can feel how painful it will be, how lonely. My heart would break a little more every single day.

We are quiet as we get ready for bed. It's only after we've lied down that he raises up on his forearm to meet my gaze.

"I'd like to marry you before she's born," he says. "I know it won't be official until the state can sanction it, but I still want to do it."

I smile for the first time since our discussion with Marie began. "Fortunately," I reply, "we happen to know a priest."

ON A SUNDRENCHED JUNE MORNING, I walk with Charlotte to the small chapel in the woods, part of the estate dating back to the 1600s. I wear a dress recovered from the ruins of the chateau and altered to fit my growing stomach—what was once a diaphanous ballgown has been turned into a maternity wedding dress that goes down to my ankles, tied under the bust with a white satin sash. Charlotte beams beside me, swinging the basket of flowers she and Lucien spent the morning picking.

"Can I wear that dress when I marry Daniel?" she asks.

I laugh. "Yes, though I hope you'll give it a few years." *And won't be pregnant.* We've reached the top of the church steps. "Are we ready, my loveliest flower girl?"

She nods and we enter. Henri waits at the end of the aisle, resplendent in a suit borrowed from Edouard. His eyes meet mine, and despite the situation I feel nothing but joy. This moment is happening because of all the things we went through, all the ways we suffered. I'd have fought so many things tooth and nail, had I known ahead of time—the broken ankle that stranded me with Henri the first summer we met, being held captive, Cecelia's birth, remaining behind with Charlotte and Lucien when the Germans invaded, letting Henri know who I really was —but they've brought us here, and because of that I would change none of them.

He pulls me against him when I reach the altar. "You're so lovely," he says, low enough that only I can hear. "I can't believe you're finally going to be mine."

I smile. "I was yours all along. Even back when I insisted I wasn't."

His mouth finds mine and I sigh happily. At last, at last, at last...I feel like I've waited my entire life to get here.

"Papa," scolds Charlotte. "You're supposed to do that at the end."

Everyone laughs and Edouard, smiling, begins to read.

Our vows are simple and said quickly, given that the church is full of restless children. But as Henri kisses me for the first time as his wife, I feel new again. As if God has, once more, decided to forgive me for what I became.

THAT NIGHT, Marie takes the children and we have the cottage to ourselves.

We retire early, and Henri carries me over the threshold, tugging the sash of my dress loose before he's even set me down. He crosses the room to light a lamp and I object.

"What do we need light for?" I ask. "I sort of assumed we'd be...going to bed."

He laughs. "Oh, we definitely will be." He removes his jacket as he crosses the room to me, then turns me away so he can unbutton my dress. "But for the last two months, I've made love to you furtively." His mouth presses to my neck, and then my ear, making me shiver. "Tonight, I want all of you—the sight of you, the sounds you make. All of it."

He pulls the dress down my shoulders and to the floor before holding out a hand so I can step out of it. I turn toward him, and his hands go to either side of my belly. "I never dreamed that in the middle of a war, my life could be so perfect," he says.

I reach up and begin to unbutton his shirt. "Not perfect yet," I reply, going on my toes to find his mouth as I pull the shirt off. "But it's about to be."

49

SARAH

June gives way to July.

I'm six months pregnant, and I've never longed for a respite from the heat the way I do now. I want air conditioning and ice. I want a shower.

But I refuse to wish these days of summer away. Because once they're gone, it will be time for us to make a decision.

We've been avoiding that conversation of late, perhaps because we both feel time slipping away. I'm nowhere near ready to be separated from him or the children. If I were to go into labor today, I know I would not be able to leave, and three months from now, I'm sure I'll feel the same.

I wake with the sun each day, my nightgown sticking to me. Toward the month's end, it's not even light out when I'm putting my head out the window, hoping to catch a bit of a breeze.

"My God, the heat is going to be unbearable today, isn't it?" I whisper to Henri.

"Take off your nightgown and I'll run a cool cloth over you."

I raise a brow. "I know where taking off my nightgown will lead."

He laughs. "If the children weren't going to wake any moment now, you'd be right. But just this once, I promise you're safe."

I pull the nightgown off and sit, relishing the feel of air on my bare skin. "I would kill for a Coke Slurpee," I tell Henri. I've explained Slurpees to him on many occasions. The name never fails to make him laugh, as it does now.

"Such a disgusting concept," he says, dabbing a cloth into the pitcher of water on the nightstand and running it over my back and then my neck, "but I promise to find you one once the war ends."

"I'm not sure you ever get 7-Elevens in France."

His smile falters for half a second. Perhaps remembering, as I am, that our daughter said we live in Virginia. There's rustling on the other side of the curtain—one restless child about to wake the others—but his hand goes to my hip and holds there for a moment. "Then I'll make you one," he says. "Because you're staying here."

I let my forehead fall to his chest, and that's when we hear it —the distant rumble of a car on the road. I know it's probably just food coming from Genevieve, or perhaps even the forged papers she's promised—she's already come through for Marta and her children, who left a week earlier for the south of France. But it never gets easier, this uncertainty. Henri meets my eye and I nod. We both know the drill by now.

We dress quickly, then I rush out with Cece in my arms, waking everyone, while he grabs a gun and climbs through the hedge to get to the front gate with Edouard right behind him. Marie, Rachel and I walk through the woods with the children between us until we reach the old church and hustle everyone inside. Then we wait, holding our breath to listen.

After a few minutes I hear someone coming through the woods and then Henri's whistle, the sign that it's safe. I throw the door open, but my smile fades. Edouard and Henri both look grim as they climb the steps.

"What is it?" Marie asks, rushing to Edouard.

He flinches. "The Germans are coming here today to repair the house. Genevieve couldn't put them off. She's got papers for Rachel and her two, plus a few of the others. She wants me to take them by foot to Versailles and catch a train to Limoges."

Her hand slides into his. "You? Why?"

"Amelie and I are the only adults here who can be in the open safely," he says, his head hanging. "But she's nearly seven months pregnant. She can't be asked to make that kind of journey on foot, and she could go into labor at any point—she can't be left alone with five children."

"And the rest of us?" I ask.

As Henri's tongue darts out to tap his lip, I already know I'm going to dislike the answer. "She's found another place for us. The driver is waiting. He'll take you and Marie and the youngest of the children, then come back for the rest of us."

I think of our daughter saying Henri was the one who *fought all the Nazis*. "I think we should stay together."

He frowns, stepping closer to twine his fingers through mine. "It's not possible. There's not enough space. I promise you I'll be there tonight." He laughs, almost to himself. "That wasn't the part I thought you'd object to."

"What did you think I'd object to?"

"We're staying in her home. In Paris."

I freeze, searching his face for some sign this is a joke. It doesn't appear to be. "She wants us to stay in the house next door to a German officer—a house where she entertains Nazis day and night?" I ask. "That's insane."

He sighs. "Perhaps. But her home is unlikely to be searched, if nothing else. Once the rest of us have papers, we'll join Edouard in Limoges."

It sounds farfetched, impossible. I worry I'll look back one day and realize it was.

AFTER AN EMOTIONAL GOODBYE, Marie and I set out for Paris, along with Charlotte, Lucien, Cecelia and Jacques, a near-silent five-year-old.

The journey is tense—only I can ride safely in the front of the truck while the others hide behind boxes in back—but our arrival is scarier. Though we pull into the alley behind the house—the servants' entrance—I can see at least six German soldiers patrolling next door. I'm sent inside and up the back stairs to the attic with Cecelia in my arms. The room is full of old furniture and paintings and covered in a one-inch thick layer of dust.

The driver and another staff member follow, carrying the children—and Marie—inside boxes. Lucien laughs as he emerges. "That was fun," he tells me, wrapping his arms around my neck as I lift him out. No one else laughs, not even Charlotte, who clings to me afterward. She's old enough, now, to understand the danger we're in.

I spend the next few hours trying to keep the children occupied and relatively quiet, waiting for Henri to come. He arrives just after dinner, pulling me against his chest and holding me tight.

"Ahem," says a voice behind him and we both turn to find a woman who must be Genevieve.

She's middle-aged and pretty, wearing a midnight-blue ball-gown that looks like lingerie, her hair perfectly coiffed. "Sorry to break up the reunion," she says, "but I'm about to entertain fifty German soldiers so this is the time. I'm working on getting papers for you but they won't be ready until the end of the week. I understand you," she says, turning to me, "have a good passport. I'll need you to run to the forger's location to check on the papers in a few days."

Henri's mouth opens to object and I step on his foot. Pregnant or not, I'm the one who's best positioned to take on a dangerous job right now.

"I know it's not ideal," Genevieve concludes, "but you're safe here. Just try not to make too much noise."

And with that, she's gone, and we set about learning how to keep eight children quiet.

THE HOURS in the attic pass slowly. The tension is constant, given the steady stream of German soldiers through the rooms below. The heat would be brutal were it not for the fans and the flow of air through the dormer windows. Food is brought up the back staircase once or twice a day by a maid who seems scared to even look at us, as if our tenuous situation might catch. On the third day she signals to me to follow her, and then downstairs gives me a scrap of paper with an address only a few blocks away.

"Tell them you're there to pick up the cigars for Herman Gunter. Do not return directly to the house, but wander through the city a bit and go into other shops until you're certain you weren't followed."

I find the building with relative ease—it really is a cigar shop, and I wonder if perhaps I'm just running errands for Genevieve instead of picking up papers.

"I'm here for the cigars ordered by Herman Gunter," I tell the man behind the counter.

He looks at me and nods, going to the back and returning with a cigar box in a bag. I take it from him, and walk to a book-seller's at the street's end, standing outside in the heat while I ensure I haven't been followed. I thumb through *Les Fleurs du Mal* by Charles Baudelaire. I remember finding it on Henri's night-stand that day, so long ago, when I snuck into his room. I called it curiosity back then, my desire to sneak through his things, but it was lust...something I'd had no experience with until him. Now, of course, there's love as well, but at seven months pregnant I'm finding that lust has taken top billing, oddly enough. I pray our papers come through soon. We could use some privacy.

I close the book and am about to put it back when I sense I'm being watched. I raise my head slowly as the book falls from my hands.

She's here.

The time traveler from 1989. She is standing just across the street and looks different in clothes from this era and with her hair pinned back, but I'm certain it's her. There's that same malevolence on her face as she watches me.

She blends into the crowd and I turn on my heel, fleeing toward Genevieve's, toward safety. I've run three blocks before I realize that if she can time travel, she can follow me on foot. All she'd need to do is return to the bookstore and follow my tracks —which means the only way I can prevent her from finding us is if I time travel myself, except if I do so, I'll lose everything I'm wearing and everything I'm carrying...namely, the documents in the cigar box. I turn, rushing back to the bookseller's, and shove the papers into a copy of *Madame Bovary*. Once they're secure, I head toward Genevieve's, stopping in the alley closest to her house.

Despite my aunt's spark, I'm still not good at landing in different places. I very well might arrive back in this alley, which opens me up to a wealth of other problems. There's no time in which a naked, pregnant female can walk about without attrac-tion attention. I take a deep breath and then focus hard on the Genevieve's attic, on the dust motes floating in sunlight and Henri's worried face as he awaits my return. I land gracelessly on the floor, relieved to see my family's shocked heads jerk toward the sound.

Henri grabs a blanket and rushes over to cover me. "Are you alright?"

"I saw her," I gasp. "The time traveler who was watching me in 1989. I saw her just now."

"Are you sure she's bad?" he asks. "Maybe she's just a family member? Another granddaughter of Katrin's?"

I glance from him to Marie, my heart beating hard. The fear in her eyes reflects my own. It will sound paranoid, voicing my thoughts, but I know what's happening is precisely the worst-case scenario Marie once suggested could occur: this woman is working her way backward, looking for the right time to strike.

And I'm worried she's found it.

"I'm sure she was bad, Henri," I whisper. "I'm sure."

50

SARAH

Genevieve sends a maid to retrieve the papers from *Madame Bovary*. She's angry at me for leaving them behind, and since I can't tell her that I time travel, I have to let her remain so. "Don't ask my staff to save your hide if you won't save your own," she says to me. "From now on, you get those papers yourself or you don't get them at all."

The next day, four of the children leave for Limoges, where Edouard waits. Marie watches them longingly, wishing she were going with them. "It'll happen eventually," I tell her.

"I hope so," she says. She turns her worried eyes to me. "I don't think you understand how bad this is."

I laugh. "Our situation? I assure you I do." I'm now farther along than Yvette was when she gave birth to Cece and trapped in a swelteringly hot attic.

"Not that. The time traveler," she says. "It's exactly as my mother described. If someone wants to stop you, she can just keep going backward. What if she sees the next set of forged passports? She won't even need to try to find you here. She'll just need to find out where Henri once lived. She could kill him back before the two of you ever met and none of your time with him would exist."

"Enough, Marie," barks Henri. "She's worried enough as it is. And if the time traveler wanted Amelie dead, she'd have done it already."

"Maybe she doesn't want Amelie at all," she argues. "Maybe she's just waiting for the child to be born. And if she fails to steal her the first time, then she'll just keep following us, or going back to do things differently."

Henri leans forward, nostrils flaring, jaw set hard. "You think I don't see through this? You're trying to scare her into going forward with the baby. It won't work."

Tears spring to her eyes. "I'm not trying to scare her," she says. "Or maybe I am, because I'm scared. Don't you understand how much danger we're all in? Not just us and our children, not just time travelers. Anyone *alive* is at risk."

"Easy for you to say when you lose absolutely nothing by having her leave," Henri says, sliding his hand through mine as he rises from the table.

"I'd be willing to lose everything in order to make it happen," she whispers. "Just like our mother did."

"Another easy thing to say," he replies, turning for the other side of the room with his arm wrapped around me tight, "since you'll never be asked to do it."

That night, with the windows open, there's just enough airflow to make the room bearable. I lie next to Henri, listening to the steady beat of his heart beneath my head. Memorizing it. Marie's words from earlier today are still with me. As much as I want to resist them, I can't deny what she's saying. It isn't about this single time traveler who's potentially a threat—it's about the threat inherent in our gift, how any of us could wreak havoc. I sense this evil in myself, but it's kept in check by my love for Henri and the children. What if it wasn't? How far would my desire to harm carry me? An innocent man has already died because of it. I'm certain there would be others.

Henri's lips press to the top of my head. "It's going to be fine," he says. "Marie is being paranoid. There's no way this time traveler can trace us."

"She found me in 1941, when you're the only person alive who knows my name here," I whisper. "She may have resources we know nothing about."

"We've been through too much, survived too much," he says. "I won't give you up simply because my sister is panicking."

I think of all our time together—that blissful summer and fall before I was held captive, and all the time since. Marie is right...any time traveler could wipe it from existence if she wanted. I don't want to die, but more than that, I don't want what exists in the past to be stolen too. I don't want it to happen to *anyone*.

He tips my chin up to kiss me, his mouth firm, demanding. I respond, my need matching his and I can feel the vibration of his groan under my palm, now pressed to his chest. His hand slides from the curve of my waist, down to my hip, and as our kisses grow reckless and desperate, his inhales sharpen. He crushes the fabric of my nightgown in his fist, struggling to restrain himself.

My thighs squeeze tight, as if it will dull the pain of wanting him like this. I allow my hand to graze over the front of his pants, relishing the hard outline of him there.

"You're soaked right now, aren't you?" he whispers with a quiet groan. "Open your legs. I need to feel it."

I shouldn't—it will only make the need worse—but my legs part and when his fingers slip between them, air hisses through my teeth.

He rolls me to my back, pushing the nightgown around my waist. "I can't wait anymore, Sarah."

I glance over at the children and Marie. "They could wake— we can't."

"We can," he says, climbing from the bed, "and we will."

He moves through the darkness, stacking chairs along the side of our bed, and then draping a blanket over them—creating a partition from the rest of the room, though one that could easily topple and wake the entire household.

"If that falls, we'll have an entire platoon of drunk Germans up here investigating," I whisper.

"Then," he says, lying on the bed and pulling me above him, "let's make sure it's worthwhile."

Genevieve appears in our rooms early the next day. I blush, grateful that Henri deconstructed the chair and blanket wall before anyone woke this morning. "I'm told the rest of the papers will be ready soon," she says. "Two more days and you will all be free to go to Limoges."

Marie and I hug, as best we can with our burgeoning stomachs, and Henri presses his lips to my forehead. "Thank God," he says. "It's almost behind us."

I sit with a still-drowsy Cece in my lap while Henri plays jeu de barbichette—the slapping game—with Charlotte and Lucien.

"You're terrible," I sigh. "They'll get expelled if they try to play that in school."

Henri's eyes crinkle at the corners. "Not in France they won't. You're too soft."

I laugh. "I think we both know that's not true."

Marie is lying on her side, her feet next to my hip. "What do you think the home in Limoges is like?" she asks.

Henri's smile tips up at the corners. "I don't care, as long as my wife and I no longer need to share a room with you all."

Marie laughs. "She's over seven months pregnant, Henri. You'll have no need for privacy for quite some time, believe me."

His eyes meet mine and hold. I bite down on a smile, just before a *thud* from the corner of the room draws my attention.

A naked woman is on our floor, on her hands and knees.

I freeze, some piece of me realizing what must be happening before I've put it all together.

Me. The woman on the floor is me. And I'd only be jumping backward like this to give us a warning.

"Go," she says, her chest heaving. "Go now."

Henri rushes over and kneels in front of her. "What happened?"

"Two days from now," she says, looking at me. "You will go to the cigar shop and they'll tell you your sister was already there, a girl with eyes just like yours."

All the breath leaves my chest and I lean forward, holding tight to Cecelia. "Eyes like mine means a time traveler," I whisper.

She nods. "She was demanding to know when the papers would be ready. She insisted that you were leaving the next morning—which means she knows *ahead of you* the day you will go."

The bedspread twists beneath my hand. "So we have to get out now, ahead of her."

She nods. "Even that may not be enough. There are a thousand ways she can find us."

Henri and I stare at each other. "We'll just have to go without the papers," he says.

"But how?" I ask. "It's daylight. You can't be seen at all, and *someone* is going to ask for identification, whether we walk or take the train."

He drags a hand through his hair. "I'll ask Genevieve for the truck," he says. "Get the children ready."

He runs for the stairs and already the naked me on the floor is vanishing, which means we've changed how things go two days from now. I just hope we're changing them for the better.

Marie and I exchange a worried glance. "There's something we're missing," she says. I've never seen her so pale and worried.

"What do you mean?"

"She can time travel, but we're acting as if she's human. It can't be this easy to escape her."

I tug at my hair. "I know," I whisper. Whatever is wrong with this plan, I'm too panicked right now to figure out what it is.

I help the children with their shoes, while Marie stares sightlessly out the dormer windows. "Marie, can you pack our things?" I ask, but she doesn't even seem to hear me. Genevieve and Henri come in just as we're done. "The truck isn't here," he says. "It won't return from Limoges until tomorrow."

I stare at him. "I don't know what to do."

"Just wait," says Genevieve. "I'm sure this—"

That's when we hear it—the pounding at the front door. Henri and I look at each other, and I see it then, the failure in our plan. "She's always going to know when we leave," I tell him, feeling faint suddenly and leaning against the wall for support. "She got her information from some point in the future, and each time we change the plan, the information she received, the dates that led her here...they change too. She knows it as soon as we do."

The pounding on the door increases.

"I don't know what you're talking about but they're about to break down the door," says Genevieve. "You need to get out of here. Leave through the basement. In the closet you'll see what looks like an air vent. Behind it is a tunnel which will lead you across the street."

"And from there?" I ask.

She meets my gaze, her face bleak. "From there you run."

She heads for the stairs, but Henri, Marie and I remain absolutely still, stunned speechless. Asking us to crawl out a manhole and run with the children in the middle of the day is tantamount to suicide. We need a car or we'll never make it. Marie presses her hands to her stomach and swallows hard.

"I can do it," she whispers with tears in her eyes. "I'll get us the truck. Meet me at the Pont de l'Alma in five minutes."

Before I can ask what she means, her clothes fall to the ground and she is gone.

"No," I whisper after her. I'm too late. I doubted her, all those times she insisted she would give up everything on behalf of the prophecy, but she may have done just that. If she isn't carrying a time traveler, she won't be pregnant when we see her next.

"Sarah," Henri says, putting two guns in his waistband. "We need to go."

He sweeps Lucien up in one arm and Cece in the other and heads for the stairs. Charlotte and I are at his heels.

We reach the basement just as the door upstairs opens and the floor above us echoes with the sound of stomping boots. I stand frozen, listening.

We cannot beat her. If there was time, I could go find out how she knows about us and perhaps stop her. But there's no way I can do that now.

And this is why the prophecy matters, why so many people were willing to die for it—because no matter what we do here and now, she can keep going back, tracing us through previous weeks and years to catch us unaware. We escape today and eventually she'll show up somewhere in our past—Nanterre or even Saint Antoine, that first blissful summer with Henri—and destroy us.

This is why my daughter needs to exist. So she can bring into the world something with the power to stop all of it. Until it happens, we are endlessly vulnerable.

"I have to kill her," I tell him.

He shakes his head. "No, just go. Get into the tunnel. I'll hold them off until you're gone."

"It won't matter, Henri!" I cry. "Listen to me! Until she's dead she'll just keep going backward to find us."

He holds my face. "There's not time for that right now," he says. "Just get ahead of her. And if that fails, save yourself. Save our daughter." His lips press to mine. "This isn't the time for weakness, little thief. You were chosen to bring her into the world for a reason. Show the universe it hasn't made a bad choice."

"Henri—" I cry, wanting to beg him to consider any other way.

He stops me, kissing me hard, one last time. "I love you," he says. "Wherever the other side is, I'll be waiting for you there." He lifts me into the tunnel and hands me Cece.

I allow myself a single, final moment to take in his face, and he holds my gaze until I go, scooting backward through the tunnel as fast as I can. I push up the manhole cover and climb out, hearing the sound of gunfire as I lean down to pull the children to me. Henri, alone, is facing whatever is behind us, and I have no way to help him—no weapon, no time. I could jump back a day and try to kill the time traveler responsible for all this, but the children would be dead before I'd succeeded.

"Take Lucien's hand," I tell Charlotte, with tears running down my face. I lift Cece in my arms and we begin to run, cutting through alleyways toward the Seine.

It's all futile, though. I don't know what the time traveler is after, but if she doesn't get it, she will just go back and do things differently. She's been tracing me, or us, for years, waiting for the right moment to strike, and now that she's found it she isn't going to give up. She'll just send the police to Genevieve's sooner. She can go back endlessly, and one of those times, she'll succeed.

It's still early, and only one truck sits down at Pont de l'Alma —a fish truck. I'm not sure if it's the truck Marie promised or some fisherman loading up his daily catch, but I run toward it anyway.

Edouard and Marie step out, and my stomach drops.

Marie is no longer pregnant.

"I'm sorry," I whisper. She shakes her head, trying not to cry, and takes Cece from me, while Edouard lifts Lucien into the back of the truck and climbs in after him.

I hug Charlotte tight and bury my head in her hair. "I have to go back to take care of some things. I'll be with you as soon as I can."

"Please, Mama," she begs, clinging to me. "You said you wouldn't leave. Let me stay with you!"

"I know," I say, choking on a sob. "But first I need to make sure things are safe for us, and I need you to be brave."

She clings harder. "I don't want you to go," she weeps. "I don't want you to go back there."

It all feels wrong. It feels wrong that I'm breaking my promise. It feels wrong that I am asking so much of her when she's so small. "Charlotte, I—"

Suddenly, a shot is fired. It pings off the back of the truck and ricochets into the grass. My head jerks upward. Soldiers are firing on us from the bridge, and the time traveler stands on the hillside, watching it unfold. I swing my back to them, protecting Charlotte. "Get in the truck!" I scream, trying to pull her hands off me. She is crying, clinging hard as if she can protect me. I feel fire in my shoulder, a pain so searing I nearly drop her.

Her grip loosens and I thrust her toward the back of the truck, into Edouard's arms. That's when I realize she's no longer fighting, no longer moving. Her eyes are open, sightless, her dress soaked in blood. A small hole in the center of her chest where the bullet entered, the same bullet that went through my shoulder.

No.

I stare at the hole, at her empty eyes.

I understand in a second's time and yet I understand nothing. It's Edouard who recovers first, who yanks me into the truck before I'm shot again. There's a sharp pain in my abdomen but I ignore it.

"No," I whisper to him, looking at Charlotte. "No, no. We can fix it!"

Edouard lifts my face. "You can't fix this, Amelie. I'm sorry."

Cece and Lucien are weeping, bullets are flying at the truck, and Charlotte—my sweet Charlotte who wanted to marry Daniel and live in Nanterre forever—is dead.

Shock and grief seem to empty me. Marie begins driving and I can only stare at my little girl, desperately trying to come up with a way to undo this. I begin shaking her, as if it's a sleepy morning in Nanterre and she is refusing to wake. Edouard grabs my shoulders. "Amelie, she's gone," he says. "You need to pull it together."

I look at him and hear his words, finally. And my grief is replaced by rage. Not clear and cold and rational the way it's been in the past. This time I want to burn the world down. I want to kill those soldiers and the time traveler and everyone they've ever loved.

Henri wanted so much for me to put this behind us. But suddenly I know, in a way I never did before, that I am meant to feel this way. That I am meant to be ruthless, and to stop at nothing to keep the child inside me safe.

And I will start with the time traveler who made all this happen.

I picture her, standing on the hillside, and I land behind her.

There's nothing dramatic about it. I don't give her a speech about how she needs to pay for what she's done, and I don't ask her what she was after—warning her of my presence in any way will just provide her time to escape.

My arm goes around her neck and then, with the other hand, I snap it, just the way I was trained. She crumples to the ground. There's no victory in it. She's just another casualty, one of many who will die to bring the prophecy to fruition.

The soldiers firing at the truck turn their guns on me, but I'm already time traveling away, picturing the manhole cover by Genevieve's as hard as I can.

I land, but another of those pains seizes my stomach and sends me to my knees, gasping. It makes the bullet wound in my shoulder seem minimal by contrast. A contraction, I suddenly realize. I should jump to my own time now, but there's a chance Henri's not dead. If he still lives, I can fix this. I can jump back to kill the time traveler sooner, before she put this plan in motion.

I begin to climb through the tunnel. My eyes adjust to the dim light—and I see a body at the other end. I crawl to it, knowing what I will find.

Henri.

His eyes are closed, and he looks boyish with those long lashes sweeping his cheeks, like a child who snuck off somewhere and fell asleep along the way. I press my lips to his cheek. His skin is cold, and I know that he is gone. I know it, and yet I remain beside him, trying to find an answer.

"Henri," I cry. "Come back. Just come back."

Another contraction hits, and my body jerks in response. I'm fading, being pulled to my own time whether I want to go or not.

I fight it for only a moment. It's what Henri wanted. It's what I already knew I had to do. I press my lips to Henri's, one last time.

And then I'm gone.

51

SARAH

I land not in the tunnel, but on Genevieve's basement floor, mid-contraction and in too much pain to push myself up, though I know this home must belong to someone else by now. I hear footsteps, running, and in a moment there's a hand in mine.

Cecelia—*adult* Cecelia—is beside me. "I'm here," she says. "You won't have to do it alone this time."

The contraction ends and I sit up, pressing my hands to my face, weeping. "Henri and Charlotte—"

Her hand is on my back. "I know."

I only want to go back to him and yet I'd be refusing to give him the one thing he asked of me. My breaths are huge and gasping and painful, wrenched from my lungs. Another contraction comes and I can barely tell one kind of pain from the other.

"You need to focus now," Cecelia whispers. "You're about to bring my sister into the world."

She's right. I know she's right, but I don't think I can go through life without him and without my children. I just want to return to Nanterre, to a time when we were happy, and stay as long as I can.

And if that's not possible, I just want it all to end.

I look toward the tunnel, to the place where I just left Henri.

"He isn't there, Sarah," she says softly.

A sob wracks my chest. "Where is he? Where was he buried?"

She squeezes my hand. "All is not lost, and all is not as it seems. There are things that lie ahead which even you can't imagine, and I think your story with my father isn't over. You will come to believe this yourself, in time."

"What do you mean?" I ask. "Is he not dead? If he's not dead I can just go back. I can kill the time traveler before she did all this and—"

"It's too late for that," she says. "But I think it best that you discover the rest as it unfolds. You want the future ahead of you, I promise, and it's time for it to begin. Are you ready?"

I think of Henri. *This isn't the time for weakness, little thief,* he said. *You were chosen to bring her into the world for a reason. Show the universe it hasn't made a bad choice.*

Our wedding day seems like so long ago, but I remember the moment when I entered the church. I was glad then for all the ways we'd suffered because it brought us to where we were. Perhaps, one day, I'll be glad for this too.

HENRI'S DAUGHTER is born an hour after I arrive in 1991.

She is tiny and perfectly formed, long fingers and a tiny pursed mouth that reminds me so much of her father that I burst into tears at the sight of her. I miss him. It's only been minutes and I miss him, and I don't know how anyone can expect me to go through the rest of my life feeling this way.

"Was it true?" I ask Cecelia, gazing at my daughter. "That things aren't what they seem? That my story with Henri isn't over?"

She smiles. "Do you think I'd lie about something like that?"

"What about Charlotte?" I hate it, that pathetic, hopeful note in my voice.

Cecelia's smile fades. "She's buried in the Loire Valley. A beautiful spot on a hillside, beneath a large oak, near where Lucien and I grew up."

I pull the baby closer to my chest as the tears stream down my face. I've lost so much. Charlotte. Henri. Even Cece and Lucien. I can visit them, but they will no longer be mine. All I have left is this little girl in my arms, and something surges in my blood, a new kind of protectiveness, the sort that borders on insanity.

Anything that threatens her, anything that stands in her way... I will destroy it without a moment's thought. From now on, there is nothing to live for but her, and I will exist only to keep her safe.

52

SARAH

1995

Quinn sits on the floor of Cecelia's library, the very image of her father, with a book spread open in front of her. She's only five but has been reading for over a year, one of many ways she stands out. There will be more of them soon, once she comes into her power.

I know the time traveler responsible for Henri's and Charlotte's deaths is gone, but I still picture her on every corner, waiting to steal Quinn from me. I saw her here once, watching Quinn and me as we walked down to the Seine from Cecelia's home. She posed no threat—the visit must have occurred before she died. My life is moving forward, but she seems to be working backward from some point in the future, and the fact that she never attacked Quinn or myself tells me it was someone else she was after, that day in 1941. I can't ask her since it might change the past, not that she'd tell me anyway. I suppose it's a mystery for my daughter or her children to solve in the future. One of many.

I tap on the frame of the door to get Quinn's attention. "I

heard my little girl was in here," I say as she looks up, "but I guess I'll keep looking. I only see a big girl in this room."

Her face breaks into a wide smile and she runs to me, circling my legs with her small arms. "I *missed* you," she says earnestly, and my heart squeezes tight with pain and joy at once. I was gone for three weeks this time, visiting Edouard, Marie, Lucien and Cece back in the 1940s as I do each summer. Marie and Edouard are their parents now. I'm glad for it, as they had no more children, yet it hurts all the same. Cecelia and I remain close, and she is thrilled by my visits to her childhood, but Lucien is already changing from a rambunctious boy to the serious young man he'll become, and he has little time for a doting American aunt.

My entire beautiful past—it's like a splinter in my heart that won't budge.

"You've gotten taller," I say, lifting her into my arms. "Stop growing so fast."

Her arms tighten around my neck into the fiercest hug, and then she is scrambling back to the floor to show me the book she's been reading. She holds up a picture of a home—no, not a picture: an architectural rendering. That ever-present sorrow climbs into my throat. I wish Henri was here. I wish he could see how like him she is.

"It's Monticello," she says. "Thomas Jefferson designed it himself. Can we go?"

I blink back tears. "You want to go all the way to the states to see a house? We live in a city full of magnificent architecture."

Her gaze drops down to the book as if she's confused. "I...do," she says. "I don't know why. We're just supposed to go."

There's something in the way she says those words—*we're just supposed to go*—that makes the hair on my arms stand on end. There are moments when it seems as if she's being directed by a force outside herself, and this is one of them. I'm terrified of the direction that force is sending her, even when I know I should yield to it.

I swallow and force a smile. "Then I guess I'd better start planning a trip."

That night I tell Cecelia about Quinn's request, searching her face. She knows where my life is headed, through the tidbits I shared going back to visit her as she grew up. "Quinn wants to go to Virginia," I say. "We're going to stay, aren't we? Something happens there that convinces us to stay."

She gives a small laugh. "No matter how many years you know me, you still try to get me to reveal your future."

"My own personal palm reader," I reply with a smile of my own, "but one who refuses to tell me anything of import."

"When it matters, I'll tell you," she replies.

"So you're saying this doesn't matter?"

She shakes her head. "No. I think it probably matters most. But I already know you're going to do the right thing."

TWO WEEKS later we are driving into the mountains of Virginia, heading to Monticello. It's August, searingly hot, but Quinn wants the windows down and rides with her eyes glued to the landscape, quiet and intense. She reminds me of an animal in the wild—the way it goes alert the moment it senses something nearby.

She nods when I ask if she's okay but doesn't even look at me as she continues to stare, hands clasped tightly in her lap.

My heart beats harder, scared of what it is she's sensing. Cecelia told me, once upon a time, that I wouldn't change this future that lies ahead of me if I could, but I still long for the husband and children I left behind. I pray that future she's referencing isn't any sadder than it already is.

"There's something—" Quinn says, suddenly, pointing at an exit. "I want to go there."

It's just a generic country road that appears to lead to nothing, and we've got a full agenda of gallery visits before we head to Pennsylvania to see my brother Steven and his wife. *Exploring country roads in the middle of nowhere* is not on the list.

"Honey, we'll miss our tour if we stop now. Maybe we can stop on the way back to D.C."

"Please," she begs. There's a desperate note to her voice I've never heard before.

Reluctantly, I turn off the highway, driving through a podunk town with no signs of life aside from a gas station that isn't even open. But she is sitting up straight, as if sensing something spectacular up ahead, her gaze intent on the small houses we pass.

We continue on until we hit a different small town—the type with a Main Street and tall white houses from early in the century.

"Can you turn?" she asks, pointing up ahead, and when I do, we reach a quiet, well-heeled subdivision where the houses back to trees. "Here," she whispers. "It's here."

There's a certainty to her voice that brings goose bumps to the surface of my skin.

"There isn't anything to see here, honey," I tell her, pulling over to the curb. "These are private homes."

Just then, two shirtless little boys about her age come running around the side of the house, chasing each other. Quinn watches them intently for a moment and then takes off her seat belt. "I'll be right back."

I watch, dumbfounded, as she climbs from the car and walks to them. She's a quiet child, normally. Reserved. I've never seen her do anything like this before. The boys—twins, nearly identical but not quite—suddenly stop whatever they're doing and stare as she approaches.

Through the open window, I hear her speak to them for the first time.

"Hi," she says. "I'm going to be your neighbor."

I open my mouth to correct her, and then...I don't. There's

something happening here and I'm not at the heart of it—she and these two boys are.

They both stare at her for a moment and then one of them frowns. "Well, you can't come in our treehouse," he says. "No girls allowed."

But the other one watches her, his head tilted as if considering what she's said, weighing it, and then shrugs. "I'll let you in," he says.

She looks at him for a long moment, so long that it's awkward, but he's watching her too. I get a chill up my spine. "I have to go now," she says. She sounds wistful. "But my name is Quinn."

"I'm Nick," the boy replies.

I glance at the mailbox. *Reilly*, it says.

Like Luna Reilly, the time traveler who tried to fight off Coron in 1918 and died for it.

My hands grip the steering wheel. I want to tell myself it isn't possible. But as I look at the two of them there, my daughter and this little boy, so spellbound by each other, I know what I'm seeing. Two of the first families in my daughter, and—I am guessing—the other two in him.

Four pieces of the puzzle, in the same place at last.

53

SARAH

There were no homes for sale, but with enough money almost anything can be purchased, and we move into a house a few doors down from the Reillys one month later.

Our lives change immediately—Quinn's life, most of all. Until now, she was a tiny city dweller, and our days were spent in galleries and parks, with Cecelia's bodyguards lurking discreetly behind. Now, she is a small wild thing with bruised shins and dirty feet, gone from sunup to dusk. Always off with the Reilly boys. She likes them both, but it's Nick she's drawn to, Nick she prattles on about as we eat dinner.

"Nick's dad is a doctor," she says one night, climbing into the tub. I've avoided the parents as much as possible, and I do my best to avoid the boys as well. It's easier not to get close to people.

"Hmmm," I say absent-mindedly, filling a cup with clean water to wash her thick, unruly hair. Henri's hair, though long and lit with gold from these days out in the sun.

"What was my dad?" she asks.

My heart clenches. It's been five years. Is there ever going to be a time when the mention of him, the memory of him, doesn't ache the way it does? "He was a soldier," I reply. "He died in the war. I told you that."

"But what *else* was he?" she persists.

"He wanted to be an architect. And he was someone who loved you long before you were born."

"I wish I could see him," she says. "I wouldn't even talk to him. I just want to see him."

I close my eyes. The mother in me wants to forbid that trip she'll take in a few years, but doing so could change things. And aside from the day I lost him, I wouldn't give up a single piece of what we had, exactly as it was.

"Yes," I say simply. "I wish you could too."

QUINN'S GIFTS begin to unfold, as I knew they would. She has Marie's ability to travel anywhere, anytime, with ease, and she has my ability to be in two places at once. At first, I'm constantly having to cover her tracks, changing the past so no one remembers the many times she accidentally disappeared in public. Eventually, I pull her out of school and teach her myself, waiting until she can control her gift on her own.

One afternoon she comes home and tells me she accidentally disappeared in front of Nick. I fix it, as I often do, after she goes to sleep. Changing her past means it no longer exists. Nick isn't supposed to recall anything about it, and neither is she. The problem is...they do.

"Nick doesn't remember seeing me time travel yesterday," she says the next night over dinner. "But he says he *dreamed* he saw me disappear."

The fork falls from my hand.

"Do *you* remember it?" I ask.

She nods. "I remember it both ways," she says. "I always do, if Nick was there."

I slowly breathe out. Some piece of her is holding on to a piece of him, even when it no longer exists. I don't understand the import of it, however, until a few months later.

It's a Saturday, and Quinn's just run off to the treehouse. I watch as she goes and walk back inside to find two naked little girls sitting on my kitchen floor. One blonde, one brunette. Time travelers, both of them.

For a moment I'm so astonished I can only stare. They are far too young to have that kind of ability—younger even than Quinn when she followed me and Henri.

"Who are you?" There's something familiar about them both, though I can't place it.

They glance at each other, suddenly uncertain. "We wanted to see our mom," the brunette says. "And to meet you."

I am obviously not their mom, so they must mean...Quinn. And I can see her in their faces. For a moment I am thrilled, and then I remember something else...one of those things about my kind I'd nearly forgotten, something I never dreamed would be an issue: the rule of threes, which ensures that only three time travelers can exist in one family line.

It means one of us must die.

And I'm the one they're here to meet, so I suppose I know who that is.

I press my hand to my heart, feeling an ache that is now familiar. Usually, it's over the losses in my past. This time, it's over the loss in my future. I wanted to be there for Quinn as her future unfolds and I won't be. I won't live to see her have these two little girls, or to become a part of their lives. I won't be around to protect them all.

I force a smile. "I suppose we haven't met before. What are your names?"

"I'm Amelie Rose Reilly," says the brunette carefully, in that formal way small children sometimes do.

"We call her Milly," adds the blonde. "And I'm Luna."

I stare at them for a moment. It should have been obvious to me from the start, what I've been seeing in their faces, the thing I couldn't identify. It's Nick. In their smiles, in the blonde's coloring. Three of the first families are accounted for—Reilly, Durand and Eber—and I'm sure the fourth is there too.

These two girls are the circle of light, from the prophecy. I don't know what it means, but I know I'm in the presence of it.

Tears sting my eyes. "And how did you manage to land here together like this?"

They both shrug. "We can always find each other," explains Luna.

Like Quinn and Nick's ability to remember each other, no matter what I erase, I think.

I ask them about their lives, and they detail a perfectly normal childhood, aside from the time travel. They go to school and they play. There's a pool in their yard and their father has taught them to swim. They tell me their favorite subjects, the teachers they like and the teachers they hate.

"And grandpa taught us jeu de barbichette," offers Milly. "But he said you wouldn't like that so we shouldn't tell you."

My mouth falls open. "Your *grandfather*?" I ask, my voice cracking. They must mean Henri. Who else would have taught them the game? Who else would have told them I hated it?

For a moment I merely envy them—what I wouldn't give to a spend an hour in his company, something I never do since it could rewrite our past. Then I realize the danger they could be placing all of us in with those visits. Not simply because of the time they're going to, but because any information they give him could change everything that takes place afterward. "Girls, does your mother know you're going back that far? It could be very, very dangerous."

"We don't go backward to see grandpa," says Milly. "Well, maybe we do?"

She turns to Luna, who shrugs. "We see him on the island. Time is different there."

"You'll see him there too," adds Milly. "He told us you would."

My skin feels stretched so tight over my bones that I'm worried I will split open entirely. "That's not possible," I whisper. "Your grandfather died in 1941."

They look at each other again. "We should go," says Luna.

Milly opens her mouth to argue and Luna yanks on her hand. They disappear before I can even open my mouth and I remain behind, staring in shock at the space where they just sat.

Is it possible? Could Henri actually still exist somewhere in the world, somewhere I could go without rewriting the past? It must be what Cecelia meant when she said our story wasn't over.

I curl up on the floor, wanting it to be true so much I feel sick with hope, wanting it so much I think I'll die a little if it winds up being false.

It's late afternoon in France, Cecelia's busiest time of the day, but she answers my call immediately.

"I met the twins," I tell her. "You knew, right? This is what you meant when you said our story wasn't over?"

"Yes," she says. "I'm sorry I didn't tell you more. I just thought it should all happen as it was meant to."

It was probably the right decision, but now that I know I can't help but push for more. "Do you know anything else?" I ask, gripping the phone tight. "Do you know where the island is?" I could go there. I'll go tonight and bring Quinn. I don't care where we have to go or what we need to do to get there.

"I've spent a small fortune trying to find the island, to no avail," she admits. "Which isn't to say it doesn't exist. There are thousands of undiscovered islands on the planet. It seems as if it's a place you can only reach in their time. That's what you'll come to believe, after the twins visit you again."

"But why only in *their* time? Why not now?"

"You tell me," she says. "These are your people and your legends. You tell me."

I think about the story, the very little I know about the island and what lies ahead for it. *The four families can't come home*, the legend says, *until they are united once more*. United once more in the twins, who don't yet exist.

"Maybe the island can't exist, at least for us, until the twins do," I venture. My eyes close and I sink into a seat, burying my head in my hands. "But if the island won't exist until they're born, and I'm going to die *when* they're born...how am I going to see him?"

"Maybe you don't actually die," Cecelia suggests softly. "Maybe you just go there instead."

The possibility of it makes my heart soar—I miss Henri every minute of every day, and there's an emptiness inside me that no one else could fill—but it breaks me at the same time. "I'll die when they're born. I'm okay with that but..." My voice rasps. I always thought I'd be there to protect my daughter, that she'd always be able to lean on me. "Do you know how long I'll have with Quinn? Did I stop going back to see you at a certain point?"

She hesitates. For a moment I think she's not going to tell me, and then she does. "Yes, your visits stopped," she says. "She and Nick...you've already seen it yourself. They'll be young when they fall in love, and they'll be young when the twins are born."

"I don't have that long with her, then," I whisper.

"No parent ever has long enough," she replies. "You just have to treasure each moment as it's handed to you."

I'm not the only one who will suffer over this, though. Quinn's going to have to live with the knowledge that the twins' births killed me. "I wish there were another way. It's so much to put on her when she's already got the entire prophecy on her shoulders."

"She's a strong girl and she'll be a strong woman, just like her mother. I think you were chosen for a reason—because you'll do whatever is required to make the world a safer place, through the twins."

I close my eyes, knowing she's right. Until the end comes, I will be happy for each moment I get. And I'll do everything I must, no matter how much it pains me, to make the prophecy come to fruition. For everyone who's died trying to make it come true. Henri, most of all.

QUINN RETURNS from another day with Nick, lit through with a small, wild joy, a bright light only he brings out in her. She climbs into my lap, her head resting against my chest, and my throat squeezes tight. This time with her is more fleeting than either of us can realize, but I'm only losing what every mother does, eventually. There will always come a day when your child is too big to be held in your arms, when she no longer wants to sit in your lap or curl up against you at night. A day when she leaves home, when she creates her own family, when you are separated by death.

We all, in the end, have to give up the things we love, and I am no exception.

Even so, I would not change a thing.

54

HENRI

1941

The Germans who rushed into Genevieve's basement are dead, but I know I don't have long either. I'm weak, not thinking clearly, but if there's any way to reach Sarah, I have to try. I crawl into the tunnel, hoping to follow her and the children to the Pont de l'Alma, but the effort takes the last of my strength. My eyes close and I picture her— my sweet little thief. She became a lion, in the end. She'll do whatever is necessary to keep our daughter safe.

Time passes. I'm sweating and feverish. I dream that I'm in the vineyard, and Sarah is walking toward me, lush and smiling, wearing the white dress with the small roses. The world is green and new, and in my wife I see everything good, everything I want in the world. "Take off the dress, Sarah," I whisper when I reach her, and she laughs, batting my hands away.

"Madame Beauvoir is here," she says. "She'll see us."

"Good," I reply, pulling the dress off her shoulders, "maybe she'll stop visiting so often."

She begins pulling me, farther into the fields where we won't be seen. The pain I felt before is ebbing and in its place is a drowsy sort of contentment. If she is leading me to heaven, I'm ready to follow.

A HAND on my shoulder rouses me from the dream, and when my eyes blink open, Sarah is beside me. The pain in my back and chest has spread, has begun to fill me, and I don't think I have long. "You need to go," I whisper. "You can't be here now." I'm having a hard time gritting out the words.

"It's fine," she says, laying her head on my chest. She's shivering with cold, and her voice is faint. "More than twenty years have passed, Henri. The children are grown, and happy. It will all happen as it's supposed to now."

She feels the same and in the dim light she looks the same, but slowly, I begin to understand. "You came back to die with me."

"I came back to go on to the next place with you," she says, her voice barely above a whisper. "But even if there isn't one, it's enough, the time we had. You and our family—they were worth all of it."

My lips press to her head. She releases a single, long breath, and then she is still. I hold her against me. "Take me with you, Sarah," I whisper. "Wherever it is you've gone."

My eyes shut and the pain leaves as I sink somewhere heavy and dreamless. But Sarah is tucked against my chest. Our children are safe and we are together.

She's right. It's enough.

I WAKE SLOWLY, eyes blinking against the bright sun. I see a small stone house and a barn, similar to ours but not quite the same, surrounded by a vineyard, one that's flourishing in the summer air. For a moment I think I'm back in Saint Antoine—that I've fallen asleep in the orchard as I occasionally did—until I look in the distance, where I see a tall white steeple and the bright, clear blue of the sea.

I'm on an island. And I think of it then, my mother's stories about the mythical island where we'd all be reunited one day. I mostly thought it was a fairy tale...but was it?

Wherever I am, though, I don't want to be here without my wife.

I push off the ground, realizing the pain in my back, in my chest...is gone, as if it never was. I lift my shirt. There are no wounds from the bullets that entered my chest, no scar from the knife that cut me when I was held captive, but the marks of my childhood remain—a small white line on my thumb from an accident with a saw, a burn mark on my inner wrist.

It's not as if I've died and been made perfect. It's as if I've simply returned to some earlier time.

"Sarah?" I call, starting toward the small stone house. Something crashes inside the barn. A sound much like the one Sarah made when she first came to us.

I run toward it this time, and enter to find Sarah standing before me, naked and confused. She looks exactly as she did that first day, but when her eyes raise to mine, I see everything I'd hoped to in her face. Love and the start of a joy she's terrified to let herself feel.

"Is this real?" she asks, her voice barely a whisper. "Is it really you?"

I take three long steps to pull her into my arms. I just saw her, and yet it feels as if we've been apart a very long time. "Yes."

She begins crying, face pressed tight to my chest. "I've missed you so much. Every day and night for more years than you can imagine."

And even though it seems to me no time has passed, I feel

something coming together inside me, a hole that is finally closed. Nothing in my life has ever felt warmer or sweeter than this, her pressed against me, solid and real.

"Are we—" She looks around, at the untidy barn and the roof that sorely needs repair above us. "Are we in heaven?"

I smile. "I don't think so. There's a church down the way and surely in heaven, church is beside the point. I think we're on the island. The one from my mother's stories."

"I wasn't sure," she weeps. "I didn't know if it would work out like the twins said."

I freeze. "The twins?" I ask. "Did we have twins?"

She laughs through her tears. "No, our daughter did, or is about to anyway. Quinn's the product of two first families, and Nick—her husband—is the product of the other two, I'm certain. And the twins are the circle of light. From the prophecy."

"And it all happened because of you," I say, my hands framing her face.

"It happened because of *us*," she replies.

I lean down and kiss her. I don't want to stop. My mouth presses to her jaw, to her temples, to her cheeks. She is too warm and real to be a dream. "Please tell me this isn't going to end."

"I don't think so," she replies. "I think maybe we're in a place where time works differently, a time that existed before our deaths. And now we're waiting for our granddaughters to set the world right."

"But I can't time travel," I argue. "You might be able to go back in time, but how did I?"

"I don't know. That's a mystery for Quinn and her daughters to solve," she says. "But you can always ask the twins yourself when they come visit us."

"*Visit? Here?*" I ask, kissing her again. "Nothing you're saying is making sense."

Her smile is so joyful it makes me ache. "I suspect we have a very long time to go over the details."

I push her hair back from her face. "Yes. But my wife is naked, and we appear to have this entire place to ourselves. That's enough for me right now."

She goes on her toes and presses her lips to mine. "Then take me inside, and let's begin our next chapter."

THE END

Sarah and Henri's story isn't entirely over. Find out how to get a free bonus epilogue on the next page!

THE FREEBIES!

For a bonus epilogue about Sarah and Henri's life on the island, subscribe to my newsletter
https://bit.ly/AcrossEternityBonus

Want a free novella about the sweet, steamy beginning of Marie and Edouard's relationship? Subscribe at
https://bit.ly/PriestE

Want a place to discuss the book and figure out what it all meant? (And get updates on a future book about the twins!) Join us on Facebook in the Across Eternity Spoiler Room.

ACKNOWLEDGMENTS

As I write this, we are two weeks into a quarantine that may last for months, and I've never been more grateful than I am now for the online community of readers and fellow authors who've become friends.

The members of the Across Time/Across Eternity spoiler rooms have been especially magical during this period, as well as the months preceding it. They inspired me when my interest lagged, and their enthusiasm for these books pushed me to work harder than I ever have before, solely because I didn't want to disappoint them. Thank you all, from the bottom of my heart. You're a big part of how Henri and Sarah's story evolved.

Thanks to Emily Wittig for these gorgeous covers and the many people I leaned on to help me tell a very tangled tale: my content editor, Tbird London; my editor, Stacy Frenes at Grammar Boss; Julie Deaton for a first round of copy edits and—because I couldn't stop revising—Janis Ferguson for the second round. Thanks also to my beloved beta readers: Shannon Vick Alley, Kimberly Ann, Faye Hooker-Graves, Amy Burke Mastin, Katie Meyer, Brenna Rattai and Erin Thompson.

Patrick, Lily and Jack: I promise I'm done talking about World War II. I mean it this time.

ABOUT THE AUTHOR

Elle O'Roark spent many years as a medical writer before publishing her first novel in 2013. She holds bachelor's degrees in journalism and arts from the University of Texas, and a master's degree in counseling psychology from the University of Notre Dame. She lives in Washington, D.C. with her three children. *Parallel* is her first paranormal series.

Made in the USA
Las Vegas, NV
03 December 2023

82018543R00201